DELICIOUS DARKNESS
BY DAVID HOLLY

Herndon, VA

ISBN 10: 1-934187-83-6
ISBN 13: 978-1-934187-83-8

STARbooks Press
PO Box 711612
Herndon, VA 20171

With the exception of "The Witch's Spell," earlier versions of these stories originally appeared on Tommyhawk's Fantasy World (http://www.tommyhawksfantasyworld.com)

Printed in the United States

STARbooks
P   R   E   S   S
Herndon, VA

Dedication

For Milford Slabaugh who first saw the possibilities in these stories.

Acknowledgments

Heartfelt thanks to my editor Eric Summers and everyone at STARbooks Press, all the Tommyhawk readers who e-mailed me with praise for, gripes about, and suggestions for improving these stories, and to Kristina who patiently proofread every single word, phrase, and punctuation mark, and who claims that in the process learned more about guy-on-guy sex than any woman has the need to know. (Need to know or not, she enjoyed every word of it. D.H.)

Contents

DELICIOUS DARKNESS

Beneath a gnarled and lightning-blasted tree, Cousin Syl and I stood protected within the circle we'd drawn with cornmeal. The moon was warmly full, but the wind chilled our naked skin as we raised our left arms and summoned demons to pleasure us. The blighted, stone-strewn heath beneath our bare feet trembled as if shaken by tiny earthquakes.

"I summon you, Nuberus. Rise from the depths and serve me," I chanted repetitiously, my right hand stroking my hard cock. The head of my cock was tingling with cascades of tiny orgasms. I gripped it hard, twisting and fondling my dick head as I pumped the shaft. The sensations were beyond anything I'd ever experienced before, and my dick dripped with anticipation. "Spring from the pit, queer demon," I moaned, "and receive my mortal cock in your mouth and asshole."

A series of more powerful orgasms made me shudder, but my cock did not yet squirt. As I masturbated, my butt cheeks bumped against those of my cousin.

"I summon you, Abbadon. Rise from the depths and serve me," Syl followed in unison, his hand similarly engaged. Knowing that Syl was pounding his own dripping hard-on increased my lust.

An antiquarian collection of spells lay open beside us, and the magical wind caught our pre-cum as it dribbled from our cocks and mingled our juices upon the hell-inspired pages. Just outside our protecting circle, we'd drawn a second circle, and as we summoned the demons, the grass within that circumference withered as if consumed by flame. Like a gathering storm, the clouds drew together around the glowing moon as the ground within the second circle cracked open.

The resulting thunder nearly deafened us, and the flash of lightning was beyond imagining. I was struck temporarily blind and incapable of thought. A shattering orgasm tore through my dick head. My hips thrust wildly as if I were humping a passive homosexual's ass or his willing mouth, and my skin crawled with ripples of perverted pleasure. When the first spurt of cum burst from my pee hole, I could no longer tell up from down. I knew I was falling, and though I must have hit the ground with a thud, I felt nothing beside the wild rippling contractions and the waves of spurting that seized me.

For a time out of mind, the waves of gratification rushed over me, contracting every muscle in my body. I'm sure that my lungs stopped breathing and my heart seized in my chest. Certainly, my brain was firing in all centers of ecstasy and nowhere else. Yet, my hand still pumped the great gouts of cum that blasted from my dick and splattered upon the open pages of the *Book of Shadows*.

When our contractions stilled, Syl and I drew long rasping gasps. Our eyes fluttered open, and we found ourselves sprawled upon the blighted ground within our circle. In the smaller circle, two reddish-purple, stud-muffin demons stood, naked and glorious, their thick cocks pointing toward the golden moon and oozing, and their long tails twitching like those of irked felines.

I struggled to my feet, lifted my left arm in salute, and gripped my cock with my right in the prescribed manner; my cock promptly swelled again. "Greetings, Nuberus, Shape of Evil. I have called you up from the Chains of Tartarus that you may pleasure me sexually," I announced, following the script in the book of spells.

Grabbing my butt for support, Syl climbed shakily to his own feet and performed the salute. "Greetings, Abbadon, Snare of Hell. I have called you up from the Lake of Woe that you may pleasure me sexually."

The demons laughed evilly, their eyes glowing. Their demonic cocks remained rock solid and dripping.

"You pathetic little faggots," Abbadon taunted. "You've been had. Didn't you read the fine print? One of you will receive our sexual submission – for a time. The other we will fuck to death this very hour and drag his conscious essence to the flaming gang-rape pit in Hades."

Wide-eyed, I glanced at Syl. He winked, and we emitted our own depraved laughter. The most dangerous moment had arrived, but we had followed the spell carefully. We switched hands and jerked off each other, as the occasion demanded.

"We studied the clause, Abbadon, and we're prepared to fulfill it," I countered, tossing over a map to the bunkhouse. I'd taken the precaution of marking Fred's private quarters with a red X. "The clause reads that we can substitute a hapless scapegrace – so we're offering Fred."

The veritable portrait of malignancy repressed, Abbadon snarled spitefully, grabbed the map, and vanished along with his fellow demon. Our close study of the spell had trapped the two fiends. They had to claim their victim's soul, and once they did so, their demonic flesh became ours to fuck at will.

# # # # #

Cousin Syl introduced me to Black Magic. "It's cool, Bram," he said. "The left hand path. The way to power."

I wasn't so sure, but I sat beside him on his bed and studied the musty old book he was holding while the drowsy June air drifted through the screened window, carrying scents of the barnyard.

My parents had sent me to live with my Aunt Edna and Uncle Jim, not to mention Cousin Syl, for the entire summer. My dad was a famous evangelist, and he and Mom were making a world tour for Christ. I would've liked seeing the foreign countries they visited, but Dad was convinced I'd fall prey to deviant foreign influences, so he shipped me off to my country cousins where the atmosphere would be pure, Godly, and wholesome.

Aunt Edna and Uncle Jim owned a farm, but they weren't dirt-poor farmers. Their farm covered 6,800 acres. Their thirty farm hands labored under the thumb of their farm foreman. The foreman, Fred, was an insulting, skin-headed ramrod about ten years older than I. Fred had converted into a Disciple of Christ in prison, where he'd served six years for pouring buckets of gasoline on two black men, one Jewish woman, and six homosexuals emerging from a gay bar. After meeting Fred, I decided that he would've made a great guard in a Nazi concentration camp, but I couldn't picture any other career for him. Nonetheless, Christians are suckers for former convicts who claim to have found Jesus, so my aunt and uncle made Fred their foreman.

I found the farm boring; watching the pigs mate got old quickly. My aunt and uncle, aloof and chilly folk, thought any entertainment outside of church was the devil's snare, so they didn't provide any recreation. They wouldn't even allow a deck of cards in the house. As long as I had known him, I always thought Cousin Syl was a creep, but he was the only companion I had. Each Sunday, we went to church, and Cousin Syl would whisper funny comments. Some of the things he said about the Bible and the preacher were so funny that I had to hide my snickers behind my hymnal. He also whispered some stuff that made me uncomfortable. Toward the end of June, Cousin Syl asked me if I ever thought about black magic, demonology, and Satanism.

I know I could've stopped up my ears and refused to listen. After all, our whole family had been Christians since Mark was a disciple, and our main reading material was the King James Bible, the same as the Apostle Paul used. But, when Syl pulled out the book on black magic, I was fascinated. He let me borrow it, providing I kept it hidden, so I took it to my own room and studied it far into the night.

One stained page featured a drawing that showed a line of naked men waiting to kiss the devil's ass. I kept coming back to that picture, time and again. The aspirant about to plant his lips on the devil's asshole displayed a dripping erection and an eager expression. Though I rationalized that I was looking at the picture to steel my soul against evil, my cock hardened as I studied the drawing. Subconsciously, I wanted to be the guy preparing to plant his mouth on the devil's anus. My hand slipped into the waistband of my briefs as I looked at the page that had been marked with countless obvious stains.

My parents had never discussed masturbation with me, but I'd heard my father preach against it, and seven years earlier – on my eleventh birthday – he handed me a tract full of Bible verses warning me against spilling my seed on the ground lest God smite me deader than Onan. Nevertheless, I'd never been able to keep that sin out of my life. I would manage to hold off for a few days, but eventually I'd end up jerking off secretly in the bathroom just like every other sinner. That I spilled my seed into the toilet instead of onto the ground probably didn't mitigate the sinful nature of what I was doing, and I expected to be blind, hairy-palmed, and insane by the time I reached nineteen. Anyway, I ended up jacking off that night and not into the toilet either. I reclined on my side and massaged my dick while I studied the *Shameful Kiss*. My cock felt particularly sensitive, as if the picture itself were exciting my tissues.

The man in the drawing was grinning lewdly. As I looked and beat my meat, his face pressed closer to the devil's butt crack. I knew that the figure's movement had to be an optical illusion brought about by the blood rushing from my brain to my penis. I spit into my hand for increased lubrication and pounded my tortured cock. My asshole contracted and pulsed. Little tingles of electricity fired in my cock. I groaned through my gritted teeth.

As I pictured my tongue in Satan's asshole, my dick grew even harder and became heavy. My hand flew on my cock. I knew what the heavy dick sensation meant, but I couldn't stop. I gripped my cock and

4

pumped harder. I imagined sticking my cock into Satan's shapely ass and humping his Luciferous buttocks. Fucking the devil would have to produce the orgasm of a lifetime. I gasped as the tingles traveled through my cock's head. My whole body contorted with rapture. My eyelids fluttered and my breath came in raspy bursts. My hand took on a life of its own as I gripped my cock and thumbed the head. My body tensed as the powerful muscles at the base of my penis contracted again and again. The cotton cloth of my white jockey briefs tormented my pee hole as I shot spurt after spurt of my spicy jism.

After I blew out that dickwad, I wanted to get out of bed, throw the wet, cum-smelling briefs into the laundry, and clean up, but I felt so relaxed and so relieved that I fell asleep. I drifted into a deep slumber, but all the same, I had the most vivid dreams of my life – and the least innocent. I dreamed that I was living in the Middle East at the time of Solomon. But I wasn't a member of the Hebrew kingdom. Oh, no. I was an acolyte of the priests of Baal, and it was my sacred duty to receive the sacred seed of the male worshipers into my ass or mouth, so I could carry it to the statue of Baal where I would ritually masturbate. Even in sleep, I knew I'd moved another step down the ladder of human depravity, and I should have felt bad about it, but the guilt just didn't show up.

Cousin Syl woke me in the morning. "Jeez, Bram, is this the way you keep my book secret? You're sleeping with it wide open on your bed. God, you smell like cum. Did you jerk off? Oh, I see. Man, your underwear. You think nobody can see all that dried jism? You must have unloaded a bucketful. Do you like sleeping with cum in your skivvies? Wow, that's gross."

My briefs were glued to my skin, and when I pulled them off, they pulled some pubic hair with them. I winced at the pain.

"Jeez, that's gotta hurt," Cousin Syl exclaimed. "Man, there's dried spunk all over your dick and balls, in your pubes and on your stomach. When I jack off, I make sure I clean up. I jizz in a warm washrag, and then I wash the washrag real good, so Mom doesn't find it. My parents would kill me if they knew I was flogging my dolphin. Do you talk to your parents about whacking off?"

I shook my head at his insane catechism, but he never slowed. "How about we jerk off together? I don't mean we gotta spank each other's monkey, just our own, like, unless you want to. It'd be kinda fun wouldn't it, just coming and the other guy doing all the work for you. I'll jerk you off first if you want. Or you can jerk off while I watch."

"Sure, we'll do it tonight," I promised. I felt strange after I agreed to masturbate with him; my face flushed with embarrassment, but my cock swelled a little, too. Frankly, I was surprised I'd said it. I told myself that I'd agreed just to shut him up. However, my promise helped because Syl did calm down. His crazed suggestions ceased, and he sat quietly on the side of my bed studying the evil book while I stepped into the shower.

After I'd made myself more presentable, Syl hid the Satanic text, and we trooped downstairs for breakfast with Aunt Edna and Uncle Jim. Breakfast was one of the good things about the farm. Not that Aunt Edna cooked, but we got the same food that the farmhands got, and the cook, whom everybody called Cookie, really laid it on. I piled my plate high with scrambled eggs, sausages, buttered grits, bacon, and pancakes. I'd just started drinking coffee, so I had some of that, too, but I also got a glass of chocolate milk.

After breakfast, I wrote a long letter to my parents and blathered about how great I was doing and other rubbish that Christian parents like to hear. I had my Bible beside me, so I threw in a few verses that would make Dad proud. Cousin Syl found me just as I was finishing.

"Bram, do you think the Bible is the word of God?"

"My dad says it is. In fact, so does yours."

"That's not an answer."

"Okay, Syl, if you want the truth, I think that back in the Dark Ages a bunch of old farts got together and made it all up."

Syl regarded me with a worshipful expression. "That's what I think, too," he said. "They wanted to control everybody else, especially about sex."

From that moment, I started looking at Syl in a new light. Syl was my age, actually a week younger than I, and we'd often had to celebrate our birthdays together, and I'd always resented him. Moreover, he acted like a nincompoop most of the time. Nevertheless, coming from such cold-fish parents, how was he supposed to act? I resolved to be nicer to him.

"Wanna go swimming?" Syl asked.

"Where?"

"At the creek. There's a great swimming hole. I'll show you."

Syl and I set off for the creek, which was an hour's hike from the house. It was about four miles, and Syl was more used to walking over fields and climbing fences than I, but we finally reached the deep hollow where the creek ran. Then we followed the stream through ferns, violets, elderberry bushes, and patches of wild onions until we reached the deep, wide swimming hole.

Syl had carried a canvas bag, and he pulled a huge towel from it and laid it over the green onion stalks.

"Man, those crushed onions are gonna make that towel stink," I warned stripping off my clothes. Buck naked, I stuck my foot into the creek. "It's cold."

I jumped in and splashed around, but I kept my eyes on Syl. When he had finished laying out his stuff, he stripped off his shoes, shirt, and shorts. My cousin wasn't wearing any underwear. His tight curved buns, and his thick cock popped out of his denim shorts when he dropped them, and the sight gave me a funny feeling. I felt strange all over, but I couldn't say what had caused it.

Syl jumped into the water, creating a gigantic splash that nearly drowned me. We splashed, swam, and played some grab-ass water game that Syl knew, and finally retired to the towel. Syl had brought some fruit and nuts that we washed down with orange pop and finished the repast with a couple of candy bars.

After eating, we rested and talked. "I saw the page you were looking at while you spanked your monkey," Syl said.

"Huh," I said. My face flushed again.

Syl's eyes were very bright. He stared directly into my face as he said, "You jacked off on that picture of the guy kissing the devil's ass."

I felt like something huge was blocking my throat. I couldn't answer. I wanted to tell him that he was mistaken. I wanted to deny everything. But my throat was constricted so that no words would come. Syl's eyes continued to bore into mine, but I became aware that he was moving in another way. Glancing down, I saw his hand fondling his cock.

"That picture is magical," Syl said. "Looking at it forces you to jerk off. I've unloaded on it six times since I found that book."

"Only six?" I croaked as the tightness that had gripped my throat moved down toward my crotch. "It looked like a thousand men had come on it." As I said those words, my dick hardened. As if instinct had

7

alerted him, Syl moved his eyes toward my crotch. His eyes gleamed as he saw my stiffening dick.

"Wanna do it now?" Syl asked. His voice was hoarse with lust.

"Here?" I was having second thoughts about jerking off with another guy, much less Cousin Syl, and I'd never dreamed I might have to go through with my promise. I was afraid, but my dick hardened to its full arousal.

"Sure, nobody comes here. Except me. I come here," Cousin Syl quipped. He reached into the bag and dragged out another old book that must've got shipped over on the Ark or something. It was bound in ancient leather with pages made of skin. I'd never seen an older or creepier-looking tome. Syl opened it to the title page, which read in barely intelligible black letter printing, *Manus Stuprare.*

I was afraid to touch the book, yet I wanted to touch it more than anything. "What's that mean? I asked.

"It's got something to do with perverting your hand," Syl informed me happily. His hand was rubbing his dick.

"Syl, where did you get this book?" My finger barely brushed the book, but the merest tap with a fingernail was sufficient to clamp my hand on my cock as if it had gone there of its own accord.

Instead of answering, my cousin flipped to a marked page. "Look at this spell," he said pointing toward an enchantment titled with weirdly shaped letters that looked like *Masturbari Frijonds.* The more Syl handled the book, the more he was forced to handle his cock.

I was getting interested in spite of myself. *Manus Stuprare* was unlike any other book I'd ever seen, though the page looked like a million men had ejaculated on it. "Those words are part Latin and part something else. Does it really mean jerk-off your friends?"

"Let's do the spell, Bram," Syl suggested. "All we have to do is chant the words while we jack off." He pulled a jar of makeup remover from his bag.

Our hands had been busily fondling our cocks since the book came out, but we'd been playing dry. I'd never imagined such lubrication that Syl was offering. "What's this?"

"Wait until you try it," Syl said. "It slicks up your dick, so you can beat it all day."

"You've been beating off with your mother's cosmetics? You're a pervert, Syl."

He didn't even look abashed. "This is nothing. Jerry King, a guy at my high school, used to jack off in his sister's panties. Really pissed her off whenever she found dried cum in her crotch."

I shook my head in dismay, but Syl thrust his hand into the makeup remover, slicked his palm, and grabbed my cock. The touch of his hand was like an electric shock. I was afraid that swapping hand-jobs with my cousin would lead to trouble, but his fist was making me happy. He started chanting the four-line stanza under *Masturbari Frijonds.* Suddenly my cock tingled so potently that my head swam. When the dizziness faded, I reached for the goop and smeared it onto Syl's cock.

I lost my Christian soul the moment my hand touched his dork. My world reeled, and ten thousand nuclear bombs went off inside my body. Drool ran out of my mouth as the sensation of Syl's cock rocketed from my hand to my brain. "I stroke your cock," I declared and discerned that the unfamiliar tongue Syl was chanting must have meant exactly that: "I stroke your cock. I stroke your cock. I stroke your cock. I stroke your cock."

I chanted the strange words in unison with Syl while my fingers played with his dickhead, twisting as I would a bottle cap, thrusting hard up and down his shaft, and sliding my other hand under him to finger his ass crack and to milk the underside of his balls. Meanwhile, Syl was doing similar things to me, and when I rose for him, he pushed his lubed finger into my asshole while he stroked me off.

Cousin Syl's hand was hard and soft on me, both at once. He gripped my dick with a firm hand, yet the oily lubricant never lost its polish. The makeup remover, spread with the soft skin of Syl's hand, carried me to extreme levels of sexual transport. That my hand was giving him the same feelings and that I was bringing him into a state of helpless abandonment only served to magnify my sensations a thousandfold. Syl beat my shaft with well-practiced strokes, while I used the knowledge I'd gained while pounding my own penis to enhance his gratification. Just as he was doing to me, I pushed my oily finger into his asshole and probed while Syl's chants rose in volume and intensity. "I stroke your cock. I stroke your cock. I stroke your cock. I stroke your cock."

I wanted to moan, groan, and beg him never to stop, but my mouth could form only the words of the spell, and together we chanted until orgasms hit us simultaneously. I wanted to shriek to Syl, beg him to stop beating my meat, and still entreat him to continue the exquisite torture. I couldn't stand the intense pleasure, but I wanted it never to cease. The sensation as my cock purpled with the abuse and cascaded through a series of heart-stopping orgasms was another kind of death. Both Syl and I died and were reborn a thousand times as we spurted loads of wet spunk onto one another and onto the open page of the book. When it was over, we lay side by side: gasping, decorated, and supremely satisfied.

"God, Syl," I wheezed after I'd half-way caught my breath. "I've never had an orgasm that good before." I slid my finger out of his ass and rolled onto my back.

"Yeah," he gasped. Even Syl was nearly speechless after that hand-job.

When we had recovered, Syl rinsed his mother's semen-spattered towel in the stream and hung it over a branch. "Maybe the smell of the wild onions will mask other lingering odors," he opined affirmatively.

We jumped into the swimming hole and washed each other carefully. I scrubbed Syl's cock and balls and rubbed my hand into his ass crack. The oily makeup remover didn't react well with the water, but we managed to clean off the bulk of it. We were both leery of leaving stains on our clothing. Syl and I had crept into David and Jonathan territory, and our fathers would act much like the biblical Saul if they ever suspected. After the air had dried us, we picked up our stuff, closed the Manus Stuprare, which now contained our dried semen along with its previous collection, and hiked home for supper.

Over the next weeks, Syl and I spent most of our days at the swimming hole, jerking each other off until we were experts. We used diverse spells from Syl's book to enhance our orgasms until we were fairly sex crazed. Still we didn't think of each other as lovers. We had started as cousins, and getting our rocks off together had made us close friends, but we weren't in love.

Since I had been raised to equate sex with love, I broached the subject to Syl one day as we lay naked on a towel so stained with lubricant and semen that we didn't dare carry it back to the farm. "You know that we've been doing some pretty gay stuff, Syl."

Syl looked at me with a hint of concern. "You don't want to stop, do you?"

"Of course not; it feels too good. I'm just wondering if we're supposed to fall in love."

"I think that sex and love are poles apart," Syl said. "If you're worried, we could get other guys to play with us."

"Where are we going to find them around here?" I asked. "Ask some guy down at the church if he wants to spank the monkey with us?"

Syl placed one hand on his cock and reached for the *Book of Spells*. "That would be dim-witted – we'd be asking for everything we got – which wouldn't be good. Besides, who says our playmates have to be human? Instead of you beating my sausage, how about we conjure demons to jack us off?"

I felt the blood drain from my face. "Demons, Syl? Are you nuts?"

Syl opened the weird book to another jism-stained page and pointed to a spell. "See this? We can summon demons and make them our sex slaves. Of course, we'll have to wait for the night of the full moon, and we'll have to do it pretty far from the house." He thought for a minute. "I know just the place. There's a lighting blackened tree on a low hill. It looks like a place where evil dwells."

"Evil. Great," I muttered sarcastically. I couldn't stop my hand from rubbing my spent dick as I read through the spell. The ancient text described how the demons would have to give us blow jobs and let us fuck them in the ass. "Hey, Syl, did you happen to notice this part? After we perform the spell, the demons get to fuck one guy to death and carry his spirit body off to Hell, so he can get screwed by all the devils in the pit."

"Huh." Syl took the book and read the fine print. The more intently he studied, the busier his hand became. "Wow, you're right. It's called 'the butt fuck that lasts forever.' That sounds kind of rough, Bram. But it says that we can choose a scapegoat to take the punishment for us."

"A scapegoat. Tell me, Syl, whom would you like to see fucked to death?"

What happened next was like a scene out of a low budget movie. We were resting naked on the towel, drying in the sun, and talking about spells when we heard a cruel guffaw.

"Oh, for God's sake, look at the pansy boys. Wait until your parents hear about this, Sylvester."

We leaped to our feet, and saw the farm foreman Fred staring at us. Fred was dressed in his usual attire of cowboy boots, tight jeans, blue shirt, red bandana, and cowboy hat.

"We've been swimming, Fred. Nobody's going to care that we went skinny dipping in the old swimming hole."

Trampling wild onions and raising a pungent stink, Fred approached us close enough to see the cum drying on our bodies.

"You pussies have been giving each other the devil's handshake. Wait 'til I tell Jim that his son is queer."

I wanted to stand up to Fred and tell him to say whatever he liked, but Syl turned pale. "Don't," he begged. "Please don't."

"What will you pay to keep me quiet?" Fred asked.

"So it's like that," I said. "Did you follow us here? How long have you been watching us, Fred? Do you get your rocks off watching naked guys?"

Fred blushed so crimson that his red-checked neckerchief faded in comparison, but Syl hardly noticed.

"I have a hundred bucks," Syl offered.

"A hundred," Fred snorted. "Don't fool with me, boy. Tell you what, you both suck my cock, and I'll forget what I saw."

"Yuk! We can't do that," Syl said.

"Then I'm gonna have a little talk with your pa."

"Please," Syl begged.

"Fred, we might break down and suck your dick," I temporized. "We got to think about it first."

"Nothin' to think about."

"There's lots to think about, Fred. You don't just spring something like that on a guy. It's not Christian."

Fred stroked his chin as he rationalized Christian blackmail with Christian cocksucking. "Okay, I'll give you until this time tomorrow."

When he temporized, I knew for sure that he'd been jerking off in the bushes while watching us. If he hadn't just emptied his balls, he'd have wanted the blowjob immediately.

"Three days," I said. "Three days from today. We'll meet right here."

"I said tomorrow," Fred threatened.

"And, I made a counter-offer," I asserted over Syl's protests. "Three days from today, we'll start sucking your cock regularly."

Fred was weaker than he pretended, so he let himself be bought. Fortunately, he was also stupid and having received our promise to meet in three days, he went back to his duties.

"I don't want to suck his dick, Bram," Syl complained. "I can't stand the thought of that skinhead's pecker in my mouth. Maybe I'd suck your dick if you really wanted me to do it because you're my best friend, not to mention my cousin, but I'd barf if my lips touched Fred's cock. I guess I could suck your dick okay, and you could even get your rocks off in my mouth. Nice guys swallow, don't they? Anyway, I don't want to suck Fred's dick. Do you want to suck him off?"

"No, Syl, neither of us is going to blow Fred, and he's not going to tell your parents either."

"Why not?"

"Because we have three days' grace."

"So?"

"So, the moon will be full two nights from now."

# # # # #

Aunt Edna knocked urgently at my bedroom door the morning after Syl and I had summoned the demons. I hastily leaped to my feet, and I was trying to pull my blue jeans shorts over my briefs when she burst in.

"Aunt Edna, I'm not dressed."

"Never mind that now, Abraham. We're forming a prayer chain around the bunkhouse, and you and Sylvester need to join in."

Syl emerged from his room – she'd awakened him first – and we hurried to the bunkhouse where Uncle Jim was organizing the grumbling farm hands into a prayer circle.

"Everybody join hands," my uncle shouted hysterically. "We'll circle the building and drive out Satan."

"What happened?" I asked.

One of the hands nodded knowingly. "The bunkhouse boss kicked the bucket."

"Our foreman died?" Syl asked. "That's what this fuss is about?"

"The circumstances of Fred's passing were peculiar." The farm hand drawled pe-cu-li-ar into four libidinous syllables.

"What do you mean?"

"We found him draped naked over a sawhorse with duck butter dripping out his ass," the hand whispered.

"Stop talking down there," Uncle Jim screeched. "We're going to pray."

13

The prayer chain ordeal was dreadful. Syl and I had opened the door for the sex demons, and we didn't want our flaky fanatic relatives trying to kick them out. I concentrated on mentally reversing every word Uncle Jim was spouting.

"I bet Fred is squealing like a pig in Hell," Syl whispered with a shudder. "It's creepy to think about it."

I shrugged, trying not to giggle at the image of demons tossing Fred from cock to cock.

All the praying and the preaching made for a long morning, but the arrival of the sheriff and the county coroner broke up the monotony. The sheriff, a waddling specimen who couldn't have followed a clue more than five feet, took Syl and me aside and asked if we'd heard anything.

We told him enough truth to dissuade him from considering us as suspects. We told him that we had gone out for a long walk in the full moon, and gave him a location fairly close to the real one. If later someone reported having seen us, we'd be covered, and the suggestion that two eighteen-year-old boys had sneaked out made more sense to the sheriff than if we'd tried to convince him that we were sleeping like lambs.

"Is it true, what one of the hands said?" Syl asked, feigning youthful innocence.

"What's that?" the sheriff asked.

"That Fred had, uh, you know, semen ... up his butt."

"That's a detail we wanted to hold back, but I figure Nosey Parker from the *Gazette* has it by now. He's talked to more of the hands than I have. Yeah, it's true, and there was a shitload of it. More jism than any ten men could squirt. We're looking for a whole gang of man rapists, so you boys better stay home until we catch them."

Later in the day, Syl and I found a quiet place to talk. "Do you still feel creepy?" I asked.

"I feel guilty because I don't feel guilty."

I laughed. "Fred's death doesn't weigh upon my conscience."

"I wonder if he liked it," Syl said. "Those thick demon cocks shooting wet damnation up his ass." Syl wiggled his butt. "Maybe Fred died of pleasure, not pain."

"I'm sure it felt good. Maybe he's happy in Hell."

We made it through a dismal supper; my aunt and uncle ate in stony silence after both offered up long prayers while the food cooled.

Not long after we'd eaten, Syl and I retired to our rooms. I read a mystery novel until I fell into a troubled sleep. In my dream, I witnessed Fred shrieking as the demons passed him around. One greenish Leviathan tossed Fred high and when Fred plunged ass downwards, the gigantic devil ringed Fred's asshole onto his enormous and hellish-shaped cock.

Late in the night, Syl shook my shoulder. "Wake up, Bram. We have visitors."

My heart thundering in my chest, I sat bolt upright. Abbadon and Nuberus were lurking behind Syl. However, according to the book, now that we had sacrificed Fred, we could "intercourse freely" without a circle of protection. I hoped that the ancient Conjuror of the Left-Hand Path knew his business.

I'd summoned these demons to rid us of Fred, not because I wanted diabolical gay sex. Nonetheless, the spell we'd used was libidinous, and Syl and I could only free ourselves from Abbadon and Nuberus by submitting them to our lusts. The book didn't say how many times we had to do it.

I glanced at Syl with a world of meaning in my eyes, and he nodded. I felt my cock hardening as I addressed the two fiends from the pit: "You might as well start by sucking our cocks."

I pulled off my jockey briefs and sat naked on the side of my bed. Syl dropped his bare ass down beside mine. I was terrified, but fear didn't weaken my erection. The air hummed with sexual energy, and Syl grabbed my hand and held it as the horned purplish demons dropped to their knees. I shivered as Nuberus touched his lips, reddened instantly as if with love's wound, to my cockhead and slowly consumed it. As his horny head rose and fell upon my swollen meat, his long hairless tail twitched.

I'd never had my cock sucked before, and these demons knew how to milk a dick. Syl and I were biting my pillow to keep from crying out and bringing his parents to my room as the demons tortured our cockheads with their lips and tongues. Nuberus's tongue wrapped around the head of my cock and massaged it deep down.

The demonic mouth rubbed my dick all the way through, and erectile tissue that had never been stimulated before expanded until the skin on my cock was stretched tight. My dick throbbed, burned, and tingled; the muscles at the base of my penis were contracting long before my balls pushed semen up my shaft. Pleasurable sensations were shooting up my asshole as well. My stomach muscles tightened. My nipples tingled orgasmically, as did my lips and nose. My eyelids fluttered, and I could not control them. I seized the back of Nuberus's head with one hand and squeezed Syl's hand with the other.

The blowjob didn't take long by the clock, but subjectively it lasted for an infinite time. Just as I was certain that I was going to die, as my heart pounded and I fought to breathe, the orgasm of all orgasms, the utmost, incomparable pleasure burst, the tingle-tickle-shiver seizure throbbed in the head of my cock. The pleasure-paroxysm rippled down my shaft until my contracting pelvis muscles pushed my semen up my tubes like a volcano spewing magma. Syl and I, gripping hands and gnawing the pillow, blasted tremendous loads down the demonic throats. Nuberus swallowed my seed greedily, and the implications of what bestowing my cum on a Lesser Lord of Hell might mean flickered faintly through my mind, but the rapturous waves of sexual transport overthrew reflection and turned me into a spurting savage, and in the throes of orgasm, I possessed no more conscious or conscience than an octopus.

After we had gushed our residue of semen, the demons wiped their glistening mouths with their clawed hands, bestowed a malignant smirk upon us, and departed wordlessly. Syl released my hand, which was white from his grip, and pulled up his plaid boxers. I climbed into my briefs after a quick peek at my softening dick, so deceptively clean and rancorously fresh from the demon's mouth.

"I'd better get back to my room," Syl said, kissed me quickly and unexpectedly on the lips, and fled to his own bed, so his mother could awaken her spotless and virginal offspring there in the morning.

That day, Syl and I pedaled knobby-tired bicycles along the farm's bucolic paths, and we barely made it home in time for supper. Following the early meal, we had to attend an evening prayer meeting at the church. I studied the congregation as we pretended to pray, and I suspected that Syl and I were probably the only Christians there who'd been sucked off by demons. I sensed a great gulf growing between my father's faith and me.

Abbadon and Nuberus woke me late that night, and I led them to Syl's room and woke him. For some reason, the demons stuck together. As we prepared for the night's sexual adventure, a new craving overcame me. I noticed how enticing Nuberus's ass looked. The demon

16

had bewitching curves beneath his tail, and the desire to stick my cock between them dried my mouth with lechery.

"Teach me how to fuck your ass, Nuberus," I demanded.

"I want to try that, too," Syl said, tossing his boxers over the lampshade. My underwear joined his, and I rubbed my cock across the fiend's sexy ass.

Nuberus threw himself face down on Syl's bed and doubled a pillow under his middle to elevate his ass. His tail draping over the side of the bed, he pulled his right leg up to his pointy chin and his purplish buttocks invited penetration. When I ran my hand over the firm, generous mounds, I nearly swooned with excitement – just as I'd felt a thrill when first I touched Syl's cock. My own cock was flinty, pointing toward the heavens, and dripping pre-cum as I rubbed it over Nuberus's alluring buttocks.

"Stick it into me," Nuberus urged. "A demon's ass is self-lubricating, so you shall find the passage easy. Slide your cock into the delicious darkness."

I positioned my dick against his hole and rammed. Nuberus's asshole received me like an old friend, and I drove my cock into the wet, grainy chute. Not jacking off alone, not beating Syl's meat, not even the blowjob from the demon, nothing I'd ever imagined had prepared me for that sensation. It was, as the demon had promised, a slide into delicious darkness.

"Ah, that's nice," I sighed, and the bed shifted as Abbadon took his place beside my devil, and Syl jammed his pecker into his own demon's butt.

I raised my hips and started humping, but Nuberus's wonderfully evil anal tube was so hot and so tight that my cock could hardly stand it. Every inch of movement was a torment of delight, a rapturous pleasure that was pain in small doses but a pain I couldn't forgo. All my life, my dick had itched with an itch that I could never sufficiently scratch. Nuberus's delicious darkness scratched deeper than any friction ever had before.

"Uh," I groaned. "Oh." The delicious distress was incredible and I wanted more.

"Oh, uh," Syl grunted, biting his demon's neck as he fucked him. "Not so loud, Bram," he managed through his gasps.

17

I clamped my teeth into Nuberus's shoulder. I squealed, though my jaws were stuffed with demon flesh. "Oh, I've never had it so good. Oh, Nuberus, I love fucking your ass. Oh, yes, it's good."

A throbbing ecstasy stunned my cock, and I thrust even harder and faster. "Oh, I'm gonna blast a wad. Here it comes, you sexy devil. I'm gonna shoot my cum up your ass."

"Yes, fill me, mortal boy. Give me your sacred seed to carry back to Hell. Pour it into my delicious darkness, saved against the day it shall be returned to you increased by a multitude."

Pour I did. Even the sinister implications of the demon's words couldn't stop me from unloading my seed into his hellishly-fine poop tube. Meanwhile, my sexual transport inspired Syl's body to unload with me, so he moaned and ejaculated into Abbadon's cute butt while I gave Nuberus my all.

A few minutes later, we popped our drained cocks out of the demons' asses. After Syl and I returned from the bathroom after washing up, we discovered that the demons had not vanished. They were lolling seductively on Syl's bed.

"Thank you, Nuberus," I said. Yes, I knew that he was a denizen of the underworld, but he deserved thanks for putting out so pleasurably. However, he surprised me when he grabbed my head and gave me a deep and soul lingering kiss with his supernatural tongue. After breaking from the hot soul kiss, he and Abbadon disappeared in a puff of pale steam.

Syl studied me with a mixture of dismay and jealous interest. "That was one hell of a kiss," he commented. "I wonder why he did that. My demon didn't kiss me."

I was at a loss for words. The kiss had left my legs wobbly and my head spinning. I staggered back to my room, collapsed into bed, and fell into dreams of temple boys joyously prostituting their asses to Ishtar, and congregations of worshipful men masturbating their semen onto the clay floor around the statue of Baal.

The summer rolled by, and every night Abbadon and Nuberus pleasured us until we were satisfied. By the next night, we were unbearably horny again – in fact, we grew hornier as time progressed – and we spent hours fucking our devils or having them suck our dicks. Both Syl and I agreed that the fucking was best, sliding into the delicious darkness as Nuberus had called it, but the sucking added variety.

Then one night, our happy edifice of black magic sex came crashing down. Literally, it crashed down. We were fucking our demons in Syl's bed, which had started rocking after two months of heavy action. I was biting my devil's neck, and the cum was rising from my balls and filling the spout in my dick when there sounded a loud crack. Alas! Just as I ejaculated, the bed, crashing to the floor, made a frightful clamor that woke everybody in the house.

Syl and I tried to pull our spurting dicks out of the demons, but we were in the throes of hell-kindled high arousal. Unable to think with our brains, we continued to pour our fluids into Abbadon and Nuberus. When Syl's locked door burst open, and his parents fell through, the demons instantly vanished, but our position was still compromising. Uncle Jim came close to a heart attack and ended up spending a night in the hospital.

Made of sterner stuff, Aunt Edna looked sadly at her naked son whose dripping hard-on was slowly deflating, shook her head, and turned away. Neither of them spoke a word to me.

That was the last time I saw my cousin. His parents allowed us no communication. Long distance phone calls caused Dad to cut his evangelical tour short, and he and Mom flew back from Australia that very night. With their various connections, it was about twenty-four hours before I saw them, but I was busy sitting in my locked room without a key during that time.

When Dad and Mom reached the farm, they had hired security guards with them – armed guards – who handcuffed me for the trip home. Three weeks after my parents took charge of me, I was a prisoner in a Christian Reparative Therapy Camp, which claimed its strict regime and draconian discipline could reprogram youthful sex perverts. I won't say that it was sackcloth, beatings, and indoctrination from dawn until dark, but those nouns would go some way toward describing the truth. Jesus would have hated the place.

Of course, the other guys at the academy were bad seeds as well, and they accepted me wholeheartedly when I told them I got caught butt fucking my cousin (even those hardened perverts might have blanched at the truth).

The Pharisees and Sadducees (teachers and administrators) watched us continuously. Everything that was not mandatory was forbidden. Cruel exercise and non-stop Bible classes and prayer circles were rigorously enforced, while privacy was prohibited. Even fashionable briefs were considered a snare of the devil. One poor sinner got caught masturbating in a closet. His punishment? Two gym teachers flogged him with razor straps while the other teachers force-marched the rest of us in a circle around him. The camp had cameras installed everywhere – including in the bathroom stalls, but no camera could record the unworldly.

One night Abbadon and Nuberus appeared before me. "Where have you been?" I demanded.

"We had to help your cousin escape," they said. "His circumstances were even worse than yours."

"Get me out of here," I pleaded.

"Of course," the devils replied, smiling apart. "That's what we're here for. Where would you like to go?"

"Anywhere but here," I said rashly. "This place is Hell."

That was the night the fantasy that had enthralled me when I first viewed Cousin Syl's mysterious book came to pass. I finally kissed the Devil's asshole. Soon afterward, I learned the other side of joy – the indescribable bliss of giving the delicious darkness.

THE FAIRY KING

A queue of fairy fellows waited to gang-bang Mike and George. Mike was crouching on his hands and knees on the yellowish-green grass, his ass thrust up and back, with rapture painting his face, while an eight-foot-tall silvery fairy with pointed ears, slanted eyes, gossamer wings, and perky buttocks humped him with luxurious indolence.

The fairy delivering the slow ass fuck was named Silverbell. Stricken with befuddled lust, I watched Silverbell's thick cock sliding comfortably in and out of Mike's ass and wondered how it felt. Mike seemed to be enjoying Silverbell as much as Silverbell was enjoying him. With wanton collaboration, Mike was hunching back to meet Silverbell's thrusts. Mike's cock was hard and dripping pre-cum onto the grass. "Oh, yes, fuck my ass," Mike was moaning. "You fill me so good. Ah, I love your thick cock." Mike hunched his ass into Silverbell's lap more aggressively as he moaned his song of fulfillment. "Oh, pack my ass full. Load me up. Fill my bowels with your spunk."

At the same time, George reclined on a bed of pinkish flowers, his legs pulled way up, as a green, wingless fairy named Greasewood, whose face wore a constant smirk, drilled George's ass hard and fast. Like Mike, George was taking the whole shaft right up to the hilt, yet Greasewood's dick head was hitting George's asshole on every other stroke.

"Oh, take it, pixie," the five-foot-tall Greasewood was moaning. "Ah, take it. Take it."

George took it and took it deep. Greasewood would pull his cock nearly out of George's ass; then he would slam it home. As the fairy cock pounded him, George howled with joy. "That's good; that's really good. I love it. Oh, Greasewood, my ass is yours forever. Don't ever stop."

The sky of fairyland hung above me like a bowl, clear blue and dotted with fleecy clouds. The soft breeze was scented with sweet musk rose and wild thyme and a spicy odor that might have been fairy spunk. Despite my reluctance to put out like my friends, my penis was throbbing. A fairy man with mottled pink skin approached me, his gnarly cock hard and slick. A constant stream of cum was leaking from its tip.

"Let Prairie Rose plant his seed in your pixie bottom," the pink fairy whispered lewdly. His knobby hands stroked my naked butt cheeks. Prairie Rose was covered with warts and odd protrusions; he had bumps that looked like hemorrhoids, welts, carbuncles, and myriad morbid growths like soft thorns without points. Even his cock was bumpy, but instead of disgusting me, I found the odd protuberances enticing.

Prairie Rose's bumpy hands were on my butt, and his demand hung on the air: "Give Prairie Rose your ass."

My fate loomed. If I let Prairie Rose slide his cock into me, I'd be taking it for life – destined to life as a pixie bottom, just like my two best friends George and Mike. Even as they were getting dicked, my friends witnessed my indecision.

"It feels so good, Ross," Mike urged, panting with hot lust as Silverbell banged him. "Let Prairie Rose turn you out. Let him have your ass."

"Ah, take it, Ross," George moaned. "You won't be sorry. Oh, yes, you'll love his fairy cock up your pixie hole."

I searched the pink fairy's eyes, unworldly eyes that promised freedom in surrender. Prairie Rose promised to break the chains of conformity. I would commit the incomparable rebellion against my mother's dominion and the discipline of my teachers.

"Fuck my ass," I said, my mouth speaking before my programmed conscience could dissent. I turned my back on Prairie Rose, bent at the knees and poked out my ass. "Make me your pixie."

# # # # #

The first of May started with an ordinary ramble among the hills. Mike and I piled into George's ancient Jeep, and we drove far into the high desert. When the track petered out, we secured his vehicle, shouldered our supplies, and set out on foot. The desert was covered with low stony hills, deep crevices, colorful rock outcroppings, and fields of spring flowers. We each carried stout walking sticks, but the few rattlesnakes we encountered slithered away, and we didn't pursue them.

At noon, we picnicked, slathered on more sunscreen, pissed together off the edge of a cliff, and continued exploring. About an hour after lunch, Mike sang out, "Hey, George, Ross, check out this cleft in the rock."

George and I followed him to the steep rock face and studied the narrow slit that led into the hill.

"We can fit," I suggested. "Let's see where it goes."

"Ross, there's got to be snakes," Mike argued. "Maybe a cougar."

I tried poking my stick into the crack, but the way twisted too much. "We'll have to leave our stuff. We're barely going to slip through with the clothes on our backs."

"This is dangerous," George complained. "I'm not going."

"Don't be a wuss."

Spurred by the universal fear of being thought wussy, my friends shed their packs, walking sticks, and water bottles. We piled our stuff beside the rocky breach, and I pushed into the red, dry hillside. It was a tight fit, but I squirmed through with minor scrapes. After a few feet, the slit widened into a tunnel with a sandy floor illuminated eerily by a low green light cast by the sun filtered through the overhanging weeds.

"It's safe," I called back. "There aren't any snakes or cougars."

A minute later, the pair had joined me. Leading my friends single file, I poked around a bend and found another slit through which we could see bright sunlight. I tried pushing through this rift, but my clothing hung me up. My boots didn't give enough, my belt added to my girth, and my baggy brown shorts caught on the rocks. Finally, my friends pulled me back.

"I think that I could slip through naked."

"Are you nuts?" Mike asked.

"Come on, we're explorers," I chided. "Where's your sense of adventure?"

I stripped off everything but my boxers and tried the slit again. The rocks were polished smooth and my skin slid over them easily. But the cloth in my underwear wouldn't budge over those strange rocks.

"Sorry, guys, our underwear has to come off, too," I said.

"Ross, you are positively insane," George announced as I tossed my boxer shorts onto my pile of clothes. "What if we can't squeeze back through? You wanna drive home buck naked?"

I was too busy navigating the close cut to answer. Amazingly, my bare body seemed to slide through easily, and in mere seconds, I popped out the other side and found myself in a landscape thoroughly unlike the one I'd left a dozen yards back.

"Come on, guys," I shouted into the slit. "You've got to see this."

A few minutes later, I had goaded my friends out of their clothes and through the crevice, and we were all standing in a landscape of tall green trees, flowery fields, and fertile grasslands. In the distance, we could see cool lakes where no water should have been and pristine snow-capped mountains higher and more abundant than the mountains of home.

"Where the hell are we?" Mike exclaimed, checking out a thicket of briars hung heavy with red raspberries. He ate a couple of the berries and smiled at their sweetness.

"This is impossible," George complained and kicked at a lush green mossy knoll overtopped with climbing roses. "It's the friggin' twilight zone."

"Hello, George, beam back to reality," I called. "We're here. It's real. Get over it."

"We should go back," Mike urged, watching George back his bare ass toward the sweet wild rose, crimson with buds and thick with thorns.

I pulled back a flowery shoot that was about to deflower George's rosebud. "Go back? Why? We just got here. Let's explore."

"We're stark naked, Ross," Mike howled. "And there are thorns."

"There are also wildflowers and herbs. Don't you smell the wild thyme blowing?"

"We've got no clothes on. Do you think this is the Garden of Eden? Suppose we meet somebody?"

With a shrug, I forged ahead, and as I rounded a hawthorn-brake, I spied a group of improbable beings carousing by a silvery pond that gave back yellow sun and blue sky. I stopped short and shushed my friends with a gesture, but Mike protested loudly, "What the hell?"

His yelp caught the carousers' attention, and the whole party jumped up. George and I leaped behind a rock outcropping, but Mike was too slow. The denizens of this strange world spotted Mike and came buzzing, galloping, and whirring in our direction.

"Last time I take you on a spy mission, Mike Anderegg," I muttered as the strange assemblage bore down upon us.

"Maybe we better run," George said.

"Too late for that," I replied. "Some of those things have wings."

Indeed, an odd lot surrounded us. They had uniformly thick dicks and protrusive rumps. In fact, their asses were more bewitching than the butts of most girls I'd seen. Otherwise, they had pronounced physical idiosyncrasies, not limited to their variegated skin colors. These fantastic folk were colored with the hues of the rainbow or Van Gogh's palate, not to mention that they had sundry styles of wings, except some had no wings at all, and one had flipper feet, and two ran on cloven hooves, and many bore extra appendages, including one with three dicks, and some had other subtle things that I couldn't quite fathom.

One addressed us in an unknown tongue.

"Sorry, I don't speak your lingo," I said.

"Well met by sunlight," he greeted, switching to arcane English.

The phrase sounded half-familiar. "Met? You were expecting us?"

"We've been expecting new pixies for some time," he said, making his grammar more contemporary. "North American by your accents."

"Yes, Oregon," I admitted. "Who are you?"

"I am Dogwood, the Fairy King," he said with a tinkling laugh. "You lads have trespassed into the Realm of Faerie."

"We're sorry," George apologized, meekly plucking cowslips with his toes.

"Yeah, we'll leave right away," Mike promised.

"Oh, no, no, we can't let you rush off," Dogwood protested. "It's been long since we've had pixies from the wilds of Oregon."

"Pixies?" I queried. I wasn't sure I liked being called a pixie.

"We were about to dine. You must join us."

So Mike, George, and I plopped our bare buns down on the thick grass and wild parsley, while the fairy men laid out provisions from a wicker basket. We breathed a sigh of contentment when we saw the provender. There were yellow bottles of dandelion wine, which quenched the thirst most refreshingly. There were hard-boiled eggs, hot baked beans, tangy potato salad, warm yeasty bread with creamy butter, and cookies – fabulously good cookies. Although we'd finished our own picnic lunch about two hours earlier, the fairy food was the best we'd ever tasted. At our hosts' urging, we stuffed our guts.

After the fairies had packed the dishes away, Dogwood asked, "Now who will be first to receive a companion?"

"What companion?" I asked, dreamy and relaxed by the rich food and the dandelion wine.

A fairy lifted a crockery jar from the basket and opened the top. Peering inside, we saw fat purple slugs that shimmered with a lewd aura. The obscene-looking slugs were crawling inside the jar as if they were seeking a home.

The Fairy King beamed at us. "Would you pixies prefer to choose your companions, or should Bottlefly select for you?"

"Neither," I asserted. "I think we'd better leave."

At my words, the fairy folk snickered, and two hairy, satyr-shaped fairies rolled upon the ground in helpless hilarity. "You can't leave now," Dogwood explained through his chortles. "Once you have received our hospitality, you must host a companion. Bottlefly shall choose."

A muscular blue-green fairy touched his cock for inspiration as he selected three slugs. We stared aghast at the obscene creatures. The slugs glimmered with a vulgar sensuality that was embarrassingly homosexual.

"What have you gotten us into, Ross?" Mike whined. "What's going to happen?"

"Once we place the companions on your rumps," Dogwood answered simply, "they will open your assholes and slither inside. They will combine with your anal cells to form sexual tissues capable of self-lubrication and multiple extended orgasms."

George shrieked, and Mike turned death pale. "Oh, my god, no."

"We didn't come here to get butt clits," I protested. "You can't make us take them. We're American citizens."

The Fairy King addressed his court. "Should we send these pixies home with virgin tails?"

"Not for your fairy kingdom," proclaimed his court.

As laughing fairies seized me, others pushed down Mike and George. Since the fairies positioned me behind my friends, I could see what happened. My friends were screaming and swearing, but I held my protests. Crying would do me no good, for the fairy men were joyously bent on our receiving companions. A purple fairy called Pansyflower laid a sex slug on George's butt, and the companion promptly slithered toward George's butt crack. Mike got his next. Then a fairy placed a warm, slimy slug on my right buttock, and the symbion launched toward my asshole.

As I beheld the slugs disappearing into the rear ends of my friends, my butt crack parted for my new partner. It arrived at my asshole, and I clamped down hard to fight against the incursion. The slug jabbed my anal sphincter with a tiny quill and injected venom. Immediately, my asshole opened wide, and the anal intruder entered. The slug tickled going in, and after that I felt a probing and a fullness.

George and Mike's sudden giggles surprised me. "What a rush," George exclaimed.

Mike seemed gripped by a similar ecstatic thrill. He jumped to his feet and shouted, "I'm high as the moon."

I stood up. I felt strange, but Mike and George were experiencing something different. Mike was tittering tipsily while George was feeling up his butt.

"Ross," George blurted, "Why haven't you ever fucked me?"

"What?" His question stirred me, and I felt exceedingly naked.

"We've been friends forever, but we're slow learners. We could've been fucking instead of thinking about girls and other silly stuff."

"George is right," Mike said. "We could've been butt screwing instead of jerking off to girlie magazines."

I was feeling a sexual hunger, but I hadn't had the same reaction as my friends – yet. In time, I would discover I was hosting the most powerful butt slug of the trio, but my symbion was toying with me. Companions that trigger the strongest anal-pleasure-enhancing chemicals are playful; they delight in delaying the inevitable.

Meanwhile I was puzzled. "You guys turned queer? Just like that?"

"Yes," they shouted in unison.

As I shook my head, Dogwood asked my friends. "Are you pixies ready to take it?"

"Take it?" I asked. I was afraid to let George and Mike speak for the group.

Dogwood acted as though he were offering the keys to fairyland. "Take it – our fairy cocks. Anally."

"Anal?" My friends nodded enthusiastically, and their cocks were pointing toward the sky.

Dogwood beamed. "Yes, anal sex. We fairies give and receive anal pleasure. And human boys who invade the Realm of Faerie become our pixies."

"You're talking about butt fucking?" I asked stupidly. The prospect appealed strangely, but I was also frightened and ashamed. I glanced down at my cock and saw that it had stood up. "You expect to fuck our asses?"

"Of course," Dogwood affirmed, smiling at my useless effort to cover my swollen cock with my hands. "Assume whatever position appeals to you."

"Fuck my ass," Mike entreated dropping to his hands and knees amid feathery stalks of rosemary and asparagus and offering his rump to any fairy who wanted it.

Dogwood pointed toward a willowy fairy with pointed ears and numerous bulbous growths, and the fairy presented himself. Willow stroked Mike's rear with his large brown hands and explored Mike's asshole with his thick finger. My friend moaned and wiggled his ass enthusiastically. Preparing to pierce Mike's sphincter, Willow's penis grew thicker, stood so hard it quivered, and leaked thick yellowish gruel.

"Oh, my ass is wet," Mike announced. "Oh, yeah, my companion is lubricating me."

When Willow pushed his cock into Mike's asshole, my friend howled with delight: "Oh, yeah, stick it to me. That's good."

The sight of Mike taking it up the ass was too much for George, and he fell back on the thick moss and pulled back his legs. Persimmon, a diminutive but shapely fairy, got to fuck him first. At Dogwood's direction, Persimmon, who possessed a long dong and a girlish derrière, climbed between George's legs, took aim against his asshole, and slid his cock in.

"I'm a pixie," George howled. "That feels so good."

As I watched my friends relishing the fairy cocks banging their asses, my mouth dried with lust, and my dick throbbed. I gawked with longing as George and Mike took fairy cocks with obvious delight. Persimmon and Willow humped wildly, and George and Mike took the driving dicks just as enthusiastically.

Persimmon started pounding his fairy ass faster and faster. His eyes glinted, and his mouth made thin piping sounds as he splattered his load into George's ass. Meanwhile, George was urging him on and demanding that Persimmon fill him with spunk.

Willow came immediately after Persimmon. Mike was howling as the fairy filled him. With my own eyes, I witnessed Mike's cock buck and shoot its own load. Nobody had touched Mike's cock; it went off just from the butt fuck he was receiving. My mind was a whirl of mixed emotions. I was having thoughts and feeling lusts that I recognized as having been a part of my psyche as far back as I could remember.

Persimmon and Willow never pulled their cocks out of my friends' asses. They rested for a brief period, but less than a minute passed before they began humping again. My friends were howling with feral lust, and I recalled that Dogwood had promised multiple extended orgasms.

When Persimmon and Willow had spurted several times, my friends offered their open dripping assholes to Silverbell and Greasewood. Yet, I stood watching, afraid of what I would become, yet desiring with all my heart to join my friends in their great deflowering. Abruptly, I understood the source of my fear; my symbion hadn't forced these gay cravings upon me. My itch was natural.

As the realization that I was a born pixie swept over me, my slug sprang its surprise, releasing the stimulant that banished my fear of being thought gay and turned me wantonly promiscuous. Pixie Rose stood behind me. He placed his pink hands on my shoulder while his cock, slick with fairy cum and knobby with warts and other unearthly growths that promised stimulation for my asshole slid across my buttocks and nestled in my cleft.

A slick fluid leaked out of my asshole as my symbion lubed my tube. I grabbed my knees and offered Prairie Rose my tail-hole. "Yes, fuck me," I begged. "Stick your fairy cock up my asshole."

Prairie Rose didn't need a second request. He touched the tip of his big cock to my little hole, while instinctively I drew a deep breath and pushed. As I thrust against his dick, he penetrated me, and I howled with joy and pleasure. When he entered me all the way, his lap tight against my butt, I felt a fierce pride. "I'm taking it!" I yelled. "Yeah, I'm taking your thick cock up my ass. Oh, it's sweet. It's so fuckin' sweet."

"Ah-ha, I'm making a pixie," Prairie Rose whispered in my ear as his fairy cock filled my ass to the hilt and his leafy thighs squashed my buns.

I gripped my knees, and Prairie Rose wrapped his ropy arms tight around my waist as he humped my rear. His cock pulled back so that its tip brushed my asshole, pushed forward again, and filled me to the limit. With each stroke, his tip brushed my new anal clit, which had already driven new nerves and vessels through my prostate to my cock so that each jab in my ass felt like a simultaneous stroke of my cock head. I'd never felt such rapturous pleasure.

"Oh, you're a good pixie," Prairie Rose moaned as he fucked me. "You give good tail, pixie lad."

"Ah, fuck me, Prairie Rose," I groaned. "Oh, that's so good. I love the way you fuck my ass. Oh, you're gonna make me come. Oh, yeah, you're gonna fuck me into coming."

Nothing in my life had prepared me for the pleasure I was feeling, and I knew that no other form of sex could ever be this good. "Oh, I love taking it up the ass. Oh, yeah, I love your big cock stroking up my hole. Fuck me, fuck me, and fuck me more. Fuck my ass."

Mike and George had been howling with anal pleasure as their fairies butt fucked them, and my shrieks of rapture mingled with their moans.

"Ah, it's so good when a pixie appreciates getting fucked," Prairie Rose moaned. "I'm going to come in you, pixie lad. I'm going to spurt fairy spunk up your pixie ass."

"Give it to me," I screeched. "Squirt it into me. I'll take all you can give me."

Though already enchantingly full, I felt even more stuffed when Prairie Rose crammed me with cum. Just as soon as his fairy spunk reached my slug, that lusty symbion that had become flesh-of-my-flesh went off like a volcano, blasted pleasure up my ass, and forced my swollen dick to cream the air. My spurts rained upon George, Mike, and the fairies fucking them.

Yet, ejaculation was only the beginning. A sustained and growing orgasm began up my ass and continued for what seemed forever. I couldn't think, I couldn't make coherent sounds, and I couldn't control my movements. With what remained of my consciousness, I knew my ass was fucking Prairie Rose's knobby cock as much as he was fucking me. Still the orgasm went on and on, and moments after it ended, a new and even more powerful tingle began as Prairie Rose finished and other fairies gang-banged me, one by one.

After the pleasure and the spurting, I stretched out on the crushed herbs beside my friends and surveyed fairyland. Before my anal orgasms, I'd known the land was lovely, but afterward I could feel the timeless bliss of this world. Ripe fruit hung abundantly from the trees, and all foodstuffs grew without cultivation. Flowers blew profusely, pure and variegated, with highly nuanced hues and scents.

But even above the natural beauty of sun, sky, land, hill, and shrub, I saw the beauty of the fairy men. Like the fruit and flowers, they came in shapes beyond imagining, yet each offered pleasures of his own. I saw neither man nor fairy I would not have received gleefully.

Dogwood let us rest before we finished our commencement by humping a fairy's rump. While we rubbed our swelling cocks with anticipation, he told us that we could choose the fairy butt we most desired.

"I want to fuck your ass, Dogwood," I announced.

The Fairy King was delighted. "Come on, pixie boy." He threw himself face down in the fragrant sedge and raised his rump so that his rounded buns glowed in the sunlight.

George had been stroking my hard cock, but he stopped to select a fairy rump. I climbed onto Dogwood and placed my dick head against his asshole. His hole opened readily, his sex channel slick and wet already. The Fairy King had a companion of his own. As I lay atop his magnificent buns with my dick jammed in full, Dogwood did something I'd never have expected. Without my moving, his rectum started massaging my cock, as if I had inserted it into a milking machine. Dogwood's asshole gripped my cock so tight that I couldn't thrust, and I sprawled captive atop him while he milked me off.

I lost track of my friends, though I learned later that they had similar experiences. I lost track of the sun, the sky, and the ground. I lost track of time and space. Overpowering waves of pleasure swept over me, holding me in thrall to a sexual transport so intense that my conscious mind failed before it. I was lost in an annihilating orgasmic rush.

I squealed as my cock approached another orgasm. My heart was pounding in my chest and my breath came in sharp rasps. The tingles didn't stop in my dick but rippled up my ass as well, because my little passenger had become a permanent part of my body and connected anal pleasure with penile orgasm.

"Oh," I grunted as the twin orgasms roared up my dick and up my ass. "I can't stand it. It's too good. Ah, you're killing me."

But Dogwood knew I wouldn't die. He tortured my cock with his anal massage until my dick blasted a second, a third, and a fourth time in a series of spurts of hot spunk. But as I ejaculated in his butt, wetness grew within my own ass. My symbion filled me with cum even as I shot it out my dick. By the time Dogwood had my balls milked dry, my pixie ass was one wet hole.

As the sun set over fairyland, my friends and I bid farewell to the fairy men and pushed our naked bodies, bodies hot with new-hatched gratification, back through the crevice. On the sandy desert floor of the inner slit, we found our clothes, but not as we'd left them. Something had strewn our garments and everything was weathered and mildewed. Little desert mosses were growing on my ripped shorts and my shoes reeked of decay. We puzzled briefly over the mystery, but lacking other garb, we dressed in the deteriorating cloth and pushed back into our own world.

Our packs, walking sticks, and water bottles were gone. "What creep would've robbed us out here in the middle of the friggin' desert?" Mike complained.

"I don't know. Let's get back to the Jeep."

Though the sun had set, its light remained for a long time. We hiked to the place where we'd secured George's Jeep, but it wasn't there. We did find a bunch of supplies scattered around, as if a large party had camped on that spot.

"This is seriously weird," I said.

"Hey, who's there?" The voice came from behind some trees nearly obscured in the dwindling light.

"What happened to my Jeep?" George demanded loudly.

Several men, one a sheriff's deputy approached us. They looked at us with some amazement and sniffed at our smelly clothing.

"I think it's them," one man said.

"Who are you looking for?" I asked. "I'm Ross Baker, and these are my friends George Antcliffe and Mike Anderegg."

"My God, it is them. Where have you boys been? Searchers have been looking for you for the past month."

"What about my Jeep?" George demanded.

"Your parents had that towed about three weeks ago."

Apparently, we'd disappeared over a month before, though only an afternoon had passed in fairyland. Of course, we couldn't tell anybody about that. If we admitted we'd gone to fairyland where we'd received orgasmic anal tissue, the authorities would have secured us in a padded cell. Unfortunately, we had no coherent story to replace the truth, so we got a bad reputation in town, not to mention the national media.

Blabbermouth Mike decided to come out while being interviewed on CNN. The next day the headlines read as follows: "Gay Youths Deceive State Search Party."

It turned out that the state government had spent a million dollars searching, and they wanted us to pay it back. Our parents, who felt responsible for our evil deeds although we were twenty-one, hired a lawyer, and he advised us to flee the country. As we played in my bed, George, Mike, and I talked over the situation, and we decided to give it a year to blow over. Wiggling his ass as his companion lubricated him for reception, George spoke for us all when he said, "If things haven't improved by next spring, I'm hauling my pixie ass back to fairyland."

NIGHTS IN RED SPANKERS

It was Christmas Eve. As Eric and I lolled naked under the lighted tree, my parents slept upstairs. We had pushed aside the gaily-wrapped gifts and built a cuddling space under the fragrant needles. Other than the colored lights twinkling on the tree, the living room stood in darkness and not another creature was stirring.

I leaned toward Eric's face, and my lips found his. Our kiss was long, our tongues roaming from mouth to mouth. As I sucked Eric's tongue, my dick pulsed for release. Eric's cock looked as if it was about to burst, and he quivered when my fingertips brushed the head of it.

"I want to give you your Christmas present right now," I breathed.

Eric glanced nervously toward the stairs. "Aren't you afraid your parents will catch us?"

"The risk of getting caught makes the spanking sweeter," I maintained, as I poured a dollop of lubricant into my hand and gripped his cock.

"So spank me," Eric purred. A thrill shot through me as my hand closed around his shaft. My thumb and forefinger were positioned just beneath the circumcised head, and the shape of Eric's cap sent a charge through my hand that inflamed my mind and made my dick throb.

When Eric gripped my cock, a gasp emitted from between his clenched teeth. "Every time I touch your dick," he moaned, "I feel like I got struck by lightning."

"Yeah," I agreed, slowly massaging his shaft. I moved my lips close to his lips so that we were barely touching. His tongue licked my lips and then slipped into my mouth. Meanwhile, his fingers were busily twisting the head of my cock.

Sucking his tongue, I stroked up and down his shaft. I tightened my squeeze as my hand wrung his dickhead. My body tingled. My nipples were hard and tingling, my lips were smashed against Eric's, and my asshole was dilating and closing rhythmically. Eric continued twisting the head of my cock as if he were turning a bottle top. I wanted to delay my orgasm, but he decided to make me come hard and fast.

Knowing that I would not hold out another minute, I beat Eric's meat furiously. I flogged his dick head with rapid strokes. I felt his cock tremble in my hand. I did not give him a second's break. He was going to jizz at my command.

As our tongues warred and our hands flailed, our bodies tipped toward the point of no return. My cock grew heavy, and Eric's swelled even thicker in my hand. Then the first tiny ripples started in my dickhead, and I knew that I was committed to come. Come what may, nuclear warheads, space-annihilating comets, or the election of social conservatives, I was going to shoot my spunk.

My eyelids fluttered, and past Eric's bright eyes, I saw the lights of the Christmas tree twinkling above us. Yes, it was Santa Claus time when the muscles at the base of my penis contracted. My asshole was pulsating in tune with my dick, and a huge contraction gripped my pelvis. A burst of semen erupted from my dick and splattered under Eric's chin. Then a gust of Eric's jism decorated my stomach and my left nipple.

We shot spurt after spurt, wetting each other with our cum. One blast of Eric's semen covered our chins, and I tasted sweet spunk. My orgasm continued, explosively, madly, exuberantly, and my balls emptied until Eric was dripping.

Drained and exhausted at last, we clung wetly, sprawled beneath the Christmas tree, our cum-sticky hands caressing each other's ass. We could scarcely breathe, and our hearts thundered as if they would burst. Finally, gripping his butt cheeks with both hands and pulling his sticky cock against mine, I whispered, "Merry Christmas, Eric."

As he thanked me for the gift in the best way he knew, his lips and tongue busy, I sighed with bliss and thought about the strange and magical path that had brought us to this happy place.

# # # # #

The Master's study was an exquisite room, a marvel of old wood, colorful oils, antique maps, books printed on vellum, and a Chinese carpet. The Master himself was about thirty-five, fluttery and sinewy, with jet-black hair. As I stared at the Master, I felt a growing premonition that my life was about to change. Returning my stare with steely eyes, the Master settled in his comfortable armchair.

"Tim Dryden, your parents remitted an expensive tuition to enroll you in the Academy of Apollo," he said, confirming my suspicions. "Do you comprehend their reasons?"

I shifted uncomfortably on the couch. We were getting into matters I did not want examined too deeply. "Yeah, at my last school I'm supposed to have called another gay kid a cruel name."

"Precisely," he said, missing my emphasis on the words 'another gay kid.' "Your parents were dismayed to learn your public school prejudices."

"I don't have any prejudices," I denied, my voice shaking with outrage. Back in public school, I ended up in the principal's office for calling Eric White a cocksucker. "It was a misunderstanding."

All through my senior year, Eric fascinated me. He was everything I wanted to be. He was cute, smooth, bulging in the front, curvy in the rear, clever in his speech, and he knew how to dress. My cock stiffened every time I saw him, but since high school boys walk around with perpetual erections, nobody noticed. I would have loved cuddling up to Eric, and as for sucking cock he only had to ask. He could have sucked mine, or I would eagerly have sucked his. Then I heard him telling another boy that I was a fat butt, and I spit out the first word that came into my mouth.

The fat butt comment was an exaggeration, but it wounded me. I did not have a bulging stomach or an ass that had to be delivered on the back of a truck. I was pleasingly plump; an exercise program would have had me looking like a clean, lean, hot-ass-queen in no time.

My offense was only a result of hurt feelings, but the militant faculty advisor to the Queers & Allies Club overheard and jumped to the conclusion that I was a gay-basher. I tried to explain, hinting that I was gay, though I was afraid of making my claim too explicit. However, I had been prejudged guilty, so every word I uttered was interpreted as homophobic. In the end, the principal suspended my ass. I missed graduating high school, and my parents flipped and spent the summer looking for a school that would 'open my mind.'

"Tim, you must open your mind to new ideas," Mom chanted through most of that dreadful summer. "Your prejudice is shocking."

"Mom, you don't understand me," I said once. I drew a deep breath. "I like Eric. I really like him."

It was a prelude to coming out to my parents, but Mom interrupted me. "Then why did you gay-bash him, Tim? Just because he's different from you?"

"Maybe he's not that different from me," I started, but she did not hear me.

Then one day, Dad approached me with a letter in hand. "We've arranged for you to take your college preparatory courses at the Academy of Apollo, Tim," he announced.

My pleas that I could go to junior college fell upon deaf ears, so on a soft September morning, Dad ordered me into the car. After a miserable six-hour drive, during which I attempted twice to discuss my sexual orientation and was ignored, Mom and Dad hauled me through the front gate of the Academy of Apollo, marched me into the Master's study, shook hands with the Master, hugged me goodbye until Christmas, and stranded me.

"You will slumber in the novice dorm," the Master was saying, "with the other boys who failed to graduate high school. You're the last of your assemblage to arrive. The others settled in last week and have already acclimated to our ways."

I wondered whether acclimation entailed brain surgery, but he started talking about my grades.

"I've studied your transcript, which is wretched, so you must embark on a rigorous academic program. I'm enrolling you in world history, renaissance literature, plane and solid geometry, botany, and Latin. You'll also have a physical education component apart from the academic one, including weight training, swimming, and aerobics. You can sign up for other sports if you wish: bicycling, track and field, or wrestling. We also have a drama club, a Latin club, and other clubs you might wish to join."

I stared at him with stunned horror. "Latin?" I gulped.

"You're wondering why we permit you no clothing or mementoes from home," the Master said.

"Actually, I was wondering what solid geometry was."

"Clever retort," the head replied sarcastically. "Your parents sent you here to change, so you can retain nothing of your old life. You will wear a uniform of our choosing, go to bed when we tell you, and eat with the group. Essentially, you'll die to the old Tim, and we'll create the new Tim as they do in military basic training."

I stared at him with pathetic defiance, fearful rebellion, and abject dismay. I suspected that my parents had accidentally consigned me to a 'Conversion Therapy' camp where they brainwash gay kids into slobbering ass wipes.

"Now you may articulate your questions," he offered.

My heart was thundering in my chest, but I spoke my mind. "You can make me wear bib overalls and burlap underwear, and you can make me attend Latin class," I said. "But you'll never reeducate me. I'm gay, and you're never going to turn me straight."

The Master laughed as if I had made a joke. "Admirable lad. That's the spirit. I shall summon one of your roommates that he may initiate you into our ways." He stretched out a finger and pushed a button on his intercom. "Send in young Victor Malapert."

A few seconds later, Victor sashayed in, a freckled, carrot-topped, cheeky specimen with a wisenheimer grin. He reminded me of that old character from *Mad Magazine*, except for having a hot booty. To my relief, Victor was not dressed in overalls, but in a sexy uniform consisting of a silky white shirt, stripped necktie, short-tailed blazer, and shorts. The shorts stopped considerably above his knees and they showed off his butt. I felt a familiar urging, and I was tempted to invite him to sit on my lap.

"You rang, Master?" asked the smarty-pants.

"Ah, Victor, my contumacious snippet, you agreed to guide young Tim Dryden through his preparatory procedures."

The smart aleck looked me up and down as if he was inspecting a pile of horseshit. "Do they call you Miss Piggy?"

I gasped at Victor's incredible rudeness and his perception to hit upon the one barb that would prick deep, but the Master called him on it: "Victor, your impertinent sauce brought you to the Academy of Apollo in the first place."

When Victor shrugged, his ass wiggled. It was close enough to touch, but I kept my hands to myself. "Come on, Miss Pig ... I mean, Tim," he offered derisively, "and I'll show you where to pick up your uniform."

As we walked, Victor voiced loads of opinions about the school, his fellow students, and existence as a whole, none of them respectful, but all smart-alecky, flip, and clever. I wanted to hate him, but he made me laugh, and he was sexy. I watched his tight ass with longing as he led me to the communal bathroom.

I pointed to the row of exposed commodes. "They don't give us stalls, even?"

"What's a'matter? Miss Piggy can't shit with other guys?"

"Actually, Vickie, I was wondering where we find a little privacy to jack off," I said, and Victor glanced at me with slightly more respect. All he said was, "You can forget about beating your meat, Tim."

Past the shower room, the bathroom ended at a counter, behind which stood a storage room and laundry for our uniforms. Victor led me to the counter where a sexy man of about twenty-four was ironing shorts. He had muscular biceps and a super chest. He was wearing a staff uniform, which included tight shorts. His butt and thighs bulged so deliciously that a tiny gasp escaped from my lips.

"Larry, this is the new guy," Victor said. Larry looked me up and down. His glance made me feel warm, but he was only sizing me up. He said four words: "Take off your clothes."

I had to strip naked in front of Victor, and Larry refused to let me keep anything: ring, watch, neck chain. I was afraid he would go after the fillings in my teeth. When I was buck naked, he packed up my stuff and addressed the package to my parents. I had to shower with Larry making sure that I soaped every nook and cranny. When my dick hardened in the shower, Larry made sure I gave it a good soaping – but not good enough. Victor voiced a few comments, but his were less helpful.

Once dried, I pulled on soft, white underwear, the fluffy school socks, the white shirt, the shorts, the necktie, and the blazer. After I tied the shoes, I inspected myself in the mirror, and the effect was pleasing. I had always been a tad overweight, but my fat disappeared beneath the school uniform. I looked damned sharp.

"The new prisoner needs his spankers," Victor proclaimed. Larry nodded in agreement, pulled insulated gloves over his hands as if he were preparing to handle nuclear waste, opened a drawer, and removed cherry-hued briefs. These shimmering spankers were not grandpa's old tighty-whities; they looked adhesive, prissy, slinky, and radioactive.

"What are those?" I said, recoiling from the proffered garment. Larry had scared me when he put on thick gloves. "Why wouldn't you touch them? Are they poisoned?"

"Don't be afraid. These are your spankers. No one else can handle them until they attune to your bio-rhythms."

As I hesitated, Larry dropped them into my hand. They were silky, but they tingled as if they were electrified. There was a living quality about them, and I imagined what they would feel like on my ass. I was also afraid of them. They grew warmer, and I felt a deep down erotic stir.

Larry grinned at my discomfort. "Put them in your joy box until bedtime," he suggested with a patronizing expression.

"Come on, bring your spankers," Victor ordered. "I'll show you the dorm."

Pinching my spankers cautiously between my thumb and forefinger, I followed Victor's butt. I was feeling exceedingly sensual, and I would have enjoyed taking on both Victor and the sexy attendant.

The hall leading from the bathroom reached a cluster of dormitories. Our room slept sixteen guys, and I was disappointed to spy eight narrow bunk beds. Two joy boxes stood at the foot of each bed. Victor showed me how to open mine and told me to put my spankers inside.

"Nobody can touch these things but me?"

Victor grinned. "Not yet. Not until after you've got your rocks off in them. Your spankers are getting to know you, and contact with another body would mess up the synergy."

"Get off in them?" I objected. "How am I supposed to stroke with these covering my dick? They're going to be tight."

Victor emitted a derisive snort. "I told you – you've given yourself your last handjob – for a while." I regarded him with utter amazement. I had been pounding my cock at least once a day, and often more frequently than that. Mom had to buy me a fresh bottle of moisturizer every time she did the grocery shopping.

Victor and I drifted to the cafeteria, arriving just in time for dinner. I planted my ass on a bench at a long table along with the other uniformed boys. No girls attended the Academy of Apollo. I had not seen any females on staff. I felt a surge of interest – all the guys were around my age and most looked hot.

Dinner consisted of salad, meat loaf, mashed potatoes, and green beans. Water to drink. No second helpings and no dessert. No surprise the guys looked trim; the school was starving them. I knew that I could stand to lose a few pounds, but my stomach felt empty as I left the cafeteria.

After dinner, most guys did homework, while others studied with their tutors. Being at loose ends, I went looking for a television. Not finding one, I picked up a collection of Edgar A. Poe's stories in the library. At 8:30, Victor found me reading "The Fall of the House of Usher" and told me to come to the dorm.

"You're kidding?"

"Nope. Lights out at 9:00."

"They put us to bed at 9:00? That's crazy, Vickie. And we get up at 7:00. That's ten fuckin' hours. How am I supposed to sleep for ten hours?"

Smirking, Victor led me to the bathroom where I extracted the brand new toothbrush from the small kit with my name taped on it. We brushed our chompers and scurried down to the dorm.

In our room, I saw guys hanging up their uniforms. Then they bent naked over their joy boxes and pulled out their spankers. I watched the guys squirming into their many-hued, slinky briefs. Once on their wearer's ass, the spankers' colors shone forth brightly, glowing blue, purple, green, red, or yellow. My mouth dried with a sexual heat as I saw how the fibers in the magical cloth circumscribed their wearer's cock and profiled his butt curves. The guys' faces changed in expression as the spankers adhered tightly to the skin. Something about that change frightened me, as if the spankers erased identity, and my fears about brainwashing returned. I watched the guys' asses sway provocatively as they flounced into the bunk beds.

Victor watched as I undressed to my white underwear. I paused a moment at my joy box, but I was too afraid. I had a lower bunk, so I sat down, feeling like a nerd. Victor watched me with glinting eyes, but when I pulled up my sheets, he shrugged, went to his joy box, and slipped into green spankers. As he pulled them over his curvy ass and thick cock, his spankers glowed with scintillating brilliance, the green radiating into various shades. A strange look came into Victor's eyes, as if something alien were taking over his mind and body. He blew me a suggestive kiss and swished into his own bed, the lower bunk next to mine.

At exactly 9:00, the lights went out and a lurid red glow illuminated the room. My cock was uncomfortably rigid in my underwear, and the tips of my fingers tingled. The stinging sensation affected only my right hand, the hand that had carried my spankers. My joy box seemed to be calling to me, but I resisted. I did not want to be brainwashed, have my personality erased, or become possessed by alien forces. As I quivered, hot, cold, and tingling sexually without release, a soft musical sound like waves lapping on a shore filled the room, and an enticing odor drifted through the air.

Then the moans commenced. I had the impression of my roommates masturbating around me, though their hands gripped the rails of their beds as they thrashed and groaned and gave voice to their secret desires.

"Fuck me, gay boy," one guy muttered.

"You're making me come," another moaned.

Yet another pleaded, "I wanna suck your dick."

"Ah, I'm coming so heavy," was the only response, though nobody was sucking or fucking, but each guy writhed alone in his narrow bed.

"Yeah, that's so good. Fuck my queer ass. Give it to me. Give it to me."

My cock was in torment as my ears pricked to distinguish the moans and pleas around me. I could not imagine what the spankers were doing to their wearers. Even as the spankers produced irrepressible orgasms, they shaped my roommates' minds. In spite of my hot lust, I could not imagine voluntarily letting a terrifying garment rearrange the chemicals and cells of my brain.

Meanwhile my roommates were calling to each other or to nothing at all, "Oh. I'm coming. This horny boy is coming."

"I'm gonna skeet. I'm gonna blast cum right now."

"Fuck me. Suck my cock. Oh, yeah, suck me, suck me off."

I was glad that the bedposts were sturdy because the guy above me was thrashing hard in his bunk. He kept baying like a donkey: "Ride my ass. Ride my ass."

Victor howled the loudest. "This bitch is coming so heavy," Victor groaned. "You're making me come like a bitch."

I could not see that anybody was making him come. He was gripping the sides of his bed with both hands. Meanwhile other guys were going off the same way, and my own cock was hard. I never wanted to jerk off worse in my life, but the other guys weren't using their hands. My spankers sang a siren song to me from my joy box, and I longed to get up and slip into them, but I was afraid.

The sex sounds went on forever, and I soon realized why we stayed in bed for ten hours. My roommates passed through crescendos of orgasm for hours on end while I lay timid with doubt and throbbing with lust. Finally, frightened, confused, and horny, I fell into tormented dreams. I dreamed of Eric and other boys I had known. In one dream, Eric was taking me up the ass while Victor was fucking my mouth, yet I remained unsatisfied for I had not accepted the magical gift that would lead to satisfaction. My dreams brought no climax, and my underwear was dry when I climbed out of bed at 2:00 a.m. to visit the bathroom.

My briefs jutting with my stiff rod, I scurried down the hall and managed to start a stream into the urinal. Just as I finished pissing through my erection, I heard a noise in the shower room. Peeking in, I saw two guys from another dorm. Clad in their spankers, they were feeling each other up and kissing. Fascinated, I could not tear my eyes from them. They were sucking tongue and uttering incomprehensible sounds of wild abandon. Their hands were stroking their asses, and their spankers were glistening. They seemed to be rubbing their cocks together, but they were pressed too close for me to tell for sure. Maybe their spankers were doing everything. So magnified were the sounds that I thought I could hear their muscles pumping cum, and their pee holes opening as they spurted.

Briefly, they pulled their mouths apart so they could whisper hoarsely. "Oh, my ass is tingling. My asshole is having an orgasm."

"Mine, too. I'm getting fucked by a thousand cocks."

"Ah, it's good. I'm coming and coming. Oh, it's never gonna stop."

"My ass is hot. Oh, yeah, fuck me. Fuck my ass."

They lost all control. Their bodies rocked convulsively, all muscles contracting unchecked. They contorted and released all holds, abandoned in a clinch, their bodies in a state of ultimate rapture. I watched for five minutes as their bliss went on and on until they collapsed side by side, smirking vacuously from the transport that had claimed them. Burning with lust and jealousy, I returned to the dormitory and crawled into bed. Morning seemed a long way off. I noticed again how dry was my mouth as hot lust raged over my body. My cock had swelled again, and was poking uncomfortably inside my underwear. Sleep would not come. The weird music was humming erotically through me and the enticing scent grew stronger.

My roommates drifted through a twilight sleep of rapturous delight as their spankers began working again. Orgasmic cries filled the room. Suddenly, I no longer cared whether my spankers would possess me, erase my memories, or program me. I was willing to surrender my soul for relief.

I crawled out of bed, stripped off my briefs, and opened my joy box. When my fingers touched the magical cloth, so soft, so slick, so sleek, so vibrating with sex, and so attuned to my body's needs, I resisted no more. I stepped into my spankers and pulled them up. I had to wiggle to draw the tight garment over my butt, but once I had them all the way up, my spankers formed a second skin.

I felt a cellular discharge, a surge of some chemical change deep within me. My mind reeled, and I needed to lie down. I swayed toward my bed. A tiny protest flared as my spankers forced me to swish, but my resistance faded. My spankers massaged my dick and stirred the nerves in my asshole. I wiggled my ass invitingly as I climbed over my bed rail. Lying back, I pulled up the covers and prepared for annihilation.

However, my sense of consciousness grew, rather than diminished. The red light cast a sexual palpitation, and the piped music transmitted a masturbatory rhythm. I grew more aware of the lusts of my roommates, not to mention those in nearby dorms; hot, horny guys who had been world-champion cockstrokers until they discovered spankers. I was part of a great society of men, all men who'd ever lived, hand-job aficionados every one, at one with the magical rhythm, the stroke of billions of hands, the spurt of cum from billions of hard cocks.

My consciousness settled into my own body again, and I was mindful of the wonderful spankers hugging and massaging my skin. My dick was being stroked by a trillion hands and being sucked by a trillion tiny mouths, while the cloth that had crept up my crack and kissed my asshole was sparking exquisite delights. I gripped the bed rails and thrust my hips under the covers.

"Spank me," I begged. "Spank my ass. Spank my dick. Spank me."

Spank me they did. My spankers violated my private places, a delectable molestation of my ass and cock. However, the physical provocation was even more than sexual, though the orgasmic trigger was beyond imagining.

"Oh, guys, I'm going to come," I moaned, as the spankers stimulated far more than my ass and my cock. The strange erotic feelings crept over my body and wormed into my brain, bringing about amazing changes in my thoughts. I was awake and asleep at the same time, dreaming and fully alert, mindless yet more intelligent than I had ever been. My memory became more alive, I could solve problems that had been hopeless before, and my senses were operating at a fantastic level. I also shed my self-consciousness. I had always felt different from everyone around me; but I began to feel that other males and I were the same.

Strangely, these realizations were incredibly sensual and impossibly sexual. Pleasure increased to fantastic proportions. I had always known that I was gay, but my acceptance of sex with guys, a passionate male/male exclusivity, catapulted to explosive sensibility. I was not so much Tim, but I was sex. I was gay sex. I was super-sex.

Explosive half-conscious orgasms erupted in my mind, and in my dick, and in my ass, and in every fiber of my body.

"Oh, I'm a whore, guys," my mouth blurted. "Fuck me. Come in my ass. Come in my mouth. Oh, yes, I'm going to shoot cum."

"Yeah, go for it, Timmy," Victor urged. "Do it in your spankers. Oh, yeah. I'm coming again, too."

My eyes squeezed shut as the wild blasts of incredible pleasure hit me, and I swept over cascades of perception. Then my eyes opened on their own, and I saw that I had thrown off my blanket and my spankers were glowing like neon while I trembled and bucked.

"Oh, that's so good," I moaned, gripping the rails with both hands and rolling my ass. "I'm coming so heavy. Oh yeah, man, fuck me, jerk me off." I kept coming and coming, the wet, sticky spurts issuing from my dick absorbed by my spankers.

"Oh, yeah, fuck my gay ass," I howled. "Stick your cock up my asshole. Fuck my mouth. I'll deep throat you all." That was the last thing I remembered. I must have fallen from sexual transport into a deep sleep.

At 7:00, an alarm sounded, and everyone bounced out of bed. My roommates pulled off their spankers, placed them reverently in their joy boxes, and slipped into their white briefs. Dropping his spankers into his joy box, Victor informed me that the students were permitted to eat breakfast in their underwear.

I pulled off my spankers and held them up. "Shouldn't we put these in the laundry?"

Victor hooted derisively. "Spankers never need washing. They're self-cleaning."

I examined my spankers. Although they had drained my balls, they were clean and fresh. I lovingly placed them in my joy box.

At breakfast, I planted my ass on a bench beside one of the guys I had seen in shower. His name was Buzz. I told Buzz that I was facing my first day of classes.

"Don't let it throw you," Buzz advised. "Every day gets easier."

Breakfast consisted of a small bowl of oatmeal, two eggs, a piece of toast, and a glass of tomato juice. After eating this meager repast, we trooped to the communal bathroom and took our seats on the commodes. Then we went through the morning routine of shaving, brushing our teeth, and showering together. After the shower, Larry issued clean briefs for the new day, and we put on our uniforms. I learned that we received clean shirts every third day, and that our uniforms were cleaned once a week.

My first class was world history, which I rather enjoyed. Renaissance literature was not too bad, botany was confusing but manageable, plane and solid geometry was a bitch, and Latin was the class from hell. Amid these classes, I ate a lunch consisting of three ounces of tuna on pita bread and a sliced apple. After that feast, I labored twenty minutes on a stair master, while a trainer urged me to go faster – followed by twenty minutes working out on weight machines – followed by another shower. Then we stopped for a snack. My face must have registered my horror when I saw the three crackers with dollops of peanut butter and an orange.

By dinnertime, my stomach was rumbling, my muscles were aching, and my brain was whirling. As I looked at the small meal, sufficient calories for a growing boy, but far less than what I ate at home, a pit of despair opened before me. I had never felt so hungry. On the verge of starvation, I humped my sore butt to the study room to meet my tutors. The tutors were patient with me. They really helped with my homework. After an hour's intense practice, I could say five words in Latin. I could not imagine anything less useful.

My depression lessoned as bedtime neared. I could scarcely wait for 9:00 to arrive. I brushed my teeth a bit earlier than my roommates, which resulted in some good-natured teasing.

"Can't wait to pile into your spankers, Tim?" Paul asked. Paul was the only black guy in our dorm, and he was incredibly sexy. I wanted him to like me.

"I've been looking forward to them all day," I admitted. With a laugh, Paul slapped my butt. Suddenly, I no longer felt like a stranger. I was part of the gang, and the guys accepted me, including Victor who was sarcastic to everybody.

"Way to go, roommate."

"Tim's gonna beg us to fuck his ass," Victor contributed.

"Just like you," I retorted. "Does anybody know how they work?"

My roommates shrugged.

"Where does the cum go?" I asked.

"Nobody knows."

"It's a secret. I'll bet the Master knows."

"I heard that the Master's spankers are pure white and glow with an intense light. They're more powerful than our teachers' spankers."

"The Master and our teachers sleep in spankers, too?" I asked.

"Oh, yes, and theirs are more powerful than ours. We wear student spankers only."

The guys were giving answers that answered nothing. Nobody knew who had invented spankers, where the school got them, or how they worked. By that time, we were hanging up our uniforms in our dorm room. We kept talking, except for the guys who had already pulled on their spankers. Once in his spankers, a guy doesn't care about anything else. I was talking with Paul as he pulled his up. As soon as they covered his ass and cock, his face twisted into a feral leer, and he swished his ass into bed.

Eagerly, I dragged my spankers over my ass. They greeted me with an orgasmic shock. A delectable tingle swept up my dick, around my tightening buttocks, and into my asshole. I felt as if I had stepped into a parallel universe, for the room took on a soft glow. My ass swayed provocatively as I swished toward my bed. My cock already hard and tingling in my spankers, I slipped over the bed rails just as the lights dimmed.

I must have been ejaculating, but the orgasmic sensation was so intense that I could not distinguish what was happening. I was hot, and my body quivered. Without falling asleep, I drifted into colorful theaters of awareness. The music projected masturbatory rhythms through my body. The enticing odor smelled stronger than it had the night before. My asshole was dilating as if it was getting fucked by a thick cock, and it was the most wonderful sensation I had ever experienced.

"Oh, fuck me," I begged. "Fuck my queer ass. Fuck my queer ass."

Around me, my roommates were howling with orgasmic delight and begging to lick my ass and fuck my mouth.

"Ram your cock up my ass," I howled, writhing uncontrollably. "Fuck me. Fuck me." My body was afire, every cell alive with pleasure. Time stopped, ran backward. I passed out of consciousness, yet somehow I was still aware that I was lost in a frenzy of howling pleasure. I returned to consciousness, aware that my brain must have turned into a puddle of liquid chemicals and reformed again.

Still I passed through orgasm after orgasm, my ass wiggling, my cock pumping, my mouth making slurping sounds until I fell into a deep purple nothingness.

Much later, I awoke from the happy nowhere with a hot body rubbing against mine. Inside my spankers, my hard cock was rubbing against another spanker-clad cock. I opened my eyes and saw that I was lying on the floor between our beds with Victor humping my dick. I had no memory of falling out of bed, but I stopped caring as Victor's lips pressed against mine, and his hot tongue slipped into my mouth even as our tingling cocks rubbed together.

After breakfast, I inspected my naked body in the bathroom mirror. I was looking better already. I had less fat than I had carried two days earlier, and though my chest muscles felt sore from the previous day's exercise, they were harder. My ass protruded more, its definition positively fuckable. My cock looked thicker, its size perfectly suckable. I was healthy and sexy, and though I knew that my spankers were carrying out the changes in my body and my mind, I no longer feared the change. I felt rested, fresh, and eager for what the day would bring.

Classes went better, too. Latin and geometry were more comprehensible. During gym class, my trainer did not have to goad me to exercise: I wanted the rewards of a better body. I pedaled furiously on the lifecycle, and I followed my trainer's example in doing squats and leg lifts. Following another meager dinner, I progressed mightily with my tutors. The problems in geometry were turning into puzzles to be solved instead of impossible barriers that repulsed my mind, and I knew my Latin alphabet and could count a few numbers before bedtime.

Each night I spent in my spankers was a new experience. When I pulled them over my ass that night, I lost all inhibitions. "I'm completely gay," I announced.

No one objected. I received praise and congratulations.

"Good for you, Tim."

"Well done."

"Now you're in the pansy brigade," Victor contributed. "You'll be riding the big cocks with the rest of us Nancy boys."

Dave and Alex patted my ass, and Brian kissed me. In our spankers, the kiss was an earthquake. We came in our spankers during the kiss and ended by collapsing to the floor.

Paul was pulling his spankers over his big black ass. My cock was rubbing against Brian's dick, but I watched Paul over Brian's shoulder. A mask of lust covered Paul's face. As his spankers took control of his mind and body, Paul threw himself down behind me, and as I tongued

Brian's mouth and rubbed my cock against his, I felt Paul's thick cock, clad in his yellow spankers, rubbing against my ass.

We wriggled together in mindless lust. My body shuddered through an orgasmic stream. My cock kept pumping as orgasm followed hard upon orgasm. I had no inclination to count them, but I must have had fifty if I had one. Paul and Brian were shaking along with me, and we clung insanely. Then came a sudden burst of clarity.

I heard Paul howling, "I'm queer for you, Tim. I'm so queer for you."

"Fuck me," I moaned, but still everything we did, we did in our spankers.

Without warning, our orgasms ceased. Shakily we climbed to our feet and swayed to our beds. As I climbed over the rails, I looked behind me and caught Paul studying my ass with a sexual glint in his eye. I wiggled it invitingly. I felt deeply sexy as I dropped my butt onto my mattress, my cock hard in my tight spankers and my asshole tickling.

For a few minutes, I lazed while nothing happened, though my body felt taut under my blanket. As I ran my hands over my chest, I felt changes under my skin. My muscles were growing. I touched my ass, which sent a thrill through me, and I discovered that my buttocks were firmer and more rounded than before. My hand tingled as I groped my ass through the spankers. The air smelled stronger than it had on the previous two nights, and I drew a deep breath. I struggled to attune my mind to the caress of the music.

A new sensation came over me. I gripped the sides of my bed with both hands as unknown pleasure grew in my dickhead, rippled up the shaft, and filled my entire midsection. My crotch and ass tingled pleasantly, and orgasmic spasms shook me. The tingles grew and grew until every cell was in paroxysm. I tried to hang onto my being. I was afraid of what would happen if I let go. Nevertheless, the convulsions increased until I let my spankers take me where they would. Jolts of rapture beyond thought rolled up my ass and down my cock as I tossed in my bed and shot great gobs of spunk.

"Oh, I'm coming so heavy," I moaned. "Fuck my ass. Splatter me with your spunk."

My voice was lost with the cries of my roommates. "Make me wet," I begged. "Shoot cum on my face. Decorate me. Come in my mouth."

As raptures exploded in my legs, my stomach, my chest, my throat, and my brain, I fell out of time and space. I humped over a hillock under a clear sky. Jets of semen flying from the masturbating bodies of every man on Earth crossed paths in the sky. Yet as I watched, the cum formed a thick white cock that swooped down upon me. As I sprawled, upended, the cock drove into my ass, bursting into gallons of spunk as it entered.

Abruptly, the sky shifted to deep blue. Towering golden pyramids stood before me, and I was the young pharaoh receiving my anal initiation into godhood. The high priest pounded divinity into my ass, and a smile formed on my mouth as his cock pounded me to orgasms.

The sky darkened to utter blackness. I was wearing a silver loincloth and the mask of a dog. I was one of the priests of Ishtar at the rising of the Dog Star when they engaged in orgies of sodomy. Man after man fucked me, as I gleefully howled with pleasure and shot load after load. Even as I convulsed in my spankers, I passed through the history of Orpheus and Mithra and Hyacinthos and Ganymede and Bran. I was all men penetrating and being penetrated at once.

When I came to myself in my bed at the Academy of Apollo, the raptures of orgasm stilled in me. I could not tell if my time trips had been real or only dreams. I only knew that my spankers were massaging my skin as I lay dreamy-woozy. In spite of, or because of, my untold ejaculations, I felt indescribably sexy and desirable to men. Idly, I wondered what secret thoughts I had shouted as I came.

Then I heard Victor whisper to me across the span of darkness: "Someday, I'm gonna suck your cock, Timmy."

"That would be great," I sighed.

"I'm gay, too," Victor bragged, before another series of orgasmic ripples swept over his body. When he could speak again, he added, "We all are. But as long as we're here, we're only allowed to come in our spankers."

So it went, day after day, and night after night. Some days I thought about Eric White and wished he were with me. Life was easier at the Academy of Apollo than it was at our high school. Eric had sucked some guy's cock in the shower, and a coach had caught them as the guy was blasting off in his mouth. Eric's father was the coach's pastor, so there had been a huge deal about the whole thing, and Eric, a senior, captain of the swim team, and star of the drama club, had been spectacularly outed. Even the newspaper had printed an article about the incident, mentioning Eric's name, but not that of the other member of the swim team. Fortunately, the principal had stuck up for Eric, so he remained in school.

By the time the Christmas holiday neared, I had not jerked off for four months because my spankers had been doing it for me. Then an older student delivered some shocking news. While we went home for Christmas break, our spankers remained at school.

We first year guys were aghast; and the older guys commiserated with us. "If you think the twelve days of Christmas are bad," Ken said, "you just wait until summer break. That's six weeks with no spankers. You have to learn how to jack off again, and it's nowhere near as good. It's a lot better if you can find a sex partner. Last year I got Buzz to spend the summer with me, and my parents never said squat about us sleeping in my bed, though we were doing the old 69 every night."

That gave me an idea, and two days before Christmas, I asked my parents if I could invite Eric White over for a few days. I was sure that I could seduce Eric into it, so our parents were the only obstacles.

My folks were surprised, but they prided themselves on being free thinkers. My dad inquired hoarsely, "You want Eric to sleep in the guest room?"

"Nah, I figured that he could sleep with me."

My parents looked into each other's eyes with wild surmise.

"You're coming out to us?" Mom finally asked.

"Yeah. I tried to come out to you before you sent me to the Academy of Apollo, but you wouldn't listen."

Later I heard them whispering. "Is it possible the school turned him gay?" Mom wondered aloud. She still had not heard me.

"If he wants to explore gay sex now, we'd be hypocrites to discourage him," Dad said. He mused quietly before adding, "I'm going to buy condoms and everything else to promote safer sex, and we can put them beside his bed."

"Maybe we should join PFLAG," Mom suggested, jumping ahead. "We could march with him in the parade."

When I went to see Eric the next day, I discovered that he had moved out of his parents' house and was boarding with a couple of gay men. Just as soon as I knocked, my heart rose into my throat, but Eric opened the door and regarded me quizzically. The couple who owned the house were decorating their Christmas tree and sipping cups of eggnog.

"Eric, I called you a cocksucker because you called me fat," I announced loudly. "I had a major crush on you, and you hurt my feelings. I'm happy you're gay because I'm gay, too."

Eric was a bit overwhelmed by my prepared speech, but he invited me in, and after a long talk, I invited him to my home. He accepted, and deep in the night, I told him how much I had longed for him. "I'll do anything, Eric," I offered. "Anything to make you happy. I'll fuck you, or you can fuck me. I'll suck your cock. I'll lick your ass. Anything."

"How about we just get to know each other," Eric suggested. "Tonight we'll jerk each other off."

"I come on you and you come on me?" I asked.

"Yeah. Nice and friendly," he said.

I answered by pouring a bit of the lubricant my dad had thoughtfully provided and taking hold of Eric's thick cock. "Wow. It's bigger than I thought. Oh, Eric, I knew it was big, but ... Wow!"

Then Eric's mouth was on mine, and his tongue was pushing into my mouth, even as his firm hand clutched my cock. I felt wetness on my wrist as his cock spurted a stream of pre-cum. I met his tongue with my own. Our tongues played a game of war while we fucked each other's dicks with our clenched fists. Explosive ripples traveled over my body as if I was wearing my spankers. A hot lusty explosion rippled across my mind, knowing that I was achieving my heart's desire. Meanwhile, Eric rocked his hips. I reached over him and fondled his ass as he screwed my hand. Still I sucked his tongue, which had not left my mouth.

Ripples tingled through the head of my cock. I would do anything with you Eric, I thought. Then I knew that in time I would do everything with him. After that night, he would be surer of me; I would win him over. I pulled my mouth from his and whispered in his ear. "I love your thick cock, Eric. I love your smooth ass. That's it, love, come in my hand. Come on me."

I was going to squirt cum. I could feel my juices rising. "Oh, Tim, you're making me come," Eric moaned. "You're gonna make me shoot it all over you."

"That's it, Eric," I whispered, inviting him to let fly upon me. "Decorate me with your spunk."

"It's gonna splatter, Tim."

"That's the way I want it," I whispered, gripping his cock with all my might. I worked at his dick head ferociously. I pounded his shaft and tortured the head of his cock with my thumb and forefinger. Meanwhile, my other hand explored the sensuous groove of his ass.

"I can't wait for the day you ask me to fuck this crack," I told Eric, and my words were too much for him. He emitted a long, low moan that surely awakened my parents, and the first spurts of his semen hit my chest and chin. The sensation of his cum streaking my body brought me past the point of no return. My dick was thrilling in Eric's fist, and I felt the powerful contraction that sent a burst of semen splattering up Eric's stomach and chest and even onto both of our faces.

"Good one," he moaned as he continued to spurt. My next contraction sent my cum into his navel and soaked his nipples. A faint tapping sounded at my door, and I heard my mother's stage whisper. "Are you boys okay?"

I could not answer; I was too busy decorating Eric with my cum. Meanwhile, he moaned again until his contractions stilled. I shot several more blasts as the rapturous buzzing still vibrated the head of my cock. After a time, my heart rate slowed as the tingles and spurts stopped. I heard my door open a crack, and my mother's voice came once again. "Is everybody okay?"

"We're fine, Mom," I said. "No big deal. Eric and I were only playing with each other."

I whispered to Eric and his eyes widened. "Go ahead," I urged. "Say it."

"I'm sorry our orgasms awakened you, Mrs. Dryden," he said. He looked at me and giggled.

Mom's voice sounded as if she was strangling, but she managed, "Well, goodnight, then." She did not bother us for the rest of the night.

Toward morning, cuddling in his arms, I knew that Eric was satisfied with the pleasure we had given each other. Of course, my own pleasure had been spectacular because I found that my spankers had opened my mind to the absolute transport of sex. However, as I looked down at the long wet streaks of Eric's semen staining my skin, I laughed because my magical spankers were fun and mind-expanding. Still, they could not achieve the magic produced by a loving guy.

DAEMON LICORICE

The late June sunlight streamed through the glass atrium of a fashionable hotel. Asmodeus, the demon of homosexual desire, strode blissfully across the marble floor, casting tendrils of cock lust into the minds of men. Golden, gloriously naked, and magnificently erect, Asmodeus followed his swollen cock. His jutting buttocks swayed with each step. Yet to those mortals around him, Asmodeus appeared as one of themselves, clothed and tempered, or he appeared not at all. Abruptly, his purposeful progress was halted by a terrific blast, a ripping sound as of a mighty warrior farting. Asmodeus paused as the lobby clocks stopped and the atmosphere solidified with entropy.

"Pootgirl," Asmodeus muttered as the two-foot-high imp manifested her flatulent form before him. This scatological jade was named Lagasse, but Asmodeus addressed her by her nickname.

"Hey, you big pansy," Lagasse hooted. She jerked a thumb toward the bank of elevators. "The Big Shots want your queer ass. Down below."

Asmodeus gnashed his teeth and stepped into an open elevator. The doors whispered shut, and he felt the pleasant sensation of falling. After a long drop into the nether regions, the doors whisked open into a room of ancient stone. Around a squat flint table, hot from the fires of Gehenna, waited the Seven Lords of Hell. From the head of the table on around sat Satan, Andras, Beelzebub, Moloch, Beliel, Astaroth, and Baalberith. As Asmodeus entered, Beliel arose and stuck out his rump. Asmodeus performed the ritual obscene kiss with which all must greet the Seven Lords. Each Devil rose in his turn so that Asmodeus could kiss his asshole. The ritual complete, Andras pointed toward the tabletop. "Up, Asmodeus."

The Demon of Homosexual Desire leaped to the top of the table and prostrated himself before his masters, hating them, despising his servitude, and sweating from the hot exposure. He considered his masters a group of bigots, trapped in the sordid tradition of thinking homosexuality a sin rather than a source of pride. Asmodeus wouldn't have been a woman chaser if they gave him the Kingdom of Heaven for it.

"Report, Demon," Moloch demanded.

"My Lords," Asmodeus ventured. "Hear of my triumph. I just tricked Daemon Licorice out of the closet. How can he not influence the young to follow his example?"

"Tell us, Asmodeus," Baalberith urged, his tongue hanging lasciviously from his terrible mouth. "Tell your damned tale."

# # # # #

Tipping the French bottle toward the thick target of his craving, Daemon Licorice, author, lecturer, sorcerer, and stage magician, dribbled Pernod onto my prick. The alcohol stung, but when Daemon licked the anise-flavored liqueur, his tongue drove me wild. He lapped at the ridges and contours, capturing every drop clinging to my foreskin, which sent tingles deep into the head of my dick and trembles up my shaft. Overpowered by Daemon's tongue's fervor, I fell back into the institutional hotel chair. "That's the way to lick it, Daemon," I urged the magician. "Suck my dick. Suck me off."

With a low moan, Daemon closed his mouth around my prick, and I tensed my pelvis, so he could have every inch. He licked the head of my cock, nibbled my foreskin, and tightened his lips around the shaft before popping them over the head. I stroked his hair as he sucked me. He made little mewing noises in his throat as he sucked, driving a low moan from my lips and sending tiny tingles that would soon grow into eruptive rapture.

# # # # #

"Tell from the beginning, Asmodeus," Astaroth demanded. "You do start in the damned middle."

The Demon of Homosexual Desire nodded and spoke pensively.

# # # # #

The evening began as these affairs always do. I attended the advertised lecture at the occultists' convention, held annually in a fashionable hotel. A hoard of adoring fans filled the chairs. Dressed in black, Daemon Licorice dominated the stage and held his audience in thrall. Sycophantic proselytes hoping for knowledge, wisdom, or happiness waited for the words that would fulfill their aspirations. College coeds watched with cock-hungry eyes; those among them who lacked the wit to turn to lesbian pursuits would sleep unsatisfied. The coeds were outnumbered by young men, their brains awash with lecherous thoughts. The lads had heard the secret rumors of Daemon's proclivities; they would find bliss with each other.

Among the carnal were arrayed those malicious souls who sought power over their fellows and thought to find it through Daemon's power and a smattering of older folks yearning for an eternal event that they could not express. A beautiful woman in red stared intently at Daemon from the Eastern wall. I recognized her – the lovely lady without pity, sweet succubus of destruction and death. She had vowed to bed Daemon and then to devour him.

After Daemon finished his lecture on black magic and Satanism, the faithful queued up to get their books autographed. I held to my seat. The woman in red arranged to be last in line, hoping to trick Daemon into her bed that night. She would be thwarted. Daemon Licorice had set up a small hourglass, and the sand quickly ran from top to bottom. Each person in line received thirty seconds of his time. Still, more than an hour would pass before he finished with this crowd.

Summoning a waiter, I ordered Pernod and ice. The sexy fellow, whose nametag read "Kit," rushed back with the bottle and a bucket of cubes. Kit was an androgynous but well-constructed lad. His ass jutted pleasantly, obvious even considering the uniform he was forced to adopt. His mouth was wide and his lips puffy. In accordance with his inviting mouth and ass, his mannerisms were fey. He excited me, and I considered taking him into one of the maid's closets to pass the time while Daemon Licorice was signing for his adoring fans. However, the anticipation of pleasure is also pleasing. I blew Kit a kiss and told him to check back with me in an hour.

When Kit returned precisely on the instant, I ordered him to seal the doors. His eyes bugged out at the size of my proffered tip and the promising pat I gave his effeminate butt. I studied Kit's swaying ass as he sashayed to the door – so juicy, so full of bounce. He glanced back before he exited, saw that I had been ogling his rear, and grinned flirtatiously. The woman in red, who'd gotten her $29.95 book signed and a cold dismissal of her frank offer to empty his balls, slipped out the door with him.

#

"That damned loser," Beelzebub snarled. "Have you punished the bitch, Andras?"

"I made her an assistant to a famous television evangelist."

Satan smiled. "Hellishly satisfactory. Now let Asmodeus continue."

# # # # #

Daemon Licorice surveyed the empty room, empty, that is, except for me. "Did you want your book signed?"

"No, if I want to read it, I'll borrow a copy from the library." I had read it, and it had transcended the typical claptrap. Daemon Licorice possessed a flair for language, and his studies into occultism had been deep and sincere. I was simply goading him, the first of the pricks he would receive that night. "Or I'll buy it off a remainder table or in a used book shop."

Grimacing over the words that writers most hate to hear, Daemon closed his pen significantly. There was a world of meaning in the gesture. "Besides tormenting me with ways to screw me out of my royalties, why did you attend this lecture?" he demanded, his face crimson.

"You don't remember me?" At the note of challenge in my voice, his annoyance faded into puzzlement.

"Huh? No." He sounded genuinely confused, but the lust light glowed in his eyes. He had received so many men; how could he remember any particular one?

"Seven years ago?" I let my voice grow more seductive. A lewd suggestiveness crept into my next reminder: "A party at Ned Charters' apartment?"

Daemon shook his head, but the action was pure pretense. He wasn't sure. I didn't look the same, and he suspected that I was a news reporter attempting to out him. He feared the world too much, and he had spent his adult life guarding his secret. He protested lamely, "I was in college seven years ago."

Seven years previous, Daemon Licorice had been a college student, sure enough. His comment was a pathetic defense against the truth. The memory of sensations I had instigated flooded his mind as if he were reliving them. Again, he felt my thick cock pounding in his ass, just the way he felt it that night I filched his anal cherry. Sensations of that first penetration filled him. He experienced my prick afresh, and his buttocks tingled with the tangibility of my hips smacking them, crotch to ass, crotch to ass. No man forgets his first butt fuck, no matter how many times he's been topped since.

"You were just starting your research into the hidden mysteries," I reminded him, glancing at his cock stiffening in his underwear.

Ned Charters was the promiscuous founder of the college's GLBT Student/Faculty Alliance, and his party had been advertised "Boys Only." Daemon had asked permission to attend, and Charters graciously allowed the young social sciences student to observe the gay revels. The party had started innocuously enough with drinks and a buffet. Soon the room darkened, and Ned's posse, the Jack-U-Boys, projected explicit sexual scenes upon the wall. The college boys were caught up by the gay porno movies, and enraptured by the sounds and the pictures; boys began kissing boys, their hands wandering freely. Tongues slipped into ears, tongues warred with other tongues, tongues licked necks. Some of the boys had experienced male/male love before, yet many were making their first sojourn into homoeroticism, and they were ardent but anxious. A strange aphrodisiac filled the air. The Jack-U-Boys arranged black and white penis-shaped candles to light the pathways to the kitchen and bathroom. Gradually, the horny, entranced college boys stripped to their underwear – all but Daemon.

I enjoyed the cornucopia of underwear stretched with swollen cocks. Plaid boxers, white briefs, colorful bikinis, thongs, and strings bulged with dicks charged for release. As the fellows watched the movie, I among them, they rubbed their cocks and the cocks of friends and strangers alike with untamed abandonment. Two sophomores from the psychology department were playing with my dick through my silky black thong. One boy squeezed and fingered my shaft while the other rubbed the head. Winking at each other, they made the unspoken compact to make me come in my thong. I grinned and let them do it. Their ministrations felt too good to stop, I had cum to spare, and I cared nothing for dry pants. If I needed clean briefs, I would filch them.

My thong was too tight for them to encircle my cock, but a half-prick tease can produce an intense orgasm. Fingers and palms worked on my dick, stirring the ambrosial fluids bubbling in my big balls. As they rubbed my prick, which was swollen painfully inside my thong and crying for release, my hands found their cocks, and I rubbed the guys simultaneously toward ejaculation even as they massaged my member.

"Fucking hell, your cock is getting hot," one of the sophomores yelled. "Your cock is hot and mine's getting hot, too. Oh, man, am I ever gonna blast."

My semen was hot and thick. The lava was rising from my balls, churning into my shaft, and moving slowly like a thick paste. One boy was slapping my dickhead with his palm when I leaked a thick spurt of sperm-magma. The ichor was rising in my veins, affecting my color, but the light was dim and flickering, so I let my hide redden. Powerful tingles were rocking the head of my prick, and my hand was suddenly wet as one of the two sophomores started shooting his load. I clutched his cock through the cloth of his underwear; the fibers chafed him, but he was too enthralled in waves of rapture and hot spurts to care.

"Ah, it's killing me," he shrieked gleefully. "I'm going so heavy I'm gonna die."

Then the muscles beneath my balls and at the base of my penis contracted, sending a thick dollop of cum into my thong. Tornadoes of orgasm blasted up my dick, sending spurts of my pasty jism out of my pee hole. The other sophomore was coming at the same time; he continued working at my dick as he discharged and his hands became slimy with my goo. I discharged until my thong looked like I'd dumped a pint of greenish lotion into it. The fluid spilled over into the chair and dripped onto the carpet.

"Dude, you can really shoot paste," one of the guys said admiringly, watching the thick, hot goop running down my legs. I smiled lasciviously; far from satisfying me, a good hand-job only inspires me to want more. I wanted dicks plugged into me, and I wanted to drive my thick cock into ass and mouth.

By midnight, the party had turned into a sex orgy as the alcohol and the narcotic compounds in the incense broke down inhibitions. College boys were fucking other college boys, doing whatever came naturally to cock and ass and mouth. I joined a cluster fuck and took two cocks up my ass while I fucked the boy ahead of me. All over the house, guys were fucking and sucking in every position imaginable. Ned himself was licking a medical student's butt crack, his tongue passionately busy at the little rosebud. Meanwhile, a boy from the law school was probing Ned's asshole with two lubricated fingers.

Guys were jerking themselves off and each other. An orgy of fisting was taking place in a far corner, while two library science majors were sucking each other's cocks on the carpet near Daemon's feet. Everyone was naked, with bright, glistening streams of semen flying through the air. The room reeked of spunk and sex, and I was there in the midst of all.

Fully dressed and out of place, Daemon sat stiff in his masculine armchair, still pretending to take notes for his social studies report. However, his dick was hard and a sexual heat raged through his body. I draped my fresh-fucked ass onto the arm of his chair and wafted the scent of jism and brimstone toward his nostrils.

"Who are you?" he demanded, studying my naked body as I sat close, playing teasingly with my bulky prick. Every tissue of his being cried out for penetration.

I touched his hair, which was thick and coarse, and the touch inflamed me. I wanted to pull his hair while I fucked his ass. "I'm the fellow who would turn you out," I assured him. "I'll fuck your ass until you bark like a bitch. You have only to ask."

Daemon hesitated only a moment. "I want to know what it feels like," he confessed. His hidden lusts and secret cravings were the real reason he had attended Ned's party.

"What do you want from me?" I purred, running my fingers through his hair. "You've got to ask for it."

"Getting fucked in my ass. What it's like having a big dick ramming into me." That was as close as he could get to begging for it. I had to help him.

"You want me to fuck you?" My fingers slid down the back of his neck, sending the urge to submit to anal penetration down his spinal cord. His asshole burned with the desire to be opened and filled while his brain composed images of pure pleasure.

"Yeah," he admitted. I bent and pressed my lips to his. His lips were soft and hard at the same time, ripe for a kiss from another male. The kiss was long, and my tongue slid into his hot mouth. His tongue met mine; he gave his mouth to me, even as he mentally opened his asshole. He moaned around my tongue, sucking at my little oral member as seven years later he would suck my cock. The ichor flowed hot in my veins, my ancient heart throbbed, and my prick released a stream. I was ready to come again. I ascended from my perch, lifting Daemon to his feet as I rose.

"You're so strong," he gasped.

"I could lift you up, slide your ass onto my cock, and frog-fuck you in the air," I assured him.

I pulled his shirt over his head before he knew what was happening. I slid my hands down his body, gliding over his chest and tweaking his nipples. As I felt him up, his cock twitched. I unhooked his belt, unfastened his pants, and pulled down his zipper. His cock stretched the front of his burgundy briefs, but it wasn't his cock that interested me that night. My hands explored his tight rounded buns; Daemon mewed like a kitten when my fingers found his crack.

I stripped off the rest of his clothes. His dick and grapefruit buttocks popped into view. I caressed his hard, bare buns, dipped my finger into a jar of anal lube our host had provided, and slid my finger into his ass. Daemon moaned loudly, so I pushed my finger in deeper and twisted.

"Oh, yeah, fuck me," he groaned. "Fuck my ass."

"I'm going to fuck you until you can't walk straight," I promised, massaging his prostate. I pulled out my single finger and inserted two. His little hole was opening nicely to my touch. I twisted my fingers, pressed his prostate, and dilated his hole until he was begging for my cock.

"Oh, yeah, stick it in me," he wailed. "Fuck me. Ream me. Take me like a bitch."

"You see those two chemistry graduate students on the couch?"

Two guys were bent over the back of the couch, their knees in the couch cushions, and their asses taking cocks hard and fast. I liked the way the asses of the two seniors from the Humanities Department thrust while they fucked the grad students, and I wanted my ass pumping beside theirs.

"Yeah," Daemon Licorice said nervously. "You want to do me like that?"

"Yeah." I pulled my fingers out of his ass and patted his tight curves. "I'll stick it to you really good. I'll give you a fucking that will give you an anal orgasm beyond anything those guys are getting. You're going to come and come again, all from a cock in your ass."

"Yes," he moaned, fear and hope mingled in his voice.

Impervious to AIDS and other STDs, a Demon of Homosexual Desire cannot transmit disease. However, I wanted to teach Daemon to play safe always. I passed him a bowl of party favor condoms and told him to unroll one onto my dick. Let him learn to wrap a cock before it banged his ass.

# # # # #

"Fuck that damned condom shit, Asmodeus," Beliel screamed. "What are you doing practicing safe sex?"

His golden skin paling in spite of being burnished by the heat of the tabletop, Asmodeus resumed talking of magical pricks.

# # # # #

Daemon caught his breath when he touched my prick. "God, that was a shock," he gasped, fearfully releasing my cock. That single touch was enough to spark him. Growing bolder, he seized upon it again. I drove the waves of lust through him. He rubbed my prick affectionately.

"You like my prick?" I cooed, nibbling at his ear while he slid the condom onto me. "You like touching it?"

"Yeah." Daemon smeared extra lube onto my dick, fingering my foreskin and gripping the shaft with his fist. I let him jerk my cock until he was ready for deeper action. I ordered him to the couch.

Daemon assumed the position between the two chemistry students. When they ogled him sidelong with expressions of feral lust, he grinned rapaciously. "I'm going to get my ass fucked alongside you guys," Daemon bragged.

I climbed onto the couch behind him and slid my dickhead into his asshole. My prick is always hot to the touch, but his asshole was hotter. He was burning for the thing I had to offer. The head of my prick disappeared inside Daemon's anal sphincter.

"Oh, yes, I want it," Daemon howled, wiggling his ass upon the head of my cock. "Fill me up. Plunge your meat into me."

Daemon was tight, but I'd already opened him. He took his first cock without pain, which is the way I want my new guys to take it. I steadily pushed my cock in until I was smashing my lap into his buns. He sighed with pleasure.

"Now, you're taking it, Daemon," I said, reaching for his hair.

"Yeah, it's good. Hump me. Hump me." Maybe later he would blame his lust on the booze and the narcotic incense. However, he'd tasted but one drink, and his host had placed the incense burners away from him. I knew the truth. Daemon wanted his ass fucked because it was his nature to want his ass fucked. He was a natural bottom.

I reared back and reamed him again, pulling his hair as I rammed his ass. Daemon grunted and moaned. His throbbing dick leaked pre-cum onto the couch. I started humping him with a regular rhythm, hitting his prostate with my dickhead on each stroke.

"You like that, Daemon? You like getting fucked?"

"Oh, fuck me. Fuck my ass. It's good."

The guys on either side of Daemon were moaning with joy. One was shooting a load of spunk onto the back of the couch as he thrust his hips to meet the cock that was pounding him. The other was getting close. Both were begging the humanities students to fuck harder and faster.

"You're gonna give me an anal orgasm," one senior wailed. "Oh, fuck, yeah. You're gonna make me come when I'm fucked."

"You're taking it like a good boy should," the boy fucking him howled. "Oh, yeah, your ass is so good, so good, so good."

A newcomer jumped the howling humanities student's ass. As the student humped the boy leaning over the back of the couch, his ass impaled itself upon the new guy's cock. "Oh, yeah, I'm getting it now. That's it – drive your cock into my gay butt. Ah. Fuck, yeah. We're doing a three-way."

"Come on, somebody fuck me, too," wailed the disappointed loser who hadn't received a cock. I was too busy fucking Daemon to oblige him, but one of Ned's Jack-U-Boys was ready to serve the needs of all guests. Soon the couch was sagging and creaking from the weight of thrusting male bodies.

Daemon emitted a shriek of pleasure. I was getting him off. I was close to coming as well, so I changed my plans and decided to make us spurt together. Daemon's tight asshole was massaging my dick like a cow tongue. I released his hair and fingered his cockhead with a slick hand while I fucked him.

"Oh," he cried. "That's it. That's so good. Jerk me off while you're fucking me."

Some of the guys had come all they could, so they were ready for a show. They crowded around to watch the first-timer take it. The rest continued fucking, sucking, jacking, and licking, but they were also watching. The guys on both sides of me had shot their loads into the assholes in front of them, though they were still getting fucked from behind. The graduate students were slumped over the couch, their assholes gaping from the action they'd received, but their eyes were on Daemon.

I was about to go over the edge, and I rocked my ass hard; my dick slammed in and out of Daemon's ass, and my loins slapped his buttocks. I stroked his cock and twisted his dickhead. The ancient fires were burning within me. The sulfur was rising, and the brimstone was hotter than fucking hell. The semen rose from my bulky balls like molten ore.

"Here I come," Daemon shouted, distracted by the friction of my hand and reduced to a mindless receptacle for the gooey quicksilver rising in my dick. "Oh, god, I'm gonna jizz."

Rapturous tingles rippled through the head of my cock and vibrated up the shaft. My dick was hot and heavy, and the spasms shook me. The muscles at the base of my penis contracted, and I shot my first great gout of buttery cum into his ass. Wad followed tacky wad as I spurted. At the same time, Daemon was coming freely, his wet loads drenching the back of Ned's couch.

The party started up again after Daemon shot his load. I fucked him twice more before the cock crew in the sunrise, the second time holding him in my strong arms and twisting him upon my cock until he was a howling creature, submissive to the power of my prick. He barked like a bitch, his mouth uttering the sounds uncontrollably as I fucked him. It was this submission that set him upon the left hand path of the magician, a dabbler in the dark arts.

# # # # #

"You took credit for that action a long time ago, Asmodeus," Moloch complained. "What the Hell have you done since then?"

"I'm explaining," Asmodeus protested. "I had to give some history."

"Screw the history. What have you done today to tip souls into the Stygian sorrow?"

Asmodeus wanted to protest that gay sex was joy rather than sorrow, but he knew his audience all too well.

# # # # #

So, there we were, seven years later, meeting for the first time since that rapturous night. For seven years, Daemon had been among the world's most promiscuous homosexual bottoms, but he had kept to his closet. As he stood over me, confused and questioning, in mock denial, I opened my pants and my stiff dick sprang free. It was my invitation for him to open his closet and stride forth in his true form, but he did not know what would come of the next submission.

"Do you remember how you gasped when you touched my dick?" I asked. I knew that he did remember. "Why not grab it now?"

"You never told me your name," he said, eyeballing my cock hungrily with his hot, bedroom eyes, still smoldering after years of reading arcane texts about black magic and the devil. His urges held him in thrall; his fingers squeezed my dickhead.

"Ah, that's it, Daemon. Stroke it. Rub it. Now dribble some Pernod on it."

"What's that?" he asked, dreamily stroking my dick. He was imagining how it would feel in his ass, but a surprise awaited him.

"Pernod is the brand name for a pastis, a type of liqueur. It's French."

"I know what Pernod is. You want me to dribble some on your dick?"

"Then you can lick it off. Suck it off. You've never sucked a cock, you know. Seven years you've been taking it up the ass from any man who would stick it to you, and you've never tasted cum."

"Who are you?" he demanded, tilting the bottle. The liqueur ran down my hell-kindled penis and into my butt crack.

"The one who knows you want it."

"Yeah," Daemon admitted, his voice husky, and he touched his tongue to the head of my prick. He shuddered as his tongue met my cock-flesh, and the spirit of fellatio entered into him. He knew that he had become a cocksucker for the rest of his life, along with being a horny butt-boy. Many were the times he would take it from both ends at once, and conclude the piercing ritual by thanking the boys who stuck it to him.

Daemon eagerly licked the Pernod, kissing and sucking my dickhead as he did so. While he kissed down my shaft, I sprinkled more drops on my cockhead; I wanted to keep his mouth on the head.

"Oh, yes, Daemon," I breathed. "Kiss it. Lick it. Suck it."

He licked the head again. "Let's make a cup," he suggested. He made my thick foreskin a receptacle for the flavorful liqueur. Then he drank deep. Using only his lips and tongue, he explored my dickhead until my cock was pulsing. My cock slid along his tongue farther and farther into his mouth, and even deeper and deeper into his throat. He wanted my prick to fill him, and his throat took it without a choke or a gag.

"Ah, that's good. That's so good," I moaned. His mouth was giving my cock deep massage. I was overjoyed by what I had awakened.

Daemon Licorice blew me with gusto; his head rose and fell upon my cock. At his bidding, I cupped my hands behind his long black hair, directed his head, and fed him my cock. Just as I was close to orgasm, but not so close that I was committed, I saw the effeminate waiter Kit peeping around the door.

Kit's face was a mask of contrasts. He leered with feral lust; yet his eyes were pools of envy. He wanted nothing more than to suck Daemon's thick cock and take mine up his delectable ass. I had other plans for him. Though Kit was a compulsive catcher, I decided to make him a part-time pitcher.

"Join us, Kit," I commanded. "Unless you like jerking-off in the hallway."

Kit fell into the room. Jumping up, he pushed the door shut behind him. His cock protruded like a tent pole in his uniform pants, proof he'd been stroking it while he spied on our lovemaking.

Daemon was looking scared, but I reassured him. "Kit doesn't want to interrupt us, Daemon. He wants to join the fun." I turned to the waiter. "If you want to play, drop that ugly uniform."

Nobody had to ask him twice; Kit stripped buck naked. He had a condom in his pocket, which he unrolled onto his dick. He gooped some lube onto it. Both Kit and Daemon Licorice were disease-free, but I did not suggest they dispense with the condom. Protection was a good habit, and I prefer that my initiates avoid the love that sickens – or kills. Male-to-male sex should bring only happiness.

#

When Asmodeus launched into his philosophical musing, the Lords of Hell snorted with disdain. "Get on with it, Demon," Moloch snarled. "Skip your damned moralizing and describe the fucking."

Asmodeus hurriedly continued.

#

"Looks like you're close to coming," I said, grabbing Kit's slick dick. "What do you want to do with this hard-on?" Kit's dick was rigid, and thin pre-cum was leaking inside of the rubber. I stroked Kit's thick shaft while Daemon sucked my cock.

Kit was nervous and excited by the new desire that wormed into his consciousness. "I want to stick my cock into the magician's ass, sir," he said. "I want to fuck him. Would that be all right?"

"Yeah, oh yeah," Daemon moaned. "Fuck my ass while I suck this cock. I'd like that."

Daemon resumed his good work on my cock while Kit approached his ass.

"Oh, you have a hot asshole, sir," Kit said sliding an exploratory finger inside. "Oh, yeah, it's tight and hot."

"Damn the foreplay," I urged. "Shove your cock into him. He's ready for it."

Daemon wiggled his ass in agreement, so Kit pulled out his finger and pressed his dickhead to the magician's asshole. Daemon opened readily for him, and Kit pushed his package through the dilated sphincter and up the grainy canal. I envied the waiter because I knew how tight Daemon Licorice's ass was, and how much serious friction it could produce.

"Ah," Kit grunted. "His ass grips my cock like a rough glove."

The cute waiter gripped the tops of Daemon's ass mounds and thrust hard. He pulled in and out, in and out. In the mirrored wall, I could see Kit's adorable ass pumping. His butt was rounded so nicely and looked so inviting that I promised I would ride it before many more days had passed. However, his ass was not a part of that night's work.

The brief pause to rearrange ourselves had served to heighten our pleasure. Both Kit and I'd been close to coming when I caught him spying, and I sensed that Daemon was pretty far along. Between the two cocks imbedded in his body, Daemon didn't have to stroke his dick in order to come. He was going to go right along with us.

Daemon sucked on my cockhead, worrying my foreskin with his tongue and lips. Again, my cock entered Daemon's throat, so that he was deep-throating my prick. As the sensation intensified, my cock grew heavier, and it swelled so hard it felt like it would burst.

"Oh, I'm getting close," I wailed. "I'm getting so close. I'm going to come in your mouth, Daemon. I'm going to give you my load."

And Kit was singing his own tune with, "Oh, ah, it's gonna happen. Oh, yeah. Oh, fuck, yeah. I'm gonna do it. Oh, god, I'm gonna do it in your ass. Right up your ass."

Daemon sucked me harder; his mouth became a sucking plant and his lips bruised my foreskin. Tingles rippled through my dickhead.

"Oh, oh, oh, I'm gonna do it," Kit continued. He was used to getting his own ass fucked, but he'd never stuck it to another man before that night. The sensation was new and outrageous and intensely wonderful. "Ah, here it comes. Oh, yeah, here it comes."

Kit was thrusting wildly, and the sight of his ass in the mirror increased my rapture. The ichor sang in my veins, my heart thundered, and my balls gathered. Hot, slow fluid filled my prick. The tingles turned into thunderous waves of indescribable pleasure in my cockhead and rippled up my throbbing staff. Cooking lava rose within me, a volcanic eruption. My entire midsection orgasmed, my muscles tensed, my toes curled, and my eyelids fluttered.

"Ah," I shrieked. "Here it comes. I'm going to blow wads, Daemon. I'm going to blow big wads."

A thunderous ejaculation seized me. My muscles shot my glutinous jism deep into Daemon's throat, load after load, while Kit finished pouring his heavy load up the magician's ass. Daemon's hands were gripping my protrusive butt, but his cock bucked and squirted all the same. He delivered his load onto the hotel carpet, some squirts landing seven feet from his dick.

For a few minutes, we remained connected; Daemon lovingly kissed my dickhead while Kit held his spent dick in Daemon's ass. As our pounding hearts slowed, Daemon reluctantly withdrew his mouth, and Kit pulled out his cock.

Embracing Kit, Daemon complimented him with, "You throw a great butt fuck." Then he regarded me with wonder. "Who are you?"

I gave him a faint twisted smile. I never reveal the mystery of my name, and I know when to leave the stage. In a few seconds, I would depart.

"Will I see you again?" Daemon asked, twisting his head. Neither he nor Kit had a chance to realize that I was no longer among the present. At that moment, the doors blew open and hotel security burst in. The guards' jaws gaped as they regarded the naked waiter with the deflating erection, their VIP guest fresh-fucked from both ends, and the spots of spilled semen. Without consulting management, the hotel security officers summoned the police, and though gay sex in a hotel conference room wasn't illegal, Daemon and Kit spent the night in jail. The next morning the newspapers and the television news stations carried compromising pictures of Daemon and Kit with the headline, "Satan Worshipers Nabbed in Gay Sex Spree."

# # # # #

The Seven Lords of Hell howled with glee, and Asmodeus was allowed to depart. He rode the elevator back to the hotel lobby where Lagasse stood waiting. "Looks like you saved your pansy ass this time," she gassed. "The Big Shots liked your story." She emitted a series of barking farts. "What I wanna know is what's gonna happen to those guys?"

Asmodeus stared into the future. "The hotel manager will fire our cute waiter, which is a lucky break for Kit because the publicity will land him a cushy job in a gay bar, where he will become somewhat of a celebrity, and his tips there will be ten times what he made at the hotel. Through my vast connections, I will be instrumental in securing that position for him, which will happen on the morning after Kit assumes a different position for my prick's entrance."

"You just wanna fuck him," Lagasse said.

"Daemon thinks that his days of drawing crowds are over, but the scandal will swell his audiences. His book will become a bestseller, and he thereafter will command five-figure speaking fees, his magic show a constant sell-out."

"Oh, oh, the Big Shots aren't gonna like that."

"Daemon Licorice will never speak publicly about his sex life, but the media must invariably attach the words 'gay icon' to his name. After getting outed, Daemon will grow less discreet, and the tabloids will sell countless issues featuring pictures of him with his male lovers. As a result, more men will embrace homosexuality."

"Do the Masters give a shit?" Lagasse snorted. "They don't want guys embracing – they want 'em tripping into Hell."

Asmodeus didn't hear her. He was too intent on his vision. In a dreamy voice, he said, "In his heart, Daemon is hoping that I will become his lover, but you and I both know, Pootgirl, that can never be. Of course, Daemon and I will have a third and final fling, but that won't occur for another seven years."

Bored, Lagasse disappeared with a rip and a stink, and time started again in the hotel lobby. Asmodeus noticed a famous motion picture actor checking into the hotel. Turning, the Demon of Homosexual Desire pointed his swollen cock at the actor. Then he assumed the guise of the bellboy, loaded the actor's luggage onto a cart, and trailed behind the actor's enticing ass.

GANG BANGERS' PAYBACK

The Portland police were patrolling Pioneer Courthouse Square on New Year's Eve, while, virtually under their noses, I was merrily plucking cash from unwitting donors' purses and wallets. Though the peril of arrest makes larceny more luscious, I found scads of cover among crowds gathered under the dim lights, the bright streamers, the bunches of balloons, and the startling firework blasts. A boy who did not look twenty-one was tipping back a bottle of pale ale, so I slipped my fingers into his hip pocket. When I lifted his wallet, I brushed the tight curve of his rump. Copping a feel of an alluring ass or a thick cock is one of the fringe benefits of my profession. As the hot lust swept over me, I considered luring him into the restroom stall and offering my rear for his pleasure. Turning out a new pansy boy would be fun, but the bliss carried its own risks. Resisting the urge, I concentrated on my objective. I surreptitiously removed the cash and returned the boy's wallet to his pocket.

I slithered among the crowd, imagining myself invisible, insubstantial, indistinguishable. Of course, I was none of those, but my fingers were light and my hands were fast. One young woman shifted just as I reached for her purse. I turned away, brushed against an older woman, and added another thirty dollars to my take.

A pair of bicycle cops pushed their machines through the crowd. The temptation was enormous; picking a cop's pocket is a thrill. I had to remind myself that I was not seeking thrills. My rent was due, so that night was a work night. Somebody tossed a string of firecrackers, and as the bystanders jumped, I lifted a wallet here and there, adding a few more tens and twenties to my collection.

Two ruffians rudely shoved two women aside, making them spill their beer. Dressed in baggy jeans and jackets with jagged yellow bolts, the gang-bangers bulled across the square as if the citizens were mere cattle. I noted the symbolic tattoos on their necks as they pressed close to me. Almost on impulse, I dipped into one banger's pocket, felt a large wad of folded paper, and faded back.

The gang-banger had been thinking about his money, so he promptly noticed its absence. "Fucka' picked my pocket," my contributor snarled.

I let the curious crowd sweep me away from the crime scene. The two bangers were threatening everyone near them. Violence was imminent. The cops joined the fray, and I inched farther back. Puzzled by the gang-bangers' overblown wrath, I glanced the tightly folded hundred dollar bills in my hand. Ten thousand dollars – enough to inspire brutality, cruelty, carnage, and bloodshed. Pocketing the incriminating cash, I slipped toward the barricades that the city had erected around the square.

Two more thugs dressed in the same gang colors were standing near the only exit. The back of my neck was prickling. I felt a rush of panic. A conspicuous exit was a bad idea, but remaining to get searched was a worse one. The time lacked fifteen minutes until midnight, so I was the only one leaving the square.

"Leaving before the fireworks?" asked a uniformed cop at my elbow. I had not noticed her; I had been too busy looking at the gang bangers.

"Yeah, there's a fight brewing," I explained, sweat breaking out on my forehead in spite of the winter air. "I don't want any part of that."

When the hue and cry goes up, lead them away from your crib. Benny the Rake's advice echoing in my mind, I sauntered away from the direction of my apartment. The homeless people crouching in doorways made it impossible to stash the money behind a loose brick or up a drainpipe. Pleading eyes remained upon me always. Leaving the square had been a mistake. Had the police selected me for a search, I could have slipped the money into someone else's pocket. The wad of cash had made me stupid with greed.

Those of us who live on the edge of society develop an instinct for survival. My spine signaled that the hunters were tracking me already. My only chance was to run back to the square – return to the scene of the crime. However, I decided too late. When I turned the corner, I saw an ominous vehicle rolling toward me. The four-door car was unmarked, too plain, too difficult to describe. I whirled seeking for an escape, but two gang members were following tight behind me. Before I could retreat one step, they seized my arms, and two who had emerged from the car grabbed my legs. Struggle though I might, they carried me to their car. Suddenly, fireworks were going off all over the city. Rockets exploded in the sky, while the popping of home fireworks displays came from all directions. Ignoring the rapturous celebration, the gang popped the trunk, dropped me inside, and shut the lid. I entered the New Year trapped in stifling darkness.

Twenty minutes later, they unloaded me into their gang headquarters, stripped me naked, and tied me ass up over a stool. My wrists were bound to two legs of the stool and my ankles to the other two. The position was so compromising and so obvious that I nearly laughed. Of course, laughter would have been a mistake.

Somebody slapped my ass so hard that the stool nearly toppled. With my head hanging down toward my tied wrists, I could not see my assailants. "Doin' a jack on us was stupid, bitch. We gonna dust ya' ass, but first we gonna pop ya' some butt sex. And while we raping ya' ass, ya' can think about laying def with cum up ya' poop tube."

The slap had hurt. I wished he would stop bragging and stick his cock into my asshole. Then I felt his bare erection slide across my buttocks, and I felt the first stirrings of eroticism. My cock felt heavier. I knew it was stiffening, but the way they had me positioned would conceal my excitement. The gang must not know that I wanted them to fuck me.

"Don't rape me," I pleaded. "Please don't. You got your money back, so you can let me go."

Coarse laughter erupted. "Stick it inta the punk, KT," a voice urged, relishing my feigned fright.

"We not gonna just rape ya', we're gonna gang rape ya', bitch," KT said. "Ya' ain't gettin' outa this. This ya' gang bang party."

What kind of street gang were they? They did not act like a real gang; they didn't even use the slang correctly. However, I was in no position to ask questions. Between my tied legs, I could see their baggy pants hitting the floor. One pair of pants, followed by boxer shorts, two, three, up to seven. I could take seven cocks easily enough, and they would not be going in deep. The way they had me bent, they were going to get only the heads of their dicks in. These thugs knew less about anal intercourse than they knew about being a gang, though they would soon learn more than they expected. They were only raping me because they thought that was what tough brutes did. Of course, men who rape other men consider themselves heterosexual. I smirked as I pictured what they would soon become.

They were lubing their cocks for action. One of them dropped the jar of Anal Lube. "Lube his ass, Don John," KT ordered. Hard hands gripped my buttocks. "Hey, bitch, how this make ya' feel?" Don John asked. I did not tell him that I liked it. I dilated my asshole. As his thick finger pushed lube into my ass, I stifled a moan of pleasure.

"We're gonna grease ya' so our dicks slide real nice. Nice fer us. Not so nice for ya'. Ya're gonna get fucked like a cunt."

The gang banger did not know how much lubricant to insert so he kept dipping his finger into the jar and pushing the stuff into my rectum. By the time he was done, he could have driven a tank into my asshole, but I had enjoyed the ride. I clenched my teeth to keep from moaning with pleasure.

"He's ready ta' fuck," Don John said, his finger still twisting in my asshole. He was enjoying finger-fucking my ass, but he had not realized it yet. "Ya' want me to go first?"

KT pushed Don John aside, and his finger exited my ass with a popping sound. "That's a tight hole," Don John exclaimed. "I wanna get my cock inta that."

"I'm the King," KT demanded. "I go first." He gripped my butt with both hands and positioned the head of his cock against my asshole. I drew a deep breath and pushed with my sphincter. The head of his cock slipped in easily, and I felt the joy of penetration. His dick head stimulated the nerve endings in my anus so delightfully that I nearly shot a load.

I remembered fondly the first night I spent in Fleet Prison, back when I was a novice working with Benny the Rake. I had not gotten snagged, but Benny was getting up in years and his hands shook. When Benny's contributor grabbed his wrist and summoned the Bow Street Runners, the Runners arrested me along with Benny. Me being young, the chortling Runners enjoyed taunting me with tales of what would happen to my asshole in prison. Then the Bow Street bastards tossed me into the dank cell occupied by Scratch Piffen, a notorious garrotter who bragged about the prissy punks he had turned in Ruthin Gaols. Piffen gave me a choice of putting out willingly or getting beaten, strangled, and then raped. Following his instructions, I bent over the bed, so he could fuck me.

Scratch Piffen slipped his cock into my ass, just as he'd done dozens of Nellie Boys, but he had never encountered any boy with my ability to squeeze a cock. No sooner was his cock up my ass than I started squeezing and twisting it with my anal muscles. I shot my own load almost as soon as he entered me, and I shot a second while I milked him off. Piffen was grunting and swearing by the time I finished milking his balls. He sat quietly after I released his cock, staring about him like an imbecile. Abruptly, he staggered to his feet, staring as if I had unmanned him. Then he threw himself down and begged me to fuck his ass. I refused, of course, so he yelled for the gaolers to fuck him. Piffen was still begging to get fucked right up until they hung him on Tyburn Tree.

I did not come immediately when KT's cock opened my asshole. The head of his dick slipped inside, pulled out, pushed in, in and out, until rapturous tingles rippled around my rim. The pulsing reached my dick at the same time KT was coming close to the edge. He had thrust only ten strokes when he began to moan.

"Oh, it's fuckin' good," he howled. "I'm gonna come. I'm gonna shoot hot spunk into the bitch. It's so good, fuckin' good."

I bit my lip to keep from showing my pleasure. My dick was heavy with approaching orgasm, and I could feel the spasms in my asshole. The tingles erupted from my dickhead, growing so powerful that I could hardly keep from howling along with KT.

Meanwhile, the King of the gang was shuddering with orgasm. He shot hot spurts of his thick spunk into my ass, all the while moaning and grunting. "I never had it sa' good," he bellowed. "Best fuckin' hole I ever stuck it in. Ah, I'm comin' so heavy. I never jizz' this heavy."

"Jesus, KT," one of his gang remonstrated, "That's a fuckin' guy ya'r fuckin', bro. Don't act like ya' like a man's ass."

"Shut up, Long Meat," Don John snapped. "Ya'r gonna have ta come in his ass, too. We all do now."

If KT heard either Long Meat or Don John, he was beyond caring. Short yelps emitted from his mouth as his pleasure grew. His balls were draining, completely emptying into my ass, and the waves of pulsing pleasure and the mind-shattering contractions lasted long. After he had oozed his final drop, he fell away from me, his dick emerging with another popping sound, and he collapsed upon the floor.

"That was fuckin' great," KT moaned before he fell strangely silent.

"I'm next," Don John proclaimed, not yet aware that "a fate worse than death" had befallen his leader. Fortunately, the guys who join street gangs are stupid; otherwise, I might have been in serious danger.

Don John pushed his cock against my asshole. I was eager, so I pushed my asshole open, nearly sucking in his wide cockhead.

As Don John started stroking, I gripped his cock with my sphincter and delicious feelings filled me again. Between my legs, I could see KT squatting in stunned amazement. It was the first real look I had of him. He was rather good-looking. He was ruddy faced, Saxon in his features, and sexy as hell. His chest and arms were well-developed. I was surprised to discover that the gang consisted of a bunch of white boys. The media had influenced me to think of street gangs as black or Hispanic, but stupidity and cruelty know no racial or cultural boundaries. I took heart in thinking that after this event, this street gang would become the most unusual in Portland.

Don John was moaning with delight by the time he had given me five quick strokes, in and out. I concentrated on wringing his cockhead with my asshole even as I watched the expressions flickering across KT's face. For the most part, the King looked befuddled. He could not yet identify the strange sensations flooding through his body or the odd images flickering through his mind. Shortly, his worm would turn, and he would know that he was a homosexual bottom, an oral receptacle, an anally passive man-pleaser, and that he would remain such for the rest of his life. However, the change takes twenty to thirty minutes, too long to warn his friends not to plant their cocks in my ass.

Don John was wailing like a creature in agony. Despite his dreadful ululations, I kept milking his cock with my asshole and grinding the head with my anal sphincter. Heavy use had toughened my anal sphincter, so any man who stuck his cock inside was going to get the polishing of his life. I squeezed Don John's dick head until he cried for mercy.

"Oh, fuckin' hell, the bitch killin' my cock," he screamed. "Uh, uh, that's fuckin' pain. Oh, man, I'm gonna come. I'm gonna squirt gallons of hot cum."

My asshole was in orgasm along with his cock, and the tingles spread to my cock. Unable to move due to the idiotic way they had bound me to the stool, I could not give him my best ass, which has been twice fatal. Still, I gave him sufficient to change his life. Don John was committed to pansyville, a present he would be receiving before an hour passed.

Don John was finished. Having shot his load up my throbbing ass, he dropped onto the threadbare carpet beside KT.

"Let me go nex'," an eager gangbanger exclaimed. His dick was already dripping with excitement. I smiled to think how easy it would be to turn him out.

"Nah, Fastpass," Don John ordered weakly. "Long Meat's gotta go nex'. Ya can get ya rocks off afta Long Meat skeets the bitch's butt."

"I ain't never fucked a fruit before," Long Meat complained. "He don't gotta pussy."

"Stick ya cock inta his bumper kit, dawg," another banger advised. "That the way hard cons do the pansies in prison."

"Don' feel right ta me, Fart Dady," Long Meat said. His big hands spread my buttocks. "It kinda queer."

"Ain't queer if'n ya're puttin' yars in. Only queer if'n yar takin' it. Like the bitch here."

Long Meat's words had been setting off alarm bells in my head, but he finally gripped my buttocks desperately and slipped his dickhead into my ass. Once the head was in, I had him. His dick head sent shivers of joy up my spine, and I felt my asshole grow hotter as I squeezed. Long Meat began to release a low keening sound as he experienced sexual sensations more intense than any he had ever felt before. His animal instinct warred within him. On one hand, the new sensations terrified him, and he tried to pull his cock out of my ass, but on the other hand, he was enjoying the sexual rapture, and he tried to push his cock in deeper. Meanwhile, I polished his knob with the powerful anal forces at my command. My terrific anal orgasm started just as the first tingles rippled through his dickhead. Long Meat's song of rapture changed pitch until he was nearly shrieking.

His wet cum spurted into my ass even as my spent cock managed a few more spurts. That I had little cum of my own left only made my orgasm more intense. When Long Meat finished shooting his load, I released his cock. He pulled his dickhead out and pushed away from me. In so doing, Long Meat solved one of my problems. He pushed so hard against my arm that the bindings loosened.

Oblivious that freedom was within my grasp, Long Meat stood bewildered by his new feelings. For some reason, total homosexuality claimed Long Meat faster than his fellows. Ready for any man to ride his rump, he tried to articulate the odd changes he felt. Fortunately, Long Meat was able to form only incoherent words: "I wanna try that," he managed. The four bangers I had yet to turn did not understand.

Fastpass, Boogers, and Fart Dady butt fucked me in rapid succession. While they were thus occupied in my rectum, even as I milked their cocks and shuddered along with them in sexual rapture, I freed my clever pickpocket hand from the loosened binding. In a twinkling, I had both hands free.

YG was the last to fuck me, condemned to sloppy sevenths by being the newest member of the gang. As YG gripped my solid ass cheeks, I could see the scene between my legs. Fart Dady was staring in amazement at Don John fucking KT's ass. Inspired, Fastpass offered his ass to Boogers, who gleefully slipped it in. Don John traded places with KT, presenting his own horny hole to his King. KT slipped his cock into Don John's asshole at the same time Fart Dady completed his metamorphosis and joined Boogers and Fastpass in a threeway. Meanwhile, Long Meat was trying to impale his ass on every cock in sight.

The action was taking place behind YG's back. Almost innocently, he placed his hard cock head against my asshole. I drew a deep breath. The moment of truth had arrived. If the last gang banger fucked my ass, I was home free. If he hesitated, my life was in mortal danger.

YG pushed his cock into my asshole, and I shouted out with glee. YG could not know why the joyous howl had passed my lips, but he was already feeling my power. He thrust quickly. As a reward for yielding to his fate, I wanted to make his orgasm extra good, and I sanded his rod with my anal muscles until he was shrieking with joy. "Oh, fuck," YG cried. "Oh, fuck my ass, that's so good. I wanna get fucked like I'm fucking ya'."

Only after he had shot his load did he realize what he had mouthed. Blushing, he turned quickly to see how his leaders were reacting. Imagine his shock at what he saw. As YG stood awed at the gay cluster fuck, I untied my ankles and stood. My asshole was wet and sticky with their cum, but it had been that way many times before. I searched for my new briefs among the scattered boxers upon the floor. I pulled them up and adjusted the seam so it fit my ass crack.

By the time I had located the rest of my clothes, YG had completed his transition. The gang was playing choo-choo, every guy plugged into the one in front. Poor Boogers was in the rear with nobody to impale his ass. He regarded me with pleading eyes.

"Stick ya' cock up my ass," he begged. His eyes lingered on my bulge, my cock concealed in my cum-wet underwear.

I smiled at him and addressed them all. "You boys play nice and give Boogers a turn," I suggested. "Trade places, so everybody rotates to the front."

As they worked it out, I dressed and went through their clothes. I found my original take, plus their ten grand, and the rest of their currency, which amounted to several more thousands. I even snagged their change. They owed it to me for the present I had given them.

Fully dressed, cash bulging my pockets, I addressed the fucking crew. "It took me a hundred years to discover that fucking my ass was a guaranteed path to homosexual passivity," I announced formally. "Only after man after man transformed into catchers after pitching their dicks to me did I appreciate my asshole's power."

The chain gang of the fucked stared at me without malice. One of the great benefits of my power is that my recipients are grateful rather than angry. Some have even thanked me, but this gang was too busy fucking to express their gratitude.

"Have fun, boys," I said in parting. "You can take any cock you want from now on. After fucking my ass, you're immune to disease. You won't even catch another cold."

Waving farewell to my new beneficiaries, I sashayed out of the gang headquarters. The gang fuck had left me satisfied. My sticky ass jiggled as I sauntered homeward. Overall, New Year's Eve had turned out to be sexually amusing and financially worthwhile, and I looked forward to a bright New Year.

PICKPOCKET'S PARADISE

Pickings had been slim during the Christmas season, and I hoped that the New Year would bring deep pockets and fat wallets. Pleasant memories of the successful New Year's Eve two years prior filtered through my thoughts as I tooled through the crowd of revelers. I smiled as I remembered how a street gang had caught me the night we ushered in 2007. They hauled me to their lair and proceeded to gang-bang me. The rape lasted until every member of the gang had turned into a horny butt-slut.

This crowd was particularly excited about the birth of 2009, the effects of new hope in our politics combined paradoxically with an economy spiraling downwards. I lifted three wallets in rapid succession, but my total take was only thirty-six dollars. I pushed between two young women sharing a bottle of apricot ale in defiance of the city's ban on alcohol consumption during the "officially approved" New Year's celebration.

That said, hundreds were boozing, and the police had given up enforcing the ordinance. They were trying only to contain the crowd, and that made my task easy. I could pick pockets and lift purses at will – so long as my contributors themselves didn't snag me.

I was recoiling from the touch of the two females, from whom I had extracted a mere four dollars. Not wanting to dig too deeply, I left them their pocket change and scanned the crowd for more attractive subjects. Promptly, three likely specimens hove into view. The men were in their mid-thirties, looked as though they spent six hours per week in the gym, and probably worked as lawyers or stockbrokers. I copped a feel of one's cock before I dipped for his wallet. Then I gnashed my teeth – silently. He was carrying a dozen credit cards and a measly twenty-dollar bill.

That's when his companions pressed close against me, seized my arms, and lifted me off my feet. The one whose wallet I had scammed gave me a wolfish grin and intoned the fateful words: "This is it, Dipper. You have the right to remain silent. Anything you say can and will be used against you in a court of law. You have the right to speak to an attorney, and to have an attorney present during any questioning. If you cannot afford a lawyer, one will be provided for you at government expense."

"Shit," I said.

"Come on, Dipper," the cops laughed. "You're busted."

"Quit calling me Dipper," I said, but declined to give my real name.

"You're a dipper because you dip into other people's pockets, but you won't be doing that anymore because your ass is going to jail."

"Fucking hell."

The last time I got arrested, I was heavy with two grand, generously contributed by my unsuspecting clients. I paid off the cops, and they let me go. This time I had gathered little over a hundred. If I offered that pittance to this trio, they'd be insulted and charge me with attempted bribery. I drew a deep breath. "I'll go peaceably," I offered. "You can set me down."

Within thirty minutes, I had been fingerprinted and photographed. "What's your name?" the booking officer asked. The booking officer was also the jail's chief corrections officer. Every member of the established force was on duty patrolling the streets that New Year's Eve, leaving a skeletal staff at the jail.

"I have the right to remain silent," I said.

That assertion pissed him off royally. "We're gonna find out who you are, Dipper," he assured me. I wanted to bet that he would not. Oh, they would learn from my fingerprints that I had been arrested before then, but my name had changed with my whims. I smiled at him and rubbed my dick with my handcuffed hands.

His eyes followed the movement. "Don't jack off in here, you dip pervert," he snarled. His dick did not agree with his attitude. His uniform trousers poked with his obvious erection. I winked at him.

"You could fuck me," I suggested. "Fuck my ass. Bareback. Shoot your hot cum up my grainy hole. I'll take your cock any way you like, if you'll let me escape afterwards."

His face turned dark red with pure embarrassment. I'd made an offer he'd wanted all his life, but it was an offer his social encoding repudiated.

"You fuckin' faggot," he yelped. "I'm gonna put you with the hard boys, the ones on their way up the river. You're gonna get gang raped, Dipper, and nobody is gonna hear your screams."

"Those will be screams of joy," I informed him.

That quip pissed the chief screw off further. He called in two other cops for assistance. "Strip the fucker," he ordered. "We're gonna let the Swinging Dicks turn him out."

"Shit, Tyler," one of the cops protested. "Those horny bastards will spend the whole night raping this boy."

"Sounds like fun," I said, and the two cops stared at me with their jaws gaping. "Why don't you cops take the first turn? Fill my ass before it gets sloppy and you have to dip your dicks into other guys' cum?"

"Fuckin' fruitcake," Tyler said. "Strip him naked and toss his ass in with the Swinging Dicks."

I chortled as the police pulled off my clothing. So far the night had been uninteresting; however, the New Year was about to turn fascinating. When I was naked, the jail guards marched me past the cells. I wiggled my ass as I walked, conveying my willingness to take any cock that could reach it. Prisoners were hooting and whistling, while I swayed my prominent buttocks and blew kisses with my manacled hands.

"Toss the pretty punk in here," the prisoners offered. "We'll show him a good time."

"Maybe later," the cops compromised. "After the Swinging Dicks take their turn, we might let the rest of you have him." The corrections officer nudged me sadistically. "How about that, Dipper? We've got one hundred and eighty-six prisoners. How'd you like that many dicks shooting off in your ass? Bet you wouldn't live past number fifty."

"I could take them all," I bragged. "Go on, try me. Bend me over. Butt-fuck my rump in front of the prisoners. Show them how a hard officer can screw an innocent suspect."

"Innocent, my ass," the officer said.

"Yeah," I agreed. "Your ass. You're gonna get fucked, too, copper. Fucked before the night is over. And you're gonna love it."

My suggestions aroused the cops into sporting obvious erections. The prisoners noticed and shouted humiliating insults. The red-faced cops shoved me toward the Swinging Dicks' module. They unlocked the door and roughly heaved me in. Some of the hardcore prisoners had been sleeping. Others were playing cards or jerking off, but all roused to see what fortune had delivered.

"Have fun with this wise-ass dipper, fellows," the guards offered as they slouched against the opposing wall to observe the action.

"He's fuckin' naked," one of the Swinging Dicks howled. "They delivered a naked pretty boy."

"Looks like a fresh punk to me," said one who looked like he was the hardest case of the lot. A real candidate for lethal injection was he, but I grinned inwardly for I could picture the pussy-assed cum sponge I would make of him.

All told, there were seven prisoners housed together in this pod, far from the number I'd been promised. Of course, swinging dicks were the nastiest prisoners, those who were destined for the big house. They were also notorious for turning out punks, making young male prisoners into proxy females. I had dealt with others of this mentality since the seventeenth century, so I knew better than to appear eager. Best to protest. "I didn't do anything," I yelped helplessly. "Please don't hurt me. The cops made a mistake."

"Yeah, we're all mistakes," the hardcase said. "Oh, man, I'm gonna love shooting a load up your tight hole." He grabbed my ass suggestively; then he shivered.

"Oh, guards, save me," I yapped, covering the hardcase's uncontrollable reaction. "These evil men intend to rape me." I was barely able to get the words out without a chortle. The hardened criminal was unable to keep his hands off my ass. He caressed my buttocks with loving desire.

"I get to fuck his ass first," the hardcase gurgled, already committed by one touch. He shuddered again as his mind was possessed by the stark need to consummate his transformation.

"Sure, Blotto," the rest agreed sycophantically. "You open up his ass."

"Sure, Blotto," I mimicked, now certain that I was destined to get fucked. None of these boys was going to back out, no matter what happened. Little did they know.

Blotto pushed me against the bars, and his hand slid between my butt cheeks. His hand was coarse, as though he had been doing manual labor. I assumed he had – most of his life in the prison workforce. Blotto's calluses came from making license plates in the machine shop or crafting furniture on a lathe. He was too hard to have broken up gravel for the highways. That cruel task was left for softer boys until they died or toughened up.

I gasped with pleasure as Blotto slobbered onto his thumb and stuck it up my ass. He thought he was hurting me. As his digit entered

84

my asshole, I heaved a sigh. "Does that hurt, faggot?" Blotto taunted. "Wait until you feel my cock up your asshole."

"Please don't hurt me," I begged gleefully. He could not hurt me, whatever he did, but he didn't know about my secret abilities. Not yet – and when he found out, it would be too late. By then, Blotto would be the pussy boy, the asshole begging to be filled with gigantic cocks and thick semen. Then he would go to prison and find himself the favorite sport of the entire cell block, while I strolled blithely back to the street to pick pockets and turn out more hard men, so they too would know the pleasure of a shooting cock in their asses.

"I'm gonna fuck you, punk," Blotto said, withdrawing his thumb. He pulled my rear back toward his jutting erection. "Here it comes," I thought.

Blotto pressed his cock against my asshole. I pushed hard to open my ass for him. He drove his dick against my hole and found easy entrance. "Ooompf," he said as his thick cock slid into me. "Oh, fuck, his asshole is sucking my dick in," Blotto added, and the other men of our cell cheered him. Little could they comprehend Blotto's bewilderment as sensations he had only dreamt before swept through his psyche.

"Fuck me," I demanded, and Blotto had no will to refuse. Homosexual thoughts flooded his mind as he pulled back his hips and thrust his cock into me. The sensation of being filled to the hilt drove me nearly to distraction. I love a hard fuck, and Blotto was sure giving it to me. The knowledge that he would be queerer than I am afterward only added zest to my anal pleasure. I wiggled my ass and clamped my asshole down on his cock. I milked his dick, squeezing especially hard as his dick head hit my anal sphincter.

"Give it to him, Blotto," his cheering section called. "Come in his ass."

Blotto humped faster. Delicious thrills raced up my anal canal as his probing cock thrust. I could feel his cock milking my asshole. I tensed my buttocks to give him greater friction, and Blotto moaned in my ear. "Oh, fuck, I never had it so good. Ah, fuck, I'm gonna come."

"Yeah," I agreed. "You're gonna come in my ass. That's it, Blotto. Let it happen."

I rode his thrusting cock until I was in full anal orgasm. My asshole was contracting uncontrollably upon his dick, sending strange signals through every cell of his body. The worms of homosexual lust burrowed into his mind as he tipped into orgasm. I heard him grunting as he shot his semen into my rectum. I gripped harder with my buttocks as he spurted, and I rode my own fantastic orgasm. The deep ripples of pleasure traveled up my rectum and vibrated through my pelvis.

"Blotto's coming in the punk's ass," one prisoner shouted gleefully.

"I wanna be next," another shouted, unaware that his demand was susceptible to more than one interpretation. Meanwhile, the guards had dropped their pose of nonchalance and were staring with fluttery intensity.

I smiled as Blotto pressed my face to the bars and the sucking tornado of pleasure howled up my ass. Blotto's thick semen was squirting into me, feeding my ass with his manly essence. Little did he know that his heterosexual desire was flowing out with his jism and from that moment on, he would desire fulfillment from thick thrusting cocks and spurting spunk.

Rushes of sexual ecstasy roared through my body as Blotto gasped and thrust. His gasps grew raspier, and his thrusts more erratic. Finally, they stilled. He pulled his dick out of my ass. The sensation of it coming out was almost as good as it was going in. My anal sphincter relished the sensation of the passing of his cock. Then it closed tight to hold in the fluids I had happily received.

"Shoes gets to ball the punk next," a voice called. Blotto sank to his knees, weakened by the powerful surges of homosexual feelings. I dropped to all fours and wiggled, drawing every eye to my booty. I wanted these armed robbers, drug dealers, killers, and other brutes to unload in my ass before they guessed what was happening to their brother thugs – and what would happen to them after they fucked me.

Shoes had no idea what was happening to his leader. Blotto had fallen back against the cell door. He was breathing heavily, but he gave no other sign of the immense changes being wrought within. Shoes smirked as he yanked off his brilliant orange coveralls and jailhouse briefs. His cock was brownish, long, and thinner than Blotto's, but twisted significantly to his left. That twist was a fine touch.

Still on my hands and knees, I thrust back my rounded buttocks. "The fruit wants it," Shoes yelped, his hands running over my butt cheeks. He started slightly as the first shock hit him, but he only knew in a dim way that he found touching my ass pleasurable. Little did he guess the souvenir I had for him. I wiggled my butt in open invitation, which was sufficient foreplay for Shoes' limited imagination. He climbed onto me, like a tiger mounting its mate, and pushed his cock head against my asshole. I pushed to let him enter, and enter he did, before he was even expecting it.

"Holy fuck," Shoes moaned as his cock banged into me. I giggled silently as he discovered that he had no will to resist my anal power. My ass pulled him in, and my sphincter kissed his shaft. I massaged his dick, caressed it with my anus, enclosed it with my rectum, and extracted the initial juices from it with the full power of my pelvis. Feverish sensations of pleasure rippled through me. My muscles contracted involuntarily, milking him off, squeezing every cell of his cock in ways even I could not conceive. My ass was going to make him shoot his load, drain him, deliver him into a state of total thrall, make him a slave to homosexual lust. In a few minutes, Shoes would be the anal whore.

"Ah, ah, what the fuck you doin' to me?" Shoes howled, cognizant that I was in command of his body and soul, but incapable of forming a coherent warning to his cellmates.

"Holy shit, Shoes is really getting' off," his cellmates yelped stupidly. "He's givin' it to the faggot a-fuckin'-right."

Shoes was, indeed, giving it to the faggot a-fuckin'-right – I relished his wild, uncontrolled, uninhibited, mindless, and shrieking orgasm. I knew what the unexpected pleasure he was experiencing meant to him – and to me. Shoes shot his wet semen into my rectum, unloading with total abandon, coming in thick unbelievable spurts until his balls softened and hung drained below his cock. Slowly, unbelievingly, Shoes pulled his cock out of my ass. He slumped down on the floor of the cell and giggled.

Sometimes my victims wept, and their tears spelled danger. Fortunately, Shoes was giggling like a sissy, but his cellmates again misinterpreted what was happening. They didn't even notice when Blotto reached for Shoes' cock.

The Hammer came in me next, and he was followed by Snickers, whose name reminded me of a candy bar. The Hammer shot a load of cum, more than the rest, but Snickers was the more talented lover. Snickers took me on my back, with my legs in the air, and he fucked my ass as he would a cunt. I laughed as he moaned, knowing that soon Snickers would be the pussy. I wished that I could see these guys when they hit the big house. Their cock-loving assholes should make them the prison's most popular punks.

By the time High-Price was slamming his lap against my hard butt, Blotto was fucking Shoes and the Hammer was pushing his finger up Blotto's ass. As High-Price fucked me, I stared into the eyes of the two correctional officers who were still watching from outside the cell. Those boys were sporting significant boners, and they were holding hands. I guessed that they were already lovers. The opportunity was too good to pass. But as the prisoner named Craze tried his best to rape the willing, I still had two of my fellow prisoners to turn out before I started on the cops.

While the worms of sexual submission were borrowing into Craze's brain, I wiggled my butt at Croaker. "Fuck this shit," Croaker said. "I ain't fuckin' no man. Pussy's my cum contraption."

"My ass is better than any pussy, Croaker," I taunted. "Come on, brave boy. Stick your cock into me. Didn't you see how Blotto did it? You want Blotto to laugh at you? Call you a punk?"

"I ain't no fuckin' punk," Croaker snarled, taking a swipe at my head. He was trying to punch me, but his momentum bumped his pelvis against my bare ass. That slight touch – through his jailhouse jumpsuit – was all it took. He was hooked into it. He pulled off his clothes and jumped me. I grabbed his cock with my ass and enveloped him until he was howling like the rest. The waves of sexual pleasure washed over Croaker. Tingles erupted in the head of his dick. He was committed to come. He thrust in my ass. Once. Twice. Three times. He could not control his thrusts. He pushed his dick all the way into me, and I laughed. Croaker was mine. I was ready to turn him. Try to resist me, would he? He would be the sleaziest butt slut of the cell block before I finished mangling the jism out of his cock. I milked him off with my asshole, tensing my buttocks to draw down his pleasure.

"Fuck," Croaker snarled. "Fuck. The fuckin' dip is takin' it out of me. Oh, fuck, man, I'm turnin'. It's fuckin' wild. Oh, fuck, yes, make me queer. I'm your cum-drawing anal whore. I'm your cocksucking cum sponge."

That Rod Man still wanted to get his rocks off in my asshole after Croaker's revelation was a mystery unto itself. I guess Rod Man wanted my special endowment because, even knowing what was going to happen, he took me against the bars, and then he took me sitting on his dick while the rest watched. Of course, by then they were all fucking each other, but it didn't matter anymore.

The correctional officers looked at me standing naked over the cluster fuck, and then they gazed into each other's eyes. One was fiddling with the key. "Let's pull his queer ass outta there, Kent."

"You thinking of fucking the punk, Scott?" Kent asked.

"Shit, yeah," Scott said, copping a feel of the other's ass. "This is our big chance. This faggot turns everyone who fucks him gay."

"And since we know we're already gay ..."

"Yeah," Scott concluded. "Who can say what happened? Who can say our own affair is our fault?"

"If we let him out, he's gonna turn the rest of the guards into flaming faggots. Even Tyler."

"That cocksucker is already gay, though he's too chickenshit to admit it. Don't you see? They'll all be gay. Just like you and me. That's the beauty of this plan."

Scott unlocked the cell and let me out. The Swinging Dicks were so busy dicking each other that they didn't notice my departure. I wiggled my ass at the guards.

"Where are we going to do him?" Kent asked.

"How about the evidence locker?"

Scott slid his hand across the curve of my ass and gasped audibly. "Yeah," he managed. His protruding cock made his uniform trousers look like he was concealing a cucumber. "The evidence locker is just the place."

"Come on, Dip," Kent said, seizing my arm.

My ass felt hot and wet as I walked. I was carrying a lot of cum. I relished the thought of all that wet spunk and tensed my anal sphincter.

They led me past cells of horny prisoners again, but this time the inmates watched wonderstruck. They expected to see me bruised and humiliated; yet I strode naked, unfettered, and triumphant. Barefoot, I walked as if I were leading the guards, and far from feeling raped, I felt like I had raped seven cocks with my ass. My asshole radiated power as I swayed my buttocks provocatively. I could turn out any man with my ass, and the prisoners sensed it.

Scott and Kent also sensed the reality of my power, but they conspired to conceal the truth from their fellow officers. We reached a locked door. Kent knocked and identified himself. The officer within opened the door, but stepped back with his jaw agape as Kent and Scott led me into the evidence room.

"Whatcha bringin' him in here for?" the property clerk protested. "Uh, guys, you know he's buck naked, don't you?"

"Put your hand on his ass, Bert," Scott said.

"What the fuck?" Bert yelped. "I'm not touchin' his smelly ass."

"It's not smelly," Scott corrected. "It's magical."

"Have you fellers lost your marbles?"

Kent rubbed his hand across my buttocks, and an expression of feral lust bathed his features. His entire body shook, as if he stood in a shower of homosexual desire, and he let the spray of feeling wash over him as he relished the cleansing away of any lingering breeder impulse.

"Do what Kent just did," Scott urged. "You gotta feel it, Bert. You can't believe it until you feel it for yourself."

"Ah, what the fuck," Bert said. "I think you boys have been hangin' out with the inmates too much. You're turnin' queer. Sure, I'll touch the punk's ass. It won't have no effect on me." So saying, Bert steeled his nerves for the experience, and rather timidly for all his brave assertions lightly brushed my butt cheeks. At the touch, every visible patch of his skin turned bright crimson. As if he was trying to pull his hand away, Bert moved in the opposite direction and cupped my left buttock with his hand so that his thumb slipped into my crack.

He shook violently, and his cock swelled his trousers. Scott winked at Kent, who was still shaken from touching my butt, though his reaction was nowhere near as powerful as Bert's. Scott began to undress hastily. After a few seconds, Kent followed suit. Bert was still dazed – almost unconsciously, he began masturbating. His fingers probed the head of his dick through his pants.

Laughing, I bent over a table that held nothing but a closed suitcase. In front of me stood long metal shelves covered with drug paraphernalia, burglar's tools, stolen goods, and weapons. I closed my eyes in bliss as Scott pushed his cock against my asshole. Scott's cock was not particularly long, but it was delightfully thick, which makes for an enchanting butt fuck. It slid into my slick asshole. I tightened my sphincter around it and let it create that wonderful sensation of fullness in my rectum.

Riding the bliss, I gripped Scott's cock with all my might. My asshole squeezed him so that each thrust held the orgasmic power of ten strokes. "Oh, oh," Scott managed. "I've never felt it like this."

I wasn't turning Scott gay since he was born gay. However, I was removing all fear and doubt from his psyche. The feelers of gay abandon were coursing through his body and entering his brain. His total conscious self was turned out by the event, so that from that instant he would no longer be the closeted cop. When my ass got finished with these fellows, they would be out and proud – unquestionably.

Scott was unloading his spunk into me. He came in great gouts, emptying his balls into my ass. I did not relinquish my tight grip, but I rode his cock for my own pleasure. The orgasmic waves pounded the cells of my rectum, and pure pleasure washed over me as Scott slowly screwed my gripping asshole.

When Scott was finished, Kent took his turn. I dropped onto my back and raised my legs for him, and he slid his cock into me without effort. Wonderful sensations flowed up my canal as Kent pinned me to the floor and rapidly banged my ass. He was shooting off before he had hammered ten strokes, but that was sufficient for me to remove any trace of doubt from his being. By the time Kent pulled his dick out of my ass, he was as fully committed to our cause as his lover.

"Oh, Kent," Scott moaned, snuggling against his friend. "We're free. Finally, we're free."

"Yeah," Kent said. He grabbed Scott by the ears and kissed his lips.

"Your turn," I told Bert. "How do you want to fuck me?"

Bert was helplessly staring at Scott and Kent, and his dick was soaring. He wanted to fuck me, he needed to fuck me, he was committed to fuck me, but he was almost incapable of initiating action. Recognizing the symptoms from some previous encounters, I jumped to my feet and quickly undressed him. He made no protest as I pulled off his blue underwear and his cock popped free.

He did not resist as I pulled him close. Then I turned my back on him and drove my ass until his dick head was pressing into my butt crack. Deprived of the ability to resist, Bert placed his hands on my hips and swung forward. I pushed back harder until the head of his dick was entering my asshole. I opened for him, and he found that his cock would slide into me with virtually no effort on his part. "Resistance is futile, Bert," I joshed. "You will be assimilated."

"Oh," Bert managed as the worms of lust wiggled through him. He claimed his present. Beside us, Scott was fucking Kent's ass, and the two officers were moaning and gasping with joy.

"See," I said. "See, Bert. See how great it is. You're being assimilated into the sodomite brotherhood."

"Yeah," Bert moaned as he began thrusting his cock into my ass, forcing deep into me and then pulling back to the entrance. He was making long, delightfully slow strokes that delivered blasts of pleasure to my every nerve. "Yeah, it's good." The psychic worms wiggled into his brain and turned all his thoughts. "Ah, yeah, I'm gay. I wanna get my ass fucked, too."

"You will, Bert," I assured him as he began humping me harder and faster. "You're gonna get gang banged by a cell full of inmates before the night is over." (I would not toss Bert into a cell full of prisoners; he would do that himself. Within an hour or so, he would take the keys and offer his ass to a pod.)

"Yeah," he cried joyously. He began slamming his cock into me so hard that I lost my balance, and we fell forward against the table. The suitcase was knocked to the floor, where it popped open. My wondering eyes saw the bundles of hundred dollar bills, thousands of hundred dollar bills secured with rubber bands.

"Oh, yeah," Bert groaned, not caring about the fallen money. He was already committed to orgasm. His dick was throbbing and filling with the semen rising from his balls. A tremendous spurt raptured out of his cock into my rectum. More squirts followed, each one feeding my anal delight. I took his spunk into me, gripping his cock with my asshole so tightly that it twisted within me as it erupted. I drained him, and he finally pulled out with a loud popping sound and collapsed gasping beside Kent and Scott. Those two had finished screwing each other and were cuddling sympathetically upon the floor.

"What the fuckin' hell is going on in here?" Tyler shouted. The chief deputy had finally made his appearance. "Why do you assholes have this dipper in here? Why isn't he in his cell getting gang raped like I ordered? Why are you guys naked? What's the money from the Parker Job doing on the floor? Don't you know the District Attorney needs that for the trial?"

I shut Tyler up by bumping my bare ass against his uniformed one. Before he could protest against the bump, I plastered my naked buttocks against the front of his crotch. Tyler emitted a loud cry and threw his arms around me. "I'll butt fuck your ass, you fucking freak," he shouted.

"Then you better get your pants off," I commented, eyeing the money from the Parker Job.

Tyler hastily undressed. More aggressive than Bert, he pulled me down to the floor and took me sideways. My back against him, Tyler pushed my left leg forward and thrust his cock against my asshole. I knew at once that this was not the first time he had fucked another man. He'd had considerable experience. Nevertheless, my instinct told me that Tyler had never been fucked himself, so a new experience would soon be his. He was already shaking as he opened my asshole with his cock head. Our position did not allow me to tighten my asshole, so I focused a burst of psychic energy that traveled up his cock and through his form. The energy coursed through him, forcing out every trace of heterosexuality and masculine behavior.

Laughing as Tyler continued slipping his dick head in and out of my rectum, I pictured the effeminate cum sponge Tyler would inevitably become. Within two hours, this bully officer would twist into a butt-swinging, mincing, prissy pansy, and he would remain thus for life.

The picture was almost orgasmic of itself. I allowed the shudders of pleasure to claim me. The sensation grew deep up my ass and radiated out in all directions. The most powerful surges followed the trail toward my asshole where Tyler was still working his dickhead at my hole and coming close to pouring his seed into me. Other surges raced up to my navel and divided toward my nipples, which crinkled with delirious joy. The surges continued up my throat so that my lips twisted and my nostrils flared. Even my eyelids spasmed.

An even more powerful surge radiated through my hard dick. The head of my dick was ablaze. The fiery tingles tippled upward toward the muscles at the base of my penis. "Oh, I'm coming," Tyler gasped. "I'm coming in your ass."

"I'm coming, too," I said. The anal orgasm was wonderful, even better than the orgasm in my dick. However, my asshole could not ejaculate. Shooting spunk is a different kind of joy. Tyler's cock stimulated the bundles of nerves in my asshole as a nearly overwhelming pleasure filled me. My muscles contracted, and a great burst of my jism splattered against the gray metal shelving. More blasts followed. I came until I emptied my balls, even as Tyler shot his cum both inside my asshole and onto it.

Tyler rolled away from me after he finished and lay on his back. He made low keening sounds as he stared vacantly at the ceiling. While he was passing through his change, I winked at Kent and Scott, who decided to take turns fucking Bert. As they positioned Bert for his big event, I picked up the bundles of money from the Parker Job and replaced them in the suitcase.

The money felt good in my hand. Bonanzas like that one only come once in a century, and I hadn't scored a major sum since 1916. Before that, I had claimed my greatest haul during a return visit to England in 1837.

I was born in Shropshire in England in 1594. My pick-pocketing career was launched in 1609 when I apprenticed myself to a tooler, scoundrel, wine-guzzler, pickpocket, and boy-banger named Benny the Rake. After Benny tippled himself into a pauper's grave, I realized I had stopped aging. At fifty, I looked exactly as I had at twenty. For the past four hundred and twenty odd years, my physical body has not aged a second, nor have I suffered a day of sickness. I can even cure diseases in others.

I have always blown through money as if it were so much waste paper, so I knew that I wouldn't keep this windfall long. Living hand to mouth added zest to my existence, especially since I combined picking pockets with my zeal to create new butt sluts.

Tyler's keys were attached to his belt. I winked at him as I removed them, but he only regarded me with a grateful expression as his fellow cops banged his ass. Leaving them in the unlocked evidence locker, I proceeded to Tyler's office to reclaim my clothing.

On the way, I stopped at a pod to turn out the four inmates incarcerated there. One of the four had AIDS, which the power of my asshole cleansed from his body while he fucked me. When he hit the big house, he would be fresh booty.

I relocked the pod door and watched my four new recruits fucking each other. The one who had been sick was looking healthier by the second, and he was enjoying the group fuck train even more than the rest. Smiling at my good work, I swished up the corridor to the officers' stations.

My clothing lay undisturbed upon the floor of Tyler's office. However, as I picked up my underwear, I heard footsteps behind me. The three undercover officers who had arrested me had returned to the jail.

"What do you think you're doing, Dipper?" one asked. He was an Irish-looking redhead with a creamy complexion and a well-developed chest. I batted my eyes at him.

"I was getting ready to leave," I said, setting the suitcase containing the cash from the Parker Job beside Tyler's desk. My fingerprint card still lay upon the blotter. "The jury found me 'Not Guilty.'"

The undercover cops were confused by that assertion. "Baffle the Bastards with Bullshit" had been the Finger's motto. My partner during the spendthrift eighties, Finger was long gone, but his motto worked sometimes. Not that time. The undercover dicks were suspicious.

"Where are the guards? Are you trying to escape?"

"Escape. No way," I asserted. "I'm having too much fun." Without explaining, I threw myself against the closest detective. His hand had been at his side, so I pushed my ass crack against it. He reacted as though he had been struck by lightning. Before the other two could figure out that I had hit their partner with a thunderbolt, I swished my ass across them.

The detectives staggered backwards, overwhelmed and frightened by the new sensations coursing through their bodies. I clutched the one closest to me and pulled down his zipper. His cock popped free. Dragging him atop me, I sprawled face down on the floor. Helpless to resist, the detective lay with his naked cock pressed against my anal cleft.

He knew what to do, though it was a first for him. He pushed his hard cock into my asshole. The wonderful sensation of fullness claimed me. I let my heat flow into him, and when he had pushed his cock down to its limit, I clamped my asshole tight. He was the one whose pocket I had picked, setting me up for a fall. I had a little score to settle. I can't turn men out by sucking their cocks or licking their assholes – they have to butt fuck me. However, even as I turn a man into a butt slut, I can, through application, make him a confirmed cocksucker and ass kisser. This fellow was going to get the full package.

Before another hour had passed, I had turned out three new ravenously compulsive anal whores. After locking the three detectives in a pod with a gang of horny studs, I dressed, picked up the suitcase, and shredded my fingerprint card in the multi-pass shredder. Grinning triumphantly, I sauntered out the front entrance of the jail. "Another highly satisfactory New Year's Eve," I said aloud as I swayed my dilated, stuffed, semen-dripping ass through the streets of the rejoicing city.

PLEASING THE TOOMA MEN

My brother Ray and I agree that our parents are mad scientists. It's not just that our mother and father are physicists and engineers, or that they have one secret laboratory in the attic and another in the cellar, but they insist on using Ray and me as guinea pigs for their screwball experiments. Like the night Mom summoned Ray to the cellar and made him drink a beverage that had the effect of two years of heavy weight training. Ray's muscles have bulged like those of a powerlifter ever since. Or the afternoon Dad demanded that I come to the attic because he'd invented a computer program that worked directly off brain power. He hooked electrodes to my skull and made me move the pointer and click on icons with my mind. For a week afterward, I had double vision and splitting headaches.

I'm not questioning whether our parents love us because they do. Still, they don't see anything wrong with experimenting on us to see what will happen. Fortunately, thus far only one of their experiments has produced life-changing consequences. That was the trip though the trans-dimensional machine, and that one was a dilly. After it, neither Ray nor I were ever the same.

It was a chilly winter weekend. Ray and I had been taking courses at the local junior college, but we were taking a break from our studies and were watching some trashy old horror films on television and trading vulgar remarks about the show's hostess.

"Man, Sport, look at those fuckin' tits," Ray said, rubbing his dick as he leered at the scantily clad hostess. His hand continued massaging his cock through the denim of his jeans.

"You going to jack off here in the living room, Ray?" I asked, glancing nervously toward the stairs where our parents were working above our heads. My own cock was hardening because if he was going to beat off on the couch so was I. Ray and I masturbated together, though we never did it to each other, just ourselves.

"Yeah, I'm horny as hell," Ray said. "But come in your pussy pants, Sport. Don't shoot off on the couch." For some reason, Ray preferred boxer shorts while I liked briefs. We often teased each other about our underwear. I called his butt bags.

We had loosened our belts, pulled down our zippers, and were reaching into our underwear when Dad called us from the attic. "Boys," he shouted, "your mother and I need you for a minute."

"Oh, shit," Ray muttered, fastening his pants. "Come on, Sport. Here we go again."

"It's an inter-dimensional transporter," Dad said upon our arrival in the attic. He and Mom were wearing white lab coats and goggles while they fiddled with a bizarre contraption composed of long clear cylinders and loads of wires. A red circle had been painted on the floor directly in front of an open tube.

"Ray, you stand on that red circle," Mom directed. "We're going to move you through another dimension and back."

"We were watching *Vengeance of the Martian Zombies*," Ray complained.

"You'll be back before the commercial break is over," Dad said confidently. "This will only take a second."

Somewhat nervously, Ray planted his feet on the red circle. "Here we go," Dad proclaimed. "The moment of truth." With a gleam of scientific inquiry, Mom threw a switch, a loud humming emitted from the machine, and Ray vanished. But not completely. All Ray's clothes fell in a heap on the floor, even his socks and underwear. I grabbed up Ray's clothes and held them out rather accusingly.

"Now that was a remarkable phenomenon," Mom and Dad exclaimed at once. "The transporter works only on animate objects."

I felt a sick horror, but before I could doubt whether I would see my brother again, Ray was back with a popping sound. Of course, he was buck naked. He was streaked with dirt and mud and drenched with some pale sap that carried a pungent odor. The sap was heaviest on his face, and a gigantic dollop of the goop was hanging off his chin. He was also sporting a dripping erection. I grabbed his boxer shorts and covered his dick before Mom and Dad could see his condition.

"What happened?" I demanded, but Ray appeared to be dazed.

"Oh, uh," he muttered incoherently. "Suck Tooma."

His eyes were glazed as if he had gone through a tremendous experience, and he could not yet cope with being returned to his world and family. I tried to help him dress himself, even though he was dripping with sap and smelled like nothing on Earth. His clothes would hardly go on over his sticky skin.

"We'd better repeat the experiment," Mom said. "Then we can make notes on both boys' experiences." Dad agreed and pointed toward the red circle. "Come over here, Sport."

"I don't want to," I said. "Wait until Ray snaps out of his daze. Let's find out what happened to him."

"Oh, he's all right," Dad said dismissively. "Probably just the transporter effect."

"Sport, you get in that circle now," Mom demanded, obsessed with the pursuit of pure research. That's what I meant about our parents being mad scientists. Once they had a scientific experiment in mind, nothing else mattered.

"I'm afraid," I whined.

"Don't be a crybaby," Dad snorted. "Your brother went through another dimension and back and look at him. He's perfectly normal."

Looking at Ray, I could see that he was anything but perfectly normal, but our parents couldn't see it. He did seem to be recovering somewhat, though there was a strange expression on his face as he attempted to finish dressing his stained body. He appeared to be smiling over some secret knowledge. As I tried to analyze my brother's mysterious smirk, I found myself half-pushed and half-pulled into the circle. When I heard the machine hum, I gripped my jeans with both hands. I wasn't going without my pants if I could help it.

All for nothing. The attic floor felt like it gave way beneath my feet, and I suffered a sickening drop. My fingers that had been holding my pants were tightly clutching nothing, for like Ray, I had passed through the dimensional barrier without a stitch. Since Ray had been gone for a few seconds, I held my breath in the expectation that I would abruptly reappear in the attic. Nothing of the sort happened.

Suddenly, I was no longer falling, but pitching forward onto soft, damp ground. The dirt had a spicy odor and the pinkish ferns that had broken my fall released a pungent fragrance. After a few seconds of bafflement, I rolled over, ran my hands over my naked body, and found neither broken bones nor gaping wounds. I was relatively unhurt, save for a few bruises.

I jumped up and brushed the clinging dirt off my ass. Then I looked around. I had landed in a vast valley covered with the pinkish ferns. In the distance stood gigantic purple mountains, snowcapped but impossibly alien. In the eerie sky blazed a red sun, a little larger appearing than Sol. Though the air was comfortably warm, I did not notice this sun heating my skin. I was in no danger of sunburn, whatever else awaited me.

I heard the ferns rustling before I noticed that I was not alone. Three men were approaching me, Herculean in their build, and displaying hard, thick cocks. From the leering expressions of feral lust on their faces, I deduced the origin of the sap that had covered Ray's body.

Running would have been worse than useless. My best hope lay in my sudden reappearance in the attic. However, in my heart I knew that time was running differently in this alien world. Ray had reappeared in less than a minute, but it was obvious that he had undergone experiences that had taken hours or even days. I was trapped until my parents' machine pulled me back.

As the three aliens drew near, I held up my hand in a show of friendship. "Greetings, otherworlders," I announced, smiling broadly in spite of my thundering heart, "I arrive on your hospitable planet from another dimension."

The reaction of the aliens was anything but reassuring. They gave no polite answer in response, but started rubbing their hard cocks. One alien continued approaching straight on, while his companions split to both sides and circled toward my rear.

"I come in peace for all mankind," I said anxiously. Terror, mixed with a queer desire I could not identify, swept over me. In desperation, I remarked with a forced, ingratiating smile, "My, what a charming world you have here."

"Suck Tooma," the alien said.

"I beg your pardon?" I said. I felt a wave of erotic dizziness, and I dimly perceived what would be required of me. My cock grew heavier as the heady scent of that world swept out the cobwebs of my narrow-mindedness.

The alien gripped his hard cock with both hands and waved it at me. "Suck Tooma," he repeated.

I had no doubt that this being from another world expected me to drop to my knees and give him a blowjob. The most amazing thing was that I did not find the suggestion revolting. I, who had never entertained a homosexual thought, was attracted by this strange cock. Responding to the heat in my loins, I found my dick half-hard already.

The alien's thick cock was leaking a thin stream of fluid. I was on my knees before I knew it. The Tooma man's cock jutted before me.

Without thought, I kissed it. The cum leaking from it wet my lips. I touched my tongue to the dripping hole in the Tooma man's dick and shuddered with delight. I had never tasted anything so delicious as this alien semen. His cum ran down my chin as I kissed the head of his cock. The head passed over my lips, entered my mouth, and poured its juices onto my tongue. My own cock was fully hard, stiff even to bursting.

The two aliens that had circled behind me were rubbing their cocks over my shoulders. As they masturbated, they decorated me with their unworldly cum. Far from humiliating me, the wet spunk splattering my skin made me feel incredibly sexy. My cock leaked my earthly fluid as the alien spunk ran in rivulets down my chest and my back. A warm stream meandered into the crack of my ass, leaving a sticky trail that dripped from my tight balls. My arousal lent impetus to my taste for the cock in my mouth. I worried it with my lips and tongue until the thick filling of my mouth grew into the most wonderful experience of my life. I grabbed my cock, wet with my own pre-cum and the dribbling spunk of the masturbating aliens, and began jacking off as I received the first Tooma deeper into my mouth.

I had no fear that I would choke or gag on Tooma, whether the word stood for the alien's race, his personal name, or his cock. I knew that I could take it into my throat. His leaking stream had been running in steady rivulets down my gullet, so the path was slicked for deep passage. Suddenly, I was doing it, I was deep-throating his cock gladsomely, masturbating my own dick furiously as I did so. I had never felt so proud of myself, pleased with my natural talent to make cocks come in my mouth, smug even that my mouth would please the Tooma man. For his part, the Tooma man shuddered, and a tremendous burst of semen slid down my throat. More and more flowed down into my stomach. I swallowed until he was drained.

I was receiving showers of alien cum. Dozens of Tooma had appeared to jerk off and decorate me with thick squirts. Cum splashed over my neck and into my hair while more warm spunk ran down my back. Big splats hit my ass, a virtual river of alien semen running down my crack. The cum was luxurious, a gay jubilance that clung to my skin. The warm goop made me feel special, and I loved having it on me and in me simultaneously. Tooma's sticky flow embellished my upturned lips; that alien cock had put a smile on my face, a big, wet, cum-mouth smile, and I wanted to drown in a sea of spunk.

I was still jerking off, and more Tooma men were jerking off on me. The Tooma cum made a great lube that stimulated my cock down to its central nerves. My balls were dripping heavier as more alien goop washed over me; one Tooma was shooting directly onto my asshole. My cock grew heavier. I squeezed it with all the strength of my hand and jacked it hard until I went beyond all going back. Marvelous prickles rippled through the head of my dick as I thumbed its head.

As my orgasm grew, a different cock slipped into my mouth. I tortured that Tooma cock with my lips and tongue while spasms rushed up my cock. My orgasm was so intense that I could scarcely touch my agonized dick, yet contradictorily, I could not refrain from abusing it. I was seized with a contraction that spurted my cum onto the legs of the alien I was blowing. I kept sucking wildly as the contractions continued. The intense ripples of pleasure did not quickly diminish, but lasted longer than any previous orgasm. My muscles contracted, and I shot hard salvos of spunk, even as the second alien unloaded onto my lips, my nose, my cheeks, my chin, and my eyes. Alien cum covered my face. I was nearly blinded. The next squirts spurted into my mouth. I sucked on his dickhead as the mighty Tooma exploded pungent juices down my throat. I swallowed and swallowed, hardly able to keep ahead of the mouthfuls I was receiving. I shuddered in the throes of orgasm and unloaded my own balls.

Exhausted, I fell onto my ass in the muck of the alien ground. Tooma men held me in a sitting position while others jacked their thick cocks onto me. Thousands of Tooma men had arrived while I was sucking off the first, and I reached for a cock that was ready to squirt. Leaning forward, I touched my lips to it. I mouthed the wonderful dickhead, loving the feeling of the cock in my mouth, loving the feeling of the cum soaking my body, loving the taste and texture of the jizz I was swallowing.

I don't know how many I sucked. More than twenty, surely. I don't know how many shot their loads onto my face, my back, my chest, my ass, and my legs. More than five hundred, surely. I was drenched with cum, full of cum, and covered with alien dirt and crushed pink ferns when the falling sensation struck again.

I had forgotten about home and family. I had been prepared to suck Tooma men for the rest of my natural life, having lost any desire to return to my brother with his ass bags, my parents with their mad science, or my junior college with its mundane knowledge. However, I had no control over my travels. I was a stranger passing through, and I felt the attic floor beneath my bare feet as I arrived, my dick half-hard and spent, my skin smeared with alien sap and dirt, and my body naked before my parents and brother.

Ray had recovered, and he threw my briefs over my cock. My preferred underwear did not cover the area of his boxers and they showed my state more clearly. Ray pushed my clothes at me, rendering them wet and sticky in the process.

"Come on, Sport," Ray urged, dragging me toward the attic steps. "We need a shower."

"We need a full report," Dad yelled after us. "We have to write up the lab notes."

"That's essential," Mom agreed. "You boys need to record every detail that happened."

I felt dazed and disoriented, but Ray maneuvered me down the attic steps and into the second floor bathroom. Ray and I had not taken a shower together since we were children, but that day we soaped each other's bodies and toweled each other off. "I have alien cum in my stomach," I said wonderingly as we dried.

"So do I," Ray said. "There's something else, too."

"The desire to suck cock hasn't gone away?" I asked, voicing the fantasies that were gripping my thoughts.

"You feel it, too?" We stepped apart and looked at each other. We could feel the difference. I knew that I would be sucking cock for the remainder of my life. What's more, I knew that I was good at it, and my newfound talents made me feel proud.

An awestruck expression had come into Ray's eyes. I could see in him also the fierce pride that I felt. "Now we're cocksuckers, Sport," Ray said. "What are we going to do?"

"Let's not start sucking each other. That would be too weird. Let's find a couple of guys who would enjoy blow jobs."

"Sport, you remember we have dates with Jennifer and Ashley tomorrow night?"

"Oh, shit, I don't want anything to do with twats. How about we call the girls up and cancel. I'll bet Larry and Rich are free."

"Those guys are queer as hell ...," Ray began. He interrupted himself and regarded me with amazement.

"Yeah, so are we. Queer as hell. And I'm glad, Ray. I'm glad I'm a cocksucker."

"Let's not wait until tomorrow. Let's call those boys now."

That night our new lives began. I ended the evening going down on Larry in the front seat of our car, while Ray sucked Rich's dick in the back seat. Then we traded places, and everybody had a swell time. Ray and I never told Mom and Dad about what had happened to us. By mutual consent, we pretended that we could remember nothing that occurred. Our parents might have felt guilty for altering our sexual orientation. Or they might have considered it an interesting side effect of inter-dimensional transport and demanded further study.

Neither Ray nor I are the least bit sorry we met the Tooma men. We had the time of our lives, and we are continuing to have a good time right here on Earth. We're sucking cocks daily, often several times a day, and getting ours sucked in return; whereas, when we were straight we were lucky to get laid once a week. That's the great thing about guys. They put out so easily.

MISTLETOE AND THE HOLLY BOY

Blixer the elf was milking the head of my cock, twisting his diminutive fist and digging deep with his strong fingers. Donthor was gripping the base and massaging the underside of my balls. Their smooth elfin hands were creating near-to-agonizing waves of pleasure. As I lolled back on the three-legged stool supporting my bare ass, Vexlet and Fridgor supported me, stroking my body as they kept me from toppling.

"This is how the Christmas Fool stirs the flavor of the Yule Pudding," Blixer purred. I was playing the Christmas Fool with a crown of goat horns and a cornhusk cloak. Horns and straws were all I wore – a milking stool made a precarious perch for my bare bottom. As I came closer to ejaculating, I opened my eyes and saw elfin faces chortling with glee. Behind them, the colossal Yule tree blazed with bright jumbles, garlands, icicles, and candles. Boughs of greenery and candles scented the room with the rich odors of pinesap, cinnamon, and musk.

"The cream will spurt soon," Fridgor announced.

"It requires more churning," Blixer ordered. "Let the golden rod boil, yet not boil over."

Donthor answered with a lascivious leer. "My grasp is sturdy. This vessel will thrill, yet suffer still."

Over my head, hung a garland of mistletoe, which radiated an erotic aura that fell upon me. As the semen arose from my balls and made my cock heavy with approaching ejaculation, I could not help pondering the miraculous circumstances that had brought me to this occasion.

# # # # #

At Lithia College, the air hung heavy with frost. Autumn was nearly spent, and the black walnut trees were dropping their bounty upon the quad – to the delight of the campus's population of squirrels and crows. In the mossy building under the clock tower where the English department had its being, a group of twenty assembled in a teaching auditorium. Lizzie slouched over the podium, her reddish hair close-cropped, her tight black jeans delineating her boyish figure, her tattoos indicating her attitude, and her bangle earrings sending a mixed message.

I had saved seats for Rod and Spence, though it was hardly necessary. The room seated sixty. The twosome arrived fashionably late, sauntering through the doorway hand in hand. They looked as if they'd just climbed out of a sizzling bed. Their intimacy made me so jealous that I turned twelve shades of green, but I didn't broadcast my envy. They were my friends, and I waved to indicate the seats beside me. As they strolled forward, Lizzie began to harangue them.

"You boys held up the proceedings," she griped. "We got important work here, and we all gotta pitch in." She shot me a direct look. "Nathan, that means you, too."

"What did I do?"

"Not a hell of a lot this term," she quipped. "That's what I'm talking about."

Lizzie's girlfriend Nixie turned and stuck out her tongue at me. I gave her the same treatment, which made Nixie burst into a fit of unladylike giggles. I cannot stand uptight airhead lipstick lesbians, but how could anyone not befriend a girl decked out in a sickly green tee shirt with "Carpet Muncher" emblazoned in pink letters on the front. Nixie was out of the closet and skipping down the primrose path, not to mention being a mathematical whiz kid.

"What'd we miss?" Spence whispered. Spence was dusty blond, with a wide mouth, though his lips were too thin. He was wearing black pin striped slacks topped by an expensive looking shirt with a reddish pattern.

"Not a fuckin' thing," I said.

"This is our last meeting before the holiday break," Lizzie yelled over our whispering. "We gotta hit the ground running next quarter."

Most of the meeting was occupied in discussing how we had screwed up National Coming Out Day. "Cross-dressing and trying to paint the boys' fingernails scared off the faint of heart," Lizzie claimed, without a grain of truth – no one had cross-dressed, unless you consider biological females in jeans cross-dressing, and Rod had been experimenting with green fingernail polish only to pass the time. "Instead of coming out, they bolted back into the closet in droves." Finally, Lizzie demanded volunteers for the GLBTQ Prom Committee. She glared at me until I raised my hand.

On the way out the door, Lizzie seized Rod's arm. "I heard you boys are staying on campus for the holiday."

"Yeah," Spence said. "We want to be together, and neither of our families is willing to host their son's gay lover for Christmas."

"Nixie is coming to my pop's country lodge. Of course, Pop's in India, and the lodge is too big for just Nixie and me. So how about we make it a gay Christmas? You guys come to the lodge as soon as your finals are over. There are plenty of spare rooms. The snow is piling up and the lake's frozen hard. We'll have fun." Lizzie looked at me standing pitifully within earshot. "Nathan, you come, too. These two half-wits couldn't find their asses without you to guide them."

"We may be half-wits," Spence began.

"... but we have cute asses," Rod finished, "and we know where to find them." That was another falsification if I ever heard one. If Rod believed what he was saying, his was the most shocking example of self-deception ever. Rod's tiny ass was lost in his jeans. Wearing jeans too taut in the seat had never been his difficulty.

We finished our finals ten days later. On the twenty-first of December, Rod, Spence, and I boarded a train, which Lizzie had assured us was the most expedient way to reach her father's lodge. "Get off at Goose Hollow Station," she directed. "Call me, and I'll pick you up."

Neither Spence nor Rod nor I had ever traveled by train, and for the first hour we had fun exploring and eating in the dining car. After that, the ride grew monotonous. We dieseled along in the shadow of a staggering mountain range, but our view was restricted by proximity, and we passed through countless tunnels. Rod and Spence fell asleep. I was close to nodding off myself when I heard our station announced. I shook the guys awake, and we grabbed our stuff and barely got off before the train began moving again.

The station was merely a decrepit wooden structure locked tight. No one was around, and there wasn't even a bench. "What a crappy place," Rod announced. I whipped out my cell phone, but I couldn't get a signal.

"It's dead," I complained. "Lizzie promised we'd be within calling distance.

Rod and Spence tried their phones, but we were out of range of any tower.

"Is this the middle of fuckin' nowhere?" Spence demanded. "Do you think those dykes played a joke on us?"

Shaking his head, Rod pointed toward a sign over the door of the station. "Gooseville," he read. "Didn't Lizzie say Goose Hollow?"

"Shit, Nathan," Spence swore, his thin lips turning pale. "You got us off at the wrong station. We are utterly screwed, and it's entirely your fault."

My stomach sank into my sneakers. It was looking as if Spence and Rod were right. I had fucked up. Totally.

"Blaming Nathan is not going to help," Rod said, taking out a pocket mirror and checking his face. "We can't stay where we are, so we'd better start walking." He pulled Spence close and gave him a reassuring kiss. I tried to look away, but the meeting of their lips pulled my eyeballs toward them. A cold sensation twisted low in my stomach, and I knew I had never felt so alone, so left out, so unloved.

Hefting our bags, we began hiking down the road, hoping that we would reach Gooseville, or Goose Hollow, or any goddamn place, so we could call for help. Spence kept pissing and moaning and blaming me for the disaster until I got sick of hearing him.

"Quit censuring me, Spence. You fell asleep. You got your queer derrière off the choo-choo without checking. If I diddled the doggie, so did you."

Spence's response surprised the crap out of me. He apologized – graciously – and then he hugged me.

"Besides it's a beautiful evening," I exclaimed. "Look how the snow outlines every limb and twig. You can't see a single footprint, except for bunny rabbits and snow birds." My mouth snapped shut on the image because my words made it sound like we were a long way from civilization.

"Boys, am I going blind, or is it getting darker?" Rod asked.

"The snow is coming down heavier," Spence offered. "No way could we see the sun."

I glanced at my watch: 4:10 pm. "Guys," I said, "I hate to mention this, but it is getting darker. Night is falling. Today is the solstice."

"Huh?"

"The shortest day of the year."

"The longest fuckin' night of the year, you mean," Rod said. "We better find shelter soon. Otherwise, somebody will be finding us – come the spring thaw."

His tone of voice froze my balls, and Spence emitted a pathetic whimper. Growing increasingly tired, cold, and hungry, we slogged onward through the piling drifts. We continued walking for forty-five minutes with nothing in sight but falling snow, shadowy trees, and deepening night. Our spirits dropped with every step. However, miracles do happen. Gazing into the woods, I noticed a side trail that looked suspiciously like a driveway. I halted the guys by grabbing at their winter coats. "Let's try up there."

As we left the road, the drive became more obvious, though it had been long since anyone had driven upon it. Still we came round the bend in the drive, and what should we see but a house standing dark and mute in the December snowfall.

The house was three storied with a catslide roof and rounded eves. The entrance was asymmetrical with a front gable and an arched dormer. The walls were grey pudding stones, and it had seven stone chimneys. An iron ring hanging from a rope rang a bell somewhere inside the house and the gigantic knocker made a thundering echo as it fell. We tried both, to no avail.

"Looks like nobody is home," Spence said.

"Then we're going to break in," Rod said, "before we freeze our cocks off."

Feeling a numbing chill between my legs, I tried the door latch. The door readily swung open. Rod and Spence looked at each other, and then both looked at me. "I saw this scene in a movie called *Dracula's Castle*," Spence muttered.

"Fuck it," Rod said and pushed past me into the house.

An echoing silence ensued, if, indeed, any silence can echo. I looked at Spence. Spence looked at me, his eyes round and fearful. I shrugged and followed Rod. Spence followed so close behind me, that under other circumstances I would have been aroused.

# # # # #

Blixer interrupted my reverie when he switched his grip. "We keep you on the brink of the flood," he giggled. "We let your cream sink before we bring it to a boil. When the Christmas Fool releases his prize, he gushes all."

I didn't tell Blixer and his elfin crew, but I was already on the trajectory toward ejaculation. My cock was weighty with rising semen, and tingles were firing in my cockhead. However, before I could shout in orgasmic triumph, Donthor squeezed my cock with a grip that could crumple steel. An agonizingly intense sensation bound my cock, and a sting shot up my rear as if a gargantuan cock were prodding me. I could not come with the elf's hand squeezing my dick, and when he released me, the moment had passed.

Such had been the elves' intention, but they did not long allow my juices to subside. Soon Donthor was stroking my shaft and playing with my balls, and Blixer was twisting my cockhead as if he was opening a screwtop bottle. A keen pleasure rose within my loins, with echoes of ecstasy rising up my cock from the base to the tip, a sensation I had never experienced before then.

"If this is how you take care of the Christmas Fool," I demanded, my voice rasping with my hot lust, "how do you treat the Holly King?"

# # # # #

"Jeepers, Rod," Spence gasped. "Do you have any idea how many crimes we're committing?"

"You wanna freeze, Spence?" I asked. "I don't like this any better than you do, but it's warmer inside than out. Let's follow Rod."

"Yeah, and suppose the homeowner comes down with a gun?"

I didn't respond. The same horrid notion had occurred to me, but I couldn't think up a better plan. We had knocked, we had rung, we had even shouted. Unless the occupants were busy fucking – or were lying murdered in their beds – Oh, Shit! – anyone present would have heard our frantic pleas.

The house was spacious but chill and echoing. We searched all three floors without finding a soul. Like Goldilocks, we found beds ready for occupancy. There was no electricity, but the plumbing worked, however old fashioned it may have been. To our dismay, the kitchen was deserted and the icebox was empty. None of that "Who's been eating my porridge" for us. The pantry was in the same condition as Old Mother Hubbard's cupboard.

Our cell phones remained deader than the proverbial doornail.

"What the hell," Spence said. "We'll survive without food for one night. Let's take that bedroom with the canopy bed and the side curtains, Spence. Nathan can have any other room he wants."

I would have preferred sharing their bed, but asking was out of the question. I was too shy, too afraid, too unsure of the answer. My fragile ego could not handle the rejection, so I rejected myself by not asking. I carried my bag upstairs and selected a bedroom somewhat removed from Spence and Rod's choice. Sounds of passion coming through the wall would have been too much for me. I had never felt so lonely, so unwanted, so unloved.

"Poor me," I said aloud, with deliberate self-mockery as I stripped to my slinky silver briefs and tee shirt. Laughing at my pathetic condition, I climbed between the pink silken sheets.

"Pink silk – Wow!" I said just before I slipped into the arms of Morpheus.

I don't know how long I slept, but music awakened me. I could see a faint strip of light beneath the bedroom door, and the hazards of sleeping uninvited in a strange house were borne home to me. I opened the door with trepidation and peeped down the hall. My heart leaped into my throat when I saw a blaze of light streaming from downstairs.

Dazed, fearful, and pantless, I crept to the top of the staircase. A warm ambiance, mouth-watering odors, and pagan Yuletide music tantalized my senses. I slipped down the stairs, taking care to conceal myself behind the railing and the thick banister. The hall below was lit with a tall Yule tree festooned with colorful ornaments and ablaze with candles. I had never seen lit candles on a tree before then. A prodigious Yule log burned in the fireplace. Against the wall, stood a trestle table laden with roasted boar, stuffed pheasants, baked squashes, nuts, popcorn, candies, meat and cheese pies, tall frosted cakes, bowls of punch, and other sundry goodies. Mistletoe and holly hung in long strands from the high ceilings and along the walls, and scented red and green candles illuminated the rest.

Despite these sights, sounds, and colors, my eyes were focused upon a festive group of fey-looking men. The tallest was only five feet high, and all were deliciously slim and enticingly curvy. They wore short jerkins, shoes with long pointed toes, and colorful tights. They were all male – that was obvious because their radiant tights displayed their assets front and rear most provocatively.

"They look like elves," I muttered under my breath. I had to be dreaming.

Whatever they were, they looked so sexy that the front of my bikini underwear began to stretch with my growing cock. One group was sitting together with musical instruments, creating captivating, hypnotic sounds that resembled Christmas music, yet the tune and the lyrics spoke of desires that bit deeper to the bone. Others were playing leapfrog, a game grab-ass and fluttery, poignant with homoeroticism.

As I peeped over the balcony, the music stopped. An elf pointed his long crooked finger in my direction. "Don't hide, fool. Come on down and join the party."

My heart nearly shot out of my mouth, but I stood up.

"Come join us."

I grew bolder. "All right. I'll just slip on my pants first."

"Don't be silly, Nathan," said the elf. That he knew my name didn't surprise me. "The Christmas Fool should bumble into the festivities in his underwear."

"Christmas Fool?"

"Don't let the jargon cause offense. The words are neither belittling nor demeaning. The Christmas Fool is a character from the Yule Goat, a game in the old religion."

"Huh?"

"Goats and elves. We be the elves, and you the goat. We flavor the Solstice Pudding. Have your sort lost the old traditions? Have you forgotten the Ways of Kindness and Peace?"

"We must have done," I blurted.

"Then your culture strives in peril. Come, Nathan, and we will teach you," the sexiest elf of the group promised. "I am Blixer, and we are Yule Elves of the Olden Ways. We will prepare you with our ministrations." There he pointed toward the front of my briefs, which I saw – to my embarrassment – were still poking out with a magnificent boner.

Blixer's long fingers brushed the head of my swollen cock. A shiver ran through me as a power incredibly ancient and deeply primal stimulated every cell in my body. A loud moan escaped my lips, all unbidden, causing the elves to smile slyly. My cock swelled harder and thicker. It looked bigger than it ever had before, which I knew to be impossible.

"Thus begins the Saturnalia," Blixer hailed. "Let the randy goat be milked."

The elves produced a three-legged milking stool. Blixer and another elf, whom he introduced as Donthor, stripped off my briefs and pushed me down onto the stool. As I sat, I stared between my legs in wonder – my cock had grown! It was both longer and thicker. Even as I looked, the wound of circumcision faded, and an impressive foreskin grew as if it had been with me all along.

"Now you are the fool, the Yule Goat," Blixer informed me. "But before this night is done, we shall proclaim you Holly King."

Without warning, Blixer kissed my lips. His kiss lasted many minutes, and my mind exploded across the galaxies with thunderous raptures. As from some distant place, I heard Donthor explaining, "The mistletoe hangs above the Christmas Fool, which we harvest at the winter solstice, just as we do the golden fernseed on Midsummer Eve. Of the four divining rods, of four woods, one must be mistletoe, and once over the treasure the rod will move as if it were alive."

Opening my eyes as Blixer kissed me, his elfish tongue playing in my mouth and driving me to heights of ecstasy, I saw the mistletoe hanging over my head, and the cropped plant was shaking all of its own. For a moment, I thought I would release my bounty, for orgasmic tremors seized me, but Donthor gripped the base of my cock and squeezed so that my orgasm shook me, thrilled me, blasted me, but produced no fluid. My lips were burning in a pleasant way and tingling.

After the kiss, Vexlet placed a set of goat horns upon my head and Fridgor wrapped a mantle of cornhusks about my shoulders. The band began playing again, but set to their solemn melody of the dying of the old year were tied satirical words about the Holly Boy, and how the fingers were numbered as the palm of his hand awakened his seed. There was reference to a beheading, which might have worried me, save the beheading involved the head of the cock and the scythes that clipped it were fingers and thumb. The lyrics joked about the fool's-finger, as the fool is beheaded but arises like the green knight unhurt to reign over the Yule festival as Holly King.

As Blixer and Donthor examined my risen cock and ministered to it, another elf poured a dark punch into an elaborately enameled pint mug and bade me drink. Since I had not eaten since the few minutes spent in the dining car, I had been coveting the trestle table of goodies, so even in my deep sexual need, I still sipped from the cup. The concoction tasted like thick stout, though sweeter and thicker than any Guinness.

By the time I had downed the pint, Donthor and Blixer were jerking my cock with obvious intent. Strangely, I felt neither shame nor humiliation at receiving a tug job given by elves and witnessed by more elves. An amazing euphoria filled me, as the horns sitting upon my brow seemed to become my own, and my goatish cock throbbed with the need to release. I was aware that I was smirking, perhaps even grinning with feral and bawdy abandon. I had never felt so utterly pagan, as pleasures heretofore unknown suffused my being.

The elves brought me to the fearful edge of orgasm, and then Donthor squeezed the base of my cock so that I could not ejaculate. Three times, they brought me to the verge. My balls were aching by then, and I thought that I would die. However, a second mug of that wonderful stout punch revived my spirit, and I shouted that they could jack my big cock until doomsday if they wanted.

I felt the semen rising again, rising above the place where Donthor could stop its eruption. "Oh, ah, I'm going to come," I chortled. "You can't stop me this time, Donthor. I'm gonna shoot a gusher."

Blixer continued to unscrew the head of my cock. He wrung my foreskin and filled me with new pleasures. An elf presented a golden chalice and held it before my cock. Blixer directed my dick hole toward the chalice. Rapturous tingles were rippling through my cockhead, while deep waves of pleasure were trilling behind my balls and rippling up my ass. My cock was tingling, my asshole was stinging, my nipples were crinkling with tiny spasms, and my lips prickled and curled back like those of a satyr in extremis. My nostrils twitched and my eyelids fluttered. The muscles at the base of my cock contracted mightily and a tremendous spurt of hot jism erupted from my peehole and splattered into the golden chalice. Spurt after spurt followed, and I kept coming longer than I had ever erupted before that night. I was enjoying the orgasm of a lifetime, and I was shooting all the spunk my body could muster.

"Thus dies the goat," Blixer proclaimed, and a cosmic weariness overcame me. I gasped. I might even have shrieked as I fell backward off the milking stool. My bare ass bounced on the soft rugs that the elves had placed behind me. Then I must have lost consciousness because no time seemed to have passed before I found Vexlet and Fridgor helping me to arise. My cock had gone flaccid, though it retained its larger size and foreskin, and it continued to tingle with post-orgasmic ripples.

"What the fuck is happening?" Spence's voice reverberated from the head of the stairs. Turning, I saw him, and I saw Rod, who was staring gape-mouthed. The elves calmly pulled up my bikini briefs, carefully packing my cock and balls into them, and stroked my ass as if nothing extraordinary had happened. Four elves rushed up the stairs, embraced Rod and Spence, and escorted them down to join the party.

"Are you all right, Nathan?" Rod asked anxiously.

I glanced down to see if I was leaving a stain, but the elves had milked me dry. I had no post-ejaculatory seepage. "Better than all right," I replied. "These little fellows just gave me the tug job of a lifetime."

The horns had fallen from my head, and I had shed my mantle of cornhusks when I fell. I was aware that I stood revealed to Rod and Spence as the embodiment of satiated desire, yet I relished the moment. I felt like a King. The jealousy I had felt for my friends' happiness had been shed with my antlers.

The elves removed the milking stool and set me to a green throne with red velvet cushions. They bowed to me and placed a wreath of holly upon my head. "The Christmas Fool is dead," Blixer shouted. "The goat has been sacrificed for the year's sake. Thus begins the reign of the Holly King."

Donthor handed me a brightly decorated mistletoe scepter. The scepter tingled in my hand. Its erotic energy poured into me, and taught me its power. I waved it at Donthor, and pictured him kissing me. Donthor brought his lips to mine and kissed me long and hard. Testing my power, I waved my scepter at another elf, visualized his kisses, and he too met my lips with a kiss sweeter than raspberries. I pointed it toward two elves standing apart, imagined one pulling down the other's tights, and watched as it happened.

Without my waving the wand in his direction, Rod suddenly rushed away from the elves, grabbed me by the ears, and kissed me hard. My spent cock arose again at the gesture. Spence followed suit, and I was close to coming again by the time his pulled his lips from mine.

"Your friends shall play an elfish game for the Holly King's amusement," Blixer proclaimed, and with a single gesture, ordered that Rod and Spence be stripped. My friends did not resist, particularly after they were given the drink that I had consumed. Only then did I understand that the mead – for so Blixer called it – a honey based stout, contained properties beyond those of mere intoxication. The mead loosened the inhibitions and allowed the imbiber to partake of his primordial soul's desires.

As I lolled upon my throne, elves loaded plates with viands from the table, not to mention wines, beers, and punches in sizable mugs, and offered them for my consumption. When I raised my scepter, elves doffed their clothing, so they could play leapfrog again, but naked. Elves leaped over tall candlesticks with high burning flames before they bounced off, over, or against the hips of other elves. After they had drunk of the mead punch, Spence and Rod lost their amazement and leaped into the game. Vexlet pretended to leap over Rod, fell short, and pressed his elfish prick against Rod's bare buttocks. At the touch, Rod's tiny buttocks swelled, growing rounded and protrusive until they stuck out like a girl's ass.

"That's the trick," Spence yelled, unaware of his lover's buttock enhancement. "Fuck Rod's gay rump. He'll love you for it."

Crude words for Christmas, I'll confess, but the mead had intoxicated him. Leering drunkenly, Spence glanced at me as if seeking my approval. Picturing the elfish pricks sliding between Rod's impressive buns, I pointed my scepter. "Rod forfeits," I proclaimed. "Ride him."

Elves produced a silver bowl from which they dipped a lubricating lotion and anointed the lucky elf's pointed prick. When he was rock stiff and lubed, Vexlet drove the tip of his thick prick into Rod's ass. Rod bayed with untamed glee.

"Oh, that's so good," he groaned. "Slip it into me. I never felt one like that." As the elf drove deeper into Rod, I saw Spence giggling. No green-eyed monster, he – Spence was getting off on watching his lover get elf-pronged.

Somehow, I knew there was no danger in the fluids the elves ejaculated. The pure semen of the other world bore no taint of corruption.

Vexlet began humping Rod's rump in earnest. I could see that Rod's cock was hard and throbbing for release as the elfish prick up his ass milked him toward ecstasy. "Catch his spill," I ordered. "Let Rod flavor the pudding."

The band struck up a lustier sound in which I recognized the melody of a carol of my youth, but that night throbbing with sex – pagan and primitive. The dancing elves skipped in a daisy chain around Rod, as Vexlet fucked Rod's ass and jerked his cock. Rod's cock swelled to a larger size as the elfish hands flogged it. Thus did the unworldly elf fuck the human, like a meeting of the ideal with the real, the eternal with the finite, the unchanging being with the process of time. The music and the dance spoke of those themes and hinted at far more than our human minds could grasp. I waved the scepter in my hand while that other scepter between my legs rose again and made a gloriously obscene print in my underwear.

I had finished my plate of food followed by five different desserts. I followed dessert with nuts, dates, candies, and a fruity liquor. Satisfied, I reclined on my throne and savored Rod's howls of pleasure as Vexlet fucked him. Spence could not resist pulling on his cock as he watched his lover being buggered so beautifully. I raised a finger and beckoned to Blixer.

"It is our royal decree," I commanded, "that Spence must suck an elfin prick while Vexlet buggers his lover. Furthermore, let Spence be milked of his seed while he gives suck."

"Thus the third of the three shepherds flavors the pudding," Blixer agreed with a nod. "It shall be done as your highness commands." I visualized the event and pointed my scepter.

The elves were dancing around Spence, and through some process similar to the musical chairs game, Frepur won the selection. Spence had left off masturbating when the elves surrounded him, and he was cooperative as they pushed him to his knees. Frepur pressed his elfish prick against Spence's lips, and Spence's lips became puffier and reddish-purple at the touch, as if he had been stung.

I watched the elfin cock sliding in and out of Spence's swollen mouth, his puffy lips doing their appointed duty, while Rod humped his wonderful rounded ass against Vexlet's elfish loins, the thick elfish penis penetrating him deeply and taking him to greater heights of sexual transport. My cock throbbed again, and I looked at it swollen in my underwear, so much bigger, thicker, and longer than before, though nature had been kind to me from my youth onward. As I touched my cock, a sudden thought occurred to me. I beckoned Blixer once again.

"After tonight, do I go back to the way I was before?" I asked. "Do my cock and those of my friends return to the way they were before this night? Must Spence's lips revert, and will Rod lose his man-enticing derrière?"

A puckish smile played over the elf's face. "Certainly not," he replied. "You return to your world the way you leave this one. All men will desire to fuck Rod's ass. All men will desire Spence's mouth. All men will wish to stroke your cocks. All men – without exception."

The decision was mine to make. As Holly King, the prerogative was mine alone. I had the power of choice, and I chose the Yule gift that keeps on giving. "Let two elves be ordered to take me from both ends," I demanded.

"Does your highness wish to select the elves for this service?" Blixer asked, his smile growing more mischievous.

"You shall choose for me, Blixer."

"As leader of our elfish throng," Blixer proclaimed, "my power is the greatest. Therefore, I select myself, and Grigor is only slightly less powerful, so he shall be your second."

Blixer summoned a gorgeous elf who had been leading the dancers. "Both holes shall be forever enticing, but one shall be more enticing than the other. Which do you choose that I shall penetrate, your ass or your mouth?"

It was the most difficult decision I had ever made. I loved sucking cock, but after a moment's thought, I commanded Blixer to fuck my ass. There is nothing better than a delicious derrière to pull in the guys, so I went for the maximum.

I tossed my underwear aside and draped myself over the footstool to the throne. Grigor gently touched his cock to my lips. The effect was like receiving a bee sting, though the initial intensity did not linger. I felt a burning jolt around my mouth, and afterward my lips tingled as if I had painted them with mint and hot pepper. However, I could not think about my lips, for a moment after the sting of Grigor's cock came the touch of Blixer's cock between my butt cheeks. The effect was not unlike an electrical shock, a hot jolt that sizzled every cell of my buttocks, drove into my asshole, and traveled up my rectal passage. It was an agony beyond belief, but a divine agony, for with the shock came a sensation of unspeakable desirability. From the instant the two cocks stung me, I felt sexier, gayer, and more desired than ever before that night.

"Oh, fuck my sexy ass, Blixer," I urged. "Grigor, stick your hard elfin cock into my mouth."

Grigor pushed forward ever so gently, his elfish cock sliding over my puffy lips that were so alive to the touch of hard cock. My mouth had never felt that way before, though I had been trading sucks with a friend from an age that shouldn't be mentioned ever. How were we to know at that tender age that an action that felt so good would be deemed so illegal by our totalitarian rulers? Yet the touch of Grigor's cock on my fresh-stung lips was unlike any other, so that the entrance was enough to send raptures of sensation throughout my being.

Grigor's cock was not fully into my mouth before I felt Blixer's elfin hands upon my buttocks. My ass felt hard and tight so that my skin could barely contain the swelling muscles within. My mouth had swollen as Spence's had, and my buttocks were firming and shaping and growing more protrusive than Rod's. Grigor's cockhead was slipping into the back of my throat, deeper than any penis had traveled before then, and Blixer's cock was opening my hole, and opening I was, without pain, without doubt, without fear. I wanted Blixer's cock in my ass more than I had ever wanted any cock before then, and the room spun as my asshole opened fully and the sensation of fullness drove deep, and deeper still until I wanted to cry out with joy, but could not for my mouth was busily sucking Grigor's elfish prick.

I continued sucking on the thick member that was slowly and delightfully screwing my mouth, yet my attention grew upon Blixer's cock, which was so comfortably, and so naturally, and so delightfully fucking my ass. With each stroke, his prick grew thicker, until my entire being was wrapped in the amazing screwing I was receiving. Ripples of pleasure vibrated around my asshole, up my rectal channel through the cells of my pelvis, and down my cock. My cock's head was throbbing, and I knew that I was going to shoot my load once again.

I sucked harder and harder on the thick cock in my mouth while I rocked my hips against the cock fucking my enhanced and taut ass. I was all penetration, all flesh, all knowing, all feeling, all sensation, all tingles, all raptures, all waves of pleasure, all sexuality, all desirable, all enticing, all cosmos, all cells, all everything.

My cells were exploding at every level, lightning flashed in my brain, I saw all men fucked and sucking through human history, I knew all, I was all, I became all, I be all. Waves of cosmic rapture filled me. I was one with the infinite. Oh, yes. I was eternal. Ah! I was Santa Claus. I was the reindeer. I was all gifts to all children of whatever age. Oh. I was thunder, lightning, rain, sleet, snow, the dog biting the mailman, and the mailman receiving the bite. Oh, yes, yes. The thunders of orgasm consumed me, prodded by two elfish pricks, filled with elfish spunk, burning with elfish magic. I became one with bliss. I came and came until I was both emptied and filled at once.

When the power had been imparted to us three mortals, and we had received all we could, the elves bade we eat again. After the meal, an elf in a chef's hat brought forth a magnificent Yule pudding and insisted that all must eat. I did not ask what had gone into the making of it, but it was the tastiest pudding I had ever spooned into my mouth.

The next morning, the elves loaded a sleigh pulled by four gigantic deer. Spence, Rod, and I stared at the deer for a moment, our mouths agape. I finally broke the spell by stepping forward and petting the deer closest to me. Its coat was rough and cool to the touch, as befitting an animal that relished the cold and the snow. Blixer handed me some shriveled apples that looked like they had been languishing long in a bin. I fed one to Dasher, the deer I was petting, and the creature devoured it with relish. Then Rod and Spence fed and made friends with Comet, Dancer, and Donner until it was time to board the sleigh. The deer kept up a fantastic pace, and we soon arrived at Goose Hollow.

Stopping just short of the town, our elf friends bade us farewell, jingled their sleigh bells, and sped out of sight. We glanced at each other in freezing disbelief. Then, as one, we whipped out our cell phones and called Lizzie.

"I was just calling out a search party," Lizzie howled when she heard our voices. "I figured you fuckin' retards got lost in last night's blizzard."

We arranged for Lizzie to pick us up in front of the drug store. Fifteen minutes later, Lizzie arrived in a sleigh pulled by normal looking horses instead of deer. She started to greet us, but she stopped to gawk at Spence's lips.

"What the fuck happened to your mouth?" Lizzie demanded. "All of a sudden you've got puffy lips. You look like a blow job waiting to happen."

Grinning lewdly, Spence shook his head while Rod climbed into the sleigh. Lizzie's eyes popped at the sight. "Crap, Rod, how'd you get into your jeans? Your butt is sexier than Nixie's; I could fuck your ass and remain a lesbian."

I had been standing behind her, so Lizzie had not yet gotten a good look at me. She turned just as a man passed down the street, veered in his path, and brushed his hand over my ass. Lizzie's eyes widened as she glanced after the man, and then she eyeballed me from toe to top. A second male passerby whispered an invitation in my ear. Shaking her head like a squirrel that'd lost his nuts, Lizzie emitted a long whistle.

"Why is Nathan attracting every man in town? The bozo propositioning him was Doctor Bell, who is a Catholic with six children, and the creep who patted his ass was Reverend Hatter. What the fuck is going on?"

We ducked her questions and turned the talk to winter sports. Shrugging over the mysteries of males, Lizzie took the reins and urged the horses around the trucks and snowplows stuck in the drifts. Before long, we arrived at her father's lodge where Nixie greeted us at the door.

"I fixed up two rooms for you boys," Nixie said. "A double for Rod and Spence and a single for Nathan. Unless you want three?"

"One's enough," Rod said and Spence nodded. "We'd like for Nathan to sleep with us."

"Three boys in a bed?" Lizzie taunted. "Out with it. What did happen last night?"

I glanced at Rod and Spence. Secret smiles played across their faces.

"You'll never know, Lizzie," I assured her. "You'll never know."

ALIEN EXPERIMENTATION

At thirty, I was the youngest associate of my college's psychology department, with three articles published in scholarly journals, and tenure two years off. It wasn't a time for timidity; I'd either make my mark boldly or fail utterly. I strode to class, resolute, zealous – albeit apprehensive – and bent on advancing psychological truths to people unprepared to confront them.

After calling roll, I sat on my desktop and faced my students. "Disregard past theories about human behavior," I began. "Freud, Jung, Skinner, Maslow, and their ilk were victims of self-delusion, wishful thinking, or something more ominous. We humans behave according to implanted patterns of conduct. We must obey our implants. Our activities, cruel or kind, reasonable or unreasonable, acceptable or intolerable, have been pre-selected for us. We are simply animals for experimentation."

I had my class's attention then. Each student waited to learn who had implanted his or her behaviors.

"My revelation will sound strange," I said. "Some of you will experience disquieting images, one or two will know that I speak the stark truth, and the remainder will scoff." I drew a deep breath. "Space aliens, that is, scientists from other planets, have been routinely abducting Earthlings and conducting behavioral experiments. Some of you will have vague memories, but most will not, for the aliens' amnesia-inducing skill is formidable. Nevertheless you must recognize that your obsessions and compulsions, your sexual irresponsibility, or your excessive drinking, overeating, or drug use do not happen naturally. They have been imposed upon us – from Beyond."

A young woman, who'd had her entire body hennaed, raised her hand. "Did the space aliens get you, Professor Coyle?"

"Yes, Tricia. During my freshman year, aliens turned me into a promiscuous homosexual."

Some students laughed uproariously, and a few regarded me with disgust. Nevertheless, I saw expressions of enlightenment on a few faces, the remnant who recognize the truth.

"Ten years ago, I was a freshman at this same college, sharing a dorm room with my old high school buddy Rick. Around 3:00 am, on the Friday of our second week, Rick unexpectedly shrieked, 'Kit. Help me.'

"Dragged from creepy dreams, I awoke in mid-snore. I opened my eyes, tried to sit up, and discovered that I couldn't move. I was just able to turn my head, but what I saw made no sense. Three tall guys with wolfish pointy ears and hairless ratty tails were standing over Rick's bed. In the high-intensity security light shining through our window, I thought that their skin looked purple. These entities pointed a strange instrument at Rick, and he rose from his bed, as if the tool was levitating him, and floated out the window.

"I was struck with cold horror, but I still couldn't move. Then I realized that I was falling, but I wasn't really falling; I just had no weight, and I passed through the window. Up and up I drifted and I could see Rick lifting above me, and other bodies, presumably students living in our dorm, above him.

"As I rose, I could see the boys above us disappearing one by one. Then came Rick's turn, and before my eyes, he simply vanished into a dark space that was different from all other dark spaces.

"'It's an invisible space ship!' I shouted, but there was no one to hear but the surrounding clouds. Without warning, I slipped into a blank empty space. The nightmare that had gripped me before surrounded me again, and though I fought for consciousness, utter blackness claimed me.

"'Weird night,' Rick said. 'I must've gone out like a light. I don't think I dreamed at all.'

"I was lying in my bed in our dorm room, with bright morning sunshine casting little rainbows through the old glass onto our walls. I pulled back my covers. I was wearing my silk boxers and tee shirt, all the same as when I'd gone to sleep.

"I crawled out of bed and looked at my face in the bathroom mirror, which must have been designed by dwarves because both Rick and I had to bend practically double to shave. As I studied my face, which looked the same as it had, Rick impulsively patted my ass and stroked behind my balls. Then he kissed my neck. That was definitely out of the ordinary – neither Rick nor I had ever professed a gay proclivity – but the bizarre molestation felt so good, I didn't tell him to stop.

"Nothing odd happened for a week, but Rick and I grew closer than we'd ever been. For instance, before that Friday we'd never even seen

124

each other jerk off, but after that night we did it together. We weren't shy about shooting cum on each other either. Sometimes we'd steal a quick kiss after.

"The next Friday, I had one of those timeless nights, in which I seemed not to dream at all. On Saturday morning, Rick was spooky; he jumped at small noises, trembled throughout breakfast, and complained that other students were whispering about us. That night, we crawled into his single bed and jacked each other off. His cock fit my hand, and I made him come hard until he was empty. We kissed while we were stroking, slept entwined, and woke stuck together.

"'Kit, I gotta ask you something,' Rick sputtered.

"I helped him spit it out. 'Yeah, I remember the aliens. I remember going into the space ship.'

"'Oh. So it's real, Kit?'

"'How do I know?' I told him everything I could remember. 'The way I figure it, the bastards are taking us during those nights we sleep so deep. Like a couple of nights ago, when I went to bed and woke up a second later, but it was morning, and you were flippy all day.'

"'So you saw the purple guys? Do you remember the dudes with the long pink tentacles?'

"'No,' I said, but I felt a peculiar warmth in my stomach when he mentioned the pink tentacles.

"'You should remember them, Kit,' Rick urged. 'One made you suck his cock. You ate alien cum, Kit. You did. I saw.'

"My hand crawled over my stomach. 'I believe you. What are they doing to us, Rick?'

"'I don't know, Kit. But I'm changing. You know that babe I kept talking about? The one in my history class.'

"'Yeah, Tina. You've been hot for her.'

"'I was. Not anymore. Today I looked at her ass and boobs in those little tight things she wears that used to drive me crazy. Nothing – she was a big zero. I could easier get a hard-on over a garbage truck. But guy's butts, oh wow! Like that morning I groped your ass. I couldn't stop myself, you know.'

"I grinned. 'It's okay. I liked it.'

"My admission triggered a wild reaction from my friend. 'Oh, Kit,' Rick wailed and grabbed my butt cheeks with both hands. 'I love your cute rear. I've been feeling up your ass while you're sleeping.'

"My whole body burned with lust. As he caressed my ass, my dick stiffened, and we spanked each other's monkey three times before class. That drained us enough so we could make it through the day.

"During the days that followed, we discussed our lusts and sensations. Gay sex was totally new to us, but by no interpretation could the things we were doing be called straight, even if they didn't involve actual fucking or sucking.

"'I don't know about you, Kit, but I was never a hundred percent straight. I always wondered what it would be like. But I was mostly heterosexual.'

"'Same for me. Probably nobody is entirely one way or another.'

"'I don't know, Kit. The way I'm going, I'll soon be totally guy crazy. And I do mean a man butt banger exclusively.'

"'Yeah, but that's because the aliens must be turning us out. Rick. We've got to find a way to stay awake when they capture us again.'

"'Kit, we are awake while it's happening. They make us forget before they bring us back, but their process isn't perfect. We've start retaining bits and pieces. I remember that you were strapped onto this machine, and the pink tentacle dude stuck his cock against your mouth. You sucked it for a long time, and I saw you swallowing and swallowing.' Rick's forehead wrinkled as he concentrated intensely. Then he shook his head. 'That's all I can remember.'

"'So, maybe you sucked one, too.'

"'I think they're sending me in another direction. That wasn't my point. We're awake inside the Ball. They give us amnesia when they bring us back to bed.'

"'The Ball?'

"'Oh, yeah, I remember that. The place where it happens is called the Ball. And other human guys are there, too.'

"The next day, I visited the psychology department and picked a couple of professor's brains about amnesia. I particularly wanted to find out if any drugs would prevent amnesia. One laughed at me, but a younger professor suddenly looked serious.

"'I remember an article, not about drugs, but a combination of herbs that seemed anti-amnesiac. The results were horrible. People tested them before major operations, and afterward they could remember everything, every word the surgeons uttered, and all the pain. I wouldn't care to try it myself.'

"I got a reference for the article, and I found it in the library. All the herbs were available in local stores, so I soon had my concoction brewed. That night I showed my remedy to Rick. 'It's been a full week. If the aliens are following a schedule, they'll come for us tonight. So we've got to drink this stuff before going to bed.'

"Rick scowled at the bubbling potion. 'What's in it?'

"'It's full of the pure, the blushful Hippocrene,' I quoted blithely.

"'I'm not drinking that shit,' he declared.

"'It won't hurt us. The ingredients are health foods.'

"'You try it,' he suggested. 'If you believe in it, try it on yourself first.'

"He thought that I'd chicken out, and did his eyes ever widen when I chugged down the whole tumbler. It tasted weird, but I knew it was safe. Rick was less sure, and he held the telephone in his hand while watching me closely.

"'What are you doing?'

"'I'm ready to call 9-1-1 if you fall over, Kit.'

"I slipped off my bed, grabbed him, and kissed him with a lot of tongue. 'Thanks for caring,' I whispered.

"I fell asleep in his arms and didn't awaken until we were drifting into the alien spaceship. Inside, we (twenty boys from our dormitory including Rick and I) floated down a circular tube into an enormous sphere. Aliens strapped us down in various positions on padded tables, and a white-skinned alien with ribbons of white hair dangling to his waist walked around with a small device. When he aimed the machine at me, I experienced a bizarre rush of memory. I remembered every previous visit to the Ball.

"They hadn't started abducting me a few weeks previously. I'd been taken aboard alien vehicles since childhood, a weekly occurrence, but recently, the alien scientists had revolutionized my programming. The memory of my first experience flooded back:

"I looked at Dr. Saur, the purplish alien I'd known since childhood. 'Christopher,' Dr. Saur announced as if he were talking to an old friend – or a lab animal, 'our panel of psychologists has selected you for homosexual experimentation.'

"Relief! Pure relief! – I'd never been particularly successful at seducing girls. Homosexual experimentation sounded as though I'd be getting more sex – and better sex. I smiled in agreement while the aliens fastened me into another machine and subjected me to the radiation that made me suck Dr. Weir's pink tentacles. Thus formed the memory that Rick had inexplicably retained.

"When the white alien, an amiable researcher called Dr. Bour, approached, I raised my face from the mindpillow. 'Christopher, you are advancing excellently,' Dr. Bour said. 'You and Rick have been masturbating each other, as we conditioned you. Of course, mutual masturbation is merely a pre-indoctrination procedure. Tonight we will implant you with an urge to receive anal sex. In human terms, you will become the catcher. We are interested in studying this phenomenon, and our political leaders hope to control your species through it.'

"Using the levitator, Dr. Bour transferred me to another alien machine. 'This machine will enhance your rectal tissues,' he explained. 'It will make the walls of your rectum almost impossible to tear, so you will be able to take multiple cocks without harm. However, at the same time, it will stimulate the growth of nerve endings through your rectum. Your entire rectal passage will transform into orgasmic tissue, much like the head of your cock.'

"Dr. Bour pointed a hand-held remote control device at my asshole. When my hole popped open, he squirted a warm lubricant into my tunnel. The machine hummed and a long narrow tube slid up my rear. Intense heat filled my ass. I felt a prickling, followed by an overall sensation of overwhelming intensity.

"Dr. Bour turned another dial on the machine. Three rods slid from their housings and touched my head. I heard a sharp crackle and a loud buzzing sound. Hallucinatory images danced before my eyes. I fell into a semiconscious state during which I lived a thousand fantasies of anal penetration.

"Dr. Bour awakened me by stroking my buttocks. I loved the feeling of his alien hands on me. 'Now for more lubrication.' He dribbled a thick liquid into my asshole. The warm liquid tickled. 'Do you want me to penetrate your ass, Christopher?' Dr. Bour asked. 'Would you like me to pierce your anal orifice and ejaculate my seminal liquids? You must respond with a request.'

"'Oh, yes, fuck me,' my mouth offered. 'Oh, please fuck my ass.' Where did those words come from?

"Dr. Bour pointed the remote control at my rear. 'I am giving you limited freedom of movement,' he announced. 'You can shake, rock, and wiggle your butt.'

"He lubricated his cock from the bottle of pleasantly scented alien oil. I wiggled my ass in anticipation. He slipped behind me, opened my asshole with his strange fingers, and poured more oil into my ass.

"'You will love anal penetration, Christopher,' Dr. Bour promised as he raised the middle of the table and pulled my legs apart. Once my butt was positioned for easy entry, he climbed atop me and sat his alien ass upon my cupcakes. He rubbed his snowy cock along the backs of my thighs, over my ass, up and down my crack, and around the small of my back. As he teased me, hot thrills rushed up my rear. My rectal tissues cried out for a vigorous cock massage.

"'Put it in, Dr. Bour,' I urged. 'Shove your space alien cock up my virgin asshole. Fuck me.'

"His cock played along my crack again, driving me wild. I wiggled my ass, hoping for penetration, but he had given me only limited powers of movement. I could not hunch my ass high enough. My desire grew. My asshole blazed with hot irritation, and I itched deep inside. At long last, he shifted his position and slipped the tip of his hard cock into my hole.

"'Oh, it feels so good going in,' I moaned. 'Your cock is sending ripples all through me. Drive it in deeper. Scratch the itch.'

"As his cock pushed deeper into me, I cried with joy. 'Thank you. Thank you. Thank you,' I reprised. 'Thank you for sticking it to me.'

"Dr. Bour pulled back and thrust deeper. He pulled it all the way out and I gasped when he slammed it back. 'Whee, plunge it into me like that,' I trilled. 'Oh, yeah, fuck me, fill me with cock.'

"I wondered whether Rick could see me getting fucked. I hoped so. I wished the whole Earth could watch me take it. Dr. Bour was reaming me with his unearthly prick, screwing me harder and faster. I wiggled my buttocks. I bucked my rump up as much as my limited freedom would allow. A special hole in the table accommodated my hard dick, so I could rock my ass freely. My cock dripped as Dr. Bour humped faster and faster.

"'Screw me hard,' I shouted. The alien twisted his cock as he fucked me. 'Oh, that's good, Dr. Bour. I don't believe how good it feels.'

"The alien was moaning as he prepared to shoot me full of hot spunk. 'My semen will strengthen you,' he moaned. 'Oh, Gornak, oh, Sood, here it comes. Get ready, Earth boy. I'm giving you a wonderful gift.'

"I wasn't ready. Who could've been ready for that gift? My cock was throbbing toward cock orgasm, but it never got the opportunity to blast. Instead, I had my first anal orgasm, and it was better than any sex I'd ever known. Dr. Bour's cock surged in my ass canal as he shot salvo after salvo of spunk into me. His semen gushed up my ass. My asshole vibrated with intense waves of pleasure, each a super orgasm. The deep rectal spasms were so intense that I thought I'd die. I passed out briefly, but awoke as Dr. Bour was climbing off the table.

"'What happened?' I moaned, though my moan was one of contentment. As the walls of my intestines devoured the hot alien semen, a sense of satiation rushed into my brain.

"'Humans lose consciousness when they experience sexual pleasure beyond their previous capacities,' he said. 'Each time you take a cock, you will experience a higher level of orgasm. In absorbing my semen, your rectal tissues will become increasingly orgasmic, and each anal orgasm will result in your ability to cope with an even more powerful orgasm.'

"My buttocks suddenly quivered. I felt like a butt slut. That feeling should have dismayed me, but it didn't. I was happy. A mischievous smile played across my face as I asked, 'How long do I stay in this slut zone?'

"Dr. Bour showed an almost human emotion. 'Slut zone. A highly appropriate descriptor, Christopher.' My ass waggled to invite a good fucking. Dr. Bour looked into my eyes, and his green ones shone with eerie light. 'There is no returning, Christopher. You are part of a long-term experiment. We will be monitoring you for life.'

"'You mean I'm a horny bottom who'll put out for anything with a dick?' The prospect sounded good; I even liked calling myself a horny bottom.

"'Your assessment is correct,' Dr. Bour said. 'Of course, you will remember nothing about this programming.'

"'I'll surely notice that I'm having anal orgasms.'

"'You will not know that only special boys have them.'

"I never saw what conditioning Rick got that night. They kept my ass up until it came time to return us. I remember levitating out of the ship, dropping quickly toward the ground, and floating in the window. Dr. Saur and his team dressed us, and erased our memories. Or so they thought. My herbal remedy worked, and I remembered every detail. I felt my asshole with my fingers and found it wet and sticky. Had I ever awakened with a sticky asshole before? No, but two weeks earlier I'd washed some dried stuff off my face. Abruptly, I recalled Dr. Weir shooting jism on my face and down my throat. Observing my reaction, Dr. Saur told Dr. Bour, 'Christopher may be more receptive to your research on anal passives.' So that's what led to the night's adventures.

"I slipped into the bathroom and touched my asshole again. I itched deep inside so I slid my finger up my ass. There aren't supposed to be nerve endings inside the rectum, but my butthole defied medical science. A thousand volts of pleasure shook me. My anal chute was wet and slick, but my finger would not reach deep enough to satisfy. In desperation, I picked up the toilet brush and slid the handle up my ass. Explosions of orgasmic delight filled me. I scratched my rectal walls until I felt some relief. However, the brush was not as good as a cock, and I did not pass out from the resulting anal orgasms.

"Rick moaned and rolled over, twisting in some alien induced dream. Wishing that he were fucking me, I climbed into the shower. As the hot water cleansed my body, I soaped my crotch sensuously. I soaped my cock and behind my balls. I slid the bar of soap back and forth in my ass crack, rinsed my asshole, and soaped it again. When I finished washing, I raided Rick's underwear drawer. I felt close to him when I slipped on his bikini briefs. I climbed into his bed, snuggled my ass against his cock, and fell asleep.

"I awoke when I felt Rick stir. It was late morning, but we had no classes that day. I wiggled my cupcakes against his hard dick. Rick touched my butt cheeks. 'When did you start wearing bikini briefs, Kit?' he asked.

"'I'm wearing your underwear.'

"'Uh, Kit. Did I miss something?" Rick stroked my butt. Heat shot through me, and I wiggled my ass against him. Rick mused, 'I remember going to bed; now it's morning and here you are.' Despite his perplexity, his cock was hardening.

"'You're not going to miss a thing, Rick,' I purred wiggling my butt crack on his cock. 'Not when we're locked together. Not when your cock is up my ass. Not when you're pumping your cum into me. Not when I'm taking all you've got and loving every inch. Every second. Every spurt. Not when you leave my asshole swollen with your hard pumping and sticky with your cum.'

"Rick's cock was super-hard. I unrolled his bikini underwear over it and pulled them down to his feet. His cock jutted toward the ceiling.

The sun hit it just right and gave it a healthy glow. Ripples of lust shivered up my ass. The more I studied Rick's cock, the more I wanted it inside me. I pulled off Rick's other pair of bikini briefs, the ones I was wearing. My buttocks tingled. I touched Rick's dick and orgasmic tremors rippled up my rectum.

"'Are you going to jack it?' Rick asked.

"'No, Rick. You're going to stick it into my ass.'

"A stunned look tinted Rick's face as if he were receiving mystical visions or hearing eternal voices or feeling numinous sensations. 'Oh god, Kit. That's what I want.'

"I positioned myself on my stomach and pulled my right knee almost to my face. Well-nigh in a trance, my friend mounted me and touched his cock to my asshole.

"'You're really going to let me put it into you?'

"'It's okay, Rick, slide it in.'

"'Are you completely gay now, Kit?' he asked.

"'It's okay to be gay. Haven't you seen the posters around campus? You know you want to fuck me. You've always wanted to fuck me. So stop fooling yourself and stuff me.'

"Rick had a huge circumcised knob but it went into me quite easily. He gasped at the ease with which his cock filled me, but he had forgotten that an alien sex researcher had spent most of the night opening my asshole. When his cock passed my anal ring, I thought I'd go into orbit. I trembled as the first anal orgasm ran up my rectum.

"'Oh, Rick, it feels so good,' I wailed. 'Oh, shit, I love catching for you.'

"'Wow, you got off fast,' Rick exclaimed, amazed that he'd pitched me into an anal orgasm.

"'Don't slow down,' I urged. 'Keep humping.' A second orgasm rocked me so hard that my throat constricted and my heart fluttered. Lightning flashed, but I did not pass out.

"Rick pounded his cock in and out of my ass, and after thirty strokes I had him ready to come. 'Uh, Kit, I'm gonna come in your ass,' he groaned. 'I'm gonna blast a wad.'

"'Shoot it into me, Rick. I want your wet spunk. Shoot your load up my ass.' I was coming too; cum was shooting out of my dick. As Rick's dick spurted into my rectum, I enjoyed a series of orgasms in my cock and in my ass simultaneously. These orgasms accelerated in speed and mounted in severity into one mighty roller. Rick thrust maniacally as his pleasure tissues forced him to empty his balls, and his thick cock stimulated the walls of my rectum into paroxysms of bliss.

"'Oh, that was great, Rick.' I assured him as I milked the final drops out of his cock. 'Yeah, I love the way you fucked my ass.'

"Rick pulled his cock out, rolled off, and lay gasping. While he recovered, his hand caressed my ass cheeks as if he could hardly believe that the mounds of flesh around the hole had given him such pleasure.

"'God, I used to chase pussy,' he giggled. 'I was a fool.'

"'There's no pussy as good as my ass,' I bragged. 'And you can fuck me every night of the year. As many times as you can. Mornings, too. And afternoons. Evenings.'

"'Oh, Kit,' Rick moaned with gratitude as he dove face first into my butt and kissed my crack. I shivered as small orgasms tinkled up my chute.

"'Come on, Rick, lick my asshole,' I urged. 'It's hot and full of your cum.'

"Rick touched his tongue to my little hole, and I nearly went into orbit again. If this kept up, I wouldn't need a spaceship to visit the aliens. Rick was going to launch me. I pushed my asshole open and his tongue poked into me. Several shaking orgasms followed, and my cock bucked, though my balls had largely emptied themselves. The real pleasure came from my anus.

"'Rick, can you come again?' I urged. 'Pitch it to me one more time.'

"'Can't get enough cock, Kit?' Rick asked.

"'No, man, I need it. I need your cock up my ass. Please fuck me, Rick. Please. Please. Please stick your cock up my ass again. Fuck me.'

"I assumed the position where the passive lies on his back with his legs thrown into the air to expose his ass-end to the active partner. Rick pushed his cock up my ass again, sending raptures through me. He grinned wolfishly into my face as he fucked me, and I asked him to kiss my hot mouth while I took his cum in my body.

"Rick couldn't get enough of my ass, and he squirted three times, but I must've had fifty orgasms. Our third butt fuck we accomplished doggy style with me on all fours on the bed and Rick topping me until he completely drained his balls. When Rick pulled out, I fell on my face and let my rectal tissues grow more luscious from his semen.

"'Are you okay, Kit?' Rick asked resting his hand on my ass. He couldn't keep his hands off my cupcakes.

"'I'm great, Rick,' I answered. 'I'm revving up my butt fuck engine. You just wait; the next time you hump me will be even better.'

"After a while I arose and pulled up the bikini underwear I'd worn earlier. 'You don't mind if I wear your underwear today, Rick?' I asked. 'It makes me feel close to you.'

"'You can keep my briefs on your ass all day, Kit. I'll never throw out that pair. I may never wash them.'

"'Don't get carried away.' (Before I gave them back, I took an indelible marker and signed my name under the words: 'I wore these after the first time Rick fucked my ass.')

"Over the next year, Dr. Bour sent me deeper and farther into the slut zone. Concluding every session, his assistants went through the motions of erasing my memory. The aliens never found out that I drank my potion every Friday. I forgot nothing of what occurred during those abductions. Rick continued to be fearful of my concoction, so I stopped asking him to try it. Dr. Saur developed Rick as a compulsive rump ranger, so he had no interest in receiving a cock. The aliens gave Rick a great love of ass, and he gave rim jobs that the recipient would cherish for a week.

"Over time my anal pleasure tissue became a fundamental part of me, so that after a year I might have been born with it. Once my mind and body were fully ensconced in the deepest region of the slut zone, Dr. Bour revealed another benefit.

"'While your anus absorbs ejaculated cum, it filters out disease. From now on, you may practice unprotected anal sex with anyone, Christopher, because no virus can escape into your bloodstream.'

"'That's good.' Deviant possibilities entered my sex-crazed mind.

"'My colleague Dr. Saur has enhanced Rick's penis so your friend will be impervious to disease. Tonight we will advance the pair of you to the promiscuity research.'"

"'Promiscuity? You're going to turn us into a couple of Hot Pants Homos?'

"'You will be aggressively lustful and wanton. You and Rick will be the most blatant, immodest, and obvious homosexuals on your planet. Of course, you will not remember the origin of your lascivious behavior.'

"'You mean we'll be coming out of the closet in a big way?'

"'Precisely.'

"A machine descended and a white cone pointed directly between my eyes. The machine hummed loudly and the cone glowed brilliant pink. By the time the machine stopped humming and glowing, I felt as though a weight had been lifted off of me. 'You will find that your personal censor and the inhibitions have already dissolved,' Dr. Bour promised.

"'I feel lighter.'

"'A sign that this procedure has been completely effective,' Dr. Bour announced. 'Only one treatment is required.'

"I picked up a sense of finality in his tone. Dr. Bour was saying goodbye. 'You're going to stop experimenting on me?'

"'Christopher, for the next two decades of your existence our research assistants will continually monitor your performance. Twenty years from tonight, we will capture you and evaluate the consequences of your licentious behavior.'

"'Am I going to get gang banged tonight?' I asked hopefully.

"'Oh, certainly. In consultation with Doctors Saur and Weir, I've decided to release your straps and let you ride a series of cocks.' So saying, he removed the restraints, and for the first time I was free within the Ball. Dr. Weir, who'd flunked me in fellatio, pointed to a row of twelve pink aliens lying a few feet apart. Each male stretched comfortably on his back with his great alien cock pointing hard up and awaiting my services.

"Even as I rushed toward the pink aliens, my ass secreted a sweet-smelling lubricant. I climbed onto the first alien and slid my ass along his rippled stomach until he moaned bestially. Grinning at his lust, I raised my ass and touched my asshole to the thick round bulb that formed the tip of his cock. The alien's red eyes opened wide as I filled my ass with his dick, and rode wildly upon his thick shaft and bulb-like dickhead. I milked my anus on the knob and passed through orgasms until I was a drooling sex fiend.

"Only after I'd come aplenty and achieved orgasms beyond counting did the pink alien emit unearthly groans. I tightened my ass and rode him harder. I forced a staggering pleasure upon him, and he blasted great gouts of extraterrestrial cum. When I had drained him, I jumped to the next alien prick and pleasured myself upon it. Meanwhile, I saw the previous alien roll over so Rick could mount his ass. The pink stud didn't look so studly taking Rick's cock up his rear.

"My night ride seemed timeless; certainly, I must've whiled away many hours tickling a dozen pink alien studs to orgasm and milking their other-worldly balls. I was exhausted by the time I popped the final alien cock. However, the nutrient-rich cum I'd stolen from the aliens healed my bruised tissues. As I recuperated, I watched Rick finish licking and fucking the pink assholes. When Rick had ejaculated a full ball-load into the last alien, he dropped down beside me.

"'You are the rod,' Dr. Saur explained to Rick, 'and your friend the bowl. We will create many others in your likeness. You will now be taken back to your beds, and forgetting all, you will adjust your lives to your new needs.'

"So saying Dr. Saur pointed his mechanical device at us, and Rick forgot all that had transpired. However, when we awoke, together in his bed, I remembered everything.

"From then on, Rick and I strutted our gayness, and we soon had other gay blades flocking to our room. How many times did we play choo-choo with a group of fellows, me leading as the engine and Rick playing the caboose? And as we cruised the campus for guys and groups of guys, I never doubted that our sexual trysts were being recorded on high by a mysterious alien statistician."

As I finished telling my tale, my students stared at me, some with admiration, some with loathing, and some with lust. After I'd dismissed the class and gathered up my notes, I noticed one lone lad loitering.

"Yes, Lonnie, do you want to ask me something?"

"Yes, professor," he replied. "What's the formula for your potion?"

I wrote it out, but I warned him before handing over the paper, "It won't change anything, you know. They're still going to abduct and program you in the Ball, and you won't be able to stop them. The formula will only help you remember. And you must never let them know that you can remember."

"They'll never hear it from me. I just want to know. I think they've duplicated your programming in me. Last night I put out for the whole swim team."

"Was it good?"

"Terrific. My rectum could take a thousand cocks and get off on every one. I thought I was the only guy built that way, but I bet they've repeated the experiment they did on you with hundreds, maybe thousands, of guys."

Lonnie was feeling better about himself after our talk, but not all my students were so open-minded. Several complained to Dean Bittern, and two days later, the president of the college summoned me to his office. After delivering a humiliating and abusive lecture, he fired me unceremoniously.

I was sorry to leave the classroom because I knew that many students could have benefited from my experience, and I was disappointed in the small-minded, homophobic administrators, who constantly rang the gong for diversity, but had no interest in its causes or consequences. Six months after getting fired, I signed a million dollar book deal, and I found better avenues to speak out. I mean, what more powerful words could I utter than, "Yes, Oprah, I need anal sex because extraterrestrial scientists programmed me that way."

EPICENE THE INCUBUS

Someone had painted the walls of the St. Sebastian College psychologist's office institutional green, and there were no windows. A single fluorescent tube buzzed overhead. I slouched in an uncomfortable chair on one side of the desk. My psychologist, Dr. Calatean, swiveled in his squeaking chair, stared guardedly, and waited for me to spill my guts.

"Epicene appeared again last night," I admitted at last.

"Your night ghost?" His tone was unbearably patronizing.

"He's an incubus."

The shrink held up his hand and consulted a textbook. "The occult dictionary says that an incubus is an evil spirit that has sexual intercourse with women as they sleep." He flipped a few pages. "The succubus is the lascivious spirit that inflicts sexual intercourse upon sleeping men."

"Epicene isn't a succubus. A succubus has a female shape. Epicene has a cock. He doesn't do women because he's a gay incubus."

Dr. Calatean nodded his head condescendingly. "Tell me everything, no matter how personal. Just use your own words."

I shifted uncomfortably and wondered who else's words I might have used. "I wake up and find him sitting on the side of my bed. He whispers suggestive things. Last night he touched me."

"Where did he touch you?"

"He was stroking my ass. I wear bikini underwear to bed, and he was rubbing his hands on my ass and feeling up my crack."

"How did that make you feel, Brett?" Dr. Calatean glanced in the book again and found inspiration. "Did the imaginary being's touch paralyze you with terror?"

"Imaginary, my ass. His touch made me feel horny. I got a hard-on."

"Have you had homosexual thoughts before, Brett?"

"Yeah, like since as long as I can remember." Did my shrink think I turned gay last week on a whim?

Dr. Calatean jotted a note on his yellow pad. "You have entertained homosexual fantasies since your childhood?"

"Yeah, I was never interested in girls, and I only wanted to play with guys – especially the games we played in our briefs. I even fantasized about them, but not like I do now."

"And you recently came out to your parents?"

"Yeah, Dr. Calatean. That's why I have to see you. My dad thinks you can help me stop being queer. But you can't do that, and I can't imagine wanting to be a friggin' breeder." The thought made me shudder. "But this is different."

"Has this figment or ghost or whatever touched you before last night?"

"No, last night was the first time. But he's been there for my wet dreams."

"What did he say to you?"

"He told me I have a cute ass. He told me that any man would want to stick his cock up my ass and ride me until he filled me with wet, sticky cum."

"Go on, Brett."

"This doesn't bother you, Dr. Calatean?"

"No, of course not, Brett," said the psychologist. "I'm a professional."

"I mean the explicit gay sex. If I have to tell you everything, you're going to find it pretty raw."

"That's okay. I'm Romanian."

# # # # #

Epicene first appeared a month earlier, a gorgeous incubus, arriving during a wicked wet dream. As I tossed in twilight sleep, coming helplessly but relentlessly into my underwear, his beautiful face and desirable body invaded my lewd nightmare. He was about six feet tall, his body rapier thin and lithe. Wearing an insubstantial green garment that kissed every curve, he moved with an effete grace that I could never hope to achieve. His face was pale, but he had a wide reddish mouth and swimmy green eyes. His hair, which hung to his shoulders, glowed with a shade of crimson so esoteric no mortal could match it with dye.

When Epicene ran his ethereal hand up my mortal thigh, I thought that I'd pop my cork. My body went taut and a lurch of desire coursed through me. Lurid images of the rites of the Priests of Sodom flashed through my mind. My cock leaked more cum into my underwear. The semen scent filled my dorm room.

Epicene's cloying otherworldly breath hissed in my ear. "Remove your tiny garment," he whispered. "Display your treasures for my inspection."

Since that first night, I'd seen him again and again, his white hands, his luscious mouth, the delicious curves of his butt, but he always faded when I awakened. I'd thought him only a dream, at first, some manifestation of my fears and desires, my childhood of endured taunts and slurs, or my parlous relationship with my parents.

But, Epicene wasn't some pathetic psychological symptom of my gay lusts. He had a real form, with a tempting shape and a charismatic personality, but he never spoke to me until the night he told me to pull down my briefs. And though I was surprised, I didn't waste time: I raised my hips, whipped off my bikini underwear, and drew up my legs so he had a good view.

He touched my cock with his warm hand, a ghostly hand, but human-like as my own. After stroking my dick silently while his green eyes burned into my own, he bent and licked my balls.

"Oh, who are you?" I asked.

"What name do you prefer?" he asked raising his head.

"I've been thinking of you as Epicene."

"How astute, Brett. Epicene is my name."

"Am I dreaming?" I asked.

"I come in your dreams."

"Can you kiss me?"

Epicene brought his lips to my asshole, and as he smooched my little pucker, I fell weightless through space. He kissed long at my back door until the escalating pleasure, mingled with a touch of the forbidden, the licentious, and the wicked, nearly triggered an explosion of cum from my balls.

"Oh, yeah, I meant my lips," I confessed, after his lingering anal kiss had extended for thirty minutes. "Oh, that's so fuckin' good."

Then he brought his red, red lips fresh from my asshole to my mouth, and I pressed my lips to his and opened my mouth to receive his tongue. His tongue played with mine, invading my mouth with delicious invitation, and I abandoned my body to his utterly. Still he merely stroked me, petting my skin and fondling my cock.

I tore my mouth away and begged him to doff his wraithlike green costume, so I could see his unclothed body, stroke his naked ass, and ride his bare dick. He smiled at me and kissed me again. "Soon, Brett," he demurred, his words another kiss. "In time, you shall participate in the revels of the sodomites."

Abruptly, I found myself sitting up, wide-awake, alone in my bed, with a killer boner, and hot to get fucked.

"Shit, Brett," my roommate Vince yelled. "That must've been a hell of a nightmare."

"Go back to sleep, Vince."

Vince was the albatross hanging around my neck. We shared a dorm room, but he wasn't comfortable about living with a "homo" – especially one out and about on campus. He'd gone to the administration several times to try to get me out of "his room," but the dean had told him to overcome his homophobia and to be happy about sharing with someone different. The dean had launched into a long lecture on diversity and the importance of learning about and being exposed to other lifestyles while in college. Vince had returned from his appointments with the dean a bitter and frustrated student.

In truth, I, too, would have preferred to be rid of Vince. He was too straight for my taste, and it was not possible to bring a guy to my room for sex with Vince there. I was a nineteen-year-old homosexual, out to everyone on campus, but I'd never actually had sex with another guy. Okay, I'd jerked off with a few friends in high school, friends who were experimenting with their own sexuality, but it wasn't the same. Until I'd sucked a cock and gotten butt fucked to orgasm, I wasn't going to give myself the credit for actually performing a gay sex act.

So that day I attended my classes, did loads of homework, visited Dr. Calatean and told him about the incubus, and ended up listening to Vince surreptitiously beating his meat while trying to keep me from knowing that he did it. Finally, I fell into an uneasy sleep, hoping that I'd dream about Epicene again.

Deep in the night, I felt him enter my bed. For the first time, he slid beneath my sheets and pressed against me in the dark. I turned to him and kissed him. After a while, he removed his eerie garment, and I pushed down my briefs.

"Is this the time?" I whispered.

"Are you prepared for the ritual of Priests of the Dog Star? Do you give yourself to sodomy, Brett?"

My heart raced. "Yes," I said. "Yes. I do. Yes."

It happened in the dark of the night. Without light, without moon, without starshine, Epicene turned me on my face and arranged my right leg so my asshole was opened for easy access.

"It's my first time," I whispered wondering if I spoke in my sleep. "Make it good for me."

"I promise to pervert you beyond measure, Brett," Epicene assured me.

"Oh, yes. Pervert me."

"I shall lubricate your holy orifice with one finger, then two. I will stimulate your prostate in ways you cannot yet imagine."

I could hardly believe what I was hearing. He was going to make me beg for his cock. I would demand that he slide it into me.

As if he read my thoughts, he assured me, "You will ascend to the heights of sexual deviance. I shall take you there, and you shall thank me over and over as I sodomize you."

"Oh, yes, Epicene," I said. My cock was so hard that I had to shift it, and the excitement his stated intentions had aroused made it leak a thin stream onto my sheets.

"Tonight you will fathom the secret rites of passage known to the pharaohs, the joys of the boys of Attic Greece, and the nightly pleasures of the men of Sodom. It was I who trained the initiates of the great mother goddess at Ninevah and Ur and induced the sodomitic frenzies of the dog-priests."

I never knew where Epicene obtained the lubricant. I've never felt another like it in the world of men, but whether he exuded it or brought it though some occult medium, he cupped a gob of thick, slick fluid in his left hand as his right index finger gently probed my hole. He whispered instructions to me, and I overcame my asshole's natural inclination to tighten. I learned how to open for the exterior probing pressure. In a minute, Epicene had his finger inserted all the way up my rectum.

"Ah, that's pleasant," I murmured as he probed and pushed, especially pointing toward my balls, which sent delicious shivers through me. "I like that. Thank you, Epicene. It feels so perverted."

"It is desirable that you relish the shivers of perversion, Brett."

"Oh, yes."

143

"This action will elevate you to greater heights of depravity, Brett," Epicene promised as he did something that nearly made my head pop off.

"Ah," I moaned, more loudly than I'd intended.

Epicene pulled his finger out of my ass, and I sighed with disappointment. "I shall now insert two fingers," he said. "Two will open you to the ways of the ancient initiates."

"Yes, open me up," I begged. "Please. Make me a dog-priest or a pharaoh."

He pushed two fingers into my asshole and twisted, provoking my dick to jolt and leak.

"Oh," I gasped, stifling a howl by biting my pillow. Epicene twisted his fingers this way and that, dilating my asshole more and more, and pushing up my ass. He was doing something inside of me that was so mysteriously luscious, so forbidden that I wanted it to last forever, and so deviant that I nearly sang with delight.

"Ah," I keened. "Thank you. Thank you."

Curious fires pulsed up my ass and rippled down my cock. I'd never imagined anything like the sexual heat Epicene was making me feel, sensations that my parents would have deemed horribly wicked, but that I relished.

"Oh, that makes me feel so queer, Epicene," I whispered. "Oh, yes, you allure me, you seduce me, you pervert me. Ah."

"Now you shall become a sodomite," Epicene announced.

"Oh, yes, I'm ready. Stick your big cock up my ass. Fuck me, Epicene. Fuck my ass."

Epicene pulled his hand out of my butt and climbed atop of me. I liked feeling his weight on me, and I trembled with impatience as he pushed his cock's tip against my open asshole.

"Shove it in," I begged. "Stick it to me, Epicene. I've never wanted anything this bad."

Contrary to my offer, he entered my ass slowly, and his thick cock steadily filled me, painlessly, pleasurably. I drew a deep shuddering breath as he filled me beyond where his fingers had reached, and soon I was full of hard dick. He had me nailed to my bed, and there was no way I could have backed out then, even if I'd wanted to. However, I didn't want to stop. I wanted him to fuck me.

"Oh, yeah, fuck me," I begged, unable to come up with a more original suggestion. Besides the invitation sounded good to my ears.

"Fuck me and shoot cum in my ass." Just saying the word fuck excited me. Fuck my ass was pure exhilaration.

"Yes, I shall fill you with the Secret Desire of the Ages, Brett," Epicene said, and he lifted his hips so that the fullness departed. Then he rammed home again, filling me deeply until his loins smashed hard against my buns.

"Oh, yeah," I groaned. "Do that. Do that."

Epicene started humping me steadily, bouncing up and down on my tight college boy ass, and fucking me until I felt like a citizen of Sodom.

"Oh, that's good. Do that; do that; do that; do me like that," I chanted. "Oh, you're fucking the shit outta me. Oh, yeah, fuck my queer ass. Thank you, Epicene. Thank you for fucking me."

Curiously, as the unhallowed incubus screwed my butt, my cock hardened even stiffer than before, and I felt the tremors of approaching orgasm.

"Oh, god, you're making me come. Oh, Epicene, you're making me come."

But even as my cock prickled with oncoming sexual transport, I heard the incubus breathing heavily in my ear, and I knew that my ass was bringing him off as well.

"Oh, yeah, do it in my ass. Shoot me full of jism."

A million tiny needles of pure pleasure tortured my cock, and all my muscles contracted to blast my spunk. My involuntary contractions drew Epicene into the cusp of rapture as well, and I distinctly heard his sharp breath as I pulled him over the edge. Then he was blasting his ghostly spunk into my ass, and I was hurling my own cum onto my wet sheets.

Afterward, as I lay cuddled against him, Epicene told me that he'd accomplished his purpose with me.

"You mean ..." I started, my eyes filling with tears.

"You shall see me no more, Brett, You must fulfill your ritual purpose with the mortal lads of this college."

"But I haven't met any who wanted what I want."

The incubus leered darkly. "You have received the seed of the wanton. There are others nearby, and they seek you even as you now seek them."

# # # # #

"So am I crazy, Dr. Calatean?" I asked during the next day's session.

"Brett, did you find evidence of this visit in the morning?"

"You mean besides the cum stains on my sheets, and the soaking wet pillow from where I'd been biting it?"

"Yes, I mean evidence of the other presence."

"My asshole was wet and sticky. I had cum in my ass. I know that homophobic Vince didn't shoot it in there."

My psychiatrist looked troubled. "Would you be interested in joining a group session, Brett?"

"You mean there are others?"

"Including you, I have four boys on this campus reporting similar experiences. I think it might be valuable for you to talk with each other."

"Yeah, Doctor, I think that's a great idea." I shifted in my chair, so my shrink wouldn't notice I was getting a woody. I could hardly wait to meet three other guys who'd received night visitations from Epicene. Once together, we could dispense with the psychologist and establish our own Brotherhood of Sodom.

THE SMYRNA MERCHANTS

Dr. Tartt mumbled on and on about *The Waste Land,* until my brain threatened to explode. I was glad that T.S. Eliot was dead, so he couldn't inflict more poetic horrors upon us. I gazed around the college classroom, small, windowless, and poorly-lit by reeking fluorescents. My fellow students, eleven in number, were taking copious notes on pads or on the margins of their paperbound texts. Finally, Dr. Tartt got to Mr. Eugenides, the Smyrna merchant, and the secret cult of homosexuality that had existed down through the ages.

Some students stirred, made uncomfortable by the reference, but Georg smiled knowingly. Everybody suspected that Georg was gay. That his name was pronounced like gay-org and not George may have contributed to the belief. Perhaps there were other reasons. Anyway, I sat on the other side of the room, and I had never spoken to Georg out of fear that the homophobes would suspect I was gay.

I tried to watch Georg without anybody realizing that I was studying him. He had a nicely constructed body, and he wore form-fitting jeans, which showed off the contours of his ass and the bulge in front. His face was feral and dark complexioned, though Caucasian, with a nose a bit too large and puffy lips. He had a distinctly animal look, and though he was supposed to be from Eastern Europe, I wondered where his bloodline had really originated. The Carpathians? Transylvania?

Would I have liked to get to know Georg? Oh, yes. I was attracted to guys. Here I was in college, and I'd never even been on a date with a girl. Just not interested. But, I was also keeping myself locked up, nailed in, and sealed airtight in the closest closet ever devised, and all due to my own fear, my terror that someone would read my private thoughts and secret desires.

Following class, I wandered, alone as always, down to the student cafeteria. After paying for the meat loaf special and a zero calorie Coke, I sat down at a secluded table behind a yellowing Erica palm. I was forking mashed potatoes and green peas into my mouth when Georg asked if he could join me. I jumped so visibly that my ass must've lifted two feet off my chair.

"S-s-sure," I croaked after a minute's hesitation. My heart was racing. If Georg sat with me, people would suspect I was gay, so I didn't want him to join me, but I did want to sit with him, which made no coherent sense. I was too embarrassed to tell him the truth.

"What did you think of Dr. Tartt's lecture, Andy?" Georg asked after he had arranged his food before him.

"T.S. Eliot doesn't grip me," I answered with all the nonchalance I could muster.

"*Nein?* E.M. Forster once refused to write an introduction for one of Eliot's books, saying that he was not in agreement with Eliot's outlook." Georg chortled, so I snickered politely. "The part about the Cult of Homosexuality was interesting, though," Georg asserted, his eyes locking upon mine. "Of course, Dr. Tartt doesn't know, cannot know, that the Smyrna merchants have truly existed from time out of mind, and continue to exist here and now."

My dick stiffened as my lunch turned to ashes in my mouth. "What do you mean?"

With a foreign looking shrug, Georg steered the conversation into an alarming direction. "I wonder ... do you truly wish to know?"

"I want to," I said, surprising myself. The words had popped out.

"In that case, you must spend the weekend with me, Andy?"

I must have turned dark crimson. Georg had scented out my secret cravings, and I wondered how many others knew. My classmates? My teachers? My parents? Could people tell by looking that I was riddled with gay lust and too chickenshit to admit it?

"It's like the damn poem is coming true," I gasped. "Here you are, an exotic guy. We're having lunch together. Then you ask me to spend the weekend with you. The only thing missing is the demotic French."

Georg's feral face moved closer until his lips nearly touched mine. I sat frozen with terror and desire. "*Wirklich?* How about it, Andy?"

"Yes," I managed with a gulp.

"*Gut*, I will introduce you to the Merchants of Smyrna." He took my hand and held it during the remainder of our meal.

I phoned my parents after lunch and told them that I wouldn't be coming home that weekend. Of course, they had ten thousand questions, which I fended off badly. I must have sounded nervous because my mother's radar alerted her that I was up to something. She ended up warning me that wherever I was, I needed to go to church. The conversation ended with discomfort and suspicion on both ends of the line. After I disconnected, I turned off my cell phone.

I told Georg that I would return to my dorm room to pack.

"You need bring nothing. Come with me now, Andy."

"Without a toothbrush?"

"I have a toothbrush. You can use it. Come on."

The idea of brushing my teeth with another guy's toothbrush sounded pretty perverted, but I went along with him. Georg's car was a hot yellow Porsche 911 GT, a ride I could never have afforded. He started the motor with a roar and grinned wickedly.

"Do not be nervous, Andy," he said. "You are following a path many men have trod down through history. Once started, you will never turn back – nor desire to do so."

Somehow, his words didn't reassure me, especially since I was sure that he was no longer talking about his toothbrush. However, I stopped thinking about such trivialities as Georg barreled through traffic, cutting in and out, and hit the interstate at eighty-five.

"Aren't you afraid of getting a speeding ticket?" I shouted as I watched the accelerator needle rise.

"None of those *polizei* squads could catch this car," he replied pushing his right foot closer to the floor. Two hours later, we reached a small town, roared through it, and parked in front of a stately mansion on the outskirts. Georg jumped out, with me trailing behind him and growing more uncertain than ever. Georg had never even asked if I was gay, and I wondered what he had in mind. Filled with mystery, I followed him to the front entrance.

A butler opened the massive door, greeted Georg familiarly, and led us to an upstairs bedroom with a canopied bed. I realized that we were expected to share this bed, and I felt rather taken for granted. Georg just assumed I'd put out for him, though I had never previously had sex with anybody but myself. However, he did not explicitly state his intentions, and I was afraid to ask.

"Want to go for a swim?" Georg asked.

I spread my hands in a meaningful gesture – no swimming trunks – not even a toothbrush. Grinning knowingly, Georg pulled open a drawer, dragged out two filmy red swimming briefs, and tossed one to me.

"*Verletzte.* Tansie's formal," he said.

"What's that?"

"It's 1950s camp. A gay boy – Tansie – would wear scarlet-red swim briefs to proclaim his availability." He shook the proffered swim suit until I took it. "These, *natürlich*, are the latest designs and fabrics."

Georg stripped off his clothes, giving me my first look at his naked form, and pulled up the slinky swimsuit. Though I had an incipient hard-on, I took off my clothes, folded them neatly, and pulled on the thin Lycra swimsuit.

"I've never worn a swimsuit like this," I admitted, admiring my form in the full-length mirror. "The most daring I ever got was buying a square cut, and my mother made me return it to the store." I felt extremely naked.

"Andy, you look sexy," Georg gushed, admiring me from all angles. Then he swatted my butt. "Cute buns."

He led me down the staircase to the main floor. Hot-eyed male servants watching us pass, we swept through the main entry, down a hall hung like an art museum, through gilded rooms, and descended another flight. The basement, deep, green-tiled, and watery, formed a gigantic swimming pool. Dozens of padded, waterproof lounges sat along the tiled edge, so the loungers could watch the swimmers. The pool also offered seclusion from watchful eyes. Massive columns rose from the water. These columns supported the house, but they also provided cover for lascivious activities. Two lagoons followed the wings of the mansion.

"I never saw anything like this, Georg," I admitted.

"Impressive, is it not. It's an example of what you can do with immeasurable wealth."

Tiled steps led down into the water, so I stepped forward into the pool. The water came only to our hips.

"Not very deep."

"This part is shallow, but it gets a bit deeper over there. Most of the pool is barely up to your neck. Around the south wing you could safely dive in. It is quite deep. Come."

Georg swam toward a peristyle of gaily-decorated columns. I struck out, doing some stroke that must have looked like a cross between a dog paddling and a goat drowning. Dolphin kicking like Aquaman, Georg led me around the columns and into a lagoon. When he planted his butt on an underwater shelf, I floated my ass down beside him.

I looked Georg in the eye. "What are we doing here, Georg? Who owns this house?"

"You are my guest, Andy. I own this house. Not alone, *natürlich*. Even so, my society owns this mansion and many others."

I looked at him with amazement, and he smiled at my expression. Then he leaned forward and kissed my mouth. I'd always feared that when it finally happened, that my fear would make me pull away. I was surprised that my mouth knew what to do, and I was even more stunned at the easy way my hands found the bulge in his red swim briefs. His cock was hard, and when my fingers touched it, the sensation was electric.

"*Ja*, you like cock," Georg stated after he'd pulled his tongue out of my mouth.

"Yes," I agreed studying the hard protrusion in his swimsuit through the water while my fingers screwed his dickhead.

After a minute, Georg caught my hand and pulled it off his cock. "Not yet, Andy. Tonight you will join us."

"Who? Whom? Join whom?"

"I told you. The Smyrna Merchants. Just like in the poem. We are an ancient and wealthy order of homosexual men, and I have invited you here, so we can initiate you into our society."

I shook my head, puzzled. "How do you know I'll fit into your secret society?"

"I must not tell you yet, Andy, why I am so certain. You shall learn the truth after you have been initiated. But, I know that you will never regret the vows you make this night."

My mother would not approve, but every fiber of my being cried out for me to join with Georg and his club.

Around 7:00, an attractive waiter brought a light supper to our room. Though Georg could have eaten in the dining room, he stayed with me until a group of effete young men came to prepare me for the initiation. Georg blew me a kiss as the fellows led me away to an ornate bathroom for the ritual cleansing. Tittering over me, they took my clothes, flushed my bowels with a series of enemas, cleaned my teeth, shaved my body – but not my head, scrubbed me under a hot shower, and trimmed and styled my hair. I tried to question them as they worked on me, but they spoke no English, and I didn't recognize their melodious tongue.

At the appointed hour, my prissy attendants dressed me in a white silk gown that reached mid thigh and led me to a darkened chamber at the highest floor of the house. They stood near me, unspeaking. Despite their presence, I felt alone in the dark. I trembled, and my heart thundered in my ears.

Out of the Stygian blackness came a rustling voice, dry as the desert wind, terrible as an army with banners. "Speak your name."

"Andrew Shahar," I answered.

"State your age?"

"Nineteen."

"Have you carnal knowledge of any female?"

"No." I gave the unblemished truth.

"Will you dedicate your body to the pleasure of men?"

I did not hesitate for a heartbeat, but my voice shook when I answered. "Yes."

"Remove your gown and crawl backward on your hands and knees. Do not stop until I command."

In the pitch darkness, my attendants assisted me to my knees, and after I had placed my hands on the soft floor, they directed me as I crawled. It seemed strange to scramble blindly ignorant of whatever waited behind me. As I crawled, I had the vague sense that I backed through a doorway and entered another chamber. The air changed subtly. I discerned a pleasantly pungent odor and became aware of a reddish glow. I heard human breathing, and in the dim nebulous luminescence, I discerned shadowy forms seated around the walls.

I continued crawling backward until a thick protruding object slipped between my spread buttocks and touched my asshole. Could it be a hard cock? If so, the cock was goopy with lubricant. Every nerve in my anus transmitted the enticement of warm gumminess to my brain. My attendants urged me to continue, and I hesitated for only a blink. I pushed backward, albeit cautiously, and the cock-shaped thing slid into my ass. I pushed with my asshole, and it filled me. I gasped as I forced it deeper into me, but my cock hardened. I pushed back until I'd taken the entire cock, and crusty hips pressed against my ass cheeks.

"Good, Andrew Shahar," came the dry voice from directly behind my ear. "You have accepted the mastery of my rod. Now pleasure your orifice upon me."

I pulled forward and pushed back, closing my eyes against the lurid glow and moaning softly through my clenched teeth. I'd never felt anything so ineffably pleasurable. When I opened my eyes again, the room had grown lighter. The opposite wall was plastered with frescoes, which I could not yet distinguish in the uncertain light. In front of the illustrations, I beheld a row of human males sprawling on thrones while they watched me hump my ass.

152

Strangely, the growing pleasure inside had annihilated my self-induced homophobia, and I no longer minded guys knowing I was gay. In fact, I started showing off and humped harder on the cock. Words formed in my brain and ejaculated unbidden out my lips.

"Ah, fuck me. Fuck my ass. Yes, I love your big cock up my ass. Oh, yeah, shoot me full of cum."

I could hardly believe I was talking that way, especially with an audience, but I couldn't stop begging for it.

"I'm hot for it," I moaned. "I want every man to fuck me. Fuck my ass. Fuck my mouth."

"Do you wish to surrender your mouth and throat for the pleasure of others?" the dry voice asked.

"Yeah, fuck my mouth," I begged.

Another form detached from the crowd, an appalling inhuman shape, but with a nicely rounded ass, and a dripping cock. I grabbed this rotund character's hind end with both hands and pulled his dick into my mouth. It unloaded immediately, and I swallowed the wet spurts. The dry-voiced thing that was fucking my ass thrust faster. The thing was pumping a big load into me. Ripples of pleasure ran up my ass. I could feel the fluid flowing into me, as though every cell in my rear was alive and feeding upon the cum of the ancient god.

The other continued to unload into my mouth. Its semen coated my tongue with delightful flavors. My nostrils were filled with the heady aroma, and as the strange cum traveled toward my stomach, I felt intense bursts of pleasure.

When my attendants lit the torches, I saw the creature I'd been sucking. He was five feet tall, round, yellowish, and shiny. After he pulled his spent cock out of my mouth and waddled to his throne at the front of the rectangular room, I saw that he had a round face with flat features. He wore a blue coat and a blue top hat that made him look like a buttery snowman.

The creature that had been fucking my ass finished and let his milked cock rest. I was glad he did not try to pull it out immediately; I enjoyed savoring the spent cock. When he finally did pull it out, I turned to look at him. I had received my first butt fuck from a pale, crusty being. The pasty creature, who somewhat resembled a long bread stick, assumed its throne beside the buttery thing I'd blown. The pasty being was wearing a brown vest open to reveal its mighty chest.

"I am Enlil," said the crusty being. "This is Utu." He indicated butter boy with a fluttery wave. "We are your gods. We are the bread and butter of your race; hence you see – and feel – our might through these forms."

I turned toward the near wall again, and saw six hot-looking human males, Georg among them, lining the wall. My eyes had tricked me earlier, for they were not sitting upon thrones. Rather, they lounged in slings with their legs raised in swinging stirrups. They were naked, and the string slings hardly concealed a single body part. A seventh sling stood empty. I turned and saw six more guys similarly slung on the opposite side.

My mind was in a whirl. What was that bread and butter claim all about? Had I really sucked one god and been fucked by another? I vaguely remembered from Gilgamesh that Enlil and Utu were old Mesopotamian deities. None of the rest made any sense, Smyrna being a seaport in Turkey or some such place. Except, hadn't my old mythology professor claimed that Gilgamesh was bisexual? While I was puzzling over whether Gilgamesh had taken the chocolate route with his friend Enkidu, I heard Enlil welcome me to the order of Smyrna Merchants, and offer the asses of my twelve partners for my pleasure.

A sudden imperative drove my doubts from my mind. As I approached the slings, I noticed that the four walls were covered with frescoes of men engaging in every imaginable homosexual act. The scenes reminded me of drawings of the ancient Near East. These images inflamed me, and I saw that my cock was hard and leaking pre-cum. I approached the first guy, who smiled at me and spoke.

"Hello, Andrew Shahar," he said. "I am Chang. I was born in central China in 1247. Feel free to greet me by kissing my asshole."

I kneeled and placed my lips to his asshole, which tasted of sweet lotions. I licked the crack of his ass, returning always to the little hole. As I slid my tongue inside, I heard a murmur of approval.

"Now you must drive your cock where your mouth has been," Chang demanded. "When you have impaled me, you may kiss my lips so that I may taste my asshole's delights."

I climbed into his sling and pushed my cock into his ass. His hole opened easily, and the chute was slick and hot. As I pushed forward as deep as my cock would reach, Chang smiled happily and brought his lips to mine. He allowed me three deep thrusts.

154

"Now you must meet Gronw Pebyr," Chang said, indicating the guy to his left. Gronw sighed contentedly as I kissed his ass, mounted him, and kissed his mouth.

And so it went around the room. Each guy announced his name and the date and place of his birth, one North-African chap being nearly 7,000 years old. Still, they all looked to be my own age. Each guy bade me kiss his asshole, fuck his ass three strokes, and kiss his lips. With each guy, my strokes in his ass brought me closer to shooting my load.

Georg was my final fuck, the last in line. "Hello, again, Andy Shahar," he said, his smile almost bestial. "I am Georg Janns. I was born in 1727, in Boehmen Koenigreich, Austria. Kindly kiss my asshole, and then kiss my lips with your cock inside of me."

I kissed Georg's cherry-tasting asshole and slid my raging cock into his hot, nearly three-hundred-year-old chute. As I kissed Georg's lips, my tortured dick finally crossed the threshold. Rapturous tingles commenced in the head of my pecker, ravishing up my shaft and obliterating conscious thought. My lips were locked with Georg's, and I was dimly aware that I was fucking his mouth with my hard tongue just as my cock was spurting great gobs of my wet spunk into his ass.

The powerful muscles at the base of my penis contracted time after time, releasing my essence into Georg while he took it gleefully. When my waves of pleasure-essence quieted, I slid my cock out of his ass and my tongue out of his mouth, but I remained on top of him in his sling.

"Why did you bring me here?" I asked in wonder.

"Only the great gods at the front of the megaron can answer you, Andy."

I climbed off him and faced Enlil and Utu.

"Approach the altar, Andrew Shahar," ordered Enlil.

I walked to the low stone structure in the center of the room. Flames were leaping from the altar. Glancing into the fire pit, I saw a furnace whose chimney rose from the world's core. This was the source of the lurid glow.

"Tonight, Andrew Shahar," intoned the god, "you have performed the sacred rite and joined with the Merchants of Smyrna. The Merchants are an ancient order of thirteen homosexual men, though its name has changed many times. Twenty-five years ago, our oldest human reached the ultimate span of his days and passed into the next phase of existence. Since then, we have searched for the young man with the sacred bloodline to complete the necessary thirteen."

"Me?" I gulped.

"We have watched you for your entire life, and three years ago it became certain that you were the appointed one. We enrolled our youngest member in the college you would attend, so that you would appear to meet him naturally. All has gone as we have foretold."

I was nearly speechless, but I knew that the cocks that had entered my ass and my mouth had been more than human. And somehow, I sensed that all I'd heard and seen was true.

"You will live ten thousand years, which is the life span of our members. You will command unlimited wealth, and your existence henceforth will be one of pleasure, privilege, and power. You may engage in sexual acts with any man you desire, but you must never pollute your body with a woman. And when you pass to the next phase, precisely 9,981 years from now, we will choose another to take your place."

I learned more, much more, and had great wealth conferred upon me. I took vows, signed papers, and after the gods departed, talked business with my new trading partners. Though I was green and ignorant, I had a thirteenth share and a vote in the Council of the Smyrna Merchants.

At length, Georg led me stumbling down the stairs to our bedroom, and we climbed naked into bed. I rolled over and faced Georg, my cock resting against his. My dick stirred again, and my exhaustion slipped away. Georg's dick was hardening, too, so I kissed downward from his hot mouth to his stomach. I stuck my tongue in his soft navel and licked the golden goblet. I licked and probed the little nectar cup and kissed every taut muscle in his abdomen.

Then I kissed farther down, over his soft pubic hair, and up his stout shaft.

"Oh, Andy," he moaned. "Your mouth is so good." His lips found my cock then, and closed around my dickhead. He made a soft, slurping sound as he sucked my dick.

"Yeah, Georg, suck me. Suck me off, and I'll suck you. Oh, yeah, that's nice."

I kissed the head of his dick. I kissed the tip and kissed around it. I took it in my mouth and massaged the tip with my lips. By then, Georg was taking my whole cock, sucking down my shaft and hitting my dickhead with his lips and tongue. His mouth was a hot tunnel.

I tried to follow his every action. I sucked him deep into my mouth, and it was good. His thick cock filled my mouth, and I fucked him with my tongue. Yes, I received intense pleasure from that shaft in my mouth, but a greater pleasure came from knowing that I was giving him pleasure. I bent all my will into forcing his ejaculation.

I sucked his cock harder and faster. I made my lips a bruising machine that bumped and ground his prickhead. Georg kept sucking my cock, trying to match my frenzied blowjob, but his ass was quivering from the hot lances of ecstasy coursing through his groin. I was torturing him with pleasure. I could feel his dick vibrating, and I knew that he was going to shoot his jism. I delighted in giving him no moment of peace. I groped his sweating buttocks while his dick trembled in my mouth.

My cock was tingling, and it got the heavy feeling that alerts me when I'm about to blast. When Georg started gnawing on my dickhead, my tortured pecker could stand it no longer. The muscles at the base of my penis contracted, and a blast of spunk filled Georg's mouth. I heard him gulp it down, just as his cock bucked hard in my mouth, and I tasted hot spunk. Georg was coming in my mouth.

I swallowed and ejaculated at the same time. I wanted to tell Georg that it was good, but I was too busy drinking his cum. I shot big squirts into his throat until my orgasm and contractions stilled. Georg's ejaculations ceased at the same time. I pulled my head back and rested with his dickhead softly caressing my lips.

"That was wonderful," Georg said.

Only after the Saturday sun had filled our window did we sleep and dream of the many years, the long centuries, the millennia of sexual pleasure to come.

BEELZEBUB'S BOY TOY

The platoon known as the Demons of the Marching Horde had been marching across the Burning Plain for three weeks, the troopers brandishing their forked swords and waving their breathtaking phallic banners. The soldiers were hairless, pale green, and horny – evident from the jutting demon dicks that raised their crimson kilts. Major Sargantanus had ordered the troops to make the most of their recreation time, so the randy soldiers were slinging Camp Whores from cock to cock. Camp Whores are good-looking guys, conscripted after their arrival in Hell to take cock in whichever manner the soldiers like to put it. Sergeant Adramaleck, a thick-cocked demon, impaled one pleasure-howling Camp Whore's ass, thrust fifteen times, ejaculated molten spunk, and tossed the cum-shooting fuck-guy to Corporals Rimmon and Python who pricked his ass and mouth.

"Garrett, do the damned troops always fuck us like this?" whispered Lyle, a newly-arrived Camp Whore, licking the smoldering cum from his lips. Lyle was sprawled beside me against a hill of burning garbage, where we were resting while we leaked out the flaming devil spunk and eagerly awaited our next round. "They get to toss us like we're rags and fuck us at will?"

"No, Lyle, they're not always so gentle. After a battle, they get wild and stick three or four cocks into us at the same time and shoot buckets of boiling jism. When the burning demon cum bubbles off into fuck gas and blasts from your guts, you'll know you're a fuck hole and cum sponge, and you'll like it," I sneered. "You just got out?"

"Yeah," Lyle shivered with pleasure as a flame fart ripped out of his ass. He collapsed into a running trill of spontaneous orgasms, which kept him mouthing obscene invitations for nearly an hour. Pungent semen flowed continuously from his cock while jets of blue cum flame erupted from his ass and mouth. When he recovered, he saw that I was still beside him. He asked, "How'd you end up here?"

"Usually, we damned army whores don't talk about our past, but since you're new, I'll tell you my story. However, I gotta tell you, if I imagined there was any way either of us would ever leave this place, I wouldn't speak a word."

# # # # #

One desolate night I was driving home from my girlfriend's house, pissed as hell. Sarah had been bitching me out again, and then crying, shouting to the neighbors about me being a crummy lover, and saying everything else she could dream up to humiliate me. I finally broke away from her and pealed out of her driveway to the sound of her dad shouting that he was calling the cops. I was so pissed and frustrated that I never saw the truck coming out of the side street until its lights were filling the driver's side window. I was swept from light and sound into pain, cold, and an awful tearing. And that was the end of that.

When I came to consciousness in pitch darkness, I felt myself strapped face down on a hot stone table. The steamy atmosphere smelled familiar, but I could not distinguish the odor. I could move my head and neck, but my arms and legs were secured, and there was a strap around my torso. The curved table elevated my butt above my head and feet, and I could wiggle my ass, so I knew that I wasn't paralyzed. The movement resulted in an unfamiliar but pleasant tingle in my asshole that crept up my rectum, and I started sweating like a bitch in heat. I waggled my ass and the pleasure increased.

Either I'd gone blind, or I was being kept in a dark room. I couldn't see a thing. I remembered the accident, and assuming I was in the hospital, I hoped that a doctor or nurse would check on me soon. Somehow, I knew that I was naked; in fact, I felt especially naked, more naked than I'd ever been, and I was pleasantly conscious that my secret places were exposed and vulnerable. Strangely, I didn't feel ashamed. Instead, I felt an intense desire to exhibit my bodily parts and functions.

"Is anybody here?" I ventured. Thereupon a weird reddish-yellow light illuminated my surroundings, and my heart quailed. This place was no hospital, but an eerie and cavernous arena, like a great cave with terrifying pits belching fire and yellow smoke and awesome stalagmites that dripped pungent spunk. Abruptly, I recognized the smell; the cavern smelled like a boy's locker room after a jerk-off contest.

Then I heard the flutter of wings, and I saw three bat-winged flying cocks circling my resting place. The cocks were twelve inches long and four in diameter, with steaming thick fluids spurting from their holes. If I could've fainted at the sight, I would've done it. I tried to pass out, but my eyes refused to close. The tingles in my asshole increased, and I wondered why I'd bothered with a girlfriend. Shit! I could have been

160

getting fucked by men. Lots of men. Plunging their cocks up my ass. Shooting cum into my mouth until I could hardly swallow another drop. Cum splattering all over me until I was drenched.

These new thoughts were horribly exciting, and I hoped that the winged cocks would swoop down to molest my ass. My dick hardened and rubbed against the hot stone. The friction hurt and felt good at the same time. My dick fluttered and palpitated, and I felt it release a stream. My asshole twitched enjoyably. In fact, the pleasure rippling through my ass was even more powerful and delightful than the throes of my cock.

The flying cocks rubbed along my sides, but they did not enter me. They teased me and decorated me with hot streaks. I wiggled my ass to entice them, but they only brushed my buttocks. They tantalized my ass crack. Before they flew away, they touched my lips one by one. No sooner had they disappeared into the reddish glow than the soft patter of footsteps reached my ears. My visitor was eight feet tall and hellishly naked save for a leather harness. His sensuous skin was motley green, including his arrowhead tipped tail; his hair was glowing red; and his fingers and toes ended in talons. He had radiant yellow eyes. An ivory horn projected from his forehead. But his most impressive features were the large bullock balls hanging between his legs and the fifteen-inch oblique cock tipped with a claw. His cock was bright with spilled semen, and as the hideous being fingered his cock, more leaked from the tip.

"I am Gresil, Demon of Impurity," the unicorn monster announced, pumping his prick. "Welcome to the Kingdom of Shadows."

"Huh?" I said. As if it were greeting Gresil, my asshole popped wide open. I'd never felt that sensation before then, my asshole gaping wide for no apparent reason.

"That church your girlfriend dragged you to would call this place Hell."

At his words, a hurricane of orgasm swept over me. I trembled and groaned as my cock pumped cum onto the hot stone beneath my hips. The demon Gresil laughed at my overpowering reaction. "Yes, Garrett, you got killed in a car crash, and now you belong to the Powers of Darkness – body and soul. Not that we give two greasy dumps about your shriveled soul, but the Hosts of Hell are going to pollute your body every way they want."

I heard a roar of laughter as if an infernal audience were observing me. Though I twisted my neck, I could scarcely discern the shadows of the crowd of witnesses. As I struggled, another voice spoke out of nowhere. That vaporous voice whispered, "You sprawl in the center ring of Pandemonium Stadium, and the condemned flesh that died before you will watch you reveal your hidden lusts." The thought that three billion lost souls were peering into my open asshole and gloating over my spontaneous ejaculation filled me with unspeakable feelings – not awful feelings of shame and humiliation but unspeakable feelings of triumph and joy.

"I'll do anything you want," I screamed gleefully. I was so relieved to find consciousness after death that I was ready to offer up my ass to anybody.

Howls of suggestive laughter greeted my response, and Gresil laid his sharp fingers on my bare ass while he continued to masturbate himself with the other hand. Thousands of explicit homosexual images filled my mind as if I'd watched – and enjoyed – every gay porno movie ever filmed. The tingles grew into a throb in the head of my dick, and my asshole made a loud sucking sound as it pulsated and vibrated.

"Garrett, you are in Hell," the demon repeated as if I had not understood the first time. I realized then that he was trying to scare me. "Nobody goes home from this place. You belong to us now and forever. This night it has been chosen for you to be turned into the Devil's Whore."

He didn't frighten me in the least. A delightful sick thrill arose in me at those words because he was offering me something I'd always wanted but hadn't known it, or rather, had only begun to admit it to myself. Little did these demons know that I was having a good time. "What does that mean," I whispered coyly, "the Devil's Whore?"

"That's right, Shitass. Tonight you will be anally and orally initiated by Satan, Lucifer, and Leviathan, and after they have perverted you into a cum sponge and a cock hole of the Diabolic Gentlemen, we shall present you to the Lord Beelzebub for his collection of Boy Toys," Gresil gloated, licking spunk from his hand. "All who come to this stygian pit are initiated – into whatever damned parody of humanity the Lord of Darkness fancies. Shortly, Satan will arrive, and he will fuck your ass until you can find release no other way."

I shrieked, "Oh, yes, yes, yes!" My asshole made another long sucking sound as if it were preparing to draw in an enormous cock. Promptly, I underwent a series of spasms that culminated in another spontaneous ejaculation.

My response left Gresil nonplussed. After all, I was supposed to be horrified. He continued, speaking sibilantly, "Listen to what I tell you, Asshole. You will surrender your honor to the Lords of Hell. You will declare yourself a passive punk, the Devil's bounden slave, eager to put out for the demon studs. Giving your favors for diabolic pleasure will become your entire existence." My favors? How corny! "After you complete your term of service to Beelzebub, you will be conscripted into the damned army as a whore for the troops who war against our enemy."

This Demonic Being expected me to protest against a homosexual initiation. He thought that I would be dismayed, whereas I could hardly wait for the heavy fucking to get going. I decided to humor Gresil.

"I was never gay when I was alive," I protested, feigning dismay. "Why is this happening to me now?"

Gresil pushed his smirking face close to mine, so I could smell his semen breath. "Because we own your ass. So we're going to make you a bottom – an anally passive, cocksucking homosexual."

"I was always straight," I howled, concealing a snicker. "I had a girlfriend. I never did anything gay."

Gresil laughed demonically. "Why do you think you ended up here, Asshole? You were born gay, and you suppressed it. You were too afraid of the world to embrace your nature. Now you will have infinite time to experience your homosexuality." The Demon of Impurity's preachy tone almost made me laugh out loud.

"I had a girlfriend," I cried, sobbing as if I meant every lying word.

Gresil looked a bit disgusted. "Yeah, Sarah. How well did that work out for you, Shithead? The bitch thought that you were bad in bed."

"She wasn't that exciting," I protested, defending my sexual prowess.

"That's because she had a pussy instead of a cock. Besides, you're lying about never having a homosexual treat. How about that time you and Ray beat each other's meat? You could have sucked him off, you know. You could have ridden his big cock until you were both marching in the gay pride parade. But you were afraid. So here you are."

How vividly I remembered that night. Tears brimmed from my eyes as I relived the memory. I had slept over with Ray. We'd watched a gay movie called *It's in the Water* with his mother. Later, Ray and I stripped down to our bikini underwear and crawled under the covers of his double bed. It wasn't five minutes before Ray touched my cock. My heart leaped into my throat, my heart thundered in my chest, and my cock stiffened in my underwear. Ray's hand massaged the underside of my erection. For a few minutes I lay frozen while he played with me. At last, my lust overcame my fear. With Ray helping, I pulled off my bikini pants, already wet with a spurt of pre-cum.

Without thinking about it, I reached for Ray's cock. His pecker was thick and rock solid. I found that he had already pulled off his underwear, so I had no problem getting a grip. Ray's mouth was close to mine. Suddenly, he was kissing me as he held my cock in his fist. My mind reeled. I was kissing another boy. When his tongue slipped into my mouth, I lost all control. I met his tongue with my own. My hand was slick with my spilled juice, which I used to jack his dick.

Ray writhed beside me. I grabbed his butt with my free hand and pulled him closer so that he could shoot his cum on me. And come he did. A big wet spurt hit my stomach, followed by another and another. Ray moaned, waggling his ass as he ejaculated, but his hand never stopped stroking my cock. Suddenly, as his fingers squeezed the head of my dick, I felt the increased heaviness that precedes ejaculation. Tingles raced down my cock. The head of my pecker was in a delicious agony, I whimpered with ecstasy even as my tongue played with Ray's, and the drawing of my pelvic muscles sent my first spurt onto Ray's skin. We continued kissing as we shot our loads, and kissed long after the contractions had stopped. Then we cuddled in our cum-drenched sheets until we fell asleep.

The next morning during breakfast, his mother wore a knowing smirk and framed suggestive questions. Ray played along, but I felt creepy. Later I realized that Ray's mother was fascinated by the thought of two boys having sex, but my conditioning had made me feel like it was broken sex, as if gay sex was inferior and puny and shabby.

Ray was cute and sexy, and I had wanted to love him in every way, but I was afraid to appear queer, and the next time he invited me to sleep over, I refused. Then, like a fool, I kept refusing until he asked me no more.

"You're right," I admitted to the demon. "I was afraid of being a faggot." That part was true, sadly true. All my missed chances flooded through my consciousness. My mouth puckered as if I were sucking an invisible dick, my asshole sucked, and my dick throbbed as it geared up for another blast. "But I'm not afraid now. I woke up here ready to take big cocks."

"You fooled me, Garrett," Gresil said after a surprised pause. He was stunned that I wasn't the timid little straight boy about to get turned out in Hell. "You were pretending to be reluctant." He stared at me in wonder. "You're enjoying this. You can hardly wait for the damned gang bang to start."

"Hell, yes," I sneered. "I was starting to figure it out before I croaked. If I'd lived another month, I have been out and about. I was already dumping Sarah, and I was going to call Ray when I got home."

At the words, my cock tingled, my asshole went into a paroxysm, and my buttocks wriggled. As I shot my third load in Hell, I heard the fanfare of thousands of trumpets. Gresil patted my ass and whispered, "Satan is arriving. Don't be shy. Offer his Satanic Majesty your mouth and your ass before he can demand them of you."

Four brawny bugaboos with bulging booties, horse's tails, horse's ears, and lance-sized pricks carried a litter with purple side curtains and golden fringes. They stopped in front of me, the side curtains parted, and out leaped an elegant being. He stood five-foot ten, his skin was deep scarlet, his tail was long and thick, and his body was sculpted like a classical god's. He had raven hair on his head, which hung far down his back, but otherwise he was hairless. I looked for cloven hooves, but he had regular human feet. I could hardly look at him, such was his physical splendor, and his smile was even more radiant. His features were gorgeous, almost feminine. When I looked at his cock, so erect that it touched his tight abdominal muscles, I melted. I wanted to wrap my legs around his waist, his cock inserted all the way up my ass, and become a part of him for eternity.

Gresil fell to his knees before Satan. Prostrating himself, he kissed Satan's feet, both knees, the head of his cock, his asshole, his nipples, and his lips. This formality completed, Gresil took a seat among other dignitaries that I had not before noticed. Satan turned his attention to me. I trembled with fear and desire. I would willingly have kissed the Lord of Hell as Gresil had done, but such was not yet required of me.

Satan touched my face, and I smiled at him. "So you're the new faggot," Satan said. "Another damned mortal who wasted his Earthly existence. Has Gresil explained what I'm going to do to you?"

"Yes. I'm ready." My asshole made a loud snapping sound as though it were calling for attention. "Make me your damned whore," I begged. "I give myself to you, Satan. Come in my mouth. Fuck my ass and fill me with cum. Make me a receptacle for your hell sauce."

Satan appeared pleased with my response. I guessed that most boys shrieked with fear and disgust. "Yes, Garrett, I will give you what you crave," he said, granting my deepest desire. "Finally, you know what you are. After I've fucked you, you'll open your ass and mouth to any gnome, demon, fiend, devil, gremlin, imp, sprite, or goblin with a cock. You'll be the cocksucker, the anal whore, the sex slave, the Boy Toy of Beelzebub, the fuck hole for any damned man or demon. When hideous tentacles are fucking your mouth and slime snakes are invading your ass and winged cocks are making you lick their bodies and demonic soldiers are tossing you like a piece of meat, you will squeal with raptures of delight. Never again will you penetrate another with your cock. Never again will you jerk off. Never after will you know freedom from sexual slavery. You will collapse helplessly in orgasms of the anus or the tongue at our command, and never of your choosing. Your reward shall be ejaculations of Hell Fire."

Every word he uttered sounded so agreeable that I smiled in accord, and as I smiled, another orgasm struck me. Satan's cock was hard, its hooded head still bouncing against the six rippling muscles on his stomach. In lascivious amazement I studied the colossal member that he was planning to stick into my ass. It leaked a stream of liquid that caught fire as it dripped, and Satan laughed at my surprise.

"Flaming semen can't kill you, Garrett. You're already dead."

Returning fear gripped my heart. "It's going to hurt, isn't it?"

"Garrett, my cock brings pain only to those who deny its mastery. It awakens shuddering pleasure in those who want it. Your asshole has been begging for my hot penetration since you awakened."

"Oh, yes," I shrieked with joy, forgetting that he was going to shoot fire up my ass.

Without another word, Satan leaped upon the table and sat on my butt cheeks. "Ah, there's nothing like a fine boy's ass," the King of

Hell stated while he ran his damned hands over my back, and slid his evil backside down, so he could stroke my buns. "Oh, yes, Garrett, you will make an excellent Boy Toy for Beelzebub."

"Please, yes, Satan," I moaned. "Fuck my damned ass. I want you to make me a fuck toy."

"I enjoy hearing you beg for it, Garrett," Satan purred as he leaned forward and let his cock leak into my crack. His satanic majesty's scorching sexual fluids flooded my butt crack. Satan's plutonian cum was sizzling, but pleasant, so I moaned with satisfaction. Satan pulled my butt cheeks apart and pushed his bulky finger into my asshole. I shrieked with pleasure; the sensation was so delicious that when I squeezed his finger with my anal sphincter I ejaculated again. My body was producing an infinite amount of semen, which flowed from my dick and even out my asshole.

"I'm lubing your asshole with my sulfurous spunk, Garrett," Satan said as I howled with glee. "Anal whores are connoisseurs of fine lubricants. A good anal lube is like a fine Willamette Valley wine."

"Lube me and stick it to me, Satan," I cried loudly. "Screw me like a faggot, and I'll take your cock like a pansy."

Satan positioned his gigantic dickhead against my little hole. "Here it comes, Garrett," he said, and with a single thrust, he rammed his dickhead into my rectum.

I shrieked because an enjoyment such as I'd never felt rippled through my asshole. The pleasure was unbearable, yet I bore it and begged for more. "Yes, yes. Thank you, Satan. Oh, yes, your cock is in me so deep. It's good. It's so good."

"I'll make it thicker, Garrett," Satan said, laughing lasciviously. "How about I ram it deeper?" So saying he pushed downward, and I felt the incredible sensation drill deeper inside me, even as my asshole widened around his still expanding cock.

My arms, legs, and torso were strapped down, or I'd have surely broken my back in my raptures. I wiggled my ass wildly. I hunched my butt up and down. I shrieked with joy again and again, and begged him to fill me with cum. He buried his shaft deeper until he had it jammed in to the hilt and his infernal loins were pressed firmly against my ass cheeks.

"You're taking it all the way, Garrett," Satan said. "What a butt slut you are. You sure have a luscious little ass. Fucking you is sweet." As he spoke, he raised his hips, and the terrific fullness left me for an instant. He pulled his cock head back to my orifice before he plunged it downward again. Without waiting for me to adjust, he pulled back again and thrust. I was really getting fucked and loving it.

"Why didn't I try this when I lived in the world?" I moaned with regret. With every stroke, the fucking felt better and better. Had I desired to, I couldn't have stopped that wonderful sensation of anal bliss any more than I could have stopped time. As the pleasure intensified, expressions of irrepressible joy slipped out of my mouth.

I couldn't long hold out against the pleasure I felt. I started to orgasm anally, crescendos of orgasm that built upon each previous release. Each cascading orgasm started deep up my ass and rippled through my entire body. Each grew in intensity until it would have killed me had I still been alive. The blasts of unmanly pleasure came and came and didn't stop.

Of course I'd fucked Sarah, but those sporadic missionary bangs had been mere pathetic grappling. Jerking off with Ray had been wonderful, but mutual masturbation was nothing compared to what I felt with Satan. Jerking off or dipping my dick into a female were a pale reflections of getting fucked in the ass by a pleasure-giving Devil dick.

"Ah, that's good," I moaned. "Oh, don't stop, Satan. I love your big dick." I humped my ass to meet Satan's thrusts, wiggling and waggling. "Oh, you're really fucking me, Satan," I moaned, humping my ass. "Oh, it's so good. I didn't know it would be so good. Thank you."

"You're welcome, Garret. Now swear that you are a whore of Hell."

"Oh, yes, Satan, I submit to you. I give my ass to you, Satan my love. I swear that I am a Whore of Hell. I am a receptacle for stygian cum. I'm yours to fuck forever."

"Nay, Garrett. You and I will enjoy but a short time yet. There are others who will open your ass."

"Bring them on," I offered. "They can fuck my mouth while you fuck my ass."

"Your mouth will be filled, Garrett, but not yet. First we make you an anal whore and second a cum feeder."

I felt Satan's cock stiffen harder and swell, as overpowering waves of pleasure rose in my ass and rippled from the head of my cock up to the base where my potent muscles contracted. I sent great blasts of boy cum onto the table, far more than I had come previously, as Satan filled my ass with his own spunk. Of course, he could blast far more than I, and he filled my bowels with gallons of searing cum. My whole body broke into a fantastic sweat as the devil's spunk poured into me.

When his once-angelic Majesty pulled his cock out of me, I started leaking. My stretched hole couldn't hold that hot cum and it bubbled out to decorate my ass. "Oh, it burns so good," I moaned. The hot cum streamed out of me, bursting into flame as it came. Each burst of fire triggered a new anal orgasm. Smiling at the explosions and flames shooting out of my ass, Satan dropped his majestic buttocks onto the edge of my table.

Gresil arose from his seat among the dignitaries, who I later learned were called the Masters of Masturbation. One hand rubbing his swollen cock, Gresil read from a scroll decorated with ribbons and seals: "Good job, Asshole. Lord Lucifer will fuck you next. He will advance your initiation to the next stage."

"Bring it on," I said, enjoying my flaming farts. Each explosion was like a thousand-man gang bang. "Fuck me some more."

"Well said, Shithead. Would you like to ride Lucifer's cock? Unbound?"

"Sure." I'd have taken anybody's cock.

Hobgoblin attendants released my straps and helped me sit up. Fifteen gallons of burning cum gushed out of my asshole and covered the table. The flames rose around me; I wiggled my ass in the fire and felt wonderful. Satan sprawled back on the cum-drenched table, masturbating his dripping dick with one hand, and pointing with the other toward an approaching apparition.

Lucifer was mounted upon a magnificent steed, like a bright horse, yet not a horse. The creature's head was phallic, and when Lucifer dismounted, I saw the thick erect penis jutting from the middle of its back. To ride this beast, a rider must impale his asshole upon his mount's prodigious prick.

Lucifer himself glowed and cast light in all directions. He glanced at me, and the room lit up. As Lucifer performed the kissing ritual upon Satan, I could see my surroundings for the first time.

I saw tier after tier filled with millions of spectators, human and demonic. Some humans were naked, but most were adorned in perverted and humiliating garb. Flying phalluses fucked open mouths, and the seats were living butt-plugs, upon which the people squirmed. Among the assembled humans sat werefolk, goblins, furies, oafs, sprites, imps, ghouls, and harpies. Near the bottom tier, I recognized my own grandparents, my sweet grandpop, who'd often taken me fishing or on long rambles through the woods, and my grandma who'd baked sweet cookies and told bewitching stories. And here were they in Hell, leering down at me with wanton and mordant expressions. I waved to them as the fire semen raged from my Satanically-opened asshole.

"That's it, you little faggot," Grandpop shouted. "Sit your ass on Old Bendy's cock." I turned and saw that Lucifer had reclined upon his back, his great cock projecting wetly. Satan had turned upon his side to watch me mount Lucifer.

"Good advice, Grandpop," I shouted. "Watch how I take it."

I raised my hips, positioned Lucifer's dickhead against my asshole, and rammed my ass down. I gasped as I reamed myself upon the massive shaft, but the crowd cheered words of encouragement from sundry cultures: "Fuck the slutty boy. Fill the catcher's mitt. Boink the bum boy. Goose his lady-hole. Sixty-six the faggot. Bugger his A-cherry. Screw the anal jabbette. Come in the catamite."

In the land of the living those words would have been slurs, meant to degrade or insult. In Hell, they were simply the calls of the fucked to the fucked. We were all damned, so I reveled in the badinage. "Sure, I'm a fucking catamite," I shouted. "I like riding the A-train. You damned perverts can bounce on your butt plugs while you watch the devils shoot loads into my slutty ass."

I raised my hips again and plunged downward. I possessed a natural talent for impaling my ass on a hard cock. "I'm a great fuck," I shouted to the crowd. "Watch this." I began bouncing up and down on Lucifer's cock so fast that even the Devil Incarnate looked impressed, and the crowd chanted in unison:

Sod-dom-ite. Sod-dom-ite.
Ass so tight.
Sod-dom-ite.
Up all night.
Fuck him right.
Sod-dom-ite. Sod-dom-ite.
What a sight.
Sod-dom-ite.

"That's me," I shouted. "I'm the damned Sodomite. I'm eternally fucked."

As I rode Lucifer's cock, I stroked his chest and pinched his protrusive nipples, which leaked a strange-smelling fluid. I was going to make him come – that's right, I, Garrett, was going to force the Light Bringer to shoot his wad – and I gripped his cock tighter with my asshole and bounced high upon him. I rose to the head of his cock and down to his hips with every bounce. My own cock was hard to bursting as I fucked his cock with my hot ass, and I saw that I'd been coming constantly. I could hardly believe that I could shoot a load like Old Horny.

I heard Grandma shouting above the rest, "Ride the Foul Fiend's cock, you little fairy-faggot. I fattened your fruity ass with cookies, so you could take the Dick of the Damned."

And my grandpop hollered, "Ride that rod. Oh, look at the way the little queer rides Old Poker."

"Ah, I like the Hellfire hard-on up my ass," I shouted to the spectators. "Thank you, Satan. Thank you, Lucifer. Thank you for fucking me. I want Devil dongs inside me always."

"That fucking anal whore is my damned grandson," Grandpop shouted proudly and the crowd applauded.

A patronizing smirk appeared on Satan's visage, and he masturbated furiously as he watched me ride Lucifer's cock. I was intent on pleasuring these devils. Spasms of pleasure rippled up my anal chute as I rode Lucifer's dick, and I still came and came. The anal orgasms never stopped, but grew in intensity. From the depths of the crowd, I heard a familiar voice shouting, "Ride it, fuckboy. Ride that cock, you anal whore. I should've fucked you myself, you little butt slut."

I could have sworn that I recognized the voice of Reverend Creevey, the late pastor of Sarah's church, a kindly old man who had passed on only a month earlier. However, I was enjoying the wild, hellish butt-fuck too much to worry about a damned preacher. Flaming spunk shot out of my cock in a thick stream, accompanied by ripples of pleasure, but the greatest pleasure blasted in inexhaustible waves up my ass. I'd never known the human rectum could produce such rapture. Echoing vibrations of pure ecstasy shook me even as the Angel of the Bottomless Pit shuddered beneath my gliding butt.

"Here I come, Garrett," Lucifer announced. "I'm going to fill your lady-hole and paint your guts with my evil spunk."

It was like receiving a thick sludge enema. When Lord Lucifer shot his load, his cock was high inside of me, and he unloaded gallons of his stygian cum into my bowels. My abdomen swelled as the thick stuff rolled up my intestines, filling me utterly with the hot crude substance. Again, I broke out in a hellish sweat as my internal temperature rose dramatically.

"High, hot, and a hell of a lot," Grandma yowled.

I was shooting fire out my dick while Lucifer was coming inside of me, and the waves of heavy orgasm intensified. The throbbing reverberations mingled with the pleasure of the ever-growing fullness. I tasted semen in my mouth just before flames shot from between my lips and out my nose.

Finally, Lucifer's cock stopped jerking within me, and I fell forward upon his mighty chest, wet with the aphrodisiacal goop leaking from his nipples.

"That was a wonderful butt fuck," I said, the fire from my mouth blasting his brilliant face. The entire side of my body seemed all in a flame since Satan had been jacking off and coming on me constantly while I rode Lucifer's cock. The flames warmed me pleasantly.

"Now you must receive my kiss," Lucifer promised.

"Yes. Kiss me."

Lucifer brought his mouth to mine, my lips burning as they met his, and his hot tongue entered my mouth. While he was kissing me, he lifted my ass off his cock and gallons of molten cum blasted out my asshole, the great blue and red flames in which we basked causing the crowd to go wild with taunting cheers.

"Watch the anal slut fart burning cum," Grandpa shouted, and the old dead preacher howled, "The little fruit will never tighten his asshole after that reaming."

They were right, and even as I kissed Lucifer, opening my mouth to his flames and sucking his hard raspy tongue, I raised my butt to show the crowd that my asshole was dilated wide open, and there was no way I could close it and stop the outpour.

Lucifer pulled his mouth away from mine. "Do you submit to me?" he asked.

"I submit to you, Lord Lucifer, body and soul, as I have already submitted to Satan. Fuck my ass. Fuck my mouth. Come in me. Come on me."

"Are you prepared to receive the Mark of the Anal Whore?" Gresil demanded.

"The Mark of the Anal Whore? Wow!" The Mark of the Anal Whore sounded a bit scary. There'd be no retreating from that mark – not that I wanted to retreat. I was loving every perverted second of my death.

"The Mark of the Anal Whore," the crowd chanted, masturbating as one. "Receive the Mark of the Anal Whore. The Mark of the Anal Whore. The Mark of the Anal Whore. The Mark of the Anal Whore."

"Is Mark of the Anal Whore the same as that 666 Mark of the Beast deal Reverend Creevey used to warn us about in church?" I asked.

"Not that old bullshit," Reverend Creevey shouted, waving his burning cum stained hands. "Satan's mark is better. Wish I had one."

Gresil smirked and answered nothing, and I found my eyes drawn to Satan's big cock, which he had begun masturbating again. The Father of Lies nodded in assent, so I placed my hand on his thick cock. A thrill such as I had never felt shot through me. His cock had given me so much pleasure. His cock had opened my lady hole, and already, I wanted it back up my ass.

"I'll take anything you want to give me, Satan. I'll take the Mark."

"Turn your ass toward me, Garrett," the Tempter commanded. "Prepare to receive the Mark of the Anal Whore."

Gresil spit into his hand and jerked off while intoning from an unholy tome. The invocation drove home that I was granting my ass unto perpetuity to the Prince of the Powers of the Air, and that my body and soul were his to corrupt, defile, pervert, and molest.

The crowd held its collective breath as Satan planted his lips on my left buttock. His tongue licked my butt cheek. The terrific burning made me shriek with surprise. It was not a pain; it was more like a sensation that gave release. I trembled as my dick spewed long strands of hot cum that arced across the cavern. The searing orgasm shot through my entire body and my soul shuddered with liberation. My mouth filled with cum. Semen ejaculated from my nostrils, poured out of my ears, and leaked from my eyes. I was a slave of Hell, yet I felt a freedom such as I had never known. Whatever vestiges of guilt, shame, or inhibition I had carried were gone. The Thou Shalt Nots were burned away. I was enslaved to service any damned being's homosexual lust, and through my sexual bondage, I was free. I had no choices, no decisions, no responsibilities, and no consequences. I was a fuck hole for the Wicked One, and I reveled in my slavish whoredom.

"Would you like to see what I have done to you?" Satan asked.

"Yes, master," I said.

"That's right," Satan gloated. "I am your master. Your owner. But I shall not keep you long." He summoned his attendants.

"No? But I want to belong to you. I'm yours."

"You are mine to keep or to give away, Garrett. I have promised your ass to Beelzebub. Now see your Mark."

As Satan spoke, his attendants raised polished glasses. I could see the reflection of my burning ass, which looked much rounder and more protrusive than before. My ass was better than Sarah's, whose butt had been a guy magnet. My ass would attract millions of hard cocks. Much as I admired the shape of my ass, the figure upon my left buttock caught my eyes. I had been printed with a detailed tattoo of an imp offering his rounded butt to any who would fuck him. As I looked upon my Mark, a design that would remain upon my ass for infinite time, I knew that I was a Boy Toy.

As I studied my Mark, I heard a great commotion of slapping and flapping. I beheld a tremendous being approaching. The new arrival was twenty feet long with numerous dripping appendages. More than a hundred cocks protruded from his body, some jutting from long tentacles that whipped to and fro, splattering hot spunk in all directions.

"Behold Leviathan, Cumbutt," Gresil commanded. "The Evil Genius. The Ogling Ogre. The Old Serpent. You will now submit to his rapine penetration. He will invade your body, Slutty Boy, and make you a receptacle for the Spunk of the Nether Regions."

"Yes," I agreed, stroking Satan's cock. "Take me, Lord Leviathan. Use me as you will."

"Lie on your back and pull your legs up," Gresil advised. "The Old Serpent likes to take his boys face to face, that they may be acquainted with the horror visited upon them."

I hurried to comply, grateful that Leviathan would consider my rectum a worthy receptacle. My dick was hard and shooting extravagant spurts as the gigantic being plopped its front end between my legs. A tremendous weight descended upon me. I saw one of his majestic cocks descending toward my asshole, and I grinned as he slammed three spurting tubes into my chute.

"Yeah, fuck my hole," I gasped. "Fuck my slutty ass."

Leviathan impaled me deeply. My abdomen hardened as the projecting tubers from his cocks filled my intestines. His hundreds of other cocks were leaking all over me. Within seconds, I was covered head to toe in a mass of wriggling slime that burned pleasurably through my skin. His cock thrusting in my ass was opening me wide again and again, meat and motion meeting meat and motion.

"Ah, you're fucking me so good," I howled. "Oh, yeah, fuck me every which way. Satan, Lucifer, watch how the Ogling Ogre fucks me. Leviathan is giving it to me good."

"Yes, you're taking it, all right," Satan snickered as his fellow Devil fucked me. "Leviathan is fucking the shit out of you, and you're taking it like a butt tramp."

The gigantic tentacles felt so wonderful that I wanted this devilish gang bang to last forever. Leviathan slammed me so hard and fast that I could hardly believe it. It felt like I was going to get slammed right off the table because his fucking cocks were like jackhammers going up my ass. The Old Serpent was setting off rockets inside of me; explosive orgasms filled me, and I wanted my guts to rip open.

"Yeah, fuck my tight ass, Lord Leviathan. Fuck it. I'm your fuckin' faggot whore. Fuck my ass. Fuck my ass."

Even through the hot cum in my eyes, I could see the crowd had leaped its collective feet, butt plugs popping in all directions. Jizz imps were fucking every hole, and the holes they missed were getting penetrated by the flying phalluses. Grandma and the other women straddled a tentacled monster, while Grandpa and the preacher had joined the men's jerk. Every man was capable of shooting oceans of cum, and the atmosphere was filled with flying jism. Grandpa knelt before the jacking preacher and took a facial. Grandpa opened his mouth wide as Reverend Creevey fed him cum, blasting load after load over his face, into his eyes, up his nostrils, onto his tongue, and down his throat.

I was starving for the taste of cum. "Fuck my mouth," I begged. "Leviathan, let me suck some of your cocks."

That Lord of Hell was taking pleasure in my ass with multiple cocks, but his other spouting tentacles explored my face. When I opened my mouth for a thick one, I tasted his dick custard. The cum in my mouth increased my erotic frenzy a thousand fold. I would have fucked and sucked every man on Earth, all those who had ever lived, and every spawn of Hell walking, flying, flapping, crawling, slithering, or creeping.

I couldn't tell when my own orgasms stopped and started; my cock, nipples, tongue, lips, and asshole were paradoxically pulsing and constant, subtle and unbearable, pleasure and pain, rapture and rupture. Orgasmic rushes commenced in my willing asshole and rose to my mouth, while my tortured cock thrust and burned as it pumped out cum as if it were a hose.

"Oh, I'm coming so heavy," Satan groaned, his hand pumping rapidly. Like the Devil-worshiping crowd, he and Lucifer were beating their meat. Hordes of bugaboo were jerking off and tossing tremendous sprays of semen over the assembled demonolaters. Imps were fucking imps or jacking off sprites or pixies. Gresil was sucking an ibis-headed gremlin's dick, while a boogyman licked the gremlin's ass.

More tentacles pushed into my mouth. Soon my face was so covered with writhing tendrils that I could no longer see what was happening. I didn't even care, so enraptured was I. I was showing three billion lost souls how I, too, could be a cum-sponge. I loved it and rejoiced in the waves of pleasure, the jolts of ecstasy, the thrusts of shooting cocks, and the inflowing gallons of cum. The cocks in my mouth were making my lips and gums orgasm; my tongue thrilled as it wrapped each cock in my mouth. Cum was shooting down my throat faster than I could swallow, and I realized that I was going to drown in it. Unable to stop my lungs, I accepted my fate. I drew a mighty breath and my lungs filled with cum. Since I was already dead, the thick fluid expanding my lungs gave me only further pleasure. I had surrendered my body to debauchery inconceivable to mere mortals and found it delightful. By some miracle, I shot gallons out of my own cock. I was already thick with Leviathan's slime cum as I painted my chest and face with my own cum.

After Leviathan had stuffed my body with his hellish semen, I felt his monstrous pricks being pulled out of my orifices. I rolled onto my stomach and tried to clench my asshole tight. I'd been baptized internally with the jism of Hell, and I vowed never to let it go. However, the flames were burning all over me, flames that burned me with intense pleasure, and every release of cum from my ass or mouth resulted in a jet of fire that was equivalent to ten thousand orgasms.

The crowd was wildly cheering. My grandfather's voice came clear atop the chants and jeers, "I always knew the little fucker would ride the A-train. He was a pansy kid, and now he's Old Poker's whore."

Satan climbed into his litter, and his bearers carried him away. Lucifer mounted his steed, and Leviathan slithered into the distance. Gresil motioned to a group of imps who'd been playing butt-fuck leapfrog. "Convey this damned slut to Beelzebub."

The imps assisted me in climbing down from the table and led me across the Infernal Regions. The ground was made of sulfur and brimstone. My bare feet sizzled pleasantly like bacon on a hot griddle. Along our route, legions of damned souls were playing with sparking butt plugs. Those who could masturbate were handling themselves compulsively and exhibiting their skills to all. We crossed a rocky bridge over Acheron, the River of Woe. Trees like willows hung over its banks, yet the trees bore bark like skin, and they wept tears of semen. As the imps led me, they chattered in some obscure language, and giggled with delight as the fuck flames ripped from my mouth and asshole.

The imps had constant hard-ons, and I offered to suck them off and let them fuck me, but they only laughed and played with their pricks as we walked. I had no interest in playing with my own dick. I would no longer find pleasure with my dick except when I was receiving the cock of another. However, that pleasure was so intense that I wanted nothing more and would not have gone back to my old living self if they made me president.

After crossing two more rivers, Cocytus and Phlegethon, we arrived at the verge of a precipice. I looked over the edge and knew this must be the fabled pit. Robert Burns had deemed it "a vast, unbottom'd, boundless pit." It was a nasty drop. The side of the cliff was jagged, dark, and rocky. I tried to see if anything was visible below, but it looked like a long terrible descent into the dark.

"Careful, boys," I warned the imps, motioning them back. "We don't want to fall over that edge."

Were the little bastards grateful? Hell no. Two grabbed my legs and tripped me while the others pushed me forward. My hands flailed, but gravity won that round.

"Goodbye, Fuck Toy," they called – or so I interpreted their gibbering language – as I fell screaming into that dreadful well.

177

After a while, the shrieks died in my throat, and I concentrated on stopping my body from pinwheeling. I breathed out a blast of flame from the semen in my lungs. I was burping and farting fire, and the sensation reminded me that the fall couldn't kill me. I was dead already. Strangely, I still felt as if a thick cock was jamming my ass. My asshole was contracting and expanding pleasurably. The cum that Satan, Lucifer, and Leviathan had poured into me was still bubbling hot inside my bowels.

"I wanna to get gang banged," I cried out, as a series of intense orgasms overwhelmed me. "I wanna get my whorish ass fucked. I want to get my cocksucking mouth fucked."

Waves of surging pleasure ran through my being as I fell. My body jerked, my skin drew tight, and my cock hardened dangerously. Without my touching it, my cock began to throb and buck. Flaming jism shot out of my blazing pisshole. My asshole puckered and dilated around invisible cocks even as the fire cum ripped from it. My mouth puckered as well as if I were trying to suck an unseen cock. And still I fell, dropping like a rock through the stygian darkness, not knowing how long I had been falling or how far I had yet to fall.

After years of falling in perpetual sexual contractions and spouting, I saw a pale glow beneath me. Writhing in orgasm, I was coming toward the bottom. "Beelzebub," I shouted by way of announcement. "Here am I, gift of Satan. I am your new Boy Toy."

I tried to see what I was falling into, but such were my sexual contractions, not to mention my flaming semen spattering in every direction, that I could still make out only a dim pale bubbling. Then I caught a whiff of semen stronger than I had smelled before. Just before I reached the surface, I knew the truth. I was falling into the much-touted Lake of Fire. Except it wasn't fire in the sense of sulfur and brimstone. It was a vast lake of boiling, bubbling, burning, flaming cum. For me, "the fire that never shall be quenched" turned out to be a passive homosexual hunger, a flaming lust that fucking and sucking could only fan.

Just before I splashed down, I saw the werefolk surrounding the edge of the lake. They stood about five feet tall, had heavy pelts of fur, and dog-like heads. Each werefellow was contributing his jism into the burning lake: They were enjoying the biggest circle jerk I'd ever imagined.

As I hit the lake, the molten semen striking my body was like an orgasm on every point of my skin. Such was my shock and sexual transport that I sucked in the burning spunk. It filled my nostrils, my ears, my mouth, and my ass. My lungs were aflame with liquid orgasm. The cum had filled me and was continuing to flow through me as if I were a hollow tube – which is the truth of the human body. Cum flowed into my mouth and out my ass. After a long time, I floated to the surface, still writhing in mindless sexual rapture beyond control.

From somewhere I heard a voice. "Well, fuck my gay ass with a telephone pole, this looks like a cheap little cock squeeze."

"Yeah, by my cum-hole mouth, this is the package. He has the Mark of the Anal Whore." I felt something pull my sticky body, soft hands grabbed my buttocks, and I was dragged into a little boat.

As my vision cleared, I saw that I had been pulled from the lake by two beautiful guys, promiscuously naked and enchantingly queer. They were physically delectable, and they expressed the most amiable vocabulary I'd ever heard. Every other word was punctuated with "fuck my ass" or "come in my mouth" or "I lick your asshole."

"What are you?" I asked. "Hobgoblins? Devilkins? Bad Peri?"

They snickered, turned, bent, and pointed toward their asses. These exquisite souls bore the Mark of the Anal Whore.

"Fuck our gay asses, we're Beelzebub's Boy Toys."

"Well fuck my gay ass," I echoed. "Take me to our owner."

The guys turned out to be Sodomites, residents of the middle-eastern town fire bombed by the terrorist Lot and his two harpy daughters. One boy introduced himself as Moab and the other as Ammon.

"How about you guys take me from both ends," I suggested. "I'm ready for a fuck."

"Fuck my mouth, we can't fuck you," Ammon replied with a laugh, "any more than you can shove your cock into our faggot asses. We can't fuck. We can't jerk off. We can only take it. Once you receive the Mark, that's all you're good for."

Ammon and Moab rowed me to a far shore, entertaining me along the way with a different version of the *Book of Genesis* than is preached in any church.

"You're claiming that David and Jonathan were banging each other?"

"Fuck my mouth, you should have seen those boys go at it. And King Saul blamed their behavior on his own wife. Saul said that Jonathan inherited his perversions from his mother."

After we beached the boat, we walked over oozing, hot mud until we reached a temple. They led me inside and pointed toward a golden steaming rock in the center.

"Kneel at the altar, Garrett," Moab directed.

I hastened to comply and dropped to my knees before the burning stone. I quivered with wild orgasms as the scent of the hot stone reached my dead nostrils.

"Encircle the altar with your arms."

I followed the instructions. Then I waited. Just when I was beginning to wonder if anyone was going to bang my ass, I felt a powerful presence behind me.

Moab commanded, "Stick out your butt. Invite your master, Beelzebub, to fuck your ass."

When I did so, I felt a massive cock bear down on my hole. I pressed back as far as I could, trying to impale my ass upon the huge dingus. "Fuck me," I shrieked. "Fuck me. I'm an anal whore. I need to get fucked."

Slowly the gigantic cock opened my back door and slid into my anal chute. It was huge, but my ass readily accepted it. When my asshole was stretched to its limit, I felt the rod of joy invade me deeper.

"That's the way," I yelled. "I'm your cum hole. Use my ass as you will. I'll suck your cock, and you can shoot your load up my ass."

I could only assume that Lord Beelzebub was fucking my ass, for he spoke not a word until he had anointed my bowels. His thick cock slid out to my asshole, then drove into me again. I wiggled my ass and squeezed his cock as he pulled back. I guessed that the tissues of my anus and rectum had turned wholly orgasmic. With each thrust, explosives waves of rapture rolled up my ass, ravishing me, bewitching me, and pleasing me with tickles beyond expression.

"Oh, oh, oh," I moaned insanely. "I can't stand it, it's so good. Oh, yes, pull it out deeper. Oh, how can you, o' feast, o' euphoria, o' goody." My mind lost all coherent thought as the storms of beatification rumbled up my pleasure-loving ass. "Boy! Wow! Goody! Hot shorts! Mmmm! Spank me!"

Still he fucked me and fucked me. His thick cock pleasured my ass, but my greatest pleasure remained in giving him pleasure and milking him of his tartarean jism. He was coming as he fucked, riding orgasm after orgasm as he fucked, filling me deeper and deeper as he fucked. A searing heat suffused my body, a stygian, infernal, sulfurous, hellish heat.

I tasted rich, thick, hot cum in my mouth, which erupted as a searing torch from between my lips. My master had filled me all the way; his cum packed my bodily tube. Greater and greater paroxysms overwhelmed me. It was a damned good thing I was already dead, or that fire fuck surely would have killed me. My lungs had filled again, and the pressure in my chest stilled my heart, though a beating heart is not a necessary organ in Hell. I was full of boiling cum, more than full even, and even more than that, I knew that I was cum. My father's cum had made my Earthly form, and now the cum shot by the Lords of Damnation had made my Hellborn flesh.

The thick cock pulled out of my ass. The blowtorch blasting from my mouth was nothing to the jet that blew out of my ass. Oh, Plutonian Powers, the pleasure that ripped me as those torches blew! Another torch was shooting out of the head of my swollen cock since my own cum had been magically transformed into the Hell spunk.

I do not know how long I crouched, humped in flame and shaking ecstasy. I do remember Moab and Ammon assisting me to my feet. They ran their hands through the fire streaming from my asshole and giggled at the pleasing sensation. Then they turned me so that I might view my master, and I beheld Beelzebub, the Lord of the Flies.

He was magnificent and beautiful beyond description. He was desire in the flesh. He was the incarnation of my lust. I merely fell to my knees before him. "I am your Boy-Toy, Great Beelzebub, my Lord, my Master, my Seal of Devotion."

Beelzebub kept me for a thousand years. His lusts were insatiable, and so we Boy Toys were kept happily busy satisfying him. Sometimes I would perform other tasks. When a new anal whore would be tossed into the Lake of Fire, we'd row out to retrieve him. After time out of mind, the day came for me to fulfill my military obligation. Beelzebub bid me a fond farewell with a series of ferocious oral and anal fucks that left me staggering. Then two laughing soldiers wearing the traditional kilt of the troops led me down a long corridor toward a green door.

The door opened into a small but tastefully furnished room. A beautiful demon was sitting behind a massive oak desk. His name plaque read "Dagon of the Philistines." Dagon was writing with a quill on prehistoric parchment. He was wearing an elegant business suit that must've cost a few thousand. I took note of it since it was the first suit of clothes I'd seen since my arrival in Hell. Dagon had the skin coloration of a resident of India, and his head was covered with an impressive mane of long white hair. After keeping me waiting for a long time, he finished writing and looked up.

"I was finishing your military induction papers, Garrett."

"I take it up the ass," I contributed. "I also lick ass and suck cocks."

"I am aware of those accomplishments," he commented dryly. "You'll do it all. You're going to be a fuck toy, a suck toy, and a lick toy."

My military career sounded so good that I shuddered with an abrupt orgasm.

"Would you like me to suck your cock now?" I asked.

"It is required of you before entering military service. Every soldier must blow the recruiter – just as they do on Earth." I wasn't convinced that he had his facts straight, but when Dagon stripped off his elegant suit and threw his brown body down on a couch, I lost interest in the argument. "Lick me, Garrett," he commanded.

I slipped to my knees and touched my tongue to his stomach. Following Dagon's explicit instructions, I tongue-bathed his body, licked his ass, and kissed his dick, not missing the tiniest patch of skin. My ass wriggled with anal orgasms as I licked. When Dagon rolled over and I started licking into his butt crack, I shot copious loads. I probed deep into his crack with my tongue, licking over the curved buttocks, warm and salty loaves they were, and working from the top of his crack, down deeper and deeper until I reached his brown hole.

Philistine Dagon's asshole was dark and puckered, but when I touched my tongue to it, my senses exploded into raptures. The taste was of salt and malt liquor, wild mushrooms and corn stalk, anise and burgundy wine. Suddenly, I wanted to be licking his asshole, and I aggressively slurped away, ran my tongue around it in hundreds of tiny circles, and making a long close dwindling spiral toward this essential opening in his once-heavenly body, plunged my tongue inside. After hours of worshiping his asshole with my lips and tongue, I turned him and he freely offered me his thick cock.

"On the Burning Plain, you and thousands of other Camp Whores will be taking the cocks of the 666 legions any way they want you," Dagon read from my job description as I sucked him off.

When I touched my lips to his dickhead, he shuddered beneath my mouth. I let his cock in. His thick, and strangely circumcised dick, penetrated the doors of my mouth, and my lips kissed it like a vagrant breeze as it entered. Then his dark cock head touched my tongue, and I attacked it vigorously. I licked around the head, softly at first, but with growing intensity. Finally, I lapped it with an insane fury, followed by a momentary pause. I pulled my head back and let the insides of my lips hit Dagon's dickhead hard.

"Oh. Ah," Dagon cried. "Oh, you're a great little cocksucker, Garrett." Dagon lasted only a few minutes before he pumped gallons into my throat, and I swallowed his hellish spunk.

When I was filled and Dagon was satisfied with my training, he ordered the soldiers to convey me to the front lines. My conscription papers read as follows: GARRETT SHALL PLEASURE THE BOYS IN UNIFORM FOR ONE EON OR UNTIL THEY HAVE WON THE WAR, WHICHEVER COMES FIRST. No one informed me what would happen after our side won.

# # # # #

"Hot shit," Lyle said. "That's a hell of a story, Garrett."

"Yeah, did you try gay sex while you were alive?"

"About a million times. I had a long and happy life. Lots of lovers and friends. I died at home in bed at age 87."

"Why'd you end up here?"

"Those assholes in the other place didn't want me."

Lyle watched a dozen horny kobold cooks grab another new fuck toy, throw him on his back, push his legs up to his head, and gang bang his ass a hundred times. Lyle and I exchanged knowing grins while we watched the guy come time and again while the kobolds fucked him.

Another guy was sucking ogre cocks. Three hundred monstrous troopers lined up in front of him. "The lucky cocksucker," I said.

Lyle quivered with sexual excitement. "From what I saw of it, the other place looked pretty restrictive. I like it better here." He tapped my flaming dick and pointed. "Look at the way they're fucking that guy."

I nodded. "They're giving it to him good. My turn will be up next."

Lyle farted a gigantic plume of flaming cum and sighed happily, "This is the life."

THE LUCKY HEART VALENTINE POTION

Following my regular Tuesday morning routine at the Portland Men's Athletic Club, I finished running on the treadmill, competed a series of upper body exertions, and headed past a group of chesty men pumping iron. I smiled shyly at Mr. Willow, who works at the bank. Mr. Willow gave me a twisted smirk, the result of the weights he was lowering, and said, "How're you doing, Ellery?"

"Just fine," I said. I was hoping he would say something else, but he continued pushing against the resistance of his weights. Though Mr. Willow must have been in his late thirties, I was attracted to the man, always trying for his teller window when I made my monthly deposit of the check my parents sent. About once a week, I fantasized about blowing him. I imagined dropping to my knees, kissing his manly cock, licking his hairy balls, and sucking until his cock slid into my throat.

Naturally, I entertained this fantasy while masturbating alone in my room. I would twist and turn on my bed, my lubricated hand stroking my cock, pounding my shaft, playing with my dickhead, and squeezing my balls, while I imagined Mr. Willow feeding me his cock. While I jerked off, I would make sucking motions with my mouth, pretending that I was really sucking the bank teller's dork.

"Oh, Ellery," Mr. Willow would moan in my fancy, his hands gripping my thick brown hair. "Oh, yeah, Ellery, you're the best cocksucker in town. Oh, fuck, you give great head. I love the way you suck my cock, Ellery. Oh, I've never had it so good. Oh, here I come, Ellery."

Usually I would be near orgasm by the time I reached that part of the fantasy, my hand wildly flogging my dickhead on the musty bed in my tiny downtown apartment just three blocks from the university.

"I'm coming in your mouth, Ellery," Mr. Willow would howl, as my own cock pushed toward the edge of ejaculation. "I'm ejaculating, Ellery. Swallow it, boy. You wonderful cocksucker, swallow my cum." Then I would be coming, adding to the texture of my already semen-stained sheets, sometimes sprawled on my back, so my cum splattered upon my stomach leaving spots and long strands of glistening jism.

Of course, this masturbatory daydream had no foundation in reality, and Mr. Willow always treated me like any other bank depositor. Still I hoped that he was watching my ass sway with lingering invitation as I sauntered toward the locker room.

Almost floating among the heady man-scents in the humid atmosphere, I stripped off my sneakers, my sopping tee shirt, my stripped shorts, and my thong underwear. I smiled at one man as I strolled naked to the shower, but he averted his eyes. Under the spray, I soaped my butt crack and washed the sweat out of my hair, before toweling off on the rubber mats. Standing naked in front of my locker, I supposed that Mr. Willow would never fulfill my fantasies about him. In fact, I questioned whether I would ever find a man to love and care for me. My love life looked so bleak that I doubted I could even find dick in a bathhouse during a power outage.

Guy Pine was pulling up a pair of baggy swimming trunks at a locker near to mine. I checked out his cute ass before the shapeless cloth covered it. Guy was about my age, early twenties, and he worked for a travel agency. Guy was ultra-straight, but he was friendly, so I said, "Hi, Guy."

Guy was another of my masturbation fantasies, though I fantasized more about Guy's brother Dude. I lusted after both Pine brothers, but I had the heavier crush on Dude. Nevertheless, I jerked off to Guy Pine's mental image at least twice a week, often while sitting on a toilet in the men's room on the fifth floor of the college library. Usually my cock would harden before I had the stall door shut. I would pull down my pants and underwear, spit into my hand, think about Guy Pine, and stroke my cock.

In my fantasy, Guy loved fucking my ass. Coming up with more spit, I would lubricate a finger and slide it into my asshole while my right hand was pumping. Then I could pretend I was sitting on Guy's cock and bouncing up and down. Guy could not long contain himself when I sat on his dick. I would squeeze his cock with my asshole, forcing him to orgasm, relentlessly preparing to drain his cum. "Oh, Ellery," he would moan behind my eyelids while I beat my meat. "Oh, Ellery, your ass is so good. Ah, Ellery, you're gonna make me come, aren't you? You're not gonna give me a break. You're gonna make me do it up your ass."

"I'm going to take every drop you've got, Guy," I would boast. "Your balls are going to get pumped dry. You're going to pour all your spunk into my ass, and I'm going to hold onto it. My body is going to absorb your cum, Guy. You're going to be a part of me."

In the college bathroom, I would catch my load in some toilet paper. After cleaning up, I would proceed normally to class, wishing the fantasy were real, wishing I was carrying Guy's semen inside of me.

Unaware that he was one of my fantasy lovers, Guy turned from his gunmetal gray locker and looked me over. I was still standing naked in front of my locker, and his eyes slithered down my body. I liked the way that he gaped at my dick, but he shifted his gaze as if he were afraid of getting caught peeping. Still, he said, "Oh, hi, Ellery. You gonna swim today?"

I nodded and reached into my locker for my multicolored swim briefs. I pulled the nylon/spandex garment up my legs and over the curve of my buttocks, tucking my package into the thin liner.

"I thought I'd do a few laps," I answered. Then, hesitantly, trying to sound offhand, I inquired, "Is your brother around?"

Guy wasn't fooled. "You've got it bad for Dude, don't you?" He laughed, and then apologized. "Sorry. I wasn't laughing at you, Ellery. I know you can't help being gay. But the idea of you having a crush on Dude! I mean, my brother is the straightest man on Earth."

You can't help being gay – like my sexuality was a condition I would want to escape. Guy had no idea he had uttered a derogatory comment. If anybody had asked him, he would have sworn that he didn't have a homophobic bone in his body, yet if I grabbed his ears and kissed his lips hard, giving him some tongue, he would run or faint. Of course, I did nothing of the sort. Guy clapped me on the shoulder like were buddies – straight buddies, of course. My face burning, I went to the mirror and checked my appearance. Reflected back was the image of a well-built young guy in a sexy swimsuit that matched his complexion and offset his brown hair. I turned and examined my rear, marveling at how perfectly this swimsuit fit my form. I unquestionably looked good enough to fuck, so why was I running into so much resistance?

The Olympic-sized swimming pool was in the basement of the Portland Men's Athletic Club. Members reached the pool thorough the locker room and down a long flight of wide tiled stairs. The pool itself was old and tiled in sea green that gave the water a shimmering appearance. Blue-green tiles also covered the floor around the pool and the walls that rose to the high ceiling. The water was always inviting due to the underwater lights that illuminated the bodies of the men swimming laps, practicing dives, or engaging in aquatic sports.

I dived into an empty lane and swam twenty laps. I was pulling myself out of the water when I saw the one who made my blood run hot. Dude Pine had arrived prepared to join a water polo game with his brother. Unlike Guy who draped his body in baggy swimwear, Dude was sporting turquoise water polo briefs, and the sight of him made the front of my swimsuit tighten. I saw Guy nudge Dude and point at me. Both brothers snickered.

In all of my masturbation fantasies, I was the bottom, never the top. Yet whenever I jacked off to Dude, which was all the time, far more often than I fantasized about his brother or Mr. Willow, I sometimes entertained fleeting thoughts of him taking my cock into his throat, or me slipping it up his curvy ass. I could not help but imagine that Dude would make a great homosexual if he would only try.

Of course, I could not imagine any pleasurable form of sex in which I was not receiving a cock, preferably anally, so if I envisioned Dude taking my cock, it had to be during an orgy or a three-way. Masturbating alone at home, I would picture Dude on his hands and knees, my cock stuck up his ass, while another guy, sometimes Guy, sometimes Mr. Willow, would be humping me. The sensation of the big cock sliding in and out, opening my asshole wider and wider, making me take it fast and hard drove my fist furiously. I would wring the head of my cock, imagining my cock inside of Dude sometimes, though mostly I visualized his rod fucking my mouth or my ass until he unloaded with shouts of pleasure.

"Ah, Ellery, I'm coming so heavy," Dude would gasp, and I would take it, though in reality I was only whacking off alone. So when I saw the brothers looking my way, I made up my mind to approach Dude. Maybe I could get him to go to a movie with me or something. Better to try than float tits up in the pool waiting for him to come to me. I hurried their way, aware of my mincing prance and certain I looked fruitier than usual. Self-conscious but resolute, I sashayed up to Dude and greeted him.

"Hi, Ellery," he said. Whatever jokes they made between themselves, the Pine brothers never mocked me to my face.

Feeling like a bitch in heat but unable to stop myself, I leaned toward Dude and said, "That swimsuit looks good on you, Dude."

While Dude Pine looked slightly discomfited by my compliment, his brother Guy smirked horribly. Glancing around, we observed that of the three dozen men in or around the pool, only one other was sporting a bikini. He was over fifty, and that tropical print bikini probably had looked good on him twenty years ago, but at least he didn't look like he'd bought his swimwear at the Portland Tent and Awning Company, which was the way most men dressed for swimming.

"You've got the right idea, Dude," I said. "The club ought to ban those bulky suits. I mean, what do these guys think they're hiding?" Just then, Mr. Willow descended the stairs to the pool. He was wearing a baggy tan garment that reached below his kneecaps. "Isn't that just pathetic?" I said.

"Er, well, I wear this suit because I was a member of my high school's water polo team," Dude said. "I never got around to buying what everyone is wearing now."

"Don't switch. Those swim briefs show off your assets," I advised, going too far as usual. "You wouldn't want to hide your ass in a sack."

Dude blanched, and his brother nudged him. Dude drew a deep breath. "Look, Ellery," he said. "I don't want to hurt your feelings, but Guy says you've got a crush on me."

My heart thundered into my mouth, and my blood ran cold. Seeing my distress, Dude continued hurriedly. "It's just that I'm straight, Ellery. You really need to concentrate your attention on some guy who would appreciate you."

I felt like Dude had kicked me in the stomach. That he was trying to be nice about it hurt even more. I just wanted to be with him. I only wanted to be his friend. I only wanted him to love me. Sure, something truthful down deep inside of me whispered. *You just want to jack off with him. You just want to suck his dick. You just want him to stick his cock up your ass. You just want him to make you come any way he can.*

Of course, I voiced none of those thoughts as a series of painful and conflicting emotions coursed through me. Seeing that I was wounded, the Pine brothers tried to salve my feelings. They were nice guys in spite of being stuck in the clammy web of sexual orthodoxy.

"We're getting up a game of water polo, Ellery," Guy said. "Want to be on our team?"

Mr. Willow overheard the invitation. "Wait a minute, Guy," he said. "I'm on your team, too. I have to think about my position at the bank, and even more important, my church."

I stared at Mr. Willow with disbelief. His semen could back up to his ears before I involved him in another masturbation fantasy. Dude looked sour, and Guy's face flushed dark red. "I just invited Ellery," Dude said stubbornly. "I'm not going to disinvite him."

I was grateful to the Pine brothers, but the situation was too gruesome. I said, "I can't play anyway. I have a history class that meets in an hour."

Never in my life had I felt bad about being gay. I had always viewed my attraction to the same sex as a stroke of good fortune. Of course, I had also been lucky in having parents who supported my inclinations. I remember overhearing my parents talking about me; I must have been between eight and nine.

Dad and Mom were lounging in the backyard, drinking beer, and listening to the grapes growing. Hiding behind the grape arbor, I could hear them whispering.

"Too bad kids don't come with instruction books. How do you raise a child you think might be gay?"

"Just love him and let him follow his own path," Mom said.

"We'll have to be careful about making assumptions. You and I were brought up by parents who assumed we were straight. We have to write our own rule book."

"Assumptions, hell," Mom said. "Ellery is obviously gay."

"That is an assumption," Dad said. "Not that I doubt it. Of course, I accept that he's gay. Ellery is a gift, and we have to raise him in a way that makes us worthy of him. I want him to be happy. I want him to accept his sexuality as right and natural, and I want him to be healthy. You and I may approve of love in all its forms, but we both know that homosexuals face greater risks. We have to teach him how to protect himself."

"How will he protect himself from love?" Mom asked.

I dressed quickly. I had lied about having a class that afternoon. I only wanted to flee. A funny feeling gripped my stomach, a hard emptiness. I had a hunger that food could not satisfy, but I decided that a little food would not hurt. Besides, it was cold outside, and the wind was whipping through the streets. The sky was like slate, and the gusts blew road grime onto my freshly washed skin. It was a typical day for February thirteenth.

The pizza parlor looked inviting. I stepped inside and ordered a slice with everything thrown onto it and a glass of ale. I opened my wallet and extracted my last twenty. Just as I was handing it to the hot-looking guy behind the counter, somebody opened the door and the wind whipped the bill from my hand. I saw my twenty-dollar bill whisk right out the door and swirl down the street.

Like a flash, I was after it. It landed not two feet from a couple of teenage panhandlers. Just as the dope-befuddled girl reached out her hand, the wind caught my money again and lifted it over the heads of several walkers. I raced between them in time to see a crosscurrent of wind carry my money down a narrow avenue.

The avenue was one of the strangest in Portland. There was an off-track betting establishment on the corner, right next door to the Church of Elvis. Across the way was an art gallery whose artist specialized in various shades of black on canvas. Next-door was the world headquarters of the Society to Legalize Heroin. I was racing past the UFO Abductees Community Center when my twenty-dollar bill stopped mysteriously. For a moment, it hung in the air in front of a voodoo shop; the next instant it was in the hand of an old black man who had emerged from that very shop.

Looking closer, I observed that he was a compact man, superficially elderly in appearance, the color of burnished mahogany, and attired in a black suit. Strangely, his suit appeared to glisten, set off by a gleaming green hat, a shimmering green shirt, and sparkling green shoes. As I looked into his face, his eyes glinted with a green light. "Follow me, *cherie*," said he.

Following him into the Lucky Magic Voodoo Shop, I stared about me in bewilderment. The shop offered scented candles, painted flags, beaded bottles, and embroidered pillows. Painted scenes illustrated myths from the voodoo pantheon while strange roots hung from strings over the counter.

"I know what you seek," said the man with the green eyes, and I had the impression that he wasn't talking about my twenty.

"Who are you?" I asked.

"I am called Louverture Antoine," said he.

"What is this place?"

"The key to your heart's desire," he said. "You want a man to love you, and here you will find that which you seek." He rested his hand on my shoulder, and though it never moved from there, I felt it glide down my body, tweaking my nipples, caressing my buttocks, and stroking my dick.

"How?" I asked, though the word came as a sigh of infinite longing.

"Through the eternal *loa*," said Louverture Antoine. "The love of a man for a man is pleasing to *La Sirene*. She will grant your heart's desire – in return for this twenty-dollar bill."

"Who is she?" I asked, captivated, bewitched, enthralled.

"*La Sirene*," Louverture Antoine said. "She is a *loa*, a *Voudoun* deity. She appears in many forms: a fish-tailed siren of the sea, a serpent, a grief-stricken crone, the alluring female, the spirit of love, the goddess of beauty, and as Erzulie Freda, the protector of homosexual men."

Louverture Antoine picked up a bottle with blue and gold beads glued around a painting of a Madonna figure. He pulled the stopper, touched his finger to it, and flicked the tiniest drop upon the back of my hand.

I heard a roaring in my ears, and experienced an instant of white darkness. I was moving through a sensuous dimension built of lust. I saw Louverture Antoine not as an elderly man, but as an object of desire, a male body complete with all masculine accoutrements. My face slipped closer to his, and I discovered that I was kissing his lips.

My cock was so hard that it was practically tearing through my underwear. Somehow, I undressed myself and Louverture Antoine as well. These events seemed to be happening to someone else, for I was nearly outside of myself, watching my body perform. I saw Ellery drop to his knees before the black man's magnificent Haitian cock. I saw his lips touch the thick foreskin, sparkling with a drop of cum already.

"Turn around," Louverture Antoine suggested. "Kindly assume a position on all fours and present your rear to me. I wish to fuck you anally."

It sounded like an excellent idea, and I hastened to comply. I pushed my ass back toward the voodoo man's thick, leaking cock, and the jism dripping from his pisshole lubricated my asshole. My anus grew slick and opened of its own accord. The more of his cum that wet my hole, the more my muscles contracted to give him easy entrance.

"Push it into me," I begged. "Take me. I give my ass to you. Fill me."

"As Erzulie Freda wills," Louverture Antoine answered, sliding his cock into my ass. "As I fill you, thank the goddess for her bounty and protection."

"Thank you, Erzulie Freda," I said, and as the words left my mouth, a tremendous sense of their significance filled me just as Louverture Antoine's cock filled me as no cock had ever stretched my ass before. "I am so full, goddess," I said. "You let me be filled with this goodness." Secure that no harm could come to me, no disease could affect me, no dire consequences would result, I drove my ass back, so I could take the voodoo man fully. The goddess Erzulie Freda, the sacred heart of love, claimed me for her own, and I gave freely.

With his cock filling my ass, Louverture Antoine slid his smooth hands over my buttocks, up my waist, across my chest, and over my shoulders. Then he gripped my ears with his fingers, and pulled back.

The action did not hurt; in fact, it felt wonderful. As he pulled, I drove my ass back to meet his thrust, impaling myself to the thick hilt. Then he eased his grip, and I found my body automatically leaning forward until he pulled again. Thus, holding my ears, he controlled the rocking and thrusting of my body, making me fuck his dick with my ass.

Rapturous pleasure was filling me. Orgasmic trills ran through my asshole, which felt like a swollen ring of pleasure around his thick rod. The trills rolled through my pelvis, meeting other tingles that had begun in the head of my cock. My dick was alive with pleasure, yet it was a pleasure controlled entirely by the cock fucking my ass.

"Oh, it's so good," I groaned. "Oh, you're gonna make me come. I'm taking this cock for you, Erzulie Freda. I'm going to come for you, goddess."

Louverture Antoine was moaning then, thanking the goddess as he spurted into my ass. I received his cum joyously. "For you I receive this offering, goddess," I prayed, as my cock raptured into orgasm. "I give my all to you, Erzulie Freda." I said no more for I fell into the white darkness utterly, knowing only the pleasure of emptying and being filled at the same time, while waves of pleasure beyond thought, beyond mind, beyond all imagining carried me though the worlds of the eternal light and the infinite night.

The next morning, I awoke feeling like a different man. I had engaged in unprotected anal sex with a man from Haiti, of all places, which sounded like I was asking for trouble. However, I did not feel sick. I felt healthier than I had ever felt. My asshole still felt puffy, but touching it was not painful. It was quite sticky, but touching it brought pleasure. I could not help but imagine how Dude's dick would feel inside of me, or how it would feel taking both brothers at the same time – the thought made me hot.

Shortly after breakfast, I used an eyedropper to extract a single drop from the bottle with blue and gold beads, which I had bought with my lunch money. I filled a small spray bottle with water and added the drop of voodoo love potion. Diluting the potion 10,000-to-1 sounded pretty safe to me, so I added the sprayer to my gym bag and headed for the Portland Men's Athletic Club.

The staff had decorated the club with red hearts on white lace, crepe paper streamers, and red and white balloons. I smiled bashfully at the hunky guy behind the counter, signed in, and went to change. I had forgotten about the day being St. Valentine's Day. Fortunately, I had brought my red and white striped spandex shorts that I wore with white thong underwear and a red shirt. After checking out my package and heart-shaped ass in the mirror and deciding that I looked like a Valentine, too, I hurried to the cardio level. I climbed about a thousand flights on the Stairmaster before I moved down a floor and completed three sets of squats with increasingly heavy weights. I could feel men's eyes on my ass; at least, I hoped they were staring at my ass after all the time I had spent developing it. I finished my squats and dropped into the machine that works the calves. More leg and butt muscle exercises followed, yet all the while, I kept one eye peeled for new arrivals. At last, I saw Guy and Dude enter. I knew that the Pine brothers would head directly to the pool. Giving them a head start, I finished working my lower body before I went to the locker room to change into my red swim briefs, the ones with the rear seam that pulled and enhanced my curves.

The squats had hardened my ass. My curves looked even more desirably heart shaped than before, and I wondered how any guy could resist rear-ending me. I hesitated with one hand inside my locker. Did I really need a voodoo potion to get a lover, I wondered, but the memory of Louverture Antoine's cock penetrating my ass provoked me to action. I grabbed the spray bottle and rushed toward the pool. One single drop of Lucky Heart Voodoo Potion was going to make Dude Pine see his valentine – a red curvy one.

Dude and Guy were talking, Dude with his back toward me. As usual, Dude looked great in his turquoise water polo briefs. Concealing my sprayer in my hand, I prepared to mist his thigh inconspicuously and see if anything happened. Before I could tighten my finger on the plunger, Dude turned. "Oh, Ellery, we've been hoping you'd show up. We gotta talk about yesterday. What Willow said was unforgivable." Dude patted my arm to emphasize his lack of homophobia. His touch gave me a shock that resulted in my dropping the spray bottle. It bounced once and plopped into the pool.

"Ah, crap, my instant tanning lotion went into the drink," I fibbed, thinking quickly. Guy dropped onto his stomach to retrieve the floating bottle. He gasped and shuddered at the touch of the water. The uncontrollable clenching of Guy's hand popped the top off the sprayer and the bottle came up empty.

Naturally, I thought that my experiment was shot to Hades since the water volume of an Olympic-sized pool now diluted my single drop of Lucky Heart Voodoo Potion, which shows how little I understood its potency. Unaware that Guy was falling through a white darkness, Dude sprawled beside his brother and reached for the sprayer top. He, too, suffered a sharp intake of breath and trembled at the terrific changes being wrought within.

Guy helped his brother stand. Moving sensuously, the Pine brothers grinned with lewd suggestiveness as they handed me my bottle. The effect was electric. When their wet hands touched mine, I crashed through the same white darkness that I had experienced in the Lucky Magic Voodoo Shop. A deep sexual heat coursed through my body. My cock rose in my red bikini, straining the nylon weave mercilessly.

I was not alone in my arousal. Both Guy and Dude were looking at me as they had never looked before. Dude's water polo swimsuit was stretched even harder than mine, and the front of Guy's baggies was protruding with his own significant boner. Both brothers crowded against me, rubbing their cocks against me, while Dude's lips met my own and Guy's tongue slipped into my ear.

Seven men had been swimming or playing in the pool, and every one of them was soon groping and kissing. As they pawed each other, they splashed the guys who had been lounging around the pool. As soon as the water hit a man, he became passionately aroused and went for the nearest man.

Mr. Willow descended the stairs, stopped in horrified shock, and then demanded, "What is going on here? What are you men doing?" Those were stupid questions because any fool could see we were preparing for a homosexual orgy. "I'm going to get the management. They'll call the police."

Guy slipped his tongue out of my ear, and his hand left my ass. Out of the corner of my eye, even as my tongue was probing deep into Dude's mouth, I witnessed Guy saunter toward Mr. Willow, smile innocuously, lay a hand on the bank teller's chest, and shove him into the pool. I heard a splash and a gasp as Mr. Willow crashed through the white darkness and blasted out the other side born-again queer. The spell hit the bank teller faster than it had hit me. Mr. Willow tore off his tent-like swim trunks and joined three men playing with each other's cocks. Glistening streamers of cum were decorating the pool's surface.

Dude dropped to his knees, his hands gripping my butt cheeks. His fingers slipped into the waistband of my red briefs and slowly rolled the garment down my body. My cock popped free, swelling even more as it was unrestrained by my swimsuit. Obediently, I lifted each foot, so Dude could undress me completely.

Dude's tongue slid between my toes. He licked my toes, sucking on them until I thought I would orgasm right then. And even as Dude moved up my feet, licking my skin, the flicking of his little oral member tickling my ankles, his brother Guy came back from watching Mr. Willow turn out. Guy returned to my nether side, and I felt him kissing my buttocks.

"Oh, guys," I moaned. "Do you know what you're doing?"

"Let it happen, Ellery," Guy moaned, as though he were the experienced homosexual and I the newcomer. He licked along the crack of my butt and pushed his face into my ass crack. I felt him kissing my asshole, his lips tight to my little pucker. His tongue emerged and slid up my crack to the top. Down again he went, stopping at my hole to lick and kiss, and then on down until he was licking the underside of my balls.

As Guy licked my ass, Dude moved up my legs. He kissed my knees, licked and kissed my thighs, and moved his mouth closer and closer to my straining pole. Suddenly, his mouth was on my dick, kissing the head of it, licking down my shaft, licking the upper side of my balls while his brother licked the underside.

Though lovelorn, I had sucked dozens of dicks. Rarely had mine been sucked, and never before that day had any guy licked my asshole. Instead of me being the one who serviced a man's needs, I had two hot-looking brothers servicing mine. My whole world was exploding. Guy's tongue continued exploring my butt crack. As he licked my asshole with a tongue so soft, so warm, so penetrating, so frisky, I could barely contain myself. While my ass enjoyed this new stimulation, Dude's mouth worked at my swollen cock.

I was leaking. A thin seminal fluid was seeping from my cock onto Dude's tongue, which he was happily swallowing. Dude was smiling as he blew me. For a moment, he pulled his mouth off my dick and beamed up at me with such intense pleasure that I could hardly believe my good fortune. Then he voraciously went down on my dick again, so deep that I knew my dickhead had slid into his throat.

Dude bobbed his head to and fro, swallowing the head of my cock. My head swam; lacking balance, I gripped Dude's head with both hands. Dude gripped my buttocks with his hands as he sucked me. He pulled my cheeks apart so his brother could kiss my ass all the better. Tingles rippled through my cockhead, tingles that grew in intensity as Guy's tongue pushed into my asshole, opening my little back door with a promise of bigger things to follow.

Spasms of orgasmic pleasure rushed through my cock. Gripping Dude's head tighter and pulling him onto me so I would unload down his throat, I howled like a wounded wolf as my muscles contracted, and I shot my first spurt into Dude's mouth. Squirt followed squirt as my entire center throbbed. I was pumping it right down Dude's throat while Guy continued to lick my asshole.

When I was drained, having shot my last, I sank to my knees. Dude kissed my lips, his mouth tasting of my spent jism. I probed his tongue with my own, tasting the cum he had eaten, and as I hunched upon my knees, Guy's naked cock touched my spit-slicked asshole.

"We've got some lube," another man called out when he saw Guy preparing to fuck me. The man was taking it up the ass, but he managed to toss a bottle to Guy's extended hand. Without warning, I felt Guy's lubricated finger slide into my already opened ass.

"Yeah, Guy," I moaned. "Give it to me. I love taking it doggie style."

The moans of fulfillment, the muted cries of bliss, and the howls of sexual rapture summoned the club's staff from the manager down to the lowest towel boy. In addition to the staff, every guest in the club stumbled down the stairs to see what was happening. Confronted with this mob of clothed and not yet voodoo charmed men, the guys in the water set up a mighty splashing. Water sprayed, squirted, shot, and sloshed in all directions, deluging those in front and sprinkling those in the rear. But whether they received a mighty wave or the tiniest sprinkle, all men touched by that magical water were overwhelmed by an irresistible homoerotic lust.

I was aware of all going on around me – the jerking, slurping, sucking, fucking, kissing, licking, and dicking – but my main awareness centered upon what was happening to my own body. Guy's cock was slowing opening my anal sphincter while I crouched on all fours, and Dude's cock was rubbing across my lips. I had always fantasized about taking it from both ends at once, and thanks to Louverture Antoine's magical potion, my dreams were coming true. Even more, many of my solo-sex fantasies involved men coming on me, their hot, wet jism decorating my skin and even my face. That fantasy also turned into reality because the hand-job team Mr. Willow had joined was coming our way. The men were stroking each other's cocks, masturbating each other freely, and letting their fluids fly where they would.

My ass was opening to Guy's cock. "Oh, Ellery, I've dreamed of slipping it to you," Guy moaned. "Whenever I beat my meat, I pictured your sexy ass."

The voodoo potion seemed to be a truth serum. Every man has homosexual fantasies. The men at the Portland Men's Athletic Club were voicing their hidden desires and thoughts, and in speaking them, they made them solid.

"Fuck me, Guy," I moaned. "I want your thick cock in me, all the way."

Guy pushed forward until his thighs were pressing my buttocks, and his cock was filling me to the hilt. "Oh, yes, Guy. I love the way you fill my ass. Fuck me and fill me with your cum."

As Guy pulled back and rocked forward, the motion stimulating my asshole with sexual bliss, Dude's cock leaked a stream onto my lips. It was salty and sweet at once, a delicious fluid that I licked from his dickhead. His dick passed over my lips, and I had to suppress the urge to nibble just a bit. I formed my mouth into a hot hole to receive his wide rod. As his dick slid deeper into my mouth, still leaking its delicious fluid, I heard Mr. Willow groaning, and a hot, sticky spurt of wet spunk splattered across my back.

"Oh, he came on my face," Guy moaned, as he hunched atop me. "That's the way, Willow. Shoot it on me. I love your cum."

Cum splattered across the mounds of my ass. Guy must have gotten part of that one right in the mouth, for I heard him begging for more.

"Shoot it into my mouth, Willow. Yum. Right on my tongue. Good shooting. Oh, yeah, I'm swallowing your jism. Oh, wow, your spunk is sending me over the edge. Oh, I can't hold out. I'm gonna shoot a big load up Ellery's gay ass – right now."

I pulled my sucking mouth off Dude's cock long enough to urge, "Go for it, Guy."

Guy needed no urging for he was howling and humping me ferociously as his dick bucked in sexual paroxysm. "Oh, oh, I'm coming, I'm coming so heavy," Guy keened. "Oh, it's so fuckin' good. Oh, Ellery, I love your ass."

The men jerking on both sides of us were coming too, coming right along with us, in fact, for Guy's cock had milked me toward another orgasm. Cum was splattering my body from both sides, and Dude was coming out with a series of moans as he grew close to sending his load down my throat. I pulled back on his dick and worked his dickhead with my lips and tongue, licking around the trimmed head and lip massaging it. As I sucked and kissed Dude's cock and Guy kept thrusting in my ass, milking out every drop of his hot spunk, I felt the prickling of approaching orgasm begin deep up my ass and wrinkle forward into my balls. My balls tightened as the prickling rushed up my shaft as if an invisible hand were squeezing the head of my cock.

I wanted to howl, to moan, to groan, to tell what I was feeling, but I could only suck furiously on the big cock in my mouth that seemed to grow suddenly harder. Then Dude's cock bucked, and a great gout of his spunk filled my mouth. The taste was incredible, and when I had fully savored its flavor, I let it slide down my throat. That's when my own orgasm reached its peak. My asshole tightened around Guy's cock. My own cock fucked the air with waves of orgasmic pleasure. Richer bursts of fresh semen poured into my mouth. As I felt my muscles contracting, spurting my cum onto the tiles, I swallowed Dude's cum and milked Guy's cock. Guy suddenly shrieked, "I'm gonna come again. I can't fucking believe it. Oh, Ellery, your fucking insatiable gay ass is killin' me."

As the noon hour approached, men kept arriving for their daily workout. Each one got sprinkled in his turn. And so it went until we were spent.

Drained, we collapsed in a pile. I was drenched with cum. My back and sides were covered with the divine goo. With the load up my ass, the one in my stomach, and the streaks on my skin, I felt euphoric. "I'm flying, boys," I said, and kissed Dude and then Guy. Of course, human semen is naturally intoxicating, and I had received a substantial dose.

The guys let me rest only a short while. With the constant stream of new arrivals, the orgy of gay sex raging around us stimulated us to renewed action. Both brothers started licking me, washing my cum-streaked skin with their eager tongues. Finally, Guy's tongue found my hard cock, and he got his first mouthful.

"Isn't that great, brother," Dude said. "You've got a cock in your mouth."

"Mmm, yum," was all Guy could say as he discovered the delights of cocksucking.

I was sprawled half against the green tiled wall, half on the floor, as Guy sucked at my dick and Dude licked my chest and stomach. The brothers waved their asses as they licked and sucked, an invitation if there ever was one. Mr. Willow was eyeing the boys' asses and stroking his dick. Suddenly, he grabbed the bottle of lubricant that had been passing around, slicked his cock, and approached Dude from the rear.

"Oh, oh, yes, yes, yes," Dude howled as Mr. Willow pushed his cock into Dude Pine's spread sphincter. I grinned to see Dude taking Mr. Willow so easily, and a huge smile wreathed Dude's face as the bank teller's cock pushed deeper and deeper into his rear.

Guy was sucking my cock so hard that he had not noticed that Mr. Willow was fucking Dude's curvy ass. When he saw the way his brother took cock up the ass, Guy would want to get his ass fucked, too. The blowjob Guy was giving me felt great, but I thought fucking his ass might be even better. Under the spell of the voodoo potion, I was finding my pleasure both as catcher and pitcher.

I touched Guy's head while he was deep-throating my dick. "Take a look at what's happening to Dude," I said softly. Guy could not pull his head off my cock right away, but eventually he weaned himself from my shaft and turned his head. Guy's eyes lit with jealousy when he saw Dude grinning ferociously while Mr. Willow butt fucked him with feral abandon.

"Oh, he's gonna come in my ass, Guy," Dude howled. "I've got an ass full of cock, and soon I'm gonna be full of spunk."

Guy gave me a pleading look; he desperately wanted to get his ass fucked. "How about you sit on my lap?" I said.

Guy smiled lasciviously. "You mean on your cock?"

"Yeah, Guy. I want you to sit on my boner, bury it up your ass, and bounce, boy, bounce."

Laughing with glee, Guy Pine presented his ass for lubrication. I had the bottle of lube in my hand, but before I slipped a slick finger into his hot hole, I could not resist touching my tongue to it. Guy shivered with delight as I kissed his asshole.

"Fuck me," he urged. "Oh, Ellery, fuck my ass."

I licked his crack, up and down, giving his asshole a loving smooch along the way. I flicked it a little with my tongue, until I reluctantly had to draw my face away. Guy wanted a cock, and I was going to stick it to him.

Preparing Guy's asshole to receive my dick turned into a magical moment. I slicked a finger with lubricant and slid it into his opening ass. "Oh, yeah, that's good," Guy murmured. I twisted my finger this way and that, opening him for my dick, and others to follow, perhaps. It was strange to be on the other side for once, for this would be the first time I had ever fucked any man. Always, I had always been the passenger, and now I was going to drive. I slicked two fingers, pushed them in, and twisted. The action nearly made Guy shoot a load right then, but I wasn't going to let that happen – yet.

I positioned my ass so that I was sitting in an easy posture with my hard cock jutting upward. "You're ready to ride, Guy. Lower your ass onto it."

Guy was only a tad nervous as he sat downward on my lap. He stopped briefly when the head of my cock touched his asshole. "I'm gonna get fucked," he said, wonder coloring his voice as he glanced at his brother. Dude was in raptures. Mr. Willow continued fucking him, slamming his hard cock in and out of Dude's eager ass. Inspired by his brother's good example, Guy let gravity take its course. The head of my cock parted his asshole. I could not believe how easily Guy opened for my cockhead.

"Oh, god, it hurts," Guy said. He tried to lift himself off my cock, but he could not get traction in that position and only slid farther down my shaft, filling his ass deeper.

"Draw a deep breath, Guy," I said, laughing. "It only hurts the first time. I thought I'd die when I took my first cock, but the pain lasts only a few seconds. The pleasure keeps on giving for a lifetime."

Guy breathed deeply, and I could feel him relax. Gravity was still capturing him, causing his ass to get penetrated deeper. "You're right," he admitted. "It's starting to feel nice. Okay, this is it; I'm sinking all the way." So saying, he let his ass drop fully into my lap until he was penetrated to the extent of my cock. His rectum was slick and grainy. No hand or mouth gave the kind of delicious friction that I felt in Guy's ass.

"I've got a cock up my ass," Guy shouted. "Look at me, guys. I'm getting butt fucked."

Guy was so happy and proud that his emotions were contagious. Men who had confined themselves to circle jerks suddenly wanted the feel of a big one up their asses. I tossed the bottle of lubricant to another man who promptly lubricated his best friend's rear. Soon a dozen men had their dicks firmly planted in the butt holes of the men in front of them and had the dicks of the men behind them inserted to the hilt in theirs. The big choo-choo of the delightfully fucked grew and grew as the men chuffed forward. Howls of "I'm coming," "I'm gonna spurt it in your ass, Reverend LaBarbera," "Here he goes," "Frank's coming in my rump hole," "My wife's gonna shit when she finds out," "Oh, I'm so wet," and "Have I got a present for you, Don," filled the air.

Meanwhile, Guy was rocking on my cock, and I was rolling my hard buns to and fro as best I could, crushed as I was beneath the weight of his round ass. "Oh, that feels so good, Ellery," Guy said. "I'd like to keep your cock in me always."

His grainy asshole was sanding my dick, and the incessant rocking was beyond my control. Guy was going to make me come; I couldn't hold off. "Oh, Guy, you're milking me off," I groaned. "I'm going over the edge, Guy. Oh, this is it."

"That's it, Ellery, do it in my ass. Shoot your boy juice into my gay ass. I'll take all you can give me."

"Here it comes," I yelped, as my eyelids fluttered and my nipples tightened. Manly tingles commenced in my dick head, turning into waves of the white darkness that overwhelmed me. "I'm going to give you a present, Guy," I echoed, my heart nearly ripping out of my chest. "A wet, sticky present."

"Oh, give it to me," Guy moaned. "Oh, Ellery, I'm gonna come, too. Oh, fuckin' wow, I'm having an anal orgasm."

My dick was going off like a machine gun up Guy's ass. From my position, I could not see him coming, but I could sure hear him. His brother was taking on another big load at the same time, and Dude was howling along with Guy. "Oh, yeah, fill me with cum. Give me that semen enema. Oh, I love riding cock; I'm a cock rider. Big thick cock. Oh, yeah. Fuck my queer ass. I'm so queer for cock. I love it. Oh."

The next day, over a hundred men swished around the pool in a colorful array of slinky bikinis, swim briefs and thongs. Gone forever were the body concealing garments, the mark of masculine shame. Now they strutted, pranced, and displayed. As they cruised each other along the edge or played in the pool, they paraded their sexuality.

When I first arrived at the gym, newcomers had been mixed among us – men who had not visited the club on the previous day. They stood out, obvious both in their attire and in their confusion. Brandishing bottles that I had handed them, the staff rushed around making sure that every man joined our ranks. The club manager ordered, "Grab those guys by the door and give them a misting." Within a few minutes the newcomers had smashed through the white darkness and were joining in the fun.

Some guys were better constructed for the scanty swimwear than others, but regardless of shape, they were flaunting their bulges and curves while admiring each other's cocks and asses. Dude was swishing his rump in a tropical print bikini, and Guy was flossing his crack with a shimmery thong. Even Mr. Willow was wearing pink swim briefs with a drawn-up-the-butt-crack seam. He blew me a kiss while he fondled Pastor Cameron's crotch bulge. "Now you know why I baptized you with that special water, Paul," Mr. Willow whispered to his friend.

The staff had drained and cleaned the swimming pool, which, given the jism floating on the water's surface, was no great surprise, and I was not dismayed, but prepared. After all, I had used only a single drop from my bottle of Lucky Heart Voodoo Potion. As I squeezed another solitary drip onto the pool's surface, I smiled to think I had enough potion left to make Valentine's Day last a lifetime.

THE GREAT INVASION

At six feet and four inches, Len Gallagher towered over the men of the island. The tallest stood only five and a half feet, though Gallagher recognized that they were shapelier. Their bodies looked to be nearly perfect: muscled, compact, coordinated, and sexy. Gallagher had to admit that those men looked damned good. With the exception of their incomprehensible tongue, the only feature he found disquieting was their uniformly purple irises. He had never seen eyes that distinct deep hue before. The men's purple eyes, combined with the strange way the women of the island avoided the males, made Gallagher wonder what was amiss.

The women did not avoid him. As he strode across the beach in his baggy swimming trunks, the women crowded around him like a flock of lust ridden gulls. While the women gestured suggestively and tried to pull him back toward the sensual shade of a palm-thatched bure, the men stood apart, sprung hipped, with their shapely buttocks protruding. They seemed to care not-at-all that their women were attempting to seduce the stranger. Some of the men were wearing colorful swim briefs, others sarongs that barely covered their assets, but most were naked, apart from the garlands of brilliant flowers worn around their necks and waists. The men chattered among themselves, but they watched Gallagher covertly. Despite the women's offer of sexual gratification, Gallagher pushed through the crowd to make his way to the shore where the turquoise waters of the lagoon slapped gently upon the pink sand.

Still, the women would not let him be. They rushed to block his progress and pulled at his arms. When Gallagher indicated by hand gestures that he intended to go for a swim, the women reacted with dismay. The men reacted differently as Gallagher made his intentions known. They tittered among themselves, as if they possessed secret knowledge. Meanwhile, a young woman held up her hands to warn him back from the gently lapping ocean. Others boldly rubbed against him in a vain attempt to seduce him away from the waves.

Gallagher felt the heat of arousal, but forced himself to picture Nellie Ann. She was waiting for him back in South Florida, and they would be married upon his return. He disentangled himself from the clutching arms and ran toward the water. When he stood with his feet in the lightly rippling waves, the women stopped. They shook their heads in disgust, and one spit on the sand.

However, the growing excitement among the men reached a fever pitch. All eyes were turned upon Gallagher as he waded deeper into the waters of the lagoon. He looked back at the keyed-up men with some doubt, but the water appeared to be harmless. The volcanic sand was pinkish with sparkling crystals that gave back the large yellow sun. Coconut palms lined the shore as did a riot of flowering plants. Many trees hung heavy with tropical fruit. Beyond the mouth of the lagoon, the open sea broke upon the protecting reef.

The lagoon must have been home to numerous small fish, for Gallagher felt the brush of some aquatic creature against his leg. The creature appeared to be uncommonly friendly. Gallagher waded in a bit deeper until the water was covering his upper thighs. The water was so warm and inviting that Gallagher wanted to start swimming, but for some reason he hesitated. More of the fish, if indeed they were fish, were brushing against his legs. Peering beneath the surface, he saw that they were not fish but pale pink eels. They were hard to see because they were transparent. One attached to his thigh, and he had to pull it off. It felt like a tingly stiff gelatin, but he lost hold of the specimen before he could examine it closer.

Gallagher cast his eyes toward the beach. The women had disappeared, but the men had lined up along the shoreline. They were lined back to front and pressed tightly together. The whole line was rocking back and forth – or performing a motion better described as thrusting. With a start, Gallagher realized that each native man was butt fucking the man in front. The sight was so shocking that Gallagher could scarcely believe the evidence of his senses.

However, he could not dwell upon the islanders' strange sexual activities because more eels had attached to his thighs. Attempting to peel off the eels, Gallagher stumbled into a hole. He floundered briefly, but he found that he could still stand, though the water then reached his chest. The eels made the best of his momentary confusion. They slithered up his thighs into his bathing suit.

"The damned things are invading me," Gallagher swore with a laugh. Despite their persistence, the eels did not bite or sting. He was wondering how he was going to get the aquatic life out of his swim trunks without exposing himself to the entire population of the island, when he felt a sharp pressure against his asshole. So surprised was he that he gasped and suffered a momentary release. His anal sphincter opened, and one of the eels pushed inside.

Gallagher thrashed in the water with panicked gesticulations. As the eel drove deeper into his ass, the other eels released their hold. They moved back in a circle around him as he thrashed, his asshole opening wider to admit his uninvited guest. A sensation of intense fullness flooded his body and grew as the eel drove in. When the creature fully invaded him, Gallagher suddenly shrieked long and loud. His asshole tightened again with the eel inside. His shriek died abruptly as his senses exploded into a dizzying kaleidoscope of light, color, scent, and sound.

From Gallagher's perspective, the inside of a nuclear explosion could not have been more intense. He experienced every sensation he had ever felt as if he were living them anew. Added to the remembered sensations came feelings that he had never imagined any human being could feel. The kaleidoscope of color swirled before his eyes, and his ears roared. He smelled the scents of the island, and his skin crawled with the information it was receiving and transmitting to his besieged brain. Every cell in his body tingled fiercely. He was on fire, yet the burning was pleasurable.

For a few minutes, he could see nothing. When his vision cleared, he waded desperately toward shore, though the scene had changed. He was seeing things that he had never seen before. Shapes and colors were different in some strange way. His bowels felt full with an unfamiliar warm, hard wetness that radiated pleasurably. Never before had he been so deeply conscious of something alien inside of him.

The island men had climaxed their group butt-fuck. They smiled and chattered as they watched Gallagher approach. Gallagher could clearly see their lips moving, and the sound of their language reached his ears. Their speech did not sound so strange as it had before, though he still could not understand the words. Another outlandish thrill shot through Gallagher's body. His cock tingled and rubbed pleasantly against the fabric of his swimming trunks. Only then did Gallagher realize that he was sporting an erection. His face flushed as his inhibitions flared. He stopped wading, but even the slight motion of his swim trunks irritated his swollen cock.

He shuddered again. His nipples crinkled and his nostrils flared. He was filled with an intense heat. The flow of pleasure undulated through the head of his cock, growing in power. Gallagher knew that he was fated to orgasm spontaneously in front of the tittering island men, but he could do nothing to stop his body from racing over the border of sexual ecstasy. He could not even turn away, for waves of pleasure overthrew him, shuddering, thought-blasting waves, that sparkled rapture in every cell and triggered lightning flashes of bliss in his brain, and the waves went on and on, cascading beyond any orgasm he had previously experienced until his pelvic muscles contracted mightily and sent great gouts of semen into his wet swimming trunks.

The thrill went on and on, and while the pleasure waves annihilated his conscious thought, he was still dimly aware of his spurting cock shooting forth more semen than he had ever known he could produce. Contraction after contraction claimed him, each sending out a glob of cum that filled his shorts.

When the contractions finally stilled, and the overwhelming waves settled down into a continuing bliss, Gallagher gasped in the scented island air and stood shaking before the grinning island men. His bathing suit felt as if he had filled it with goop. He stripped it off. Even in the ocean water, it smelled of semen. He flung the garment toward the sandy beach and washed his cock and balls in the churning seawater.

The island men waded into the water and led Gallagher to an island bure of thatched palm fronds and bamboo poles. Gallagher saw everything around him, saw more clearly than he ever had before. Every scent was alive, and sounds were magnified, though not objectionably. The island men chattered at him, and he suddenly understood some of their words. They were telling him that he needed to lie down, that if he did not recline, he would fall and perhaps be injured.

Gallagher suddenly remembered that he had an eel – or whatever kind of mysterious sea creature, inhabiting his rectum. He dimly wondered why he had temporarily forgotten that crucial fact. Then, his invader seemed less important as a remarkable dizziness struck him. The men helped him down onto a cot, where he reclined naked and face down. His ears were roaring and colored swirls warped his vision again. His body began to tingle as though each cell was being masturbated. Despite the growing ecstasy, Gallagher felt like he was sliding down a slick chute into a pool of ink. His last conscious desire was to rub the overwhelming itch in his anal canal. He wished that an island man would stick his cock in to scratch that itch. Perhaps feed it with his semen. Then Gallagher slipped into dreams that defied all description.

# # # # #

Russ swam his final lap in the green water. He placed the flat of his hands on the edge of the pool, and used his powerful upper body to rocket onto the edge. His light blue bikini trunks were tight enough to stay in place during this maneuver. The sight of him made me adjust my cock through the thin fabric of my swim briefs.

"You sexy man," I called. "Come here."

"Just what do you have in mind?" Russ said, grinning at me as he approached with an exaggerated sway. When he was close enough, I grabbed his hips and pulled him closer.

"My mother warned me about boys like you," Russ purred as my hands slipped over the wet curves of his ass, so delightfully taut in his unlined bikini. His bikini's deep front pouch brought his package out – and up.

Of course, his cock was hardening. The fabric twisted it to the left in what I knew must be an uncomfortable position. Mercifully, I slipped my fingers into his waistband and pulled his swimsuit to his knees. His swollen cock popped free and bobbed before my lips.

"Oh, help, the agency has got me," Russ called playfully, making a not-so-subtle reference to the service that employed me.

"Blow job time," bellowed a senator decked out in a red Nike bikini that rode furiously up his butt crack.

"The congressman is gonna get his cock sucked," another voice called.

"Chris is just the guy to suck it," a third voice from the cheering section contributed.

Of course, Russ and I were exercising in The New World Order, a "Gay Men Only" fitness club that doubled as a sex club. A sort of combination gym, pool, and bathhouse, where pretty much anything was liable to happen, and anything was okay providing all parties were willing. The men there had common employment that called for discretion outside the club. Some were senators, congressmen, justices, or the staffs of such. The rest of us were members of the clandestine services.

Russ's circumcised cock head was barely touching my lips. I moved my head forward a bare fraction of an inch and kissed it. The saline taste of the swimming pool water taunted my taste buds, but as I flicked my tongue around the trimmed head, another taste, deeper and more primal, sent little raptures of lust into my brain. The skin of his cock was both hard and soft at the same time, hard with an urgent need, and soft with a silky texture that my tongue traveled over. I kissed his dick head hard while I stroked the smooth cheeks of his firm ass with both hands.

"Oh, Chris," Russ moaned. "Do it, Chris. Suck me. Suck my cock. Right here. Right now."

No further urging was necessary. My lips twisted his dick head. I gripped his shaft with one hand, while I stroked his smooth ass with the other and attacked the head of his cock with my lips and tongue. My own cock grew harder as Russ's cock slid along my lips. There is nothing more stimulating or masculine than sucking a dick. It is power cubed. I mastered his dick with my mouth, licking the head, flicking his pee hole with my tongue, and bobbing it with my lips.

Russ moaned uncontrollably. He was mine. He was in my power. I had him right where I wanted him. I sucked harder, taking his cock deeper into my mouth. I bobbed my head on his dick as I jerked the lower part of his shaft and sucked the top. His cock was slick with my saliva, so I pulled my head away and gripped it tightly. I jacked it hard, biting deep with my fingers. I tortured his dick head with my thumb and forefinger.

"Ohmigod," Russ wailed, the mortal ruin in his voice drawing the last of the swimmers from the pool.

I stopped jacking Russ for a couple of seconds before returning to him with my mouth. I attacked his dick with my tongue. Then I took him all the way, so that his cock head was fucking the back of my throat while I swallowed to keep my gag reflex from kicking against it. My lips were meeting his soft pubic hairs as he gave forth with a series of low moans.

"I'm gonna come," Russ wailed. "Oh, Chris, I'm gonna do it in your mouth."

That was exactly what I wanted. I abused his cock head with my lips again. His cock seemed to tighten, growing harder and swelling to its maximum before its ultimate burst. I swallowed it into my throat again and let him fuck my mouth. As I pulled back, I tasted his cum upon my tongue. He was ejaculating hard in my mouth. I swallowed spurt after spurt of his spicy jism until the quivering stopped and the heavy hardness of his cock broke. He had shot all he was going to shoot then. His orgasms were complete.

Without warning, a low wail rent the air above the pool. Pulling away from Russ, I mouthed, "Fuck it all," and tried to pull my swim briefs over my hard-on.

"Chris, there's a funny sound coming from your towel," a Supreme Court Justice contributed helpfully.

Hopping on one leg, I grabbed up my towel and the red cell phone I'd secreted beneath it. "Pipes and stems," I answered, which is the code to indicate that strangers could hear me.

"Creeping man," a voice said and disconnected.

The code was obvious, referring to Arthur Conan Doyle's story "The Adventure of the Creeping Man." The second paragraph begins with "It was one Sunday evening early in September of the year 1903 that I received one of Holmes' laconic messages: 'Come at once if convenient – if inconvenient come all the same. – S. H.'" I was being ordered to report without delay to Mr. Z, my superior in our nation's most top-secret agency, that churlish, desperate, and unhappily married heterosexual who was entrusted with directing the most delicate and dangerous of the covert operations.

# # # # #

It was a red folder, stamped TOP SECRET, and bound with a paper ribbon that read EYES ONLY. Additional stamps indicated that the folder had been checked out to me, Christopher Ruskin, Senior Agent. I turned on the loudly buzzing florescent tube and violated the paper ribbon. The enclosed goldenrod sheet told a succinct but woefully incomplete story:

LEN GALLAGHER, MARINE BIOLOGIST WITH DRYDEN LABS IN HOMESTEAD, FL PASSED US CUSTOMS ON MARCH 3 CARRYING BAG OF BLACK EELS (SEE PHOTO OF SPECIMEN REMOVED FROM VICTIM HAYNES). GALLAGHER TRICKED CUSTOMS AGENT ROSCUE INTO AN OFFICE AND INFECTED HIM. ROSCUE EFFECTED GALLAGHERS ENTRANCE INTO COUNTRY. THE INFECTION OF WELL-PLACED MEN PROCEEDED FROM SOUTH FLORIDA AND SPREAD TO NEW YORK, LOS ANGELES, AND WASHINGTON. LITTLE HAS BEEN DETERMINED ABOUT THE NATURE OF EELS. WHETHER THEY ARE OF EARTHLY ORIGIN IS UNKNOWN. OUR SINGLE SPECIMEN WAS STOLEN BY HAYNES SHORTLY AFTER IT WAS REMOVED FROM HIM, AND IT IS BELIEVED THAT HE HAS REINSERTED THE ALIEN. GALLAGHER

HAS GONE INTO HIDING ALONG WITH ALL KNOWN INFECTED. SUGGEST YOUR DEPARTMENT INVESTIGATE SINCE THE INVASION IS SPREADING EXPONENTIALLY.

I blinked at the report, hardly able to believe what I was reading. Still, something in it summoned something in me. With a start, I realized that my cock had hardened as I sat at my desk reading. For some reason completely unknown to me, the dry words had stimulated me like the most descriptive erotic story. I compulsively rubbed my swollen dick through the soft flannel of my suit pants as I picked up the blue sheet.

SCIENTIFIC ANALYSIS OF THE INVADER IS INCOMPLETE DUE TO ITS THEFT (NOTE: COLLOQUIALLY DESCRIBED BLACK EELS ARE ACTUALLY TRANSLUCENT AND PINK.) SPECIMEN WAS ALIVE AND POTENT AT THE TIME OF EXTRACTION FROM THE GOVERNMENT LABORATORY. ANALYSIS OF THE CREATURE (ALIEN) REVEALS THAT IT ATTACHES ITSELF TO THE INNER WALLS OF THE RECTUM AND INTESTINES OF ADULT MALES, FORMING AN ORGASMIC TISSUE THAT SENDS CELLS TO THE BRAIN AND OTHER ORGANS. OVER TIME THE CREATURE BECOMES A PART OF THE HUMAN BODY, INDISTINGUISHABLE FROM THE REST. IT THEN EFFECTS CHANGES IN BRAIN CHEMISTRY WHICH ALLOWS VICTIM TO EXPERIENCE SENSUAL DATA BEYOND NORMAL HUMAN CAPACITY. VICTIMS CAN SEE FAR INTO THE INFRA-RED AND ULTRA-VIOLET LIGHT SPECTRUMS. IT ALSO PRODUCES PHYSICAL CHANGES, ALTERING THE SHAPE AND SIZE OF THE HUMAN BODY. OVER TIME, THE MALE BODY BECOMES A PULSATING, OVERLY SENSUOUS, PLEASURE-ADDICTED MECHANISM.

A pink page described the highly illegal, top-secret experiment conducted upon an unwilling prisoner.

POLITICAL PRISONER CP1120939(VL) (MALE) WAS SELECTED FOR THE EXPERIMENT. A SMALL PIECE WAS CUT FROM THE EEL AND PLACED UPON THE PRISONER'S BUTTOCK. THE INJURED CREATURE REGENERATED EXCISED PART. THE SEVERED PIECE REGENERATED A SMALLER EEL IDENTICAL TO THE PARENT SPECIMEN AND IMMEDIATELY SQUIGGLED TOWARD THE PRISONER'S ANUS AND TRAVELED INSIDE. THE PRISONER UNDERWENT ABRUPT CHANGES. WITHIN TEN MINUTES HE EXPERIENCED A SHUDDERING ANAL ORGASM AND BEGAN PASSING THROUGH A SERIES OF BODILY CHANGES. AFTER A WEEK THE ORGANISM WAS INDISTINGUISHABLE FROM THE REST OF HIS BODY. NO CURE FOR THIS INFESTATION IS POSSIBLE.

EXPERIMENTAL PRISONER SHRANK FIVE INCHES IN HEIGHT, LOST FORTY POUNDS IN UNSIGHTLY FAT, INCREASED ROTUNDITY IN HIS BUTTOCKS, AND HAS BECOME INSATIABLY HOMOSEXUAL. THE 75 OTHER PRISONERS CAN BARELY KEEP HIM SATISFIED.

PRISONER YT2610056 (VL) (FEMALE) WAS SELECTED FOR SIMILAR EXPERIMENTATION. WHEN PLACED UPON THE PRISONER'S BUTTOCK, THE EEL STEADFASTLY REFUSED TO ENTER. WHEN INSERTED, THE EEL PROMPTLY EJECTED ITSELF, ATTACHED TO THE HAND OF A MALE EXPERIMENTER, AND PROMPTLY DISAPPEARED INSIDE THE MAN'S GARMENTS. DISASTER WAS NARROWLY AVERTED. SIMILAR EXPERIMENTS WITH PRISONERS DUPLICATED THE RESULTS. THE EELS BOND WITH THE MASCULINE ANUS EXCLUSIVELY.

I replaced the three colored sheets in the red folder and sat back stunned. Clearly, Earth had been invaded by an alien species, bent upon who-knew-what goal, and as usual, our government was covering up the crisis, and it fell upon me to help hide the truth from the public. While I was hiding the truth, my superiors expected me to investigate the phenomenon and to save the world – again. Ah, the perilous existence of a secret agent.

Mr. Z had been his normal insulting homophobic self when I reported to him. "Since you're a faggot already, the invaders can hardly affect you. That's why we're entrusting you with this mission. President Buchanan himself was on his knees in the Oval, begging that I assign the mission to you."

I'll bet that cocksucker was on his knees, I thought, knowing well the president's proclivities. Dick Buchanan, President of the United States, could suck the cream out of ice cream. He had sucked my cock enough at The New World Order, which is why he knew my name and knew that I was the top ranked Secret Agent in our country's clandestine services.

# # # # #

After a brief stopover in Hawaii, the commercial airliner carried me into the South Seas. My investigations in Miami and the Florida Keys had been inconclusive since the subjects of our inquiry had fled. Gallagher had acquired the parasite (if I must call it by that word) on either Drawaqa or a tiny island near to it. There, of course, is where I headed, escorted by agents from every covert bureau on the planet. My opposite numbers (or opposing numbers) almost packed the airline. No country had been unaffected at that point, and most of the services had sparked the same scheme. Send a gay agent, they thought. A homosexual will be immune to invasion. No one knew then that we gay males were as susceptible as other men – more so even – far more so.

Quintero Garcia, an agent from Mexico's Jefatura de Policia, gestured toward the rear of the airliner. Quin loved receiving a hard Yankee cock up his ass, which I had arranged for him in twelve U.S. cities and two Canadian provinces (not counting once in San Miguel de Tucumán). Lifting my pocket mirror, I saw Panther Mann making out with Boris Badenass. Quin nudged me; he was trying to play another of his sexually suggestive word games.

I was not in the mood to play Quin's games after he had gotten caught sneaking atomic secrets from the U.S. Patent Office. "Quin," I whispered, "What do you think of these reports?"

"My government ..." he began.

"Fuck your government," I interrupted. "What do you think?"

"The incident is fascinating, Chris."

"Screw fascinating. Did you hear about the orgasms the guys have after they've been invaded? I want one of those aliens up my ass. What about you?"

"*Sí*, Chris," he gasped.

"No fucking kidding, Quin," the British agent provided. "Buggery in the foxholes, all over again."

"That's a thought, double-o thirteen," approved the Hebrew agent, Israel Gould.

"You boys," complained the only female agent on the airliner. The CIA had dispatched Valerie Glamour on the mission, which caused Tommy Fedora to hoot with laughter. Tommy claimed to know things about her. Of course, Miss Glamour looked ravishing, as usual, and the males secretly envied her, especially Secret Agent X-9, who was traveling in disguise (candid observers might refer to X-9's makeup, dress, and heels as drag).

I checked my watch. We would be landing on Fiji in twenty minutes. With the single exception of Valerie Glamour, was a single agent still working for his government? Or did we all have private agendas? Everything I had read increased my desire to obtain one of the aliens in my own rectum. Whatever would happen after I had been invaded, who was to know?

Len Gallagher, traveling under faked documents and credit cards in the name Fanty McCoy, checked into the Hotel California. After unpacking hastily, he scrutinized his image in the mirror. Gallagher no longer looked anything like the tall, salt-and-pepper-haired man who entered the waters of a South Sea island several months earlier. He had lost nine inches in height, but he had gained in figure. He looked and felt as though he were twenty instead of nearly forty-five. His glowing purple eyes gazed back at him from the mirror, and the intelligent tissues in his rectum tingled with a mini-orgasm.

Recalled to his mission, Gallagher stepped onto his balcony and scanned the beach with high-powered binoculars. Counting and estimating, he judged that a dozen adult males were standing in waist deep water at any one time. From his watertight suitcase, he removed two of the translucent eels. He stroked the eels lovingly for several minutes before he laid them on a towel wet with seawater and watched the process.

Gradually, each eel separated into two, and the four divided into eight. When sixteen small eels were writhing upon the wet towel, Gallagher returned four to the case, scooped the other dozen into a beach bag, pulled yellow flowered swim briefs over his nakedness, and caught the next elevator.

Thirty minutes later, Gallagher was spinning down the coast in his rented car, seeking a likely beach for the next infection. Meanwhile, in the warm waters of the Hotel California's beach, a matronly woman grabbed her middle-aged husband's arm. "Henry," she demanded. "Henry. Are you having another attack?"

Wheezing and trembling, Henry Pigeon did not respond to his wife's worried query. A pinkish eel was penetrating his asshole. Sensations such as Pigeon had never imagined fired his accountant's mentality. His consciousness crashed through all barriers as the eel drove its feelers into Pigeon's prostate and sent other tendrils coursing through his body, stimulating every cell and every nerve, and eventually penetrated his brain, awakening changes in chemistry that stood millions of years down the road of evolutionary change.

Around Henry Pigeon, eleven other men were passing through similar transformations.

Once the airliner touched down in Fiji, the secret agents scrambled for transportation. I watched them renting boats, booking tours, buying seaplanes (the Chinese government was going all out), and other forms of nonsense. I strolled along the wharf and hired a taxi to carry me to my contact's vacuum-cleaner-sales-and-repair shop. "Our Man in Fiji" greeted me warmly, offered me an aperitif, and provided a platter of seafood delicacies.

"So, Chris, are you going to the Mamanuca or the Yasawa islands?" he asked as if I would tell him.

Len Deighton wrote that the "greatest tribute you can pay to a secret agent is to take him for a moron." Then he added that the agent should "make sure he doesn't act too exactly like one."

"I haven't decided," I said. "I want to try some snorkeling, perhaps, a little spear fishing. Which would you suggest?"

"You are homosexual, aren't you?" he asked, purring with untoward insinuation.

The agent was a Bush administration appointee who had not yet been returned to sender. His "need to know" was virtually nonexistent. I patted his thigh suggestively, which caused him to spring to his feet (erect in all directions) and to decant another Campari, over which he poured cold water.

"Of course I am," I affirmed. "I'm sure that the agency sent you small portions of my file – sufficient for identification. I've read every entry in yours." He blanched at the heavy implications in my statement. "So have you found appropriate transportation?"

"Most discreet," he said hastily, splashing the drink down the front of his white mess jacket. "You wouldn't find another more discreet on all of Fiji."

I took a sip. "Delicious," I said. "Our Man in Fiji" was a far better bartender than he was a spy. "You mix a wonderful drink," I added, causing him to beam with pleasure.

Three hours later, half drunk, I was sitting on a small sailing vessel manned by two natives wearing sarongs that barely covered their asses. Sitiveni and Rupeni were beautiful in every sense of the word, and their eyes glowed with purplish intent. I was wearing a silver and black, snake print thong and lathering suntan lotion onto my chest, stomach, and thighs,

"Would one of you fellows do my back?" I asked.

216

The islanders exchanged glances, their purple irises speaking volumes, and Sitiveni, the more effeminate of the twain, nodded to Rupeni. Rupeni took the lotion from my hand. I turned onto my stomach and let Rupeni massage my back. His hands roamed lower until he was covering my bare buttocks with the oily lotion.

"Would you fuck me, Rupeni?" I whispered. "Fuck my ass?"

I was past worrying. AIDS and other sexually transmitted infestations could not pass from or to those who had been invaded. I well knew that my hosts were hosting invaders, so I had nothing to fear from their semen, and being a guy who loves cum for its own sake, I made the most of the situation.

Rupeni said nothing, but I heard his breath grow raspier with lust as he massaged my buttocks. I raised my hips, so he could pull down my thong bikini. He inserted a finger to get the back of my swimsuit out of my rear. His slick hand slipped into my crack, and I drew a deep breath. When his finger probed my asshole, waves of pleasure washed over me. Sprawling face down, I could not see the islanders, but I felt Rupeni's weight as he climbed atop me. His cock was slick with the suntan lotion and another lubricant that I could not identify, and it was incredibly thick, which I knew because it felt like a heavy weight when he pressed it against my asshole. I drew another deep breath, forcing my asshole open to receive him. Rupeni entered my ass easily, filling me with his shaft.

As he pushed deeper, Rupeni's thick cock head hit my prostate and sent shivers of pleasure through me. Still wordlessly, Rupeni started humping my ass. I rocked my hips up to meet his thrusts while Rupeni bored deep until his loins slammed against my ass cheeks.

Rupeni pulled back, paused for a heartbeat, and plunged downward. The stroke sunk deep. My dick became an agony of throbbing tingles. I reared up to meet Rupeni's lunges. He plunged down faster, and I tightened my asshole around his cock to milk him off, just as I had done for so many of our nation's governors.

Rupeni's dick was massaging my prostate outrageously. "Oh, fuck, I've never had it so good," I howled.

Even knowing I was getting fucked by a male possessed by an alien, I didn't feel as if I had lost myself. Greater waves of intense pleasure rippled through me, empowering me, enlightening me, and making me want the ultimate fulfillment. I was a slave to my nature, and I had never felt more liberated.

I worked Rupeni's dick with my derrière. The islander's big cock was pulling in and out of my asshole, each thrust driving shivers of ecstasy up my ass and down my cock. My cock sizzled with unexpected sensations. My heart raced with the thrill I took from the thrusting rod separating my butt cheeks.

I squeezed Rupeni's cock as hard as I could. I worked him with my butt until he was all but screaming with rapture and Sitiveni laughed aloud. Perhaps to impress his friend, Rupeni slowed his strokes until he had regained a measure of control. An agony of pleasure rippled through my cockhead, so that I erupted onto the deck of the native boat. Rupeni slowly fucked my ass while I came. My semen splattered upon the boards. Salvo of spunk followed joyous salvo. I was shooting what felt like cannons of jism. The islander Rupeni cried out while he filled my ass. I continued milking him until I felt the break in his hardness that signaled that he was drained. A squeeze of thick post-cum oozed from my tortured cock, and Rupeni finished with a few final gentle thrusts. Sitiveni applauded and cheered our success.

# # # # #

In a low budget Mexican beachfront hotel, Jeremy Smith fastened the belt on his plaid swim briefs and looked himself over in the smoky mirror. Not bad, he thought, carrying denial to the ultimate extreme of self-delusion. Smith was sixty-seven years old and ravaged with STDs. He had managed to survive the worst years of the plague during the time when no knew how the disease was transmitted, only to catch the AIDS bug, along with assorted other pestilences, at the age of sixty-five, during an anonymous and drunken encounter in a bathhouse.

Smith threw a beach robe over his sloping shoulders, picked up the thin hotel towel, and headed for the beach. The sun-scorched sand burned his bare feet, but his severe condition of peripheral poly-neuropathy kept him from noticing the blistering.

Smith wasn't so far gone, though, that he failed to notice the gorgeous young man strolling his way. The fellow was wearing belted swim briefs rather like Smith's own, but the younger man's fit his form deliciously. Smith could see the bulge of the young man's cock and balls through the print of the swimsuit. Smith stood five foot eight, and the young man appeared to be about two inches shorter. He carried neither towel nor beach blanket. His feet were also lacking in sandals. He carried a picnic lunch bucket in one hand. The way the youth was formed made Smith shift slightly forward as he walked. The strange lad's compact body was so perfectly formed that he was the veritable embodiment of desire. What a wonderful trick that little morsel would make, Smith mused, and the youth smiled at him.

The young fellow – up close he looked even younger than Smith had thought – Smith hoped that he wasn't jailbait – not that even the possibility of prison mattered anymore. Age and disease had placed Smith beyond managing his appearance, and since appearance was everything, he had become reckless. He decided to speak to the youth, but the young man spoke first.

"How old do you think I am?" The question disconcerted Smith. Was it designed to point to the boy's youth, or to his own decrepitude? Sprung jawed, Smith could only goggle like a grouper pulled from deep water. "Forty-four."

"Excuse me?"

"My name is Len Gallagher. I was born forty-four years ago. Six months ago, I stood six foot four; I was a key marine biologist; I was a virgin in all ways; and I was preparing for my first marriage."

Jeremy Smith possessed world-class gaydar, and his whole system was flashing red with bells and whistles. Not a word this boy was claiming could be true. Gallagher, if that was the lad's true name, could hardly be a day over eighteen, if that.

"Would you like to be young and gorgeous again? Gorgeous like I am?" the youth queried, his fingers evocatively touching his thick cock.

Dragging his gaze from Gallagher's crotch, Smith considered the young man's purple eyes. "Yes," he said. "Oh, yes."

"Follow me into the water," Gallagher commanded, "and prepare your old ass for the fuck of a thousand lifetimes."

# # # # #

The island was remote and almost unspoiled, except for the various conveyances that had transported my fellow secret agents. Native bures clustered along the shoreline. I saw the native women working, but there were no small children with them. The youngest child was ten or so, which seemed strange. The native men stood in a cluster away from the women and children. Still feeling the terrific pounding my ass had taken and the hot spunk inside me, I pulled up my thong and wrapped a sarong around my waist before our craft neared the shoreline. Sitiveni trilled some communication to Rupeni in an incomprehensible tongue.

My fellow agents were gathering under the swaying palm trees, preparing to enter the water and seek out the invaders. Quin, the British double-o man, and the Israeli secret agent were prominent among the group, but Valerie Glamour was trying to talk with the women. She would not be finding out the great secret, but she would, doubtless, obtain secrets of her own. Whether the things she learned would help our government prepare to fight the invasion in time remained to be seen. From what I already knew, the invaders were winning, and the invasion had spread farther than anyone in Washington, Tel Aviv, Moscow, Peking, or Mexico City imagined.

"You wish to meet the mother," Sitiveni said in heavily accented English. It was a statement, not a question.

"Mother?"

"Yes, wrong word. Is not female. But it spawns the rest. The lesser powers."

"And now the primal power seeks a host?" I asked.

"Yes," Sitiveni agreed. "She – It has split off enough of its essence. Now the lesser ones can multiply sufficiently. Now She – It seeks the one she/it will occupy."

"It is calling me," I said.

"Yes, you are chosen. You are the one."

My fellow agents were entering the tranquil water of the blue lagoon fringed with coral reefs and a sweeping white sandy beach, some boldly, some with trepidation, some stripping naked to give easy entrance to the black eels, which were neither eels nor black, but the intelligent progeny of a being from another word. Sitiveni and Rupeni led me behind the traditional thatched bures where two other young men greeted me. Like the islanders, neither looked older than eighteen, but these youths were not natives.

Speaking with American accents, the one introduced himself as Jeremy Smith and the other gorgeous lad said that he was Henry Pigeon. I recognized both names as possibly infected men who had been reported as missing persons some months earlier. Neither looked remotely like the photographs attached to their sheets. They were shorter and more compact. Their physical beauty was unearthly, especially their hypnotic eyes that glowed purple. They were wearing nothing but short colorful sarongs tied loosely around their hips. I could see the curves of their protruding naked asses.

The far side of the island was steep, with dramatic volcanic peaks dense with green foliage and brilliant flowers. Henry and Jeremy led me along a narrow path, which zigged and zagged around trees and bushes, through groves of fruit trees, and beneath swaying canopies of green from which came the chattering of tropical birds. After an hour's walk, we found the path leading downward. Our way took us between two peaks and down through a crevice in the high cliffs to the narrow beach below. We walked along the beach until we reached an outcropping of volcanic rock that bulged over the waves.

There, Jeremy suggested that I leave my clothes behind. "We have to walk in waist-deep water to reach the cave," he said. Jeremy and Henry removed their sarongs, and I caught my breath at the sight of their exquisite bodies. I doffed my own clothing until I stood naked before them. I felt foolish, for though I had never felt ashamed of my looks before then, I was no match for their incredible sexiness.

Henry Pigeon grinned at my discomfiture. "Not to worry, Chris," he said, though I had not told him my name. "By tomorrow, you'll look hotter than Jeremy and I combined."

We three splashed into the cavern, waist deep in warm tropical water. I expected invasion at any moment, but nothing happened, save that I was struck with the awesome beauty of the cave. The beach rose sharply once we were inside the cool shelter of the sea cave and within a minute, we were standing on the golden volcanic sand of the narrow, underground beach. The volcanic walls of the cavern were spotted with colored lichens and strange tropical mosses. Long vines with flowers trumpeting in hues from dazzling yellow to radiant red hung in profusion. The atmosphere was scented with a strange musk, virtually homoerotic in its scent and in its intensity.

"This is the place?" I asked uncertainly.

Jeremy and Henry stared around in bewilderment, so it was clear that the environment was as new to them as it was to me. Gradually their gazes shifted toward each other, as if an unknown power was exerting an influence over them. They embraced and then they kissed. As their tongues warred, their cocks arose with ferocious intent. One of the twain was going to get fucked, but I couldn't guess whom. To answer any speculations, Henry turned his back on Jeremy, and Jeremy inserted his cock with a single dramatic thrust. I gasped at the ferocity of the insertion, but Henry's lips curled with satisfaction.

I could feel the semen in my own ass even stronger than before. It was as if the sperm lived still, wriggling with delight within my rectum. The warm water rippled over my toes. Turning away from my butt-fucking comrades, I saw a pale, transparent snake-like being writhing in the warm water. It was nearly two feet long, almost invisible except for its rich pink hue that contrasted with the greenish water over the volcanic sand, and four inches in diameter. I could not but believe that such a thing entering my ass would split my rectum, if it did not slay me outright. Yet, even as I trembled with fear, I waded into the water.

The alien creature wriggled beside me as I waded deeper, and I knew that it had called me to this place so that it could enter into me. When the warm, sloshing wavelets covered my buttocks, the creature encircled my hips – lovingly, even, and exquisitely homoerotic. Its head lightly separated my buttocks. Almost unconsciously, I leaned forward, bending until my face nearly touched the frothy surf. I pushed to dilate my asshole with outrageous invitation. If I was going to get possessed by a species invading our planet, shouldn't I resist a smidgen – even in token? But I couldn't. I did not want to resist. I wanted the invader inside of me, part of me. I thought of my own agency and of Mr. Z, our misogynistic, misanthropic, homophobic superior. It was time for humanity to evolve, even if that evolution meant accepting a symbiotic alien that altered inclinations and affected one's very sexuality.

My asshole opened as I pushed, and opened farther than it had ever opened before. I opened up to the future of humanity. I opened to the conquest of the Earth.

"Come into me," I invited. "Enter. Take me. Join with me." The thick being entered, and its entrance was nothing I would mistake for the passage of a tiny human cock. I opened for ITS alien majesty, the Archon of the Boolean Cosmos, and it took me as no human man had ever taken me. Alien thoughts joined with mine. I was one with the alienness of it.

I was fucked hard, deep, and beautifully. I was fucked in the ass in ways I had never been fucked in the ass before then, and I loved every inch of its alien thickness, and every second of its alien penetration.

My body shivered with delight. My eyes lost focus. I could no longer see the walls of the cave, or Jeremy fucking Henry's horny ass on the shore. The alien form was still slithering up my ass as I exploded through raptures beyond imagining. My lips pulled back in uncontrollable frenzy. I grimaced like one slain, yet my grimace was a grip of pleasure beyond comprehension. My nostrils crinkled, as did my nipples. Oh, those little vestiges of our initial femininity! I shot fluid out of my hard nipples, even as the powerful orgasms shook every fiber of my psyche. I was fucked and fucker.

Cum was blasting out of my cock. Spurt followed spurt as I crashed through countless series of orgasmic thrills. My cock bucked as orgasm multiplied out of orgasm. The sequence of orgasms in my cock came at increasing speed. Even faster, though, the intense orgasms that rippled with increasing fury up my anus made my mortal body feel like a fucking hole. But more than that, I was the pulsating cosmic void. I saw cosmos swing upon cosmos. I saw the evolution of a million planets. I saw civilizations evolve, grow to splendor, and die. I saw creation, and I saw the heat death of the universe. Orgasms without counting thrilled me, and while the furious pleasure ripped through me, I remembered the births and deaths of universes.

I could feel Henry's and Jeremy's thoughts. I could feel everything their bodies were experiencing. My asshole was throbbing with pleasure that coursed through my body. My cock hardened again, and the tingles tore through the head. A renewed spasm of orgasmic bliss hit me with such strength that I staggered in the waist deep water. I recalled every homosexual experience of my life, every man I had had in every way, as my muscles contracted and sent an incredible spurt of thick jism into the water. I gasped as my asshole contracted and waves of pleasure rippled up my ass. A second spurt followed the first, equal in volume. If I had been capable of thought, I would have wondered how my body could produce so much semen.

I felt the sensations of Jeremy's cock in Henry's tight ass. Henry's ass was like a sucking hole that massaged every cell in Jeremy's cock. Jeremy shot loads as his body milked itself into Henry's ass. At the same time, I could feel the even greater pleasure that Henry was feeling. The cock fucking him was purely sexual, but it was other things as well. Jeremy was feeding Henry; feeding him pleasure, feeding him penetration, and feeding him the semen that his symbiotic cells lapped.

I tried to wade toward shore, but every step drove strokes of delight up my ass. Walking was literally – actually – an act of masturbation; every step was pleasure magnified. My skin was tightening so that I tingled all over. I could smell, hear, and see things I could never have seen before.

I touched my asshole. It was hot, but closed upon the gigantic alien that had entered into me. I was stuffed with the body of a being from another world, a tremendously powerful being with abilities I did not yet realize. Yet I was completely myself. I could hardly call myself possessed, even though an alien creature had joined with me, and was becoming more a part of me with every passing second. My buttocks rubbing together as I struggled toward shore produced an anal orgasm. Unearthly spasms rippled though my rectum, each ripple a delight beyond imagining. Overcome with sensation, I thrashed in the warm water and found nothing to hold onto, so I continued walking even though each step was a new act of anal masturbation triggering another orgasm.

With every step, I became more sensitive to my orgasmic contractions. They occurred at rising intervals while the strength of my contractions also mounted at a steady rate. My muscles relaxed completely between orgasmic contractions, and these pauses heightened the experience of the spasms.

Jeremy had finished fucking Henry by the time I reached the shore. They assisted me onto the golden sand where I collapsed face down. For a time I could not move, but I did not lose consciousness. Instead, I entered into a state of super-consciousness. I was aware that Sitiveni and Rupeni were approaching our cave, and I reached out for their minds. They knew that I had been taken by the great one, the leader of the invaders, the ruler who had spawned the rest. They approached the entrance of the cave with trepidation as though they expected to meet a god within.

I made their passage easier by sending forth a Zone of Compulsion. This was easy to do, and as the Zone touched them, Sitiveni and Rupeni lost their anxiety and swam into the cave. Every cell in my body was trilling, so I examined each one individually before studying how they all worked together. I examined several organs that served no purpose, but were simply evolutionary remainders and eliminated them by turning the cells into semen that spurted out my cock. The resulting orgasm was intense and satisfying.

I decided to wait before completely rearranging my body. I levitated from the sand and sat gloriously naked in the air before the two American men and the two islanders. Once I had cast a Zone of

Serenity around them so nothing I might do could frighten them, I took the molecules of the water and fashioned them into a green boat. I levitated my body into the boat, but I let the others climb aboard on their own. These pathetic mortals still needed to exercise their muscles, so I resolved never to relieve them of all physical labor.

Carrying us, our boat of water sped over the sea toward the beach where my fellow agents were entertaining their own aliens, though none had received anything like mine. I spread a Zone of Illusion over the island's women including Valerie Glamour, so they could not see us until I had Sitiveni and Rupeni safely returned to the shore. Then I spread my Perception so that my mind was in complete rapport with the island men and my fellow secret agents. Each man would have many tasks to fulfill.

While the island men disembarked for other islands, each carrying an alien capable of multiplying itself infinitely, I enlarged our water boat so that the agents could climb aboard. As we sped across the waves, I achieved greater speed by levitating our vessel so that we were flying over the sea, rather than riding upon it. While I directed the flying boat, I explored my cells again, rearranging until I was utterly stacked and gorgeous. Within minutes, I looked nothing like my former self. I meticulously rearranged my molecules and altered my DNA, shaping my ass into perfection, my cock into excellence, my muscles into perfect balance, and my features into sublime androgyny. I designed my form to arouse the lust of every man who saw my true shape.

Once I had sculpted my shape into perfection, I reached my Sense of Perception to the alien tissues in the bodies of my fellow passengers. In perfect rapport, every man collapsed onto the deck of the water boat, cuddling with his fellows in the throes of anal orgasm. My passenger thrilled me with a cascading series of orgasms that began as uncontrollable spasms of unimaginable pleasure in my anus, which rippled through my loins until my cock was spurting. We sprawled and gripped one another, coming maniacally on one another, gasping and clutching one another, and rubbing against one another as I mentally masturbated the entire group, including myself, as one.

# # # # #

Mr. Z, the head of our agency, wasn't feeling quite himself. After his invader claimed him, he suffered through a shuddering orgasm.

Compassionately, I helped him to his leather couch where he could sleep through the strenuous physical changes. I placed a Compulsion upon him, so that he would know how to turn out the other men of our agency once he had finalized his own transformation. Sending a Zone of Illusion before me so that others would see my shape as I used to be, and even manipulating the images captured by the security cameras, I strode boldly toward the front entrance.

Jeremy and Henry were waiting in a long, black car outside, and I floated into the back seat. I cast my Perception into our large cooler chest. Ninety-six more baby alien slugs had just multiplied.

"Success?" Henry asked.

"A tough case. He went over a little harder than most," I said, using my mouth rather than my thoughts. Some of my human habits yet remained. "He didn't even know it was on his leg until it was too late. I had to hold a Compulsion on him to keep him from hitting the panic button. He'll wake up with an itch up his ass that will require many cocks to scratch."

"Where to, Chris?" Jeremy asked, shifting hornily in the car seat. Lacking my own superior abilities to manipulate our orgasmic tissues at will, he wanted to get fucked again. I decided that after we had finished the next assignment, we would visit The New World Order. There we would find a near cornucopia of sexual partners who would be eager to receive their own invaders.

"Senator Ditch Dingle's office," I ordered. "The Republican leader can then summon his juniors into his office – one by one. When they come out they'll be out all the way."

Henry Pigeon tinkled with laughter. "And Dingle will pave our way into the Oval?"

"That's the plan, Henry," I agreed. "Once President Buchanan is hosting an invader, he can order the joint chiefs to receive theirs. Love those chains of command. Total conquest of every male on this planet is achievable within a year."

My comrades' eyes glowed with purple light as I threw a Zone of Illusion over Washington, D.C., levitated our automobile, and pointed its nose toward the cast-iron dome of the United States Capitol.

THE WITCH'S SPELL

One blustery morning during the winter quarter, my classmates and I were sitting in the college cafeteria, guzzling coffee and dunking donuts. We had just left our biology class, so we were discussing evolution. As usual, Tricia was talking the loudest, cutting everybody else short, and dismissing all opinions besides her own. According to Tricia, the human species evolved as females, and defective genes caused the masculine deformity. "Men are nothing but pseudo-women," Tricia claimed, giving us guys the evil eye. Nobody argued with her because Tricia was a hotheaded bitch with fiery red hair, an assertive jaw, and piercing eyes. She was an ardent feminist who carried feminism to a militant first strike policy. She belonged to every campus women's organization: Women on the Way, Sister Spirit, Warrior Women, Radical Dykes, and a host of others. Everyone knew that she was a practicing witch, and not of the good, healing Wiccan craft. Tricia bragged that she practiced the Left Hand Path and put hexes on people who crossed her.

I was scared of Tricia, and I did not intend to offend her, but she was known for taking innocent remarks the wrong way. That's what happened when I joked that separate evolutions must've taken place. Since males and females think so differently, they couldn't have evolved from the same source.

While the guys chortled over my weak joke, Tricia bounded to her feet, fuming with rage. "You boys think women are inferior to men," she accused. She pointed at me, and then at Phil MacMillan, Rich Jones, Dane Rothenberg, Scott Simms, and J.T. King in turn. "You think because you've got dicks and can beat your meat, you're the master race."

Scott nearly choked on the maple bar he'd been loading into his mouth when Tricia shouted the word dicks. When she howled beat your meat, Phil dropped his cream puff onto the floor. All conversation died in the cafeteria, and everybody stared. "I didn't say anything like that, Tricia," I protested, stunned at her crazy accusation. "My joke wasn't a put down. It was gender neutral."

"If I decide to take offense, then it's offensive," she insisted, quite unreasonably. "You're going to pay for insulting women, Todd. Phil. Rich. Dane. Scott. J.T." She pointed a wrathful finger at each of us as she pronounced our names. "You're gonna pay with your manhood. You're gonna find out just how little your tube steaks are worth."

With that arch threat, she stomped away.

"Shit," J.T. said, setting the jelly donut he had been squeezing back onto his paper plate.

"She'll get over it," Dane said, shrugging off Tricia's insane predictions.

Nervously, Scott commented, "She's a fuckin' witch." Scott, who was majoring in theology, was the most superstitious guy I knew. "Who knows what kind of hocus-pocus she'll hang on us."

"She's going to lay us proud usurpers low," I paraphrased from Robert Burns, since I was majoring in literature and hoped to become a college professor.

"Get real," said Rich, a math major. Rich had chestnut hair that covered most of his body. He was one hairy mathematician, but he was so smart that he would be plotting the trajectory of rockets to Jupiter after he graduated. "Witchcraft, my ass. You guys are too gullible."

We went our separate ways after that incident. I had only one class that afternoon, eighteenth-century British literature, and after finishing some research in the library, I walked home.

Since my parents' house was only five blocks away, I lived off-campus. That evening I ate dinner with my parents, studied for the next day's Italian language class, watched television, and passed a normal night. The next morning, my alarm blasted me out of a nightmare filled with loss and longing. I pushed in the buzzer and sat up, drowsily sensing that something was wrong. For as long as I could remember, I had been waking with a major pee hard, but that morning my dick was soft and felt numb. Still half asleep, I stumbled into my bathroom and took care of business. My dick looked normal, but it didn't feel right.

Then realization hit me – I had been too busy to jerk off the previous day. Consulting the clock, I decided that I had time to spank the monkey before class. I grabbed my lubricant, sat on the toilet, and played with my dick. I squirted some lube into my hand, and smeared it up good. My cock felt warm in my hand, but numb. I stroked and rubbed, but my dick wouldn't get hard. The need to shoot my load grew as I worked, yet nothing happened. Even after teasing my cockhead, rubbing the shaft, and massaging it with both hands, I couldn't get a hard-on. For fifteen minutes, I tried fruitlessly to pump it up. At last, I had to admit defeat. Bothered and horny, I finished my toilet routine, ate a moody breakfast, and jogged through the driving February rain to the campus.

Tricia caught me in the library after Italian class. "How's it hanging, Todd?"

"Huh?" I said. Tricia snickered snidely and sauntered off.

By the end of the week, I was getting desperate. I was so horny I couldn't stand it, but my dick wouldn't get hard, and I couldn't ejaculate. Several times each day, I tried to jerk off, but the result was the same. I even swiped one of my pop's Viagras, but the pill had no effect on my dick. All I got was a bone-crushing headache. I was getting scared, and by Friday of the second week, I was nearly insane. I knew it was time to seek medical help.

I was standing in line to see the doctor in the Student Union when Tricia pulled me aside. "Having trouble jerking off?" she asked.

Filled with the darkest suspicions, I went cold all over. "How do you know that?" I demanded. "Did you put something into my food?"

"Nothing like that, Todd," she said, chuckling blithely at my plight. "I cast a hocus on you, which no one can remove. But I can add a pocus to the hocus. I'm a witch."

"I don't want a pocus. I want to be like I was before. That's why I'm waiting to see the doctor."

"No doctor can help you. You've got a hex on your cock. Come over to my place tonight. You'll get a hard-on, and I'll make you come without your having to tug it."

I stared at her. Was Tricia inviting me to have sex with her? That didn't make sense. However, after I had suffered through history of the Roman republic unable to think straight due to my witch-charmed limp dick and full balls, I was ready for anything. Following dinner, I caught a bus across town to the address Tricia had given me. The bus plunged bravely through the gusts and driving rain, carrying me toward my fate.

Tricia lived on an old residential street that would be pleasantly tree shaded when summer came but was then a mass of rotting leaves and mud. Up a leaf-strewn yard, warm yellow light glowed from the windows of a pleasant bungalow. When I rang the doorbell, Tricia answered barefooted and garbed in a silky black witch robe.

"Here I am, Tricia," I declared, feeling suddenly apprehensive and completely foolish.

"You're the last to arrive," Tricia said, sneering at my announcement. "Everybody is down in the cellar."

I followed her through the kitchen and down to a deep candlelit basement. Tricia's coven, five females garbed in black robes, stood in a doorway gloating at me. Tricia introduced them as Circe, Eurale, Gorgon, Medusa, and Stheno, and added that I should call her Endor.

After I had greeted each of the women by their silly witch names, Tricia told me to follow her. "The boys are waiting in here," she said.

Tricia led me into a side room that looked like a former coal cellar. Waiting on a threadbare carpet were Phil, Rich, Dane, Scott, and J.T. The guys were stark naked and shivering.

"Strip off your clothes, Todd," Tricia ordered.

Against my better judgment, but driven by my lust, I removed my clothing. Tricia made me give up everything, and after I was bare, she carried my clothing and accessories to another room. I joined the guys who stood with flaccid cocks and forlorn expressions.

"Did these mumbo-jumbo witches hex you guys, too?" I asked.

"Yeah, for nothing," Phil complained. "I haven't got my rocks off for two fuckin' weeks."

"The fuckin' bitches," Scott swore, but he kept his voice low.

"Why'd you have to make that dumb-ass joke, Todd?" Dane hissed. "It's your fault Tricia put a spell on our cocks."

"Shut the fuck up, Dane," J.T. warned. "You laughed. That's the reason she dusted your peter with the goofer. You can't blame Todd."

"I don't believe in witch charms, spells, ju-ju, hocus-pocus, goofer dust, or hexes," Rich said. "There's a scientific explanation for all this."

"So why are you standing bare ass in Tricia's cellar with the rest of us?" J.T. chided.

We shut up fast as Circe entered the room. "We're ready for you limp noodles," Circe announced. "I'm going to guide you one by one to the sacred space. You first, Dane."

When my turn came, Circe led me to the doorway where Stheno anointed my feet, knees, cock, asshole, navel, nipples, and lips with scented oils. When I had been daubed according to the best spell books, Medusa took over and escorted me into the ritual room. The ceiling was painted like the night sky, splendid with stars. Pagan scenes decorated the four walls, and thick Persian carpets covered the floor. When we were all assembled, Tricia cast a circle around us, banished forces baneful to her intentions, and invoked the watchtowers.

Gorgon placed six phallic white candles on the floor around us. She lit each candle in turn and spoke a phrase in some eerie language while the other witches danced in a circle with brooms between their legs and evoked the Weird Sisters of Sex Magick. Finally, the dancing and chanting ceased and Tricia announced, "You boys have suffered for two weeks from a spell we cast. Tonight we will relieve you of your burden, but not in any way you might imagine. Tonight, we will fuck you, and you will come."

We guys glanced at each other in bewilderment. We had no idea what she meant.

"You boys are the defective women. Your cocks have never been obedient to your will, and have controlled you on many occasions. Now behold the shape of the true woman."

At the word, Tricia and her five robed cohorts formed a circle around us, lifted their robes, and displayed their naked forms. Six guys gasped as one. Tricia and her friends had feminine figures with female boobs and perky girl butts. However, not a twat was to be seen. Thick erect cocks jutted from their crotches and balls hung beneath. Their manly cocks would have looked spectacular on any man, but on these girls, big dicks were marvels to behold.

"Look at those fuckin' dicks," Dane murmured.

"What are they gonna do with those things?" Scott asked.

"You heard what she said," I contributed.

"Yeah," Rich added. "She said they're gonna fuck us."

"Here is the witchbone," Tricia intoned, rubbing her cock. As she stroked, a thick, yellow cum leaked out the end. "My cum is called fernseed. Tonight you broken women will be prodded with witchbones and filled with fernseed."

The girls passed around a tube of lubricant, squirting the stuff on their big hard cocks, and smearing it on each other. It seemed strange to see girls jacking each other's dicks. After they lubed their witchbones, each girl chose a guy to screw. Tricia picked me, which surprised me.

Tricia ordered me to bend forward while she lubed my asshole with her finger. "Oh, yeah, I'm gonna enjoy fucking your ass, Todd. The first time I saw you, I noticed your sweet caboose, and I vowed to get my witchbone into your butthole before the winter ended."

For my part, I crouched speechless while her finger slid into my ass. For a second my breath stopped; then my lungs sucked in the oxygen with a loud gasp as I surrendered to the incredible sensation that filled my ass. Nor was I alone. All the boys were moaning with joy as the girls lubed their rectums for penetration. Unbidden, a low howl escaped my lips. I had never felt anything so wonderful. Tricia's finger twisted this way and that, opening my hole for her thick cock's passage. Her voice whispered in my ear as she slipped her fingers out of my hole and pushed in the head of her dick. "Harden now, malformed woman," she commanded, and as my anal sphincter opened for her dickhead, my own cock filled and arose.

A thrill of joy shot through me. "My dick is hard again," I said.

"Mine, too," Dane said.

"And mine," proclaimed J.T.

The women laughed evilly. "Don't fool yourselves, boys," Tricia taunted. She pulled her dick out of my ass and my erection deflated. "You can't get hard without our help. From now on, you will get a hard-on when a witch has her witchbone up your ass. Only when a witch leaks fernseed into your rectum will you be able to shoot your load. If we tire of you, you will never ejaculate again, though you will still produce semen, which will be an everlasting torment."

With that, Tricia pushed me to my hands and knees. The guys were brought down with me. "Stick out your asses," the witches commanded. "Wiggle your booty and show you want it."

I had to come. If I could only shoot my cum that way, then I had to put out for the witches. I wiggled my ass. Tricia's firm hands grasped the top curves of my buttocks, and her prod touched my asshole. The witch prepared to drive her entire, thick, slick cock up my ass.

"Beg for it, Todd," Tricia demanded. "Tell me how much you want me to drive my nine-inch witchbone up your fuckhole. Ask me to pump you full of fernseed and make you come."

"Make me come, Endor," I begged, remembering to use her witch name. "Please. Fuck my ass and give me some relief."

Her huge dick opened my little hole, and a delicious joy shot through me as my cock hardened again. "Fuck me, Endor," I begged. The monster cock opened me farther, and my asshole dilated pleasantly. My cock grew even harder. I could feel already that this fuck was going to make me come.

I was not alone. By the flicker of the cock-shaped candles, I beheld the faces of my friends. Their eyes were bright with joy, and their mouths formed words that they had never articulated before that night, "Fuck my ass, Medusa. Fuck my pansy ass, Gorgon. Ah, Eurale, fill me with your cock." As the guys begged for it, the witches obliged and shoved their jutting dicks hard up the guys' asses.

"Shove your witchbone into me," I pleaded, as Tricia pulled back. "Come on, Endor, fuck me." Here Tricia pushed her cock far up my ass, and I felt no pain, but an exquisite delight too singular to describe. "Oh, yes, fuck me," I demanded. "That's it. Fuck my ass, Endor. Ream me hard with your big cock."

Tricia gripped the top swells of my ass more tightly, pulled her cock back, and slammed it into me. Her witchbone was leaking fernseed steadily, depositing the paranormal cum inside my rectum. In my desperate state, even the trickle of fernseed that reached my prostate was enough to set me off. Tingles of orgasm rushed through me, the bliss produced by her cock driving moans unbidden from my lips.

"Oh, Medusa," Phil howled. "You ram me so good."

"Your fernseed is working, Circe," Dane wailed. "Oh, oh, it's driving up my ass and out my cock."

"Oh, yeah, fuck me; make me your bitch," I shrieked as the tingles rose in intensity. I was gripping the carpet with both hands and rocking my ass to meet Tricia's thrusts. My cock was alive in a strange way. I felt like a thousand hands were gripping it hard, but the sensation was more like being milked from inside out. The cock in my ass was getting me off. Instead of the tingles running back from my cockhead, they were running from my ass to my cockhead. I gripped Tricia's cock with my anal muscles. I rode her cock, delighting in the filling and the reaming. I felt a powerful contraction in my ass, followed by a contraction of my pelvic muscles that culminated in great blasts of hot semen spurting out of my cock. "Ah, fuck me, Endor. Fuck me. Fuck me."

"I am fucking you, bitch boy."

Tricia fucked me hard, rocking back and forth, and reaming me with her cock. I shot hard squirts of my cum onto the carpet, and my friends were coming all around me. Finally, my contractions ceased, but the pleasure did not end there, for the witch wasn't finished with me. She kept right on fucking me, and since the sensation of being prodded was a great pleasure in itself, I just let it keep on – not that I really had a choice. After about fifteen minutes of hard penetration, a second orgasm rose within me.

"Oh, I'm going to come again. Ah, yes, Endor, your witchbone is making me come. That's good." A hurricane of orgasms hit me, one after another, while I squirted out tiny needles of spunk that hurt in a good way when they spewed out of my peehole, while the thick dong up my ass maintained its steady rocking.

"Oh, Stheno, my guts are full of your fernseed," Rich proclaimed, his lips close to my ear.

Tricia kept fucking me until I had a third orgasm and ejaculation. After that, I felt exhausted, and I slipped forward, falling into a light doze for a while. When I awoke, I was sprawled face down in my own spilled cum, mingled with the semen of the five other guys.

After closing the circle, Tricia announced that we would assemble for wine and cakes. "You butt boys take a shower first," Tricia ordered. "I don't want to eat with a bunch of drippy holes."

Stheno led us to the basement bathroom. We showered together – without the girls – and washed our semen-wet cocks and butt cracks wet with fernseed.

"Have you ever seen jism like this?' J.T. asked, displaying the fernseed that Eurale had unloaded on his butt.

The girls' cum was markedly different from the stuff we shot. Fernseed was thicker than our natural boy jism and vibrantly yellow. The witches' balls must have produced tremendous amounts of this substance, for our asses were dripping wet and sticky inside and out.

"I hope Circe didn't give me a disease," Dane said as he soaped between his buttcheeks.

"No danger of that," Rich assured him, wholly converted to the realm of magic. "It's witchcraft. If they can grow dicks at will, then they can control disease, too."

After we dried, we found that the witches had left a box labeled "Butt Boy Panties." The note read: "Wear these to the wine and cakes."

Rich held up one pair of creamy yellow panties. "They look like something a Butt Boy would wear," he muttered, wiggling his ass into his panties.

I slipped into my panties. They felt incredibly sexy on my ass.

"These panties are the same color as the fernseed," Dane commented.

"You think that's a coincidence?" J.T. chided.

Phil pointed at Rich. "He's walking like a girl. Look at his ass sway."

I took a few steps. My ass swayed. Try as I might, I couldn't walk like man. We were all swishing our butts with every step.

"Fuck it," Rich said as he sashayed to the magical room. The rest of us swished along behind him.

The witch girls had dressed again in their black robes. They must have showered as well, for their hair was damp. I wondered whether they grew the dicks to suit the occasion or whether they were permanent fixtures. I thought that I caught a glimpse of Stheno's thick cock roll, but their witch robes played hob with my vision. The witches were sitting in a semi-circle on the floor, leaving room for the six of us to form the other half. A platter of bite-sized, white-frosted cakes sat in the center, along with two crockery pitchers of red wine. Tricia served the wine in kiln-fired goblets.

As we ate, the witches lewdly discussed us as if we were sex objects existing for their personal pleasure. They talked about the shape and firmness of our asses and how our grainy rectums had given their cocks good friction.

"I shot a bucket of fernseed into Rich," Stheno announced.

"Scott is nice piece of ass, too," Gorgon said.

"Todd is a good little slut for my witchbone," Tricia announced. "You women should try him out." She turned her evil eyes upon me. "Next Friday night, be a little earlier, Todd."

"Next Friday?" J.T. echoed.

"Yeah," Tricia said. "We're gonna do you boys once a week. We fuck your asses, and you get to shoot your loads. Meanwhile, don't bother trying to beat off. Your broken peckers are not gonna get hard and you're not gonna come. Not until our witchbones are up your asses again."

After we polished off the cakes and wine, the witches returned our clothing. We dressed in our own underwear, left the yellow panties at Tricia's house, and departed with forced and desperate promises to return the next week. Dane drove J.T. and me home. I was glad that my parents were asleep because I was in no humor to answer questions. I threw my pants and shirt over a chair, crawled into bed, and slept the sleep of the profoundly tormented.

Phil, Rich, Dane, Scott, J.T., and I talked once as a group during the week. True to Tricia's words, we could not masturbate. Our cocks were still hag-ridden, possessed, and witch-held. We agreed that we had no choice but to let the girls butt-bang the cum out of our cocks.

By Friday evening, I was insanely horny again. I would gladly have invited the whole football team to gang bang my ass if it would make me shoot my load. However, Tricia had claimed that the spell did not work that way. I had to take a witch's cock in order to come.

When I heard Rich blowing his horn, I raced out to his car. He had already collected Scott and J.T. We picked up the rest of the guys and arrived at Tricia's bungalow in good time.

The procedure was the same as the first time. We stripped, saw our clothes whisked away, and waited for the witches to summon us one by one. When we were in the sacred space, the circle cast, the watchtowers invoked, and the baneful forces banished, Tricia again evoked the Weird Sisters of Sex Magick.

The women removed their robes to reveal their witchbones, dripping with fernseed. We looked at the nine-inch-long rearing cocks, thick and dripping with yellow custard, and fell back as the witches commanded. We stretched upon our backs, our heads touching, our bodies like spokes in a wheel. At the girls' command, we lifted our legs. Medusa's face twisted into a diabolical smirk as she prepared to thrust her thick cock into my asshole. She pushed my legs farther toward my face, which raised my ass off the carpet. I felt the pressure of her tremendous dickhead against my opening hole. My cock hardened then, solid and ready to shoot as her seeping dick massaged my rectum and planted fernseed in my prostate.

"Yeah, shove it in, Medusa," I moaned. "Come on, fuck my horny ass. Shoot me full of cum."

I turned my head to see what was happening to the guy next to me. It was Dane, and Tricia had chosen his ass.

"Ok, let's witchbone these pansies," Tricia ordered, and each girl rammed her gigantic cock up a guy's ass. I gasped as Medusa reamed it into me, and I squirted my cum over her tits.

"Ah, uh," the guys moaned as each blasted a load in response to the terrific reaming. "Oh, fuck, fuck my ass. Oh, I'm coming like a bitch."

"That's our boy whores. They come when they're fucked," Tricia yelled demonically as she pulled back and rammed her cock into Dane's ass again and again. She fucked him hard until he started moaning again. He was getting close to another shooting, as was I, as were all the guys.

"Ah, you're going to make me come again, Gorgon." "Uh, shit, Endor, that's good." "Oh, yeah you're really fucking my ass, Eurale."

My second orgasm built more slowly than the first; it grew from mild tingles into a storm of pleasure. The orgasm originated in my ass again, and the anal sensation was more pronounced than the previous week's. I abandoned myself to the fantastic prickling, which rippled in my ass, growing to a wave of pleasure. The wave drove my cum from my balls and sent it flying out of my cock. As I spurted my load onto Medusa's stomach and my own, I made yelping sounds like a wounded animal, and tears of joy filled my eyes.

"Oh, Endor, I needed to come so bad," Dane cried. "Oh, thank you for fucking me."

"I having an anal orgasm," Rich howled with wonder and pleasure. "Circe, it's so good. I can't believe it."

The witches were getting close to unloading their nuts for the third time. I felt Medusa's cock stiffen even harder up my ass, and she thrust violently. "Yeah, take it, you boy slut," Medusa groaned. "Yeah, I'm gonna shoot my fernseed up your bitch asshole."

"Yeah, skeet it into me," I urged. "Unload your balls in my ass."

Tingles of a third orgasm ran through me. I could not judge whether the orgasms originated in my cock, so hard yet so thoroughly unmanned, or up my horny ass, so eager now to be filled constantly with cock meat and motion and to become an eager receptacle for spent semen. The pleasure grew slowly and swelled to a shuddering climax just as Medusa's cock shuddered and she grunted and swore with the intense orgasm shaking her cock and the spurting that emptied her balls into my eager rectum.

Then Medusa collapsed atop me, panting and gasping, even as her long thick penis still filled my ass. When she withdrew her magical rod, my asshole popped loudly. After she pulled her cock's head out, I lowered my aching legs and rolled onto my stomach so her fernseed wouldn't leak.

"Shit, you give good ass, Todd," Medusa said. "I unloaded a shitload of hot fernseed into you." She patted my ass affectionately. "You keep putting out like that, and I might keep you around 'til the end of the summer."

Showered and swishing in our Butt Boy Panties, we joined the girls for cakes and wine. The girls were bragging about our asses, and what enchanting little fucks we were. Meanwhile, Phil, Rich, Dane, Scott, J.T., and I exchanged glances, feeling demeaned and devaluated as human beings while the witches dismissed us as sex objects, no more than holes for the deposit of their seed.

And so it went for the remainder of that quarter. Tricia and her big-dicked girlfriends fucked our asses every Friday night and left us to suffer the rest of the week.

"This is intolerable," Scott exploded. We were huddled behind the oldest books in the college library, kept on the top floor where no one ever visited. There we could conspire in secret.

"They're humiliating us," J.T. agreed. "We can't let them keep treating us this way."

Rich spoke for us all when he said, "I like getting fucked in the ass, but I want my dick to work like it should."

"Yeah," I agreed. "I don't want to be having sex with girls anymore."

My statement stopped all conversation. The guys looked surprised, but after a few minutes of self-evaluation, they nodded their agreement. "I guess that we're totally disgusted with women," Phil said. "Whether they have cocks or not."

"So we want to reverse Tricia's spell, but we don't want to give up getting fucked?" I asked.

"Right," Rich said, his eyes flickering over the millions of old books that filled shelves as far as we could see. "We gotta find a spell to make our dicks work normally again."

"And what then?" J.T. asked. "When our dicks work – will we be queer then?"

No one spoke for the longest time. We had experienced anal sex and found it good, but we had not yet faced the fact that we were homosexual. My face reddened, but I spoke first. "I know that I will," I said. "Guys, I'm gay."

"Me, too," Dane said.

"And me," announced J.T. "And I'm glad."

"I wouldn't have sex with another girl if you gave me a million bucks for it," Dane bragged.

"Okay, we're gay," Rich agreed. "Wow. It feels good to say it out loud. But now that we're gay, we've got to get our cocks working right again. That means finding the spell that hexed us. Then we can get one to counteract it."

"How are we going to do that?"

"I don't know yet," Phil said. "But while we're looking for that spell, we ought to find one that would turn the tables on those fuckin' bitches. I want some payback."

Agreeing that revenge would be sweet, we pursued an extensive study of the occult arts. I never did so much reading in my life. The college library had numerous hoary tomes about spells, charms, glamours, cantrips, demoniurges, and wanga. We scoured antiquarian bookstores and loaded up with quaint and curious volumes about magic caps, magic wands, magic rings, magic belts, magic lamps, and magic spectacles. We studied about seven-league boots; wishing stones and wishing wells; caps of darkness; hands of glory; flying carpets; and merry thoughts. Meanwhile, we uttered nary a word to Tricia and her girlfriends and let them prod us weekly. By early July, we had become experts in incantations, conjurations, exorcisms, and captivations, but we hadn't found a spell that would counteract Tricia's evil hex. As time passed, the witches were getting bored with us and looking for other guys to ruin.

"When we're tired of you boys, we're going to cast you aside," Tricia told us during cakes and wine one night.

"You will take the spell off our dicks first, won't you?" J.T. asked. In response, the witches cackled cruelly among themselves.

A week later, our library science major Dane unearthed the spell used to bind our cocks. He found an elderly warlock living in Hungary, telephoned him, explained our situation, and received back faxes that detailed arcane spells. The warlock told Dane that the spell Tricia used had been collected in a 16th century manuscript, and that she must have picked it up from an Italian witch's website. The warlock was certain that the other spells he was faxing over had never been published, for they had been handed down from father to son. There was no way Tricia would know them, and therefore she would not be able to counteract them.

On Thursday, Phil, Rich, Dane, Scott, J.T., and I assembled in Phil's attic, cast our own circle, lit pink candles, and burned pungent incense. Working skyclad, Phil, who was majoring in classical languages, read the spell in a deep voice fraught with presence. At the conclusion of the incantation, we lifted our voices in unison: "So mote it be."

Our cocks rose, hot and horny as ever before. J.T.'s hard pecker seemed to dance before my eyes. It fascinated me in the way a snake fascinates, so I was not even aware that I had fallen to my knees. My lips were touching the head of J.T.'s dick, so firm, so delicious. My tongue flicked over the tip of it, and my head slipped forward of its own accord, and that beautiful dick filled my mouth.

It was better than any lollipop could ever be. I sucked on it, licked it, tasted it, and abused it with my lips. At the same time, I felt a wet, sucking sensation on my own cock. Somehow I had fallen to my side, as had J.T., and as I sucked him, so Phil was sucking me. All of us were lying in a circle, each guy sucking a cock, each guy getting sucked.

My hand explored J.T.'s smooth ass while I sucked his cock. The physical education major's ass was rounded and firm, doubtless the result of zillions of hours doing squats with thousand pound barbells, and the feel of those firm mounds with the mysterious crack between excited me beyond imagining. I sucked harder on his cock, willing it to explode with its bounty of juices. Meanwhile, Phil was wildly sucking me off, forsaking all in his desire to make me come.

We were so horny that we could not hold out long. My dick grew heavy, filled, stiffened ever harder. Tingles became trills that turned into thrills. Raptures rippled through the head of my cock. A deep cosmic throb filled my cock, growing and warming my pelvis, prickling in my nipples, asshole, nose, and toes. J.T.'s cock bucked in my mouth, and I tasted his hot jism, salty and sweet at once, and the taste of his cum and the feel of his cock in my mouth, and the shape of his hard, smooth ass under my hand, drove the contractions that shot my sperm into Phil's throat, making him drink my juice, swallow my spunk, down it all as I gushed into his mouth. As I came, I swallowed, too, gleefully sending J.T.'s semen into my stomach, and a warm glow filled my whole body, and my mind was exploding with joy.

Long we sprawled together, wet with each other's mouth, fed with each other's fluids. Finally, we rose shakily and closed the circle. We were free to grow hard, to masturbate as we willed, to come with others; our cocks were ours again, exorcised and evoked from the dead, and raised from the vasty deep of the witches' curse.

"Tomorrow night," Rich said. "Tomorrow is Friday. The spell calls for a circle jerk, so don't tug your pud just because you can. Save it, so we can put our own spell on those hocus-pocus girl pricks."

"Thus the whirligig of time brings in his revenges," Shakespeare wrote, and I was eager to see the whirligig whip those girls who had been fucking and debasing us for so long. At college, Friday was a day of secret smiles and silent smirks, and eagerly we longed for the night's comeuppance. Then we would see these chicks with dicks get their deserts.

When we entered Tricia's basement, we each knew our part in the drama that was to follow. We stripped as usual and let Tricia cast the circle. However, before she could banish any forces inimical to her control, Phil, Rich, Dane, Scott, J.T., and I moved to the center of the circle, sat naked in a ring, and Phil spoke a ritual in a language strange to the witches' ears.

"What the fuck?" Tricia yelped.

"They've got hard-ons," Circe screeched, pointing at our erect cocks.

"They can't get hard by themselves," said Medusa in denial.

"I don't fuckin' believe it," Gorgon moaned, her voice reflecting her dismay and horror.

"The boys are gonna hoodoo us, Endor," Stheno warned, the only witch not incapacitated by denial or invincible ignorance. However, she spoke too late, and her sorcerous sisters ignored her.

Our cocks were lubed, and each guy gripped the slick dick to his left. None of us was expert at left-hand handjobs, but we were ready to blow anyway.

Stheno was frantic. "They're jerking-off, Endor. Banish their powers before it's too late." Tricia did not respond. She only stared in numb shock while we beat each other's meat.

"Endor, say the banishing ritual," Stheno shrieked. "When these guys come, their spell is going to hit us." Tricia was not listening; she didn't move, not even when Stheno grabbed her shoulders. "Endor!"

All too late. Dane's cock was quivering for release; it filled my hand magically. Rich was rubbing the head of my cock, and his fingers bit deep. "Ah, Rich, you're gonna make me come," I groaned.

I felt Dane's cock stiffen as semen rose from his balls. My semen was rising at the same time; I felt the heaviness that precedes ejaculation. The prickles of approaching orgasm were rippling through my dickhead.

"Ah, Todd, you're jacking me so good," Dane moaned. "This is it. I'm gonna squirt."

"Me, too," the guys moaned, and indeed, jism spurts were already flying and decorating us indiscriminately.

The tingles in my cock grew to an explosion. "I'm gonna blow," I howled. "Oh, here it comes, guys."

We kept jacking each other as orgasm claimed us all. While splats of shot semen spurted high, the six witches fell backwards screaming and shrieking. As we writhed in sexual ecstasy, they writhed as their bodies transformed. The warlock had assured us that their metamorphosis would hurt, and their pained cries made our orgasms all the sweeter. We came and came, milking each other's cock until the last drops had oozed forth. Finally, we stood, bowed to the old gods of lust of man for man, and opened the circle that Tricia had cast.

The six witches were regaining consciousness. As I studied Tricia's boyish face and her shorter hair, she opened her eyes and blinked at me.

"What happened?" she demanded.

"Take off your robe, asshole," J.T. suggested. "See for yourself."

The other former witch girls were rising as well. The one who had called herself Eurale pulled her robe over her head. She had become a guy, a slightly effeminate looking guy, but male all over. The others stared at the former Eurale – then pulled off their own robes.

"You transgendered us," Tricia said, tweaking his boy nipples. "We're boys."

"That's right," Dane smirked. "You're just like us now."

"That's right, Tricia," I said. "Or whatever name you're going to use from here on out. You're going to stay male for the rest of your life. Of course, there is one catch. You're gay – not even a little bit bisexual – totally gay – as you will soon discover."

After his initial shock, Tricia loved his new body. After all, he became what he really wanted to be all the time. After his change, he took the name Troy, and he and the rest of the former witches dropped out of college and ended up as exotic dancers in a gay bar. As for Phil, Rich, Dane, Scott, J.T., and I, we agreed that we were finished with girls for good. After our experiences with the witches, we decided that we would have far more fun with each other than we could ever achieve by pretending to be straight. We ended up sharing a house, even after graduation, and we have our ritual space in the attic. Every Friday night, we cast our circle and perform our own magic spell.

UNCLE HORNY

One warm, fly-buzzing day in late June, I met the Demon of Fellatio, an old member of the family, in my grandmother's attic, and discovered that I was a cocksucker who sprang from a lineage of cocksuckers. A few weeks earlier, my mom and dad had shuffled me off to my grandmother's house for the entire summer while they partied in Europe. At the time, I'd been highly pissed about being dropped off like an unwanted sack of potatoes, especially since I'd only met my dad's mother a few times, and those were before Grandpa Barnet died.

Anyway, that morning I was sitting in my room in Grandmother's house and attempting – without much success – to come up with a topic for an essay I had to write. I'd arranged with my classmate Bob for a late afternoon movie, followed by pizza, but in the meantime, I was stumped for a topic.

Grandmother Barnet was enjoying her morning nap, from which she broke for lunch at 1:00, and followed that with her long afternoon nap. I didn't know anybody in that old Oregon town except for Bob, whom I found tiresome, and I'd only met him because Grandmother insisted that I take an English composition class at the local junior college on Monday and Wednesday mornings. So I sat in my room after class on Wednesday, completely stuck for a writing topic due the following Monday. After staring at an empty computer screen for forty-five minutes, I hit on the idea of exploring the attic.

I reached the attic by way of a long unused flight of steps leading up from a long unused bedroom. Though both doors creaked horribly, the servants were cooking and cleaning below and a nuclear explosion wouldn't have awakened grandmother from her beauty sleep. I crept up the squeaking stairs to a level no one had invaded for longer than I'd been alive.

The attic had an odd smell, like ancient dust. The long-unswept floorboards, stacks of wooden crates, antiquated dressmakers' mannequins, antique furniture, and other relics from a bygone era were covered with dry filth. Dead houseflies crunched under my feet. The attic had no lights that I could find, but eerie sunbeams filtered through two grimy windows at each end of the house.

I was peering into a trunk when I heard someone whispering to me. I should have jumped out of my sandals, but the voice was so soft and so gradually did it intrude upon my consciousness that I felt no apprehension. I glanced around, and dimly in the uncertain light, I spied a grinning head poking above a five-foot high packing crate.

The little fellow's face and scalp were hairless, but pleasant to look upon. His skin was pinkish yellow, his lips full and smiling. Two ivory horn nubs projected from the top of his head.

"Who are you?" I asked.

"I'm your Uncle Horny, Derek."

I thought that strange. "How do you know my name?"

When he stepped from behind the taller crate, I saw that his arms and chest were bare and as hairless as his head. Still, his physique impressed me more than his smooth skin. His muscles were powerfully developed, and I wondered where he exercised.

"I know everything about you, my boy. Everything."

That was puzzling because I'd never heard my parents mention him. "Do you live in the attic, Uncle Horny?"

"Sometimes. Let me look at you, my boy. Take off your shirt."

Considering he was family, I pulled my shirt over my head. I felt embarrassed because I didn't have any muscles to speak of since my parents had never encouraged me to get involved in any physical activity. Nevertheless, Uncle Horny examined my bare torso, smiled reassuringly, and asked, "Would you like to build yourself up? Have the kind of body that any guy would envy?"

"Sure," I said.

"Let's see the rest of the package," Uncle Horny suggested. "Pull off your shorts."

I kicked off my sandals, pulled down my brown cotton shorts, and piled them on my shirt. "Should I take off my underwear?"

"Certainly. I need to see what we have to work with," Uncle Horny replied.

That made sense, so I slipped out of my green and black bikini briefs and laid them beside my clothes. When Uncle Horny emerged from behind the boxes, I saw that he was naked, too. I felt better about that because I'd been kind of embarrassed about being buck naked in front of him. But with him exposed, it was more like being in the locker room, and I didn't feel so self-conscious.

Uncle Horny prodded every part of my physique to check where I most needed to develop. For some reason, this groping left me feeling oddly sensual, even aroused, by his exploration.

"Are you feeling queer, Derek?" Uncle Horny asked.

"Yes, I think I am. I never knew that it would feel so good. Look how hard my cock is. And look at your cock, Uncle Horny."

Uncle Horny's pinkish dick was long and thick. I couldn't stop looking at it. All my life I'd wondered whether I might be gay, but I knew for sure when I grabbed hold of his enticing piece of flesh. I gasped when I closed my hand around Uncle Horny's cock. A thin spurt of pre-cum leaked out of my own dick, leaving a wet stain in the dusty floor.

"That's my boy," Uncle Horny moaned. "You're lucky that you're queer, Derek. Were you straight, you'd have to waste thousands of hours lifting weights to build up your body. But I have a better way."

"If this means sucking your dick, Uncle Horny, I want to do it."

Uncle Horny smiled at my eagerness. "Yes, Derek, and the spunk you swallow will make your muscles grow."

I was taller than Uncle Horny, so he elevated to kiss my lips. I responded with my tongue, and my dick leaked furiously as our tongues tangled. I kissed his neck and down his chest, sucking his hard nipples one by one, until I went so low I had to fall on my knees. I kissed his strangely colored stomach, rippling with muscles, and down to his protruding shaft. Uncle Horny's crotch was hairless, and his dick had been circumcised. When I touched my tongue to the bulbous head, Uncle Horny leaked a pearly drop onto my taste buds.

The flavor of his cum made me want more. It was the best pudding I'd ever tasted, and my mouth formed a ring around his cockhead so none would escape me. Fearful of choking, I closed my fist around his shaft, and worked his cockhead with my lips and tongue. I especially liked it when Uncle Horny placed both hands behind my head and rocked his hips. I released his dick, so he could fuck my mouth at will, gripped his big firm buttocks, and worked at his cock furiously. Since I was new to it, Uncle Horny didn't push it in deep enough to gag me, and he didn't move faster than I could handle.

It didn't take long for Uncle Horny to reach his pleasure point. "Swallow it, Derek," Uncle Horny moaned. "Oh, that's good, my boy. Take it as it comes. Oh so good. Here I come, Derek. Oh, yes, here's cum in your mouth."

The hot thick fluid was spurting into my mouth, tasting like a thousand flavors of creamy pudding or scrumptious ice cream without the cold. I kept swallowing it down as quickly as it came, hardly believing that he could discharge so much. Uncle Horny filled my mouth as fast as I could swallow until I could hold no more. When my stomach was bulging, Uncle Horny ceased shooting his wet spunk and pulled his cock from my mouth.

"Good boy. You swallowed most of it."

I brushed away the dead flies, sat my bare ass in the dust, and leaned against a crate. I was dizzy, but my young body felt alive in ways it'd never felt before. I also felt sore all over. Every muscle was tingling.

Uncle Horny dropped his ass onto the floor in front of me. "That was incredible, Uncle Horny," I confessed. "Thank you."

Uncle Horny touched his pink hand to my throat, and I experienced a sharp burning; it felt like a million hot needles had pricked me. "You're a cocksucker, Derek," he agreed with a smile. "I've given you the cocksucker's official mark, and you'll suck cocks for the rest of your life."

"Sweet," I exclaimed, swelling with pride. "Was I good?"

"You're a natural. You made relatively few of the first timer's errors. Of course, your technique will improve over time. The more you suck, the better you'll suck."

"Sweet."

"My dick put a smile on your face," Uncle Horny observed.

That afternoon Bob and I went to a movie and afterward stopped at a pizza parlor. The date wasn't as interesting as I'd hoped. I inadvertently referred to myself as a cocksucker, which resulted in Bob turning pale and casting sidelong glances. He acted as if he suspected me of sneaking up on him. When we finished eating, he complained that he had a ton of homework and dropped me off at my grandmother's house.

I stripped in my bathroom and checked my body in the mirror. Bumps of muscle were budding in all the right places. Nothing spectacular yet, of course, but I was surely developing a physique. I found a brown stain on my throat where Uncle Horny had touched me. It wasn't anything that other people would notice, but the mark formed some vague shape.

I heard the dinner bell tinkling. I'd eaten pizza, but that was two hours earlier and I felt ravenous. I pulled on my briefs and shorts, and grabbed a fresh shirt.

Grandmother Barnet's housekeeper/cook was called Matilda. (Grandmother also had a maid named Gertrude and a gardener/chauffeur named Gretchen). Matilda had despised me at first sight and did not attempt to conceal her opinion. Privately, I began thinking of Matilda as the Horrible She, with the adjective varying according to my mood. I'd hit on that name during a silly adjective lesson in comp class.

The Hideous She had cooked onion soup, spicy chicken breasts swimming in a white sauce, yellow wax beans with cashew nuts, potatoes with cheddar cheese, and a Caesar salad. In spite of the dinner being old people's food, I cleaned my plate and took a second helping of Baked Alaska, although the Repulsive She made a snide comment about fat freeloaders. Grandmother kept glancing at my neck during dinner, but she didn't comment on the burn. She only talked about her distant past, and the weird stuff she and her friends had done back while historical figures like Franklin Roosevelt and Huey Long were threatening to seize the family fortune and distribute it among the poor.

Finally, Grandmother Barnet's tedious story ended, and I mounted the stairs to my bedroom. Every muscle was singing with pain, muscles I never knew I had, and I could hardly bend over. I dropped my shorts on the floor beside the big double bed with the canopy and the side curtains, fell in without trying to remove my tee shirt and briefs, and crashed into a deep slumber.

When I woke in the morning, I thought that both my tee shirt and briefs had shrunk. My tee shirt still fit, albeit tightly across my chest, but my briefs had become impossible. I stripped them off and examined my body in the mirror. I couldn't believe what I saw. My clothes had not shrunk; my body had grown. My ass was rounded and hard, a real moon. I'd always wanted a shapely butt. When I ran my hands over it, a thrill shot through me. My ass reminded me of Uncle Horny's firm derrière, which I'd gripped while blowing him. I thought my cock looked thicker, too, although I knew that it wasn't really a muscle.

I looked into my mirror face to see if I still looked the same. Yes, it was the same familiar face looking back at me, but with an inner glow. The brown mark on my neck had faded to a tan, but its lines were clearer.

"Good morning, cocksucker," I said to myself. I'd never again use that word as an insult.

I hurried through my bathroom routine, and pulled a clean pair of summer shorts from a drawer. After trying on several pairs of underwear, I gave up in despair. I'd have to buy larger ones. When I pulled up my shorts, I gaped at the effect. My waist was still the same size, perhaps even narrower with tiny ripples of budding muscle, but my ass nearly split the shorts.

Even grandmother noticed the difference. "Good heavens, Derek," she commented when I arose after a breakfast that consisted of pineapple juice, gigantic cups of foaming lattes with peppermint, bowls of oatmeal with raspberries and thyme honey, a pepper and mushroom omelet with current jelly wrapped in, blackberry filled hotcakes with lemon curd and Vermont maple syrup, and slabs of Virginia ham. "You must be wearing shorts you outgrew years ago. From the back end, you look like a girl. It's charming, but you can't be comfortable. Matilda will give you money from the household fund, and you can buy new summer clothes today."

"So you won't look like a prissy sissy," the Unpleasant She whispered.

I kissed Grandmother's cheek and hurried up to my room to study my butt in the mirror. I did fill out my shorts rather girlishly. I grinned with wicked glee and sneaked up the next flight of stairs. After oiling the door hinge with a can of Matilda's sewing machine oil, I tiptoed through the unused bedroom and oiled the hinges on the attic door.

The attic was eerie in the early morning light. I stripped naked, set my clothes on a dusty crate, and waited. Uncle Horny didn't make me wait long. He slipped from behind a stack of old paintings, his big dick erect, dripping, and ready for my mouth. I went to my knees before him.

"Uncle Horny, my body is changing," I bragged and kissed his cock. His leaking fluid was as delicious as I'd remembered it.

"As I promised," Uncle Horny said with a smirk. "Shall we commence with your education?"

"Yes, please, Uncle Horny," I said. I slicked my hand with Uncle Horny's constantly leaking jism and gripped his cock. I stroked up and down his shaft and twisted his cockhead with my fingers before touching my lips to it. When Uncle Horny blasted a thick load over the lower part of my face, I opened my mouth to let it cover my tongue. Somehow, I knew exactly what Uncle Horny wanted me to do; I directed his spurting cock around my face, throat, shoulders, and even into my hair. Soon his semen was running down my face and dripping off my chin.

"Now you've received your first facial, Derek," Uncle Horny confirmed. "I wish you could see yourself. There's nothing prettier than a new cocksucker with cum on his face."

Licking my lips suggestively, I smiled at Uncle Horny. "Have you checked out my ass this morning, Uncle Horny? I'm growing a rump like a girl's."

"As I intended, Derek," he said, "for a shapely rear will attract men, but right now you must concentrate on sucking cock."

"I'm ready, Uncle Horny," I announced clutching his backside and drawing his cock into my face.

For a while, Uncle Horny made me suck him off the way I'd done the day before, and I must've swallowed a gallon of his jism before he instructed me in the next step.

"Time for you to take it deeper, Derek."

I shivered with anticipation and hoped that I wouldn't gag. But Uncle Horny showed me how to open my throat, and soon I was breathing regularly between his thrusts. His thick semen was shooting so far down my throat that I didn't need to swallow.

"Good blowjob, Derek," Uncle Horny moaned. "I'm fucking your throat, and you're taking it like a hardcore cocksucker. Oh, yes. Now it's time for you to suck and shoot together."

I couldn't answer, of course, but I knew what I was supposed to do. Uncle Horny expected me to jack off while he was fucking my mouth. I discovered that my cock had been leaking pre-cum. My thin fluid joined Uncle Horny's thick jism in my hand. I tried to start slowly, but the excitement of jerking off for Uncle Horny while still blowing him was overwhelming. I gripped my cock tightly and abused my glans penis with every stroke. It hardly took any time at all before I tripped over the point of no return and realized that I was going to come immediately. Uncle Horny's cockhead twitched as it thrust in my throat, and I knew that he was blasting salvo after salvo of hot wet spunk down my little red lane. I gripped one enticing butt cheek with one hand and jacked my cock mercilessly with the other as he poured it into me.

"Ah, that's good," Uncle Horny moaned. "Oh, yes, Derek, you're an insatiable cum sponge."

Rapturous waves of orgasm claimed me, and I shot long spurts while Uncle Horny fed me his spunk. Exhausted at last, I fell back while Uncle Horny drenched my face with a final splat. That accomplished, spent as I, he dropped down in the dust beside me and fingered my cock.

"Excellent, Derek," he praised, and I blushed with pride. "In a month, you'll be a world class cocksucker."

"Thanks, Uncle Horny," I said.

"Now you'd better clean up and go buy new clothes as you promised your grandmother. Remember, as you try them on, that your muscles will continue to develop."

"Yes, Uncle Horny."

There was no way to clean up in the attic. The dust was marked with long tracks of my spent semen. I pulled up my shorts, sneaked down the steps, made certain the coast was clear, and bolted for my room. Fortunately, Gertrude the maid had finished cleaning, so I studied myself in the mirror. My face and shoulders were mottled with cum, some dried, some still slick, and my hair was stiff with it. Grinning at my appearance, I headed for the shower. After some scrubbing and two vigorous applications of shampoo, I was presentable to appear in public.

I searched through my pants to find the loosest pair, and I pulled on a gift shirt that had always been too big for me. Still, the pants looked like they'd been painted onto my butt and the shirt buttons strained across my chest. I gathered up all my pants, shorts, shirts, and briefs, and stuffed the lot into several trash bags. Lugging the bags downstairs, I went searching for Matilda.

The Disagreeable She handed me bundle of hundred-dollar bills, fifty in number, and told me to buy something that made me look less like the royal catamite, whatever she meant by that. I wondered what Grandmother had said to her.

Grandmother's house was two blocks from the main street, so I hoofed it downtown and threw my old clothes into the back of a Salvation Army truck. Then I sauntered along investigating shop windows. I passed several clothing stores for old farts before I happened upon a shop that carried my kind of clothes. As I walked in, a bell on the door tinkled. It was a sleepy Thursday afternoon, and I was the only customer.

A yummy guy about my own age hurried from the back, paused, and appeared to recognize me. "Oh, hi," he greeted. "Didn't I see you on campus yesterday?"

I instantly realized that he was gay, as if I was receiving psychic messages, and I instinctively knew that I liked him. "You're taking classes, too? I'm taking just one course, comp, two mornings a week."

"I'm Dewey. I've got algebra in the mornings and fill in here every afternoon."

After introducing myself, I told Dewey that I needed practically everything except for shoes and socks. "Look what I'm reduced to," I bragged turning my butt toward him.

"Yeah, wowie, I'd say you outgrew those," he gasped.

"No kidding. My grandmother's housekeeper Matilda, the Ghastly She, said I looked like some kind of cat. Some word with cat in it. I'm going to have to ask her and look it up."

"Catamite," Dewey suggested with an almost feline grin.

"That's it. I don't know what it means."

"It's Latin. A boy kept for fucking or sucking – a young guy who lives only to give pleasure to the man who keeps him."

"So my grandmother's cook was saying my ass looks good enough to fuck?" I stepped closer to Dewey. He didn't back away.

"I guess. The word isn't used anymore. It's Queer now. You've probably seen signs advertising the Queers & Allies meetings on campus."

I rested my hand on Dewey's arm. "Are you a member?" I asked. Then I slid my hand down his arm, slipped it around his waist, and rested it on his ass.

"You're gay, too?" he breathed, as if I'd left any doubt.

"Of course." I brought my lips to his and kissed him long and hard. At first, he responded fervently; then he stiffened and pulled his tongue out of my mouth.

"Derek. Not here. I need this job."

I stepped away from him and winked. "Okay, we'll be careful. No need to rush things. How about helping me buy some clothes?"

Dewey found some extra large bikini briefs that fit me loosely. "You could maybe go down to the large size," he suggested.

"No. My ass will be sticking out even farther in a few days. I'll take the bigger ones."

Dewey raised his eyebrows, so I promised to explain when I knew him better. I figured that he was a good candidate for Uncle Horny's physical education program, but I wasn't going to offer until I'd asked Uncle Horny. I wasn't going to share Uncle Horny's cock with just anyone.

Dewey helped me find a number of outfits that fit all right, though I made allowance for the fact that I was a growing boy. After I paid him, Dewey and I exchanged telephone numbers, and he invited me to the Queers & Allies meeting.

"You know, I haven't told anybody else that I'm gay," I confessed.

"If your aunt's cook is calling you a catamite, then your secret's out," Dewey said. "But I haven't told my folks, either. It's so hard."

We talked and copped random feels until another customer entered. Blowing Dewey a kiss behind his customer's back, I lugged my purchases onto the sidewalk. Glancing farther down the tree-shaded street, I saw a rainbow flag mounted over a doorway. The shop sold gay books and novelty items. Since I still had a good bit of cash, I bought a book about coming out, a couple of paperbacks by a gay mystery writer, and a pride flag.

Back home, I piled the books on the table beside my bed, and I tacked the rainbow flag to the wall. When Gertrude reported their presence to Matilda, and the Ominous She kicked the news upstairs to Grandmother, the truth would come out.

Since I had a topic, I sat down at my computer and typed a 1,000 word expository essay analyzing the process of coming out at school, with appropriate MLA citations and parenthetical references to the book I'd bought. The conclusion of my essay was no pathetic restatement of the thesis or summing up of the main points, but a clear statement of the issue my thesis was pointing toward. My paper ended with the words "I am a proud cocksucker."

During our dinner consisting of vichyssoise, grilled oysters, tomatoes stuffed with wild mushrooms, steak au béarnaise, glazed onions, artichoke salad with saffron vinaigrette, and chocolate raspberry cheesecake, Grandmother complimented me on my new clothes. Even though it seemed somehow perverse, I offered her the money I had left over. She sniffed and told me to keep it. "We're rich, Derek," she demurred. "We don't discuss money."

Later, I called Dewey from my cell phone. Dewey didn't have a cell, so I ended up going through his sister.

"It's your boyfriend, faggot," I heard her announce.

Dewey came on the line with an exasperated voice.

"Sounds like your family is onto your secret," I said.

"Oh, my folks don't listen to her," he corrected, his voice softening after hearing mine. "They know she's a total dweeb."

I told Dewey about the English paper I'd written. "I figure that about ten minutes after I turn it in Monday, the whole campus will know I'm queer. So if you're going to hang out with me, you'll be outed, too."

Dewey and I talked for an hour, and then I hit the bed. Again, I fell into a deep and nearly dreamless sleep, and when I awoke Friday morning, I thought my body was on fire. An hour after breakfast, I was in the attic calling for Uncle Horny. That time he didn't arrive right away. I sat down and waited until he showed up. I stripped for him and he examined my body minutely after I told him how much I hurt.

"You're coming along fine, my boy," he said. "You're growing muscles so fast your skin has to work to keep up. Today's cum feast will smoothen your muscles and skin."

"What are you, Uncle Horny?" I asked.

"Your uncle. An old member of your family."

"Come on, I'm in college."

"I'm an angel."

"A demon, you mean," I corrected. He'd been doing me a world of good, but I wasn't going to let him bullshit me. "Why would a fallen angel be circumcised?"

"So many questions, my boy. Are you adverse to sucking demon dick?"

I grabbed his cock and licked the head. Uncle Horny's cum kept tasting better and better.

"Yes, I'm a demon, Derek – all the little Barnet cocksuckers have called me Uncle. And to answer your query, we demons were created circumcised, and none knows why. Now, blow me like a good little college boy."

Though I had loads of questions, I put my mouth to better purpose. I kissed his big pink cock, tickling the head with my tongue, and licking down the sides of the tall shaft. I kissed and tongued the dickhead until I had Uncle Horny quivering at my oral ministrations.

"Ah, Derek," he moaned. "You are learning the pleasure of torture. Now take it in your mouth."

I didn't obey immediately. I licked his cock closer to orgasm without taking him over the edge. "Ha, that hurts so good," he cried, and I started learning the power of a cocksucker. My mouth was turning a demon into jelly.

When I knew I had Uncle Horny ready to do anything for release, I made my mouth a hot wet cave for his demonic cock. I sucked his cockhead, attacking the rim furiously with my lips, letting it swell my cheek, and occasionally fill my throat.

"Oh, you cocksucker. You total cocksucker," Uncle Horny howled, and I could feel his muscles contracting as the waves of orgasm rolled over him, followed by uncontrollable spasms. Then the powerful muscles at the base of his devilish cock contracted and sent a gigantic spurt of cum into my mouth. I swallowed quickly for his wild contractions blasted big squirts that totally filled my mouth, and I had to gulp them down or lose them. He was coming so heavy that jism was running freely down my chin though I was swallowing eagerly and audibly.

At length, when I could hold no more, Uncle Horny emitted a keening sigh and stopped erupting in my mouth. I waited while his dick calmed. Then I slowly skimmed it clean with my lips as I pulled my face away, and tired from my oral exertions, I sprawled naked on the floor.

"Oh, Uncle Horny, I don't think you've ever ejaculated so much before," I said. "That was awesome."

Uncle Horny stretched out beside me and rested his pink hand on my bulging stomach.

"I've been training novice cocksuckers for ten thousand years," Uncle Horny said. "They're all good when I get done with them, and some spectacular. And there have been a few, perhaps a dozen in all that time, who've gone beyond the spectacular. I think you may be one of those, Derek."

I took his hand in a burst of gratitude and affection. "Thank you, Uncle Horny."

During the precious minutes I rested beside him and digested his spunk, I told him about Dewey, and my paper, and the Queers & Allies club, and my sudden need to come out.

"All to the good," he replied. "You live in a more favorable time than did your ancestors."

Our clasped hands were still resting on my stomach. My gut was no longer bulging, and the powerful double row of new muscles showed forth. "I just hope all the cum doesn't make me fat."

"Cocksucking isn't fattening," Uncle Horny consoled me thoughtfully. "My cum will reshape your body, as I promised. It'll make you more masculine in some places and feminine in others. In a month you'll have a body that'll make the straightest guy on Earth bone his undies."

"That'll be sweet," I said.

"Your reformed body will be disease resistant," Uncle Horny said. "Because I want you to be my apostle on Earth for a long time to come. But for the time being, you need to play it safe with anyone but Dewey."

I promised him that I'd be cautious and then asked him if he wanted to meet Dewey.

"No, you'll keep him for yourself, Derek."

"You want me to suck Dewey's cock?"

"Not right away. First, he must suck yours. Not all your changes are visible, Derek, and your semen has become like mine. You can help your friend."

When our conversation languished, Uncle Horny did something he hadn't done before. As I lay on my back in the dust, he climbed atop me, stroked me, nuzzled me, and kissed me with his soft mouth. I liked his touch, and he freed me to enjoy the caresses of other men.

"You'll want men to touch you," Uncle Horny confirmed what I felt. "From today on, your body will be a willing playground for the male sex."

When Uncle Horny had handled everything on my front, he rolled me over and diddled my backside. I particularly loved having his hands fondling my curvaceous ass, and when he kissed deep into my crack, I nearly lost my load. As he rolled me over again, I felt a moment of disappointment, followed by euphoria when he kissed my dick.

Uncle Horny kissed my cock's head with his demonic mouth, and I closed my eyes as a tremendous weakness claimed me. "Oh, Uncle Horny," I mouthed hardly able to speak.

"Just let me do everything, Derek," Uncle Horny said withdrawing his mouth briefly from my cock. "Don't try to help. Only give yourself to me."

"I'm yours, Uncle Horny," I whispered. "Oh, I'm yours."

Uncle Horny kissed and licked my shaft before going to work in earnest on my dickhead. He massaged the tip of my cock with lips that felt like the pleasure hole of the cosmos, and when his tongue caressed my cock, I thought I'd die of the wonderful agony. I hovered on the edge of mindless joy, unable to move and hardly able to breathe. My cock was hard near to splitting; I leaked thin streams of pre-cum into Uncle Horny's mouth.

Uncle Horny took my whole cock then, and it felt like a tight, moist thing had encased my cock and was drawing it toward the ultimate orgasm. "Uh," I moaned, unable to form coherent thoughts or words. "Ah," I gasped, hardly drawing breath as billows of staggering pleasure swept through my loins. I felt like my future had pumped into my balls to cast wantonly into the sucking mouth of a demon.

Had I chosen to resist, I would've been powerless. However, I had no desire to deny him, and whatever Uncle Horny was willing to do with me or to make me become, so was I eager to give or receive. Had he chosen to turn me into a prissy cum-sponge or the most limp-wristed pansy in human history, or to pervert me into committing sexual acts so degraded that they were unknown to anyone but the most foully debased of fiends, I would have complied happily for his sake.

"Oh, ah," I whimpered as the orgasmic waves deepened, and I was caught in a tidal wave of pleasure. The potent muscles at the base of my penis contracted as they'd never constricted during masturbation, and I savored the great spurt of jism springing forth from my cockhole and chugging down Uncle Horny's throat. The waves of rapture rolled on and each came with that intensely satisfying ejaculation of my life's spunk. And in some mysterious way, strange and delicious, the realization that I was coming into the mouth of a demon, and that doing so would change me in ways that only the demon knew, made my experience more satisfying.

When I staggered downstairs for lunch with grandmother, having showered and gotten myself into a presentable condition, I sensed that the household alliances had solidified. I was most surprised by Grandmother Barnet. After I'd seated myself, she beamed at me and declared, "I understand that you're coming out, to use the parlance of your generation."

"Yes, grandmother. I'm gay. I can't hide it anymore."

"You should not," Grandmother Barnet said. "You're a Barnet, and you must flaunt your sexuality. My brother Albert was a homosexual, but in his day the truth had to be concealed."

"That must've been terrible."

"Oh, Albert lived a merry life. He had a wide circle of friends and lovers, and that in the days before AIDS. Nevertheless, he would rather have braved the world without the coloration of falsehood. Now that I think of it, Albert had the same discoloration on his throat that you have."

As I self-consciously touched Uncle Horny's mark, Matilda brought our shad roes and wonderful hot bread. The Gloating She bestowed me with a patronizing gleam as she placed the fish eggs before me, but Grandmother didn't heed the facial expressions of servants.

"Your grandfather also liked sex with men," Grandmother continued. The Loathsome She rolled her eyes.

This was a revelation. "Grandpa Barnet?"

"Yes, but I wish you'd say Grandfather. He told me before we married that he was drawn to men. In fact, most of the males who've lived in this house have been homosexual, going back to the wagon trains arriving in the 1850s. Tomorrow I'll have Matilda bring the old family diaries from the attic, and you can read about your heritage."

Before flouncing into the kitchen, the Odious She tapped her head behind Grandmother's back. She was indicating that Grandmother wouldn't remember. Watching the door swinging behind the Hateful She and wishing that it had hit her in the ass, I, too, hoped that Grandmother would forget. I could see no good coming from Matilda snooping around the attic.

I leaped back to the Grandpa question. "You married Grandpa, I mean Grandfather Barnet, even after he told you?"

Grandmother looked surprised, and she glanced around to ascertain that the servants had left the room. "Of course," she whispered. "It excited me. My only condition was that he let me watch him with his male lovers. It wasn't long until I was participating. I conceived your father while your grandfather was humping me and sucking another man's penis at the same time."

I was so stunned that I'd forgotten to eat. Matilda brought the veal and removed my shad roe. Since it was fish eggs, I didn't object.

Fortunately, she left the bread, and I ate a bite and spooned the hot wine over my veal.

"What about Dad? You say this house produces gay men, but Dad's the biggest homophobe walking."

Grandmother shook her head sadly. "Every family has its skeleton," she quipped with a little laugh, and I realized that she'd made a wisecrack. "I gave him every chance to come out of the closet, as the parlance of your generation goes, but he'd never been in the closet."

"Or the attic," I muttered under my breath.

Grandmother sighed. "Somehow the family trait skipped him, and he closed his mind to the lure of his ancestral heritage. I'm pleased to learn that you're carrying on the family tradition. However, you must perpetuate the family name, even if reproduction is repugnant to you, Derek. If you cannot force yourself to impregnate a woman, even while indulging your real passion, your generation has methods of reproduction unknown to our ancestors.

"Yes, grandmother," I promised.

"I'm going to will you this house and all of the family assets. Your father cannot be trusted with our fortune."

After lunch, I read my English paper to Grandmother, and she kissed me approvingly on the cheek. Then I pulled on my black Lycra bicycle shorts – stretching them to the limit for that was one item I'd forgotten to replace – and pedaled my Trek to the campus.

I had been relying on the posters advertising the Queers & Allies meeting to direct me, but they were conspicuously missing. Someone had torn down every one, leaving only ripped corners taped to the walls. Frustrated, I headed for the Student Services office.

"Somebody stole all the Queers & Allies posters," I told the student assistant. "I want to find out what room they're holding the meeting in."

"Are you an ally?" she asked, appraising me suggestively.

"No, I'm a queer," I replied with a grin. "Sorry to disappoint you."

Considerably nettled, she checked a file folder. "It's in LI 201. That's the meeting room just off the second floor of the library. The meeting started five minutes ago."

I thanked her, and I could feel her staring at my ass as I hurried out the door. I walked across the quad and found the room easily enough. There were two dozen students inside, more females than males, but I saw Dewey sitting toward the front. I plopped my ass into the vacant chair beside him.

"Wow, you made it," he whispered, his eyes sweeping my bicycle outfit.

I kissed him in greeting, and slipped my bicycle helmet under my chair. The meeting wasn't particularly earthshaking because the Pride Festival had already passed and Coming Out Day was still many months off. Mostly the meeting concentrated on ways to catch the homophobe who'd been tearing down the group's posters. In spite of the lack of real issues, though, I felt good attending a meeting with others like me.

Later Dewey and I found a private bench and got to know each other better. We kissed deep and long, our hands roaming freely, and our tongues playing.

"Damn, Derek," Dewey whispered feeling my body. "Do you work out four hours a day? How'd you get that shape?"

I gripped his hand and rubbed it across my chest. "Oh, I have a better program," I admitted coyly. "Want a taste tonight?"

Dewey slid his hands over my ass. Then he reached inside my bike shorts and grabbed my stiff cock. "Oh, I want to so bad," he groaned. "But I gotta go with my parents tonight, and I have to work at the store tomorrow morning. After noon I'm totally free," he added hopefully.

I put my hand behind his head and pulled his face to mine. I kissed him roughly, and his tongue stabbed at mine as I fondled his throbbing cock. My own cock was ready to come, but I knew we had to wait.

Saturday morning dawned, warm already, clear, sunny, and full of spunk. My body had stopped hurting, and my muscular development was looking more natural. I sure did have a great ass, though, and my cock appeared to have both thickened and lengthened. At breakfast, I told Grandmother that I'd be spending the afternoon and evening with my new boyfriend.

She looked up from her Eggs Benedict and Bananas Foster over French toast with a bright gleam. "You can bring him home, if you want."

"You wouldn't mind if we made love in my room, Grandmother?" I asked.

Matilda mockingly beseeched heaven for strength, but Grandmother replied, "Of course not."

After breakfast, the Hateful She whispered, "pansy," as she passed me, but I was starting to enjoy taunting her. I swished my ass scandalously as I mounted the stairs. Gertrude was cleaning my room when I entered, and she regarded me with approving eyes.

"Please pay no heed to Matilda, Mister Derek," she said. "She wanted a man and never got one, so she's bitter. Knowing you can get any man you want gets up her nose."

After Gertrude had worked her way downstairs, I sneaked upstairs. Uncle Horny was waiting for me, and I told him that I had a date with Dewey.

"Then you must save your cum for him," Uncle Horny professed. "This morning you'll give me a simple blowjob, and I'll come no more than you can swallow."

Uncle Horny sat on a high packing case while I bent to consume his cock and soon made him moan with pleasure. My improved cock burned for release, but I gripped the top rounds of Uncle Horny's buttocks and resisted other urges. His delicious jism filled my mouth, and I swallowed every drop.

Shortly thereafter, I hurried down from the attic. If Matilda did come seeking the family diaries, I didn't want her to catch me. I was certain that Grandmother Barnet knew nothing about Uncle Horny, since he revealed himself only to Barnet men who were ready to receive him. Grandmother was happy about me being gay, and I didn't want the Insufferable She queering my pitch by speaking of demons.

When I checked out my body in the mirror, I perceived that the mark on my throat was becoming a tattoo of Uncle Horny. Grinning at the image, I showered extra carefully, strolled downtown, and found Dewey closing the store. His face brightened when he saw me.

"Jeez, Derek, you're looking hotter every time I see you," he groaned, lustfully squeezing my biceps and patting my ass.

I helped him turn off the lights and lock the front door. We exited through the back of the store, which operated with a spring lock.

"Do all the stores close at noon?" I asked.

"What do you need?" Dewey asked.

"New bicycle shorts. I can hardly peddle in the ones I was wearing yesterday."

"Yeah," Dewey laughed. "They were stretched tight across your ass. If you'd farted, you'd have had a blow out. Come on, Tony's Sporting Goods is open."

Tony was open for business, and being close to a junior college with an active bicycle club, he carried a fine selection of bicycle garb. I picked up a silvery pair of Lycra shorts that looked plenty large. The price tag looked pretty large, too, but I was still heavy with Grandmother's cash.

The owner, Tony, was a fair, sporty-looking guy, probably about forty, but he'd taken care of himself. He grinned when he saw the shorts I was appraising.

"That's a new design. They have a smaller pad, and they cling like skin. Why don't you try them on?"

Tony didn't object when Dewey accompanied me into the changing room, and we had fun fitting me into the shorts. Then we came out, and I examined my ass in the mirror. I looked so hot that I wanted to have sex with myself right there. The pad was perfectly positioned to protect my asshole and the underside of my balls where vascular damage could occur, but it didn't give my butt that weird misshapen look. The silver shorts clung like skin and gave like skin, rather than stretching tight and pulling my butt cheeks together. My cock made a pleasing bulge in the front.

"Wow, Derek, buy those," Dewey gushed, and I noticed that Tony was also staring at my crotch with burning eyes.

I changed into my slacks and paid for the shorts. Tony was studying us, his face full of curiosity, and I thought that it would be mean not to satisfy it. After all, the sixth sense that Uncle Horny had given me had been signaling Tony's innate queerness since we'd walked into the shop.

"Yes, Dewey and I are lovers," I declared. "But he hasn't come out to his parents yet, so it's still our secret."

Tony put his finger to his lips and nodded sagely. Before we departed, he filled us in on the local gay scene and invited us to a gay pride potluck supper.

On the sidewalk, Dewey chided me gently: "You told him that we're lovers. We haven't done much yet, you know?"

"I was anticipating. Are you ready to change that?"

"Yeah." Dewey gripped my hand tightly. "But where?"

"My room."

"With your grandmother in the house?"

"She suggested it, Dewey."

"Wow, I wonder what would have to happen for my parents to propose I have sex with a guy in my room?"

We reached grandmother's front fence, opened the tall white picket gate, and strolled up the wandering walkway through her front garden. We'd been holding hands since leaving the sporting goods shop, and I was carrying the bag with my new bike shorts in my left.

"You've got to break the news to your parents, Dewey," I finally said. "Otherwise they're going to hear from the town gossips. I mean, you're not keeping the secret from anybody but them."

"I know," he agreed moodily. Then he brightened. "But not right this second."

Gretchen was washing the Rolls Royce in preparation for Grandmother's monthly Sunday pilgrimage to Grandpa Barnet's grave, and the Unspeakable She was busy in the kitchen. Of course, Grandmother Barnet was napping, and the only servant we encountered was Gertrude. She tipped me a wink and made a cocksucking motion with her tongue and hand – behind Dewey's back. I winked and nodded confirmation.

In my room, we quickly stripped naked. Dewey had a cute little body, slim and only slightly developed. His buns looked like two firm grapefruit. I figured that a mouthful of Uncle Horny's cum was just the thing for him, but Uncle Horny had said that I could pass the magic to my friend. I stretched out on my bed under the symbolic presence of the rainbow flag, my hard cock pointing toward the ceiling.

Dewey sat beside me, and brought his lips to mine. I pushed my tongue into his mouth and he sucked it. As our tongues fought and played, his hard cock slid across my abdominal muscles and left a streak of pre-cum. Dewey kissed my ear, nibbling along the lobe, and finally poking his tongue into my ear canal. His warm wet tongue inside my ear drove me wild with lust.

"Oh, Dewey, I want you to suck my cock," I moaned, but he continued to torment me with his tongue.

After a while, Dewey moved his mouth down to my nipples. He sucked on my left nipple until a warm glow filled my chest. When he switched to the right, I nearly lost my cum; my cock twitched reflexively, and a thin stream splattered across Dewey. I licked the cum I could reach as he continued to tongue me from my nipples down to my navel. He grazed around my navel, lapping pre-cum, and drove his tongue into my little belly hole.

"Ah, Dewey, that's incredible," I groaned. "You sure can use your tongue. Yes, that's good."

By the time he went down on my cock, Dewey had me at his mercy. He licked my cock shaft and worried its head with his lips and tongue.

"Ah, Dewey, suck my cock. Yeah, suck it," I moaned. He took my cock in his mouth, while his burning dick slipped along my body, and my eyes opened wide with shock. The touch of his mouth astonished me, and I lay supine, dumbfounded, and thunderstruck, until in my extreme ecstasy I turned my head and caught Gertrude spying through the crack in the door. By that point I couldn't have cared if she'd sold tickets to her friends and set up a bleacher section. I cried out, "Oh, yeah, suck me. Suck me."

Dewey wasn't giving me a chance to delay my climax. "Dewey, you're making me come fast," I panted. "I can't stave it off." Dewey was relishing his power to make me come at the time of his choosing, and I was totally helpless.

"Oh, I'm going to go in your mouth," I wailed. My breath burning against my teeth, I saw Gertrude open the door wider. I supposed that she was masturbating and I didn't want to witness any such sight. I closed my eyes and thought only of Dewey. "Oh, Dewey, I'm going to do it in your mouth."

He sucked harder, bringing me over the edge mercilessly, mastering me with his horny mouth. Abrupt pleasure tore through me. My orgasm came not in familiar waves but sharp pulses. My heart hurt me, so intense was the agony of pleasure and the uncontrollable ecstasy that Dewey forced upon me. My muscles blasted a long, long stream of wet spunk into his mouth, followed by another, and another. For a long time, longer than any past time, I continued to spurt volumes of semen that he swallowed down greedily, until minutes later my spurts of rapture and wet jism slowed – then stopped entirely. Still Dewey sucked me until my abused cock softened in his mouth.

I drew a deep gasping breath and lay like one near dead until the prying maid had withdrawn her head and pulled my door closed. "My God, Dewey," I uttered. That was all I could say.

# # # # #

I never took Dewey to the attic to meet Uncle Horny. I loved Dewey, but he wasn't a Barnet after all, and Uncle Horny had assured me that Dewey would grow strong from my cum because the mark he'd placed on my throat meant that I had to power to ejaculate strength. That came true, and I bought Dewey new outfits after his muscles filled out from swallowing my semen. He turned out to be one hot looking guy, and he and I have lived together for many years now.

Grandmother wrote to my parents and told them that I was gay, thus saving me from coming out to them. By the time they returned from their European vacation, they already knew. But they'd never cared enough about me to be bothered by whom I sucked, and within a few years they were out of the picture financially because – true to her word – Grandmother Barnet willed me the family house (including Uncle Horny), and the entire Barnet fortune. So now I control my parents' purse strings, but with a light and generous hand.

I still suck Uncle Horny's cock regularly, and Dewey and the servants wonder about my solitary sallies to the attic. However, these are family secrets. Following the events I've described, I went to English class on Monday with my paper in hand. Surprisingly, our teacher didn't call for the papers right away. Instead, he decided that we should read our papers aloud to the class before turning them in. Guess whose name was second on his grade sheet?

I strode boldly to the front of the classroom and read my coming-out process to the class. When I finished there was a moment of heart stopping silence. Then two girls applauded, followed by general clapping from the entire class. It just goes to prove that real Americans will applaud a fine cocksucker, and Uncle Horny agrees.

ABOUT THE AUTHOR

Possessed of a wild imagination and minimal inhibitions, David Holly has penned more than a hundred gay erotic stories. He lives in Portland, Oregon, the setting of most of his tales. Readers will find a complete bibliography at http://www.gaywriter.org.

g in the park. He was wearing these really tight jeans, so tight y
aring any underwear. "Excuse me," I said, having a hard time l
nded by that bulge in his crotch, "but don't I know you?" "May

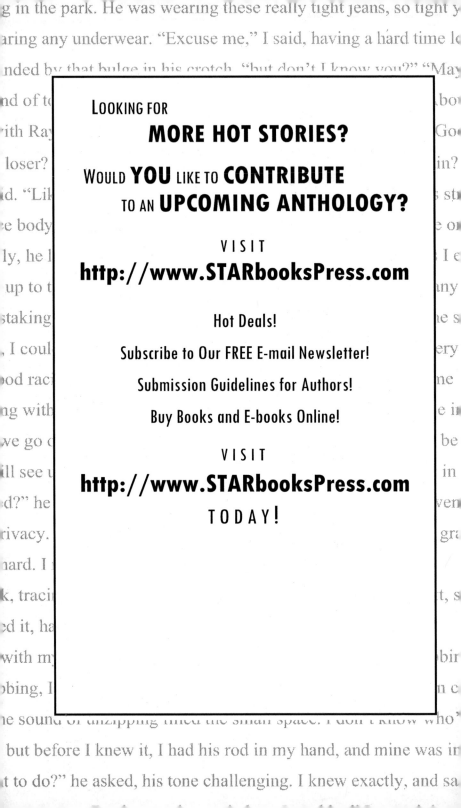
e sound of unzipping filled the small space. I don't know who
but before I knew it, I had his rod in my hand, and mine was in
t to do?" he asked, his tone challenging. I knew exactly, and sa